LOVESICK

DARKNESS BEHIND STARS

BOOK ONE

LOVESICK

POETIC LICENSE

The freedom to depart from the facts of a matter or from the conventional rules of language when speaking or writing in order to create an effect.

"I took extreme poetic license. I departed. A lot."

— TRISH

"To even comprehend it, you have to abandon the comfort of known physics. You have to reach into the unknown, into the void itself, and fucking hope some semblance of humanity survives."

— ORION

Sometimes it feels like hope.
And sometimes it feels impossible.
To every woman who has lost her power to a monster—
Take it back.

PLAYLIST

- Interstellar (Main Theme Cover) – Hans Zimmer; Gacabe (Ch 1)
- The Old Religion – Florence + the Machine (Ch 2)
- Time – Tony Ann (Ch 3)
- Send Me an Angel – DeadStar Assembly (Ch 3)
- Shadow – Livingston (Ch 4)
- Jaws – Sleep Token (Ch 4)
- Ocean Eyes – Billie Eilish, Astronomyy (Ch 5)
- The Night Does Not Belong To God – Sleep Token (Ch 6)
- Experience - Ludovico Einaudi (Ch 7)
- Terrible Love – Moda Spira (Ch 7)
- Devil, Devil – MILK (Ch 8)
- Give – Sleep Token (Ch 9)
- Dark Things – Starset (Ch 10)
- Stars Went Out – Inalery, Lxtra (Ch 11)
- Say That You Will – Sleep Token (Ch 12)
- Clarity (Acoustic) – Foxes (Ch 12)
- Pulsar – Nurali Beisekozha (Ch 13)
- Know – SAYSH, Anderson Rocio (Ch 14)

- Drag Me Under – Sleep Token (Ch 14)
- ICARUS – Tony Ann (Ch 15)
- I Found – Amber Run (Ch 15)
- Devour Me – Cenobia (Ch 16)
- Forty Six & 2 – Tool (Ch 16)
- Never Let Me Go – Florence + the Machine (Ch 17)
- Infinite Baths – Sleep Token (Ch 17)
- Dead Souls – Nine Inch Nails (Ch 18)
- Wild Heart – SPELLES (Ch 19)
- Hero – Alan Walker, Sasha Alex Sloan (Ch 19)
- Look to Winward – Sleep Token (Ch 20)
- Telomeres – Sleep Token (Ch 20)
- No Light, No Light – Florence + the Machine (Ch 21)
- Sun Killer – Spiritbox (Ch 22)
- Half Life – Livingston (Ch 22)
- Faded (Restrung) – Alan Walker (Ch 23)
- Dead in the Water – SPELLES (Ch 23)
- Tattoo – Loreen (Ch 24)
- Cosmic Love – Florence + the Machine (Ch 24)
- Lovesick – Alan Walker & Sophie Simons

I

STAR-CROSSED

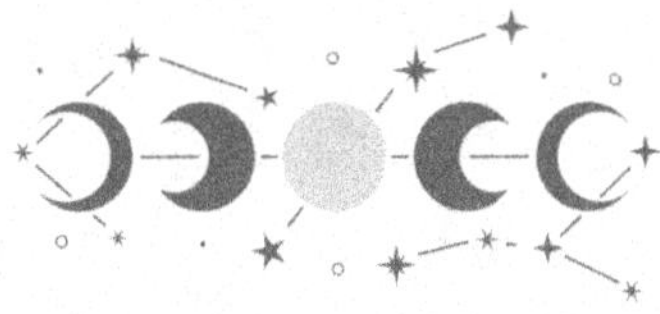

All truths are easy to understand once they are discovered; the point is to discover them.

— GALILEO

ORION: PRELUDE 9

The wind whips around me, rising into a roaring chorus as waves crash furiously against the jagged cliffside below. Even as the rain breaks and the sky clears, the misty air remains charged with a storm.

I hold the brass object between my thumb and forefinger, feel the balanced weight of it.

Sometimes, you have to lose something important to find it again. And you have to be willing to risk losing it forever.

There's a cost to loving anything too fiercely. That only after losing what we love most can we truly realize its value.

It's a cruel paradox.

With an aching breath, I lift my gaze toward the horizon.

Out there in the vast ocean is my violence. I recognized its fury before the ripples could reach me, before the vibrations could be felt. Like gravitational waves passing silently through one another, we were never supposed to collide.

That's the law of physics.

My thoughts rage like the restless sea stretched endless before me, cast in tossing black waters that absorb the fading light. Two worlds layered one on top of the other.

In the distance, that faint seam of horizon threads the space where the ocean touches sky, blurring the boundary between the two.

You need the dark to see the light.

The waves push and pull against the shoreline as I stand fixed on the rocky ledge, the towering spires of Stonehurst looming from behind. I clench the brass in my hand, my fingers as numb with cold as my body with indecision.

Soon, a blazing corona will circle a black sun, the moment of totality eclipsing the beach.

And me.

Right here, trapped in this space between, I feel that push and pull on a cellular level as gravity mercilessly dominates my atoms. An inevitability that has tormented me since she first entered my orbit.

As crosses form on the shallow waters, the tide displays the mark of danger. The gravitational pull churns the tide higher, pulling harder at the ocean.

I recognize the pattern because the science of what I do depends on it. Inherently, we are designed to recognize these patterns. It's coded in our DNA. To escape predation, to identify danger.

I should have recognized the danger in her.

With fire lashing my sternum, I remove the star-taker from my pocket and fit the piece into place, and her melodic tune sings through me, an intoxicating, haunting refrain.

Nothing is as perfectly measured as the symmetry of a reverberating tune.

Standing at the precipice, I step closer to the edge of the cliff. The waves roar, crashing higher, spitting up against the rocks. Something vicious stirs in my blood as I strip away my jacket and wrench off my tie, allowing the serrated wind to sink its teeth into my skin.

Gravity becomes secondary to this deeper, darker pull within.

With the next frigid gust, I pull in a shuddering breath. My foot slips along the rocky incline as I look down into the turbulent waters below.

I've suffered this moment on an endless loop.

There's no fear of falling in space, only the silent terror of becoming adrift. Frozen, motionless.

The void whispers, the seductive urge to jump. To surrender. To succumb to forces beyond control.

And I answer its call.

The most beautiful experience we can have is the mysterious. It is the fundamental emotion which stands at the cradle of true art and true science.

— ALBERT EINSTEIN

2
FIREFLY

The total number of stars in the universe is greater than all the grains of sand on all the beaches of the planet Earth.

— CARL SAGAN

COLLINS

My life is defined by a before and after.

Before I took my last breath, and him.

We shouldn't be so fragile that one moment out of the whole of our existence should alter us. But that's the cruel reality every victim of a crime comes to realize, just how delicately fragile we truly are when caught in the fury of a storm.

I clench my hand until the seashell crumbles. The frail, spiral exoskeleton is reduced to chalky clusters in my palm, and I let the broken pieces drop to the sandy dune.

With a resigned breath, I swipe my hand down my slacks and send a reply text to Laurel. She gets anxious when I don't check in while working a case. She's retired now, hasn't been my psychiatrist in years, yet she has always been more than that to me.

Family.

It was Dr. Laurel Montgomery who pulled the canvas away and breathed new life into my lungs.

She saved me in more ways than one.

I drop my phone into my wool-blend coat, the pressure in my chest eased enough to focus on the crime scene below.

There's a reason he chooses such vast spaces. Right out in the open, so exposed.

It's intentional.

Majority of ritualistic offenders select remote locations to discard their victims, like the woods, even though such sites are typically familiar to the perpetrator and can tie them back to the scene. They still believe there's a less likely chance of discovery. The trees give a false sense of security. Secluded. Secret.

The thought provokes the unwanted mental image of dusty green branches and the smell of earth.

But that's not him. It's not that he desires an audience; he's not bragging or unintelligent. He doesn't want to be caught, despite his choice of a public area. He has his reason, and that reason lies somewhere along this coastline.

I lift my gaze from the victimized remains to stare out over the darkened shore, the night too dense to discern much else other than the blanket of stars dusting a midnight sky. A pale crescent moon hangs partially obscured by a swipe of hazy clouds. The roar of crashing waves competes with the harsh wind as it rips through brittle dune grass and sea oats the color of sawdust to toss strands of my loose hair across my face.

The night feels violent.

"Damn, they're setting up the spotlights already." FBI Special Agent Zeke Darby moves in beside me, his towering, stocky build blocking the activity of the busy scene.

My gaze still cast on the ocean, I blink to try to keep the horizon in sight, that nearly invisible line where the ocean meets the sky. Like an optical illusion, the longer I stare at that seam, the more it starts to blur, disappear.

Darby's right. Once the crime-scene analysts turn on those beaming lights, we'll lose the offender's perspective, blurring our evaluation like the vanishing horizon.

Anxiety swells in my chest, the urgency to uncover a new piece of the puzzle before it's lost. The fear that this could be my last chance to find him steals my breath like the next gust of wind across the dunes.

Serial offenders don't stop killing. They often experience a cooldown period, or they're incarcerated for other crimes—but he's different.

He's searching for something. And I fear once he finds it and his ritual is complete, the trail to him will go completely cold.

"Least his dump sites are always scenic," Darby comments, glancing around the darkened dunes.

"We'll make sure to send him a thank-you note for his consideration." My sarcasm earns a scowl from the agent.

"Fucking smartass." He shakes his head. "I just meant, we've never had to literally sift through a dumpster or landfill. Done that more times than I want to recount."

A slight smile breaks free despite the grisliness around us, because he's not wrong. There's a sort of elegance to the offender's scenes, a sophistication. It speaks to his confidence, why he leaves his victims on display, unafraid of being caught.

He's fearless, not reckless.

Sifting through the filth and vileness of a case can make you appreciate a well-thought-out crime, even the artistry in it.

And while art isn't always beautiful, it is interesting.

The mutilated body lying below in the depression of sand is a prime example. This isn't just the perpetrator's dump site.

It's his kill site.

He works quick, methodical. Each time, faster and more efficient than the last. He's gotten his ritual down to a meticulous science.

Since the inception of this case, I've alleged that location is key, confident his victim selection is tied to the sites as much as the victims themselves. The first one was discovered buried in the Arizona desert. The remains so badly charred, fingertips severed, it took the local agency weeks to identify.

Once the media broke the story of the murder victim, he stopped bothering to cover his kills. It wasn't long before more bodies started turning up across the country, and it took two years to link the cases across states and jurisdictions.

The fact is, he's not tied to any one area, making it near impossible to predict where he'll turn up next.

The most recent vic—male, mid-fifties, Caucasian, local resident—was discovered four hours ago by a wildlife conservationist scouting the coastal interdunal swale. I only know this terminology because she repeated it incessantly while berating the Feds for tromping through the habitat.

The body hadn't even reached full rigor mortis before our plane was touching down in Salisbury. From there, it was a forty-five-minute ride into the coastal town of Bethany Beach, and then another ten-minute hike toward the Delaware Seashore State Park, where a stretch of barrier island is bounded on one side by the Atlantic and the other by Rehoboth Bay. Apparently, one of the few places left where one can glimpse a rare Bethany Beach Firefly.

Which brings my thoughts full circle as I drop my hands into my coat pockets and turn toward Darby. "Let's use the conservationist," I say.

His thick brows draw together over tapered dark eyes, then he chuckles as he catches on to my scheme. "God, you're a menace, Hol. Don't start that dark psychology shit here."

"I've told you, that's a pseudoscience," I say, for what feels like the hundredth time. "Not what I do."

Technically, there are verified studies into the art of dark psychology and its tactics. Manipulation, deception, persuasion, or any application of psychological techniques used for unethical purposes—strategies to exploit and control.

One must know how to recognize such tactics in order to counter them.

"Right, and yet, I don't hear any denial there," Darby mocks, but humor softens his eyes. "I wonder how often you've used your witchery on me." His tone deepens to take on a serious note. "You're going to piss off McCallister if you're not careful."

I arch an eyebrow in challenge. "Only if you tell him it was my idea."

He shakes his head, but the devious grin remains on his tan face. Since we paired up on this case a little less than two years ago, the field agent has been the closest thing to a partner I've ever had.

"Her name is Dr. Lancer," I say to him. "She's been advocating to get this special firefly put on the endangered species' list. I'm sure giant spotlights would disturb their natural habitat even more."

On cue, the wind carries the shrill voice of Dr. Lancer our way as she schools Agent Valdes on the mating habits of the female firefly, or what she calls the *femme fatale* lightning bug. Interest piqued, I cock my head to absorb a few facts.

With a defeated sound of acceptance, Darby situates the braided leather band around his wrist, then nods. "I'll handle it. Just don't do shit else until I get back," he warns.

I use my index finger to cross my chest.

He frowns. "That's not even where your heart is located."

As he sets off, I breathe in the salt air, considering the irony of his words. The truth is, despite claims that I'm somewhat heartless, the location of the hollow organ inside my chest is never far from my thoughts.

If Laurel were here, she'd send me a knowing glance, filled with the tense silence of our very last session before I was accepted into the FBI's Violent Criminal Apprehension Program.

I pick up my slim leather briefcase and anchor the strap to my shoulder. Feet shuffling through the loose sand, I track down the dune toward the enclosed crime scene. Caution tape sections off the low-lying depression between sandy ridges.

After I flash my lanyard to the uniformed officer standing guard, I duck under the shiny strip of yellow tape. Two Feds in basic black suits are talking to the chief medical examiner, his occupation made apparent by the tactical khakis and collared shirt emblazoned with the county ME seal.

Having escaped Dr. Lancer, Agent Valdes offers me a slight chin nod in greeting. He was assigned this case out of the BAU last year when the victim count reached double digits.

For reference, there are several departments housed under the FBI National Center for the Analysis of Violent Crime, or NCAVC. One being the Behavioral Analysis Unit (BAU), and another ViCAP.

As a ViCAP crime analyst, I'm assigned cases of a serial nature in order to document in-depth analysis and compile intelligence into Crime Analysis Reports. Geography, offender profiles, suspect lists, victims—all relevant data is provided to investigators, and also keeps the largest, most comprehensive violent offender database up to date: ViCAP-WEB.

I tuck my lanyard beneath my blazer and remove my tablet before I lower my briefcase to the ground, knowing I'll be haunted by this sand for weeks, discovering it in every crevice of the leather.

The victim has been preserved as best as possible despite the wind, which has layered a thin sheet of sand over the body, pushing up around the frame like the wall of a sandcastle. His shins show signs of pinches and bite marks from fiddler crabs and other crustaceans.

From a distance, it appears as though he merely fell to his death down the steep dune. Up close, it's the gruesome sight that denotes a violent murder, and links the crime to the Reaper killings—the moniker the FBI has failed to keep out of the media —now spanning nine states over the past five years.

The exposed victim has been stripped of clothes. His hands and legs have been impaled with steel, skewer-like rods, pinning his appendages to the earth like an insect to a board. Yet it's what's missing that gives my guy his moniker.

The head has been severed, taken from the scene.

Reaped.

It's more than the perpetrator's MO, it's his signature.

A frisson of exhilaration prickles my skin as I observe the precise, clinical slices along the victim's vertebrae.

"Griffin Klane Anders," Valdes says as he approaches from the side. "Prints just identified him. Serial predator. Wanted on numerous abductions and murder charges. Honestly, some of the most disturbing shit I've ever seen. The Bureau's been actively hunting him since he dropped off the radar three years ago, unable to bring him in." He shrugs, releasing a dry grunt. "Until now."

I look up into his tense face, features cast sharp by the pale moonlight, his graying hair windblown. "Any connection to previous victims?"

He shakes his head, pulling out his phone to scroll updates. "Nothing pinged during a cursory sweep. Keats is running a deeper analysis now. But it's not likely."

I nod once. Other than the history of dark deeds, there's been no obvious connection among the victims. Just the fact that they're all wanted for vile crimes and untraceable.

Valdes stares at the staged body, brows furrowed. "I mean…" He hesitates, voice dropping low. "Hell, this perp is taking out the trash. Maybe we shouldn't even catch this guy."

A ripple of apprehension coasts down my spine, and I force a tight smile. "Yeah, maybe."

Here's what I know: If the perp is intentionally targeting these wanted offenders, then he's using something beyond mere skill; a method of profiling and hunting that surpasses even our most sophisticated agency systems.

Valdes mutters a curse and kicks a fiddler crab away from the body. "Shit, we need a tarp."

My throat constricts, and I swallow past the sudden tightness. Before I step onto every crime scene, I arm myself with a defensive wall. But like the sand creeping into every crevice of my briefcase, trauma always finds a crack.

I bring my hands together, thumb resting over the pulse of my wrist. "Can you keep me updated on the progress?"

"Sure thing." The agent tucks his phone away before he returns to the medical examiner.

While the agents document the scene, I focus on the body, even though the victim isn't really why I'm here.

As a psychopathologist specializing in abnormal psychology and maladaptive behaviors, I've conducted over forty interviews with violent offenders. I'm here to make sure this one is captured alive, and that I'm the first to interview him.

From the moment I realized the connection, he became mine.

I'm here for him.

Aiming my tablet at the body, I snap a few pictures for my report. The skin is blanched, tissue devoid of blood. What remains has congealed on the sand at the point of decapitation.

First, he administers a paralytic to incapacitate his victim.

Then, depending on what the environment calls for, he uses either a wire bone saw or an oscillating surgical saw to slice through the tendons and bone of the neck—

While the victim is still alive.

Although the act is especially brutal, it's not done for deviant delights. The staging of the victim is too purposeful for his intent to be sadistic torture.

Whether the head is taken as a trophy or in connection to a deeper, darker compulsion is irrelevant to me. It may interest the Feds, and even further our understanding of the serial offender mind, but this one—*this* particular offender—has something far more valuable to offer.

As I move around the body to capture images from different angles, I record the pose. Each previous victim earned a unique position, even the first buried beneath the desert sand.

This victim has been placed on his left side, his front facing the ocean. His knees are curled toward his stomach. Left arm extended, right arm stretched at a forty-degree angle away from his chest.

A sudden commotion rises above the roar of wind and waves, and I can hear Dr. Lancer speaking passionately into her phone. Not long after, Darby crosses under the yellow ribbon and tunnels his fingers through his thick hair.

"That might buy us a little time," he says, exasperation weighing his shoulders. "And just to be clear, I never want to hear about fireflies again."

I turn my face away from the gust, guarding my eyes against the spray of sand. "I don't understand how they can be out here with this wind anyway."

"Unfortunately, I do. I now know more than I ever wanted to."

A smile slips along the seam of my mouth. "Like what?" I ask, knowing he's actually dying to share. Darby acts tough, but he secretly enjoys trivia and—his worst offense—documentaries.

He blows out a terse breath. Then, glancing around, he points out one of the lightning bugs. "They're beetles, not *flies*. Dr. Lancer was insulted I referred to them otherwise. The glow or light or whatever they emit can be different colors."

I watch the lone firefly flutter its tiny, winged body against the wind and land on a blade of dune grass. The bottom of its abdomen illuminates into a brilliant green glow. The bloom of light is beautiful, filling me with a foreign emotion.

"They blink in a sequence, like a code," Darby continues as he gloves his hands and crouches next to the body. "Flashing their light to create a pattern unique to their species."

I recall what Dr. Lancer said about their mating signal, how they follow a pattern to find a mate. The male will flash while the female waits to be impressed by the light display. When she selects a suitor, she'll time her flashes with his to lure him to her.

"Jesus," Darby says, tilting his head at an angle to examine the mutilated neck. "No hesitation marks. Cut clean through. He worked fast."

"Then the vic didn't suffer long," I say, my voice cut low by the wind. "Unfortunately."

Darby looks up at me with a thoughtful expression. Though I give him credit, he doesn't let an ounce of pity register in his eyes. "I also found out the female fireflies are toxic to predators," he says. "Even in death, the victim fights back."

A hard swallow scrapes my throat. Besides my superiors, Darby is the only agent who knows of my past, a consequence of his field in intelligence. He was the investigator who conducted my Personal Security Interview for the background investigation during my hiring process.

"Too bad her retribution comes a little too late," I say.

Darby glances away. "Insects have their ways, and we have ours. That's what we're here to do." He absently touches the leather band around his wrist. "Anyway, the last victim blew my theory out of the water. He's not targeting offenders who commit the same crimes. His victimology is all over the map."

"Same as his kill sites."

Like strings connected to points on a murder board, we've tried connecting every conceivable variable. Once a connection is made, it always feels obvious after the fact.

I need to be able to predict where he'll strike next.

As Darby becomes invested in his evaluation, I wake my tablet and fill out the initial findings for my report, my thoughts still clinging to patterns and the blinking, harmonic glow of fireflies.

In psychology, the Gestalt principles explain how the mind uses innate pattern recognition to organize seemingly random details, applying laws of perception that simplify the chaos.

Like how the law of connectedness helps link separate objects into a single shape. It's why our brains see a pattern even when there's no intentional pattern to begin with. Like how the flashing of the fireflies, set against the dark backdrop of a starry ocean sky, resembles the stars dotting the night.

Their glowing bodies look like constellations.

"Oh, my god." As soon as the thought strikes, I push my sleeve up, my fingers tracing the starry points inked across my wrist.

I glance up at the rolling ocean, the horizon now lost to the hazy offing. Clusters of burning stars scatter the black sky, their light reflected on the surface of the dark water.

Walking a circle around the victim, I keep my face cast upward as I pick out the distinct shapes amid the stars until I find the one I'm searching for. Then I look down at the victim, the way his body is posed.

As soon as I see it, I can't unsee it. Obvious after the fact.

"Shit." I stagger away from the body, hands unsteady as I download a sky map to my tablet, then angle my device skyward.

"Aquarius," I whisper, the excited tremble of my voice snatched by a gust of wind.

Wary, Darby eases my way. "Hey, you all right?"

Wasting no time with assurances, I rush to find a sturdy reed and yank it free of the dune. I drop my tablet and scratch a sloppy symbol into the sand. "It's a constellation," I say, looking up at the sky and using the stalk to trace the air and connect the twinkling dots. I then trace out the same design above the victim, my arm shaky with the surge of adrenaline. "He staged the victim in the shape of a star constellation."

Darby tears his gloves off, pocketing them into his pristine suit as he comes around to stand at my side. "What are you talking about?"

As I stare up into his shadowed face, I catch the microexpressions he's trying to conceal. The worry line carved deep between his brows, the tight rim of his lips.

"Look at the victim," I tell him as I scoop up my tablet. I punch in a web search and turn the screen around, showing him an image with the stars connected by lines so he can clearly see the shape. "Aquarius. The victim has been posed like the constellation. The arms outstretched…the legs curled inward."

He takes the tablet and studies the image, comparing it to the body. He glances back and forth, his silence burrowing beneath my skin like abrasive grains of sand.

"Darby—"

"Yeah." He cuts me short. "I mean, I see it, Hol. But you know it's likely a coincidence. There's a billion different star patterns. If you try to find one to match every victim, chances are, you will."

Disappointment tightens my throat. I swallow, swiping the hair from my face. "Why do you always do this."

His exasperated sigh stirs my irritation further. When he finally meets my eyes, I'm devastated by the doubt I see banked there. "To keep McCallister off your case," he says. "Just…if we do find any correlation, let me take it to him."

He stands before me like an imposing obstacle. Hand braced on his hip to part the bottom of his black blazer, tie side-swept by the wind. A fierce devotion carves his features that, I know deep down, he's only trying to protect me. That's his nature.

And yet, a flame fills the hollow pit of my stomach. This rage is always festering right below my surface. At times, I latch onto it and let it char my insides to ash. I try not to give it enough oxygen to blaze hot enough to burn those closest to me, but it's malignant, tainting every relationship.

As I feel the bubble of anger rising, I smother it. "Of course, all right," I say to ease Darby's concern.

He expels a lengthy breath. "We'll finish up here and then look through the past cases, compare the poses of all the victims. See what, if anything, it could mean. Okay?"

I nod again in reply, only hearing the crash of the waves, the howl of the wind. Seeing the glowing embers of fireflies blinking against the starry backdrop of night.

But even as I gently consent to his suggestion, my mind is racing as quick as my pulse.

I accept the tablet from Darby, the star map still displayed on the screen, and a surge of adrenaline heats my blood.

Map.

It's a fucking map.

The realization clicks into place so effortlessly, I almost feel buzzed. Desperation claws at my waning patience. Time is always against me.

"I can find him," I say, my voice softly muffled.

Darby watches me closely, that hint of worry creased between his brows, but fails to respond when the spotlights flick on, illuminating the dark beach. All around, agents begin to assemble and erect a tent.

"I was watching this documentary on Michelangelo last month," Darby says, and I can hear the solemn inflection in his tone. "It was about how he saw raw materials before transforming them into art."

Normally, I can follow his winding commentary on all the things he uses to fill his idle time, and I can even sympathize, knowing the reason he does so, but my mind is humming too frantically, impatience fraying my nerves.

"He put it this way," Darby continues. "'Every block of stone has a statue inside it, and it's the task of the sculptor to discover it.'"

Clicking the tablet off, I let him have my full attention. "What are you trying to say to me?"

"That the artist should never impose their will on the stone." He folds his arms across his chest. "I know how badly you want to make this case, but you can't impose your will on it, Hol."

A ribbon of anger coils around my bones, and my muscles burn. I can't tamp down the reactive flame fast enough to prevent my next words from hitting the air. "Maybe if you had imposed yours harder, you could've found her killer."

The immediate shock of hurt contorts his features. The resulting lash of guilt strikes back at me, my gaze falling to the leather bracelet circling his wrist. A pang of regret murmurs through the bruised organ in my chest.

"Shit. I didn't mean that—"

"I know," he says, saving me the awkward apology. He tips his head up and glances around the scene, then scrubs the back of his neck with his hand. "Come on. I saw a beach bar on the way here. Let's go clear our heads."

While he wraps up with Valdes, I grab my briefcase and start the climb toward the top of the dune. I only make it halfway before my lungs fail to pull a full breath, and my ears pulse with the struggle.

Palm flattened to my chest, I seal my eyes shut and take measured breaths, fighting back the dizziness.

One. Two. Three.

The attack fades, replaced by the dull ache of cold fury. I clench my teeth, gritty with the grains of sand, and lower my hand.

The climb up is always so hard. It's what makes us want to give up, to give in. To finally let the darkness have us.

Every day, giving in feels easier.

In a previous life, I was something of an artist. Though Darby knows this, he won't blatantly come right out with it, instead using vague metaphors to deliver his point. Still, being reminded of what existed in the before feels as raw as my sand-beaten flesh.

When I reach the top of the dune, I let the bite of wind assault my skin and glance around at the darkened habitat. Caseworkers churn within the lighted tent, the inside aglow like a firefly jar.

It's deceptively beautiful, the violence hidden within.

As the night wind intensifies, the illuminated bodies of the lightning bugs fade out, save for one errant straggler striving to claim shelter in the sea oats. She's tossed by the sand spray, pitched to the ground. Caught in the fury of the storm, the firefly is a victim of the cruel elements.

I lower myself to the grass and pluck the beetle from the sand. Cradling the insect in my palm, I realize just how delicate she is, how fragile. Even if she survives the storm, there's a predator waiting to descend on her in her weakest moment.

As she crawls along my thumb, I think about how cunning the *femme fatale* firefly is—how she lies in wait, mimicking the flash signals of other fireflies to attract and lure in a male. In essence, she tricks him, convincing the male that she's like him, allowing her to get close before she kills.

My gaze shifts to the star pattern on my wrist, the only link I still have to my before—and that's when I see it, a beacon flashing from the sand.

Hand trembling, I brush away the grains, my breath stalling as I uncover a brass object. One moment where I war with indecision, then I curl my fingers around the piece of evidence.

Darby appears at the top of the dune, all concern washed from his face. "You ready?"

My resolve never more firm, I clench the slender brass in my palm and nod. "Yes."

I will find him.

Before I stand, I release the firefly back to the sand, where a fiddler crab makes her its target.

Yet, nature gave her a way to fight back, to get even. Her veins are primed with poison.

In death, she will have her revenge.

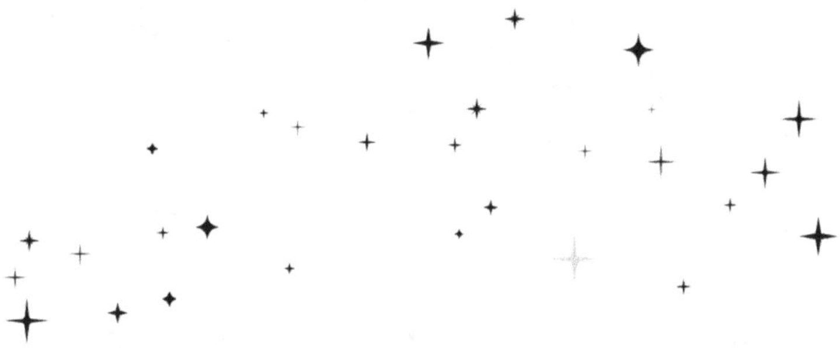

The cosmos is within us. We are made of star-stuff. We are a way for the universe to know itself. Some part of our being knows this is where we came from. We long to return, because the cosmos is also within us. We're connected to everything that ever was, is, or will be.

— CARL SAGAN, *COSMOS*

3

LUMINARY

First contact (C1): The moment when the moon first touches the solar disk, marking the beginning of an eclipse.

COLLINS

Luminary has to be one of the most beautiful words in existence. The archaic meaning is described as a natural light-giving body, like a planet or a star. In the realm of astronomy, the ancients looked to these celestial bodies for guidance.

It's also a person who inspires or influences, especially one prominent in a particular sphere. Not so unlike the original meaning, as we can see the evolution, but maybe less whimsical, lyrical.

During my preparation, I came across many interesting articles like this, but nothing—no amount of preparation or study —could prepare me for Stonehurst University.

The clack of my heels on the smooth sandstone echoes in the long stretch of hallway. The architecture is a mix of Gothic

Revival and Glasgow Style, with vaulted ceilings that lend to the elegant curvature of the arches.

The research university itself sits atop a rugged bluff overlooking the Pacific, weathered by the elements and time. Salt air drifts inside the dark, hollow limbs of the structure, carrying the scent of coastal evergreens. Towering spruce and vibrant vine maples surround the campus, their misty branches and fiery red-and-orange leaves woven into the very fabric of this academic harbor.

But there's something else—something indefinable and chilling that clings to my bones as I navigate the Kessinger Wing, some unknown entity casting a shadow everywhere I look.

As I near PAT 211, I glide my blunt nails across my forehead to sweep my long bangs aside and take a fortifying breath.

Then I pull open the exit door to the lecture hall.

The deep baritone of a male voice fills the auditorium, and a thrilling tremor travels through me. Keeping my gaze aimed at the carpeted floor, thankful for the muffled sound of my footsteps, I creep into a seat along the empty back row of tiered bench seats.

Discreetly, I set my briefcase on the floor beside my feet and look up toward the front of the theater—

And my breath immediately catches at the sight of *him*.

Keeping his back to the room, he works an equation on the blackboard, scrawling Greek letters and algebraic strings in his messy script. His smooth timbre fills the hall as he talks out a calculation, the acoustics projecting his low mutterings.

My gaze falls down his body in appreciation of the lean, muscular build of his physique. He's dressed in a tailored, all-black suit, the dark dress shirt fitted beneath a black vest, cuffs tapered close around his wrists where black leather gloves meet.

I'm struck by the sight of him, in the flesh, my heart thundering. Out of habit, I press my palm to my chest, focusing my breathing to slow the climbing rate of my heart.

He pauses, left hand held at an angle from the board, while he takes a moment to analyze. He drags his gloved fingers over the medium taper of his black hair before he begins working the equation once again.

"Black holes are extreme distortions in spacetime. When two black holes collide, it's an immensely violent event. Physicist Kip Thorne likens this merger to a cosmic whirlpool. Two intense vortexes of twisting space that send gravitational waves rippling out through the fabric of the universe. Like a storm in time." He makes a mark on the board. "As we sit here, these tiny ripples from violent cosmic events are passing through this room, passing through us, subtly altering the flow of time. With detectors like the ones Thorne helped design at the LIGO Observatory, we can now detect these faint distortions from millions of light-years away."

I can't help being drawn in by the smooth cadence of his voice. It's captivating—everything about him is captivating. While I've studied footage of him, making sure I could identify my target, it has failed to prepare me for the visceral impact of being in his presence, hearing his voice, breathing the same air.

And in the space of a skipped heartbeat, I know it's him that infuses this institution. It's his dominating force that pervades every stone and shadow.

Orion Night.

As many of the students are doing, I shift my attention around the room, where he lectures on the physics of astronomy three times a week.

Dark fabric drapes the walls between the opaque windows with black ornamentation. The entire theater is carved in stone and deep wood, reminiscent of a Gothic cathedral, something right out of a Victor Hugo novel. Antediluvian objects decorate the space. Brass globes and spinning dials. Phases of the planets and astrology from when it was a science.

My thoughts turn to the slender brass piece I keep in my pocket, trying to match it with one of the artifacts. But at this point, it would only confirm what I already know. The second I saw the man, I knew he was the one.

He was mine.

My thoughts halt as I become hyperaware of the sudden silence. I sense the moment his sharp eyes snare me, my movement caught as I look toward the front of the room.

Behind his black-rimmed glasses, Orion's piercing gaze scans the pews, seeking the change in his environment, and those striking teal eyes alight on me in the back row.

And time seems to distort, making me feel his words on a deeper level. The past, present, and future linked in one moment. As the seconds slow and speed all at once, I'm left breathless in the wake of his discerning gaze.

The intelligence banked there is startling, but it's the uncharacteristic beauty that catches me off-guard, caught in a labyrinth of lust and wonder.

God, to wield the power to devastate with a single glance is a frightening ability.

I feel the years fall away, the past dissolving beneath his unblinking catalogue of my features, and an electric charge builds between us, a palpable link to the man I've been chasing.

I'm vibrating with a dangerous mix of exhilaration and fear, unable to hide the effect he has on me. As his bold gaze sweeps over me, I feel the touch of it on my cheeks, neck, clavicle, sending a flush of heat through my entire body.

Emboldened, I lift my chin and stare right back at him, ignoring the curious glances from students. He glides his tongue over his bottom lip before he breaks eye contact, shifting his attention to his audience. In an effort to resume his lecture, he falters and stumbles over his words. Then gives a self-deprecating laugh.

Smiles.

That smile illuminates his face, and something inside me wakes.

"Damn, where was I?" Orion says, a slow smirk spreading across his full lips, and a blush burns through my skin. "Gravitational waves. The violent nature of space when extreme forces are at play. It can be…intense." His arresting gaze tracks back to me, offering another dizzying smile. "Fuck," he mutters, driving a hand through his hair. "I apologize for getting off track."

The class laughs easily in response. But I know this man never apologizes. For anything.

Being the woman who makes him lose his place during a lecture feels empowering—and seduction is nothing if not a game of power.

Dr. Orion Night may be a luminary in the field of astrophysics, but this is my domain. Strategic dark psychology and perfectly timed moves.

His sphere revolves around a branch of space science that seeks to understand the universe, exploring the life and death of stars, planets, and galaxies.

He's the brilliance behind Stonehurst Observatory's exemplary astronomy program, and the president of the university desires to keep their brightest star shining in order to continue to pull funding.

He's also psychologically unbalanced.

A liability the university has taken great care to keep under wraps, requesting in-house, NDA-contracted psychiatric measures to evaluate the level of risk to the university.

As fate would have it—with a little help—Dr. Collins Holbrook has been employed for just this purpose.

When the lecture lets out, I wait patiently for the students to clear the room. As I descend the steps, it's the moment of truth. Whether I can commit. I've never gone undercover before, and I fear he's going to see right through me, like peering through one of his lenses into space.

My background has been scrubbed by the most advanced agency software tools. A search of my name will produce a carefully curated identity.

Orion removes his glasses and places them in his vest pocket before he props his forearms on the lectern, casually watching me approach with a mix of caution and curiosity, as though he holds all the secrets of the universe behind his masked expression.

And he does. This man holds all the secrets.

I will my hand to loosen its grip on the handle of my briefcase as I stop a few paces away from the lectern. Before I'm able to introduce myself, the door to my right opens, and Dr. Banner enters.

"Ah, good. You've already met," he declares.

"Not properly," Orion says, his rich tone curling around each syllable as his gaze drags down the length of my body in obvious appraisal.

Heat flushes my face, and I school my features, trying to discern what reaction will most entice him. Innocent blush? Confident appreciation? Coolly offended?

"Well then, allow me the privilege." Dr. Banner greets me with a chaste smile, but I detect the wariness behind his bravado. Our conversation from yesterday still weighs heavily on him, his fear of this situation going badly. "Dr. Night, may I present Dr. Collins Holbrook. She's taking over the counseling services for staff."

I extend my hand toward him. "It's a pleasure to meet you, Dr. Night."

He hesitates, something akin to betrayal flickering across his face. He remains rooted to the lectern, his gloved fingers tapping the edge, my hand extended awkwardly between us.

My gaze bounces between the two men, and Dr. Banner clears his throat, his discomfort mounting the longer the seconds stretch.

Orion halts tapping, turns his attention to Banner. "I thought we agreed I'd no longer participate in staff counseling."

I slowly lower my hand. Banner shifts his feet. "Unfortunately, for the case to be officially resolved, HR and legal have mandated conflict resolution through mandatory counseling," Banner says, his tone apologetic yet firm. "My hands are tied, Rye."

A shadow falls across Orion's features. "And Prescott."

Banner straightens his posture. "Will be required to do the same to appease the board."

The tension around Orion's eyes softens when his gaze falls on me. Then that brilliant, charismatic smile unfurls. "And you'd be the therapist," he states.

I lift my chin, wondering whether this defines us as friends, rivals, or conspirators. "I'm here to offer my services in any way you need, Dr. Night."

A muscle tightens in his jaw, and some unspoken challenge glints in the depths of his eyes.

Rivals it is, then. At least, for now.

With sure movements, Orion tugs the cuff of his glove up and pushes away from the lectern. He steps directly up to me, his towering height forcing my head to tip back as he boldly steals the hand at my side, his palm sliding along mine with a claiming grasp.

"I'm sure we'll figure that out, Collins." He says my name slowly, as if tasting it, as two of his fingers rest along my inner wrist.

I sweeten my smile, trying to ignore the way the leather scent of his gloves speeds my pulse, the feel too cool against my skin. "I'm sure we will," I concede, unable to curb the slight tremble in my voice. "But please refer to me as Dr. Holbrook."

As I attempt to pull back, he tightens his hold, his long fingers sealing me within his grasp. For the briefest moment, I catch an unstable shift in his expression before his grin stretches. "We'll work on that."

He releases my hand and cuts a flinty look at Banner. "Just more bullshit bureaucracy to waste my time," he says, and Banner visibly recoils. "Don't worry, Leo. I'll play nice for the donors."

I curl my fingers into my palm, feeling the lingering press of leather. Like the predator he is, Orion's gaze catches my action.

"Listen, Rye, none of us want this, you have to understand—" Banner breaks off to collect himself. "The incident left me little choice."

Orion gives Banner the full weight of his icy stare. "Choice," he says with a defiant edge. "That's not a word you want to use with me."

It's more than a power dynamic at play here; it's what I sensed when I first entered the university, that indefinable element that stings the air, the unknown entity that whispers through the dark corridors. It presses against me, rolling off Banner in waves.

Fear.

Like Stonehurst, Orion Night presents a breathtaking exterior, fascinating and beautiful. But it's what lurks in the shadows within that's to be feared. A terrifying and dangerous duplicity.

A lot of information is dropped during this short exchange, and I hang on to a couple key details. Banner's nickname for Orion. The familiarity between them despite the obvious tension. And all the while, I watch Orion's shifting expressions.

He's as unstable as his experiments, and yet, there's no other way for me to get close to him without taking a risk.

I need access to him.

"I'm excited to be here," I say, jumping in to defuse the tension. "This is an amazing opportunity for me."

"You're interested in the study of space, is that right, Dr.

Holbrook? That's why you disrupted my lecture today." Orion watches me with a scrutinizing calmness that chills my blood.

The tempo of my heart accelerates, and I refrain from touching the place where the muscle kicks my breastbone with palpable force, refusing to display the slightest hint of weakness.

Instead, I clasp one hand over the other and press my thumb to the pulse point of my wrist. "I've always found astronomy fascinating. But more so, I rarely have the opportunity to work with someone so gifted in their field," I say, testing a stroke to his ego. "A true luminary."

It's almost unnoticeable, but I detect the slightest tic in his jaw, the dilation of his pupils. "Is that right."

"Absolutely. But I apologize for disrupting your lecture." I hold his gaze, not apologetic in the least as I lick my lips, the way he did when our eyes first met across this hall. His mouth twitches at the corner, a secret between us already. "It's my method, referred to as Naturalistic Observation. It gives me the opportunity to observe a person in their environment, whereas a therapy room could have influence on behavior."

"Observation is how we form theories," Orion states.

"Precisely." I smile.

Banner chuckles gratefully, and an indistinct grunt passes Orion's lips. "And what is your theory of me, Dr. Holbrook?"

"That I need more observation."

A true smile illuminates Orion's face, and I feel it in the backs of my knees. "So you want to watch me…with some voyeuristic method." There's a hidden dare beneath his words, a challenge flickering behind the lustrous blue-green of his eyes.

I flip my hair off my shoulder, too aware of the firing pulse in my veins. "I don't like to waste time, mine or anyone else's. Naturalistic Observation is very efficient."

At the mention of time, Orion checks his wristwatch. He then reaches under his lectern and retrieves a black leather jacket and helmet. After he slips the jacket on, he snaps the collar closed, his tongue resting in the corner of his mouth as he considers me. "We'll meet in your office once I've made time on my schedule."

I bite back my retort, carefully culling my options as my chest tightens. I can only garner what I need by observing him in his environment.

His habitat.

"Then it's settled," Banner says, offering me a strained smile before he steps in Orion's direction. "You'll give Dr. Holbrook what she needs."

"And then some," Orion states smugly, offensively, before he levels Banner with a fixed look. "So I'll expect my terms to be met. Now, if you'll excuse me. I'm late getting to my observatory."

I pull the strap of my briefcase onto my shoulder. "I appreciate your cooperation, Dr. Night."

Orion's eyes clash with mine, a gravity there that threatens to pull me in as his gaze heats, staring at me with such intensity I forget how to breathe. Then he storms from the room, his helmet tucked beneath one arm.

A breath rushes past my lips, and Banner mistakes my reaction for one of relief.

"His observatory," he mutters derisively. "I assure you, Dr. Night is brilliant despite his eccentricities. He won't be as difficult with you."

I arch an eyebrow. "If you'd like for me to believe that, then you won't mind being completely transparent about my real purpose here, Dr. Banner."

A tight frown brackets his mouth. "You have to understand, this is a delicate situation."

Where money is concerned, it's always delicate.

The "incident" transpired during an experimental test, when the observatory's unpatented particle accelerator became unstable.

Another astrophysicist, a Dr. Eugene Prescott, attempted to shut down the instrument, falling from the observation platform after a fight escalated between the two.

Dr. Prescott didn't suffer any injuries, unless his wounded pride counts. I should've been hired to help mediate, but navigating the legalities of the altercation wasn't actually that difficult, seeing as HR closed the case last week. Counseling was noted as a recommendation—not a mandatory requirement.

Proving there's another agenda here.

Anxious, Banner runs a hand down his tie. "Dr. Night is brilliant, there's no question, and what he's done for the university…" He trails off with a defeated sigh. "Years spent working in solitude, under the extreme pressure from our field can strain the most brilliant mind." He glances around before lowering his voice. "I've known Dr. Night for his whole academic career," he continues, a sadness filling his eyes. "And in that time, he's suffered a few setbacks. I just think…I consider him my friend, Dr. Holbrook."

I nod, sympathetic. "Of course. You want to make sure he's receiving the care you feel he needs."

"Exactly." His smile is thoughtful. "With the Solar Eclipse Observer Symposium less than three months away, everything needs to run smoothly. Our donors expect to see results from Orion's research. And let's just say, he has a history of being difficult where investors are concerned."

And there's the optics problem. Dr. Banner may care about his friend, may even want to genuinely help him, but he won't allow Orion to jeopardize his institute's funding.

"Let's go ahead and get you settled, shall we?" Banner offers. "I'd like for you to meet Dr. Prescott soon. His research is also quite remarkable, and he has some fantastic marketing ideas for the symposium. I think you're going to be very pleased with what Stonehurst has to offer, Dr. Holbrook." He beams with pride, and a wariness slithers into the pit of my stomach.

Brows pinched, I study Banner's guarded body language, his forced smile, and a hot blade of realization slashes through me. Banner may want to help his brightest star to continue to shine, but in the event that fails, he already has a replacement ready to step in.

With a beckoning sweep of his hand, he leads the way out of the lecture hall. I follow slowly behind, pausing in the corridor to watch my target escape in the opposite direction, his stunning silhouette slipping farther away until he's swallowed by the shadows.

The desperate desire to chase after him thrums through my veins.

Like one of the brightest constellations in the sky, Orion is a shining star in his field. The one everyone orbits around, and where all the strings on my murder board connect.

The killer I've been searching for.

The hunter.

It's taken months to locate him, and to even get this close, I've had to walk away from the safe and secure life I carefully constructed for myself.

I had to sever my connections to everything, everyone.

The law of proximity states that we're more likely to develop relationships with people within our vicinity. We connect and form friendships with those physically closest to us—classmates, colleagues, co-workers. But simply being in Orion's vicinity is not enough.

I need him to trust me completely. And there is no relationship that fosters more trust than one intimate in nature.

Yet that can't happen if he's removed from my reach.

I catch up to Banner, matching his brisk pace. "What terms has Dr. Night stipulated?" I ask, recalling their tense conversation.

"Stipulated," Banner mutters in a scathing tone. "More like demanded." He sends me a sideways glance. "Dr. Night wishes to work alone on his research. To have the entire research team relocated from the main observatory."

I churn this information over, deciding how to use it to my advantage. "I assume that's a daunting request."

Banner grunts in confirmation.

"But it's not entirely a bad one," I say, earning a confused glare from him. "At least during the evaluation period, to ensure protocols are in place, that safety measures are being taken for the symposium. It would give me the chance to observe him, to work one-on-one, providing him the attention he needs."

It would give me three months.

His sigh is heavy. "Yes, of course. I'll see what can be arranged." A hint of acceptance laces his voice. "Thank you, Dr. Holbrook. I can already tell you're going to be a valuable asset to Stonehurst."

I accept his praise with a demure smile. "My pleasure, Dr. Banner."

Not only does the *femme fatale* firefly have to shine just as bright as her male counterpart, she has to make sure no other predators smother his light.

She has to protect her male, all the while mimicking his flash pattern to lure him closer.

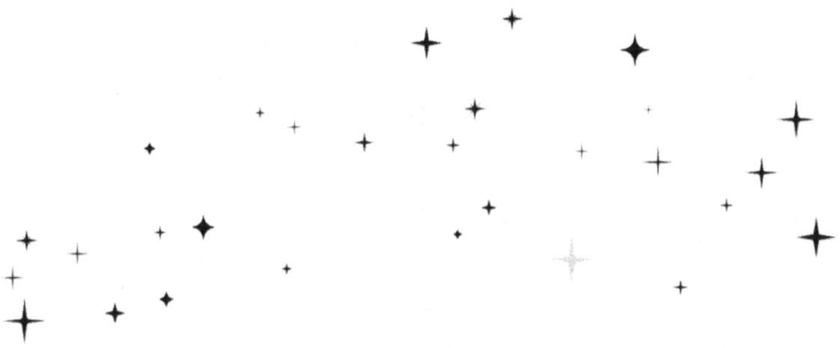

For the first time, astronomers have captured an image of the supermassive black hole at the center of our galaxy, known as Sagittarius A* — the beating heart of our Milky Way galaxy.

— MICHIO KAKU, ON THE 2022 RELEASE OF
THE EVENT HORIZON TELESCOPE IMAGE

4

SHADOW

The umbra is the darkest, innermost part of a shadow in which
all light is blocked, used especially about a shadow made during
an eclipse.

— CAMBRIDGE

ORION

My Triumph roars loud enough to nearly drown out the
storm. Rain needles my body, tires cutting across the
slick asphalt. I throttle the engine, quieting the chaos
inside my head as I push my bike faster down the winding road.

Ahead, the soaring spires of Stonehurst rise up through town.
The domed structure near the top punches past mist like a dark
beacon.

I grip the bars until my gloved knuckles ache, the rumble of
the bike chasing the static clawing at my skull, daring me to push
the machine harder.

I need the danger, the rush.

The noise has become a near-constant now. I blink hard

against the dull throb behind my eyes, feeling the pressure build at my temples like waves battering a seawall.

It started as a shadow, a lurking silhouette at the edge of my awareness. Unseen, unfelt.

Untouched.

This void slowly grew, swallowing until the absence itself began to hum with a discordant resonance.

Down the incline, I pick up speed, savoring the rush of adrenaline until the road veers off. I downshift and swerve into the congested morning traffic, slipping in and out between cars. As I'm forced to slow, I swipe my visor clear, creeping closer to the high gates of the university.

Aspen trees bend against the wind, the sun blotted out by swollen clouds. I tilt my face skyward, finding the seam of light slicing through.

It's become a compulsion to look up. After a lifetime spent searching the farthest reaches of the universe, fascinated by space and stars and planets, there's nothing on this one I find captivating enough to steal my gaze from the sky.

Plagued by more setbacks than discoveries, it's a fucking maddening endeavor. Those few rapturous moments that keep me obsessively searching, immersed in a field of quantum mechanics and observation, tirelessly working with the same four fundamental forces.

And yet, the sheer enormity of the cosmos asserts there must be something more that shapes our existence, some elusive agent hidden in the dark sector of the universe.

In astrophysics, anything dark is simply unknown.

For years, my primary focus was on dark matter—the unknown material of the universe that binds entire galaxies together, wrapping the fabric of space with an invisible, mysterious pull.

My research has since evolved, drawn to an even darker

mystery surrounding black holes, and the paradoxical theory that information is never truly lost.

My efforts to define these things we cannot see or touch have gone well beyond obsession. When you dedicate more than your academic career to the relentless pursuit of such all-consuming forces, you become something of the essence you cannot explain.

Hidden. Unknown. Warped.

And it would seem that for the second time in my life, I've been ensnared by a mysterious, all-consuming force.

Coming to a stop at the sign, my gaze catches on the woman crossing onto the sidewalk.

For one breathless beat, I'm suspended as I watch her, the world narrowing until all that exists is her soft silhouette outlined by the rain, the hurried cadence of her steps. I'm annoyed by the fact that I notice her—that I can't stop noticing her.

And right now, I'm furious over the sight of her drenched, sheltering beneath her briefcase. Livid that, even in her disheveled state, she's still so fucking beautiful she stops my heart.

The blare of a horn jolts me out of my stupor.

"Fuck," I mutter beneath my helmet. Just as I rev the engine and roll forward, her briefcase slips and splashes into a puddle, and I'm hit with an irrational surge of anger.

With a hard twist of the throttle, I swerve into the left lane, ignoring the irritated honk from the car behind as I pull my bike up to the curb.

My gaze never leaves Collins as she treks through the puddle toward the university gate. Fury pulsing through my veins, I drop the kickstand and throw my leg over before I reach into my pack.

I start in her direction, taking in her drenched hair, her thin black coat clinging to her body. As my determined steps close the distance, I hear her breathy curse as she rattles the locked gate, her breath fogging the damp air around her.

She ducks her head to start around, and I step into her path, effectively blocking her escape.

Startled, Collins brings a hand to her chest, her gaze lifting to my black visor as a shiver rolls through her. She's soaked, dark strands framing her face, nude lips pale—and too damn tempting.

The flash of fear crossing her pretty face is unmistakable, and it ignites something hot and reckless in my blood. My gloved hand curls into a fist, muscles coiling tight.

As I step closer, uncertainty draws her features together. Her mouth parts, her eyes widen a fraction, and my pulse riots as she takes a reflexive step back.

Fuck, don't run.

Just as she extends her hand—I thrust the umbrella into her open palm.

Her gaze cast upward, wet lashes blinking against the rain, I glimpse a shimmer of gold there, like a star breaking a teal sky. As her fingers slowly curl around the black steel handle, I back away, escaping to my bike just as quickly.

Satisfaction thrums through my vessels as I maneuver ahead of traffic, a smile tugging at the corner of my mouth when I pass Collins on the sidewalk, now sheltered beneath the black canopy of my umbrella.

And the adrenaline coursing through my bloodstream—fucking euphoric.

If I feed the cravings just enough, I can offset the restlessness. I can't starve them; they only grow hungrier, more demanding, until the pain in my skull is all I can feel, the roar all I can hear. But little hits stave off the worst of the urges.

I pull into my parking space and kill the engine. Rain falls in a steady rhythm as I sit back on the seat, bracing my hands on my thighs. My fingers tap out a habitual count, waiting until I see Collins cross into the covered colonnade before I dismount and cut across the quad with quick strides, rain pelting my helmet and jacket.

Face tilted toward the looming gargoyles that frame the stone arches, I climb the campus steps toward the entrance. I remove my helmet and rake my gloved fingers through my hair, the scent of wet leather clinging to my clothes. Statues and stonework echo my heavy footsteps as I wind through the labyrinth of dark corridors, turning down the main hall.

The gray morning filters in through arched windows where, just beneath, I spot Leo standing sentry near the grand staircase, his posture stiff.

Hot tension twists around my spine, and I rub the ache in my wrist as I pass him. "Not today."

"Not any day," he fires back, trailing after me. "Dr. Holbrook told me you've yet to attend a session."

As though speaking her name alone will summon her, Collins appears at the top of the landing. Rain still dampens her hair. My umbrella is anchored to her wrist, dripping to the stone. She clutches a mug of coffee, engrossed in conversation with Professor Fallon from the physics department.

The sounds of chatter and rushing students fall to a hush as I come to a stop and lean against a stone pillar. Helmet resting on my thigh, I stare up at her, my gaze wandering over her sexy skirt suit, her arm tucked close around her trim waist. Her head tips back and she smiles, laughs, and something foreign tightens beneath my ribs.

"Rye, are you listening to me?"

The impatient grate of Leo's voice tenses my muscles. "I was intentionally trying not to," I give a snide reply. At his irritated huff, a smile lifts the edge of my mouth.

Curious, Leo directs his gaze toward the top of the staircase. "Ah, I see," he remarks, and I don't like the satisfaction I hear in his smug tone.

"You haven't been able to see shit for years, otherwise you'd never have signed off on that useless VR simulator."

He mutters something unintelligible about keeping up with the times, then perks up. "She's quite the eye candy," he says, trying to sound as hip as the students.

"So that was your clever plan, to tempt me into therapy with eye candy." I send him a doubtful look.

He bristles. "Worth a try after all these years—"

My warning glare shuts him down, and I quickly glance away. "Where did you find her?" I ask, and immediately regret it.

"I didn't find her," he says. "Pam did, through the hiring program."

"*Hmm,*" I intone distractedly, caught on the starry points scattered across her inner wrist.

"She was the only applicant."

I grunt in response as my gaze traces the familiar pattern, instinctively connecting the constellation, its arrow pointing toward the dark force at the fiery heart of our galaxy.

"You heard me, right?" Leo demands, running a hand over his graying hair. "No one else even applied. You have to understand that doesn't bode well. I can barely keep a staff counselor hired on after the rumors." A hard divot forms between his brows. "Don't scare her off, Rye."

But I'm no longer listening. As though she can feel my gaze prowling over her, Collins glances my way, our eyes clashing.

And Christ, just like that moment in my lecture hall, an aching chord thrums through my chest, reverberating the sweetest melody. The constant roar inside my head fades, barely noticeable over the thundering pulse in my veins.

I never lose my thought process during a lecture, yet the instant my gaze met hers, I felt the shift, that unknown matter within me swell and recede like a turbulent wave, the ocean of my thoughts pulled into a vortex.

I've made every effort to avoid her since. Then she does shit like this morning, obliviously tromping through the cold rain—and how can I focus on anything fucking else with her walking around soaking wet?

Collins lowers her head, blinks once, twice—her smile lighting her face—before she returns her attention to Fallon.

And fuck, I nearly bound up those stairs as soon as the thought splinters my head, a mental image of smashing Fallon's drivel-spewing face through the window.

I blink back the intrusive thought. Tap my fingers in a rhythmic beat against my helmet. Blink twice more before starting the count on my right hand—

When she chances another look my way, I halt. She lifts the umbrella in a small wave, a faint smile curving the delicate seam of her mouth, and despite myself, my lips twitch.

While it wasn't my intention to frighten her before, it's unavoidable. Keeping my mouth shut is the best policy. Once those dark filaments strangle my mind, I barely have enough willpower to filter what leaves my mouth.

"I'm trying to help you," Leo says, breaking into my thoughts. His hand almost lands on my shoulder before he realizes, dropping it with a frown.

"You're trying to help yourself look better to your donors," I counter, meeting his eyes with a cool stare.

"Yes, because that's how it's done. They want to know where their money went. Like the new HPC expansions—" he ticks off on his fingers "—the fluid chambers. The quantum sensors. All the research expenses you're too paranoid to explain. I have to reassure them we'll have something to show, preferably by the symposium, but I fear it won't be enough—"

"It has to be enough," I mutter, my hungry gaze slipping over Collins. Little hits, stolen glances, feeding the craving—it has to be enough.

Because it can't ever be more.

A sharp pain slices behind my sternum, and I press a hand to my chest. It's like the first time I looked through a telescope and saw the light of a binary star explode into view, reshaping everything I thought I knew.

The aching awe of witnessing something so beautiful, so utterly ineffable, and yet knowing you can only ever admire it from afar.

A rumble of thunder sounds in the distance. The meager light fades farther into the shadows as the storm batters the stained-glass windows. I rub a gloved hand over my jaw, letting my gaze linger on Collins until she disappears up the staircase, taking the last of the light with her.

The void within senses the absence, darkening my thoughts.

Leo has gone quiet. He watches me with a guarded expression, a sheen to his forehead, like he's suddenly aware of the shift. "If you refuse counseling," he says, voice strained now, "I'll be forced to concede to the board."

Tired of his games, I dip my head close. "I know the counseling isn't mandatory," I say, lowering my voice to a lethal decibel. In fact, I have a sneaking suspicion of what Leo actually intends for me.

If he wants to push me out, he'll have to try a hell of a lot harder.

His mouth falls open, but he's smart enough to close it before another lie spills out.

"Don't bother me with Dr. Holbrook again. I'm not interested in therapy or eye candy, Leo." A sudden throb of pain assaults my skull, and I rub my gloved fingers along the side of my forehead. Pushing off the pillar, I tell him, "See you at the unveiling."

When I reach the observatory, the air is thick with the hum of equipment and an undercurrent of tension. A number of gazes lift as I maneuver through the workstations, passing fluid chambers and arrays of quantum sensors. Some of what Leo is so concerned about.

My sonic black hole.

The cylinder filled with circulating water creates an acoustic horizon, simulating the behavior of a Kerr black hole. Observing how sound waves interact with a fluid vortex is useful to my research, and nearly expensive enough to satisfy investors. A front for what lies deeper.

Prescott's eyes narrow on me as I pass, and I allow a slow smirk to twist my mouth. For the sake of the upcoming particle accelerator reveal, I've been advised to keep my distance. Not such an easy feat when he's been trying to steal my research.

I climb the spiral staircase, feeling his eyes drill into my back until I reach the dome.

The chamber is lit by the console lights, the large shutter above sealed. I drop my helmet on the desk and strip off my leather jacket, quickly changing out of my damp clothes before I slide my glasses into place. Each action uncoiling a layer of tension.

I settle behind the desk and wake the monitors. My system is air-gapped from the main facility. In the hidden sub-level beneath the observatory, I've built my own quantum computing array. Superconducting qubits housed inside an industrial-cooled cryostat, protected behind layers of encryption and a biometric lock.

I'm the only one with access.

Even if someone managed to gain entry, they'd never make sense of the photonic resonance simulations, let alone the quantum gravity models. Up here in the dome, I've mirrored just enough of the system to verify celestial alignments and run theoretical particle interactions. A curated overview meant to satisfy any curious, prying eyes.

But the heart of my obsession reaches into far darker regions—ones where quantum theory and gravity collide.

Where existence meets its singularity.

The question that haunts me, whispering at that unseen boundary.

When consciousness collapses, its pattern doesn't simply vanish. It's imprinted into quantum entanglement; encoded signatures that linger like Hawking radiation, preserved at the very threshold of annihilation.

An imprint of existence.

An echo of identity.

Memory—captured at the event horizon, forever caught in the liminal space between oblivion and eternity.

It's an impossible thing, when trying to explain something you can barely grasp yourself. And I know, the science feels heartless. Cold and sterile compared to its origin.

I glance at the telescope—my Hand of God—where I once gazed into nebulae and stellar nurseries, consumed with the beauty of the universe. Those memories being overwritten like code that can't be copied or stored in quantum.

The moment this theory came to me, as I lay beneath a starry night, my body broken, my skull cracked, gazing up at the hunter in the sky—I realized in this shattered state that, if the fabric of spacetime could ripple, it could also rip.

A violent tear right through my life.

For everything beautiful in the universe, there exists a terrifying symmetry. What is luminous and breathtakingly full of wonder is mirrored by its opposite. Shadows that are desolate and horrifying, brimming with destruction and decay.

When a star dies, its core collapses under its own gravity. Once it burns through its nuclear fuel, the heart becomes so heavy, so dense, it's crushed, unleashing a stellar explosion.

In its final beats, a star's life is beautiful, brilliant. Immensely powerful. It's also destructive, violently imploding as its energy is cut short before it darkens into a black hole.

It was once thought this ravenous void devoured everything irrevocably, leaving nothing behind. But through the dark regions of my research, I've glimpsed an impossible truth, where echoes of memory are never lost, preserved indefinitely at the darkest boundary.

Before me, a wall of screens displays three feeds. On the first, an intricate celestial map tracking cosmic events and alignments. On the second, curated data fed into the algorithm—police reports, medical histories, psychological evaluations, demographic lifestyle tracking; even scraped social media and dating app data. And on the third, a graph labeled Quantum Entanglement Entropy.

Just to check the system, I highlight a node: Annihilation 8, Jake Marlow

- Age: 64
- DOB: October 26 (Scorpio)
- Terminal Prognosis: 6 months
- Criminal Profile: Serial rape / homicide
- Entanglement Entropy at Death: 54.2% resonance
- Correlating Cosmic Events: Neutron Star Merger GW261023 (Gravitational waves detected by LIGO/Virgo) & U Scorpii Outburst (Recurrent Nova)

A linked article shows Marlow's censored body arranged as the Scorpius constellation. The instant his consciousness collapsed, gravitational waves from a distant neutron-star merger rippled through space, coinciding with the stellar outburst of U Scorpii.

These extreme celestial alignments time echoes at the boundary. Patterns I can capture, decode.

Symmetry is crucial.

A ritual that has to replicate the exact conditions of that night.

Fingers hovering over the keyboard, I hesitate, waiting to feel the slightest twinge of guilt. That visceral twist in my gut which used to plague me in the early days of my research.

Now, nothing.

Resigned, I initiate the search. It scours databases. It cross-references criminal profiles against predicted astronomical alignments. It's what Leo and the board are so desperate to get their hands on.

My quantum algorithm.

I strip off my gloves and rake a hand through my hair, tension gathering at the base of my neck.

Obsession is physical, something I feel in my flesh like a fever, a madness infecting my cells.

And yet, for a brief moment as I stood at the base of the staircase, gaze cast on her—the only light on this drab fucking rock—I felt like I could breathe.

I switch on the monitor to my left, toggling through the security feeds until she appears on the screen. And hell, there it is again, that blissful disruption.

An immediate rush that feeds the craving.

Her presence resonates with a hypnotic melody. A vibrating current that strums against my skin, softens the battering tide in my head.

Over the past week, I've watched her, lured closer as if by a receding tide. And I savor this feeling until she disappears from the screen. Even after she's faded away, her lingering notes remain, a haunting echo of a tune. It's stirring and melancholic, and it's the reason I lost myself when I first glimpsed her in my lecture hall, rocked by the force of that first powerfully struck chord.

It's been years since I've been able to hear any music.

Removing my glasses, I push away from the desk and stalk toward the controls. The shutters groan open, revealing the panoramic view of the ocean.

Over five years ago, my algorithm identified the coming solar eclipse as the thirteenth celestial event, with Shorehaven directly in the path of totality. It will align with a cosmic event so violent and powerful, I'll be able to capture echoes beyond anything I've recorded.

I glance back at the screen, where names flicker too quickly to register. My algorithm has been searching all this time, filtering, recalculating.

And I'm still waiting for one final name.

A ray of sunlight appears past the stormy horizon, and I inhale deeply, bracing myself for the cycle to begin again. As each celestial event draws nearer, the pull intensifies—stronger, more urgent—until the tidal force is inescapable, stripping away more of my will.

I have no choice but to surrender.

It started as a shadow, a lurking silhouette at the edge of my awareness—yet with every alignment, every kill, the shadow darkens, forming a dense umbra at my core.

It's the interplay between life and annihilation, radiance and void, where matter and its absence converge. A gravitational wound punched into the universe.

You have to look beyond what can be seen, past the horizon.

To even comprehend it, you have to abandon the comfort of known physics. You have to reach into the unknown, into the void itself, and fucking hope some semblance of humanity survives.

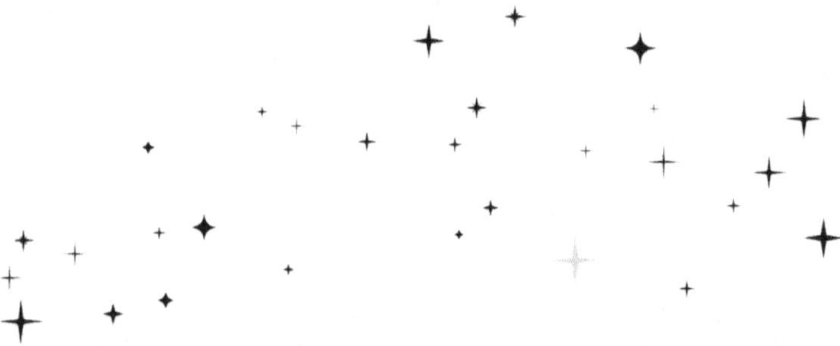

Unable to mount an effective chemical defense of her own, the *Photuris* femme fatale is compelled to spend her nights in pursuit of firefly prey to slake her thirst for toxins.

These insects employ surprisingly sophisticated hunting tactics, including a behavior known as aggressive mimicry.

— DR. SARA LEWIS, EVOLUTIONARY
BIOLOGIST, *SILENT SPARKS*

5
LIE IN WAIT

Never came poison from so sweet a place.

— SHAKESPEARE

COLLINS

There's something haunting about the misty, windswept town of Shorehaven. Despite its quaint veneer, an underlying melancholy burrows in its bones. It feels solemn.

Tragic, even.

With its soaring Gothic buildings that stand in muted tones of gray and black—cold, chipped, faded—it's like the town has been carved right from the surrounding stone by the relentless ocean winds.

I pass the high gate abutting a library as timeworn as the other towering, collegiate structures. Overhead, red- and yellow-capped trees form a broken canopy, their branches trembling.

Every morning, I walk the half-mile of the Professor's Walk from the residence hall to the university—Orion's umbrella looped around my wrist, just in case—until I reach the stone bench in the West Quad. The spot I've claimed as my own for the past three weeks.

Today, the briny scent of sea mingles with the smell of decaying leaves, the air charged with the anxious note of passing time. The hollow tick of the clocktower sounds right before the low rumble of an engine, announcing his arrival.

I set my blond leather briefcase on the ground and cross my ankles. Flipping open to a page in my book, I keep him in my peripheral vision. Past the quad and students migrating toward the colonnade, I watch him dismount his bike. He removes his helmet, swipes a gloved hand through his messy dark hair, and my breath stalls.

As much as you have to fear your target, you have to admire them. Their intelligence. Their skills. Their calculated execution. You have to be a little in love, studying them the way a lover would, memorizing every defining detail. Those qualities that make them unique, even their flaws.

Especially their flaws.

From his hair to his laced-up motorcycle boots, Orion is dressed like the night, those teal eyes that reflect stars and sea the only trace of color. When he unzips his leather jacket, I notice how the material of his charcoal suit stretches across the muscular definition. His hair falls over one eye, obscuring the scar along his forehead.

There's no denying Orion is beautiful. His body, his features. His mind.

Over the past few weeks, our brief encounters have amounted to a handful of lingering glances and fleeting smiles. I've expanded my groundwork, learning his habits, his routine, mannerisms. Mimicking him like our very own courting ritual. Small encouragements to bait him.

I don't pose a threat.

Every exchanged look is a message, so much said in just his eyes, in the tension of his jaw, the subtle curve of his mouth. Every charged, almost brush of contact is a move on our board—like two opponents facing off, inching closer.

Casually, I comb my fingers through my freshly dyed hair. I check my roots daily, keeping two bottles of cool black demi dye stocked. The cyan undertones bring out the teal in my eyes, a small but important detail.

Orion finds meaning in the symmetry of things. Like the birds that flock above the spires, moving in a flowing wave, as if the sky mirrors the ocean.

I turn a page in the book, my thumb grazing the stars dotting my wrist. The tattoo was a part of me from before. I could've covered the ink, but it's easier to maintain a cover story when you blend truth with the lies.

For now, let him believe I'm the fiery seductress who threatens to disrupt his routine. Just enough to unravel him a little.

There's an art to psychological profiling, stringing connections on a murder board like the constellations connect patterns along the stars. Ironically, in this case, when a literal web of constellations happens to be the murder map.

That night on the beach when Darby said my discovery was a coincidence, that there are billions of star patterns...it felt impossible. Although technically, as I soon learned, there are officially eighty-eight constellations across the celestial sphere.

Difficult.

But not impossible.

Once I mapped the chain of kill sites along the ecliptic, I realized not only that the staged victims mirrored zodiacal constellations, but that the date of each kill coincided with a cosmic event, like a meteor shower or planetary alignment.

Location. Event. Victim. This was the pattern.

His pattern.

The design that helped pinpoint where he'd strike next. After losing myself in astrology and—*god*—astronomy, my only logical course was to focus on upcoming events.

My gaze lifts to the banner draped across the quad that reads:

SOLAR ECLIPSE OBSERVER SYMPOSIUM

The moment I spotted the projected eclipse on the star map, I felt the connection falling into place. Not astrological—astronomical. The path the sun takes through the sky, through each constellation.

His ritual coming to completion when the sun goes dark.

So I followed the projected path of totality through each major city and town, eventually landing on Shorehaven.

I slip my hand into my coat pocket, fingers brushing the cool brass artifact I recovered from the Bethany Beach crime scene. This small piece of evidence is what ultimately led me to one of the world's foremost astrophysicists.

Engraved into the brass are three worn letters: SUO—the initials a perfect match for Stonehurst University Observatory.

Once I had a lead to explore, all I had to do was track my hunter on his own turf.

To ensure my place here, I removed every competing résumé from consideration.

While the evidence could've belonged to virtually anyone in the astronomy department, the closer I looked at him, the more the man started to align with the psychological profile.

The law of continuity is used to explore the progression of a person's mental functioning. As our thoughts and actions are connected, over time, our feelings and behaviors follow consistent patterns.

Like how our childhood influences our adult behaviors, or the way we react to certain situations that reflect underlying personality traits and past traumas.

Before the Reaper killings began, there was an inciting incident in a brilliant man's life that altered him, setting off a lethal chain of events that all emerged into a larger pattern.

One of a serial killer.

A shiver whispers up the column of my spine, and I sense the moment his eyes settle on me. I can always feel when Orion is watching, sensing the unflinching intensity of his eyes roving over my body.

It's the primal pull of predator and prey, that instinctual awareness of lurking danger.

Tucking a stray lock of hair behind my ear, I glance through the stone arches toward the parking lot, and my gaze collides with his.

Orion leans against his motorcycle, arms folded across his chest. Even from this distance, I can see the lift of his mouth, one corner pulled slightly higher, betraying his guarded expression like a splinter of light breaking the night.

My pulse quickens as a flush of heat ignites beneath my skin. Even as I succumb to his undeniable charm, I never forget the threat hidden behind that deceptive beauty.

His cunning, meticulous nature. The dark compulsions of his personality. These characteristics are evident in the fitted gloves he never removes, the obsessive drive for perfection, the fixation on his research.

And yet, I've glimpsed tiny cracks in his controlled exterior. Hints of instability, of vulnerability, flashes of reckless impulse. There's an undercurrent of pain that flares behind his high, stony walls, revealing something fractured at his core, something damaged. At times, it can hurt to simply look at Orion, as if no matter how desperately he tries, he can never be whole, unbroken.

It's because of this contradiction that he's unlike other predators of his kind.

He has an expiration date.

The clocktower chimes, and as my hunter is drawn away, I close my book and rise from the bench. I slip beneath the arches of the colonnade, sensing a ripple of tension even before Dr. Banner steps into view.

He strides toward me, movements as brisk as his tone. "Dr. Holbrook, a word."

Despite the unease threading my nerves, I fix a smile into place. Unfortunately, I know what he wants to discuss.

Since I arrived, I've mediated squabbles over stolen lunches. Counseled faculty through depression and burnout. Tending to just about every faculty member here *except* Orion.

"I'm sure you've already heard about last night's unveiling," Banner says. At my hesitation, he adds, "The particle accelerator…the initial test run for the donors."

"Right." I nod, brightening my smile. "I trust everything went well."

He exhales, shoulders sagging. "No. In fact"—his gaze narrows—"it appears someone tampered with the control software. There was an override, causing the system to fail the moment Dr. Prescott powered it on."

Dammit, Orion.

My climbing heart rate pulses in my ears. "That's unfortunate—"

"Unfortunate doesn't cover it." He gives a short, humorless laugh. "This stunt not only cost the university financially, it puts our research at risk. We just… We can't sustain any more setbacks."

Like always, I feel the instant his eyes find me. My gaze flicks to the far end of the walkway where Orion lurks, shoulder braced against an angelic statue, helmet gripped in his hand, fingers tapping. He observes our exchange intently, making no attempt to conceal his interest as his mouth slants into a smoldering smile.

My hold tightens around the steel handle of the umbrella, the one he gave me to shelter from the storm. I recall him standing before me in the rain. Imposing. Striking. Protective in a way that felt possessive.

When the female firefly lies in wait, she's not merely waiting to be impressed; she's studying her suitor. Learning his flash patterns. Deciphering his intent in his signals.

And Orion's signals are too damn erratic. Unless sabotaging the instrument had a deeper purpose, his rash behavior doesn't align with the meticulous predator I've spent years profiling.

"Dr. Holbrook," Banner says, regaining my attention. "I need to know how much longer this evaluation period will take. It's been nearly three weeks already."

Drawing my hands together, I rub my thumb over the faint pulse in my wrist. "I've already implemented safety measures and completed the protocols with Dr. Prescott for the symposium," I say, keeping my tone neutral. "Has there been any progress in relocating the research team from the main observatory?"

"Unfortunately, the board isn't too eager to make changes." He adjusts his stance, exhaling audibly. "Let me be candid with you. Dr. Night has potentially discovered something groundbreaking in his research, something that could put Stonehurst on the map. The board feels relocating Dr. Prescott from the observatory isn't ideal."

An icy current of unease slips through me. They have their own eyes on Orion. "Understood," I say.

Banner eases closer, lowering his voice. "It pains me to say this, but if your approach isn't working, we may need a more decisive measure." With a heavy sigh, he reaches inside his blazer and produces a folded document.

Wary, I accept the paper and unfold it slowly.

"If I'm being frank, the ideal scenario might be if Dr. Night weren't present during the symposium. If he were somehow… detained." He holds up a hand, as if it's just an innocent suggestion. "Placed under observation, just temporarily."

I skim the page. It's a referral for a mandatory inpatient psychiatric evaluation. The dates of which conveniently coincide with the symposium. My name and credentials are printed at the bottom, awaiting my signature.

And there it is—the agenda.

Banner hired me to be his scapegoat. My only purpose here is to declare Orion unsound and have him removed.

"It's just too risky," Banner continues, trying to justify himself. "We can't afford any incidents or interference during the symposium."

I slip the document into the pocket of my briefcase, my gaze inadvertently seeking Orion down the walkway as I fight to smother the fire in my stomach. "I can see how heavily this is weighing on you," I say, injecting a grain of sympathy into my tone. "Especially considering everything Dr. Night has contributed here."

Banner glances away, but not before I see the flicker of guilt in his eyes. "Dammit," he mutters. "I just keep hoping Rye will come back around."

I place a gentle hand on his arm. "You've mentioned how stressful this field can be," I remind him.

"It's more than that," he says, almost to himself. "Maybe there's just too much loss for one person to come back from."

I withdraw my hand. "I don't follow. There hasn't been any mention of that in his file."

He releases a humorless laugh. "No, there wouldn't be. Not in our field, when the mere suggestion of instability can ruin a career." He straightens, pulling away. "I've done my best to protect him, but sometimes it feels like Rye is hellbent on that ruin."

My grip tightens on the handle, heart rate rising. "If my method hasn't been effective, maybe it's time I try a more direct approach."

Banner nods in reluctant agreement. "You shouldn't blame yourself. Academia is full of secrets." His gaze drops to my briefcase, underscoring his point before he offers a strained smile. "Have a good day, Dr. Holbrook. We'll speak again soon, I'm sure."

With that, he strides away, leaving me standing in the colonnade. I draw in a slow breath, loosening my grip on the umbrella, my pulse pounding in my fingertips.

"Shit," I mutter.

I turn to find Orion moving against the tide of students, his eyes fixed on me. As he approaches, he studies me curiously, like an insect he's just torn the wings from.

"You look bothered, Dr. Holbrook," he remarks, leaning into my space, close enough that his shoulder comes within an inch of brushing mine.

Heat spills through my veins as I angle my head to meet his gaze. "You're always so observant, Dr. Night."

A hint of amusement flickers behind his eyes. He drags a gloved hand over his mouth and stalks away. As he reaches the arched column, he glances over his shoulder.

Smiles.

And that smile… A little cruel, a little hungry. A little entirely too beautiful. It makes my heart clench, sending blood flowing in reverse. A physiological response to my chosen male.

But while the *femme fatale* firefly may have the luxury to lie in wait, I no longer do.

Before he disappears from view, I mirror his smile, clutching the umbrella to my chest as if his protection is what I desire. What I *need*.

The art of seduction isn't solely a psychological tactic—it's a surrender of the heart.

According to Banner, Orion's inciting incident spans more than a single moment, the damage running deeper than those tiny cracks.

To get closer, I need to do more than mirror him. I have to reveal some of my own cracks, letting him see the fracture lines.

Normally, I'd draw him out by creating intimate moments, becoming an anchor for him with subtle touches. Intertwining myself with his positive, pleasurable emotions.

Because once your target relies on you to bring them pleasure, the cold denial of your attention brings them pain.

And pain is the ultimate conditioning tool.

Yet Orion presents a complication here with his aversion to touch. Without that simple anchor, I'm forced to be more creative.

I pivot and head in the direction of my office, my heels striking the sandstone in a sharp staccato that echoes the firing beat of my pulse.

Whether protective or possessive, my hunter is a predator, a creature ruled by instinct and driven by a primal impulse he can't deny. While Orion may be unlike others of his kind, all predators have the same innate weakness.

And nothing lures a predator more effectively than the scent of wounded prey.

If I attracted one monster, I can attract another.

If foundational information disappears into a gaping maw, the notion of a 'past' itself may be in jeopardy—we couldn't even be sure of our own histories. Our memories could be illusions.

— STEPHEN HAWKING, ON THE BLACK HOLE
INFORMATION PARADOX

6

GRAVITY

You can't blame gravity for falling in love.

— ALBERT EINSTEIN

ORION

Through the panoramic window of my observatory, I focus the monocular on Collins crossing the leaf-covered quad. All around, the clear ocean sky vies for my attention, yet I can't take my eyes off the breathtaking view below.

Shoulder braced against the cool windowpane, I tighten my grip on the compact telescope. After grinding a new lens, the image quality is unmatched, bringing her close enough to burn.

Her legs are bare below the hem of her stylish skirt, where eight little buttons hold the pleat of fabric fixed, the suit jacket coming to rest an inch above the skirt hem. It's just provocative enough to be distracting, but still professionally tailored to her petite body.

Dark waves bounce along the curve of her back as her heels

punch down with purpose, carrying her toward the arched colonnade, the overcast afternoon doing nothing to mute her striking presence. Though she's trying, it's impossible for her to blend into the scenery. She's calling attention just by breathing.

Whether Collins realizes it or not, her presence has caused a disruption. I've fine-tuned this institute the way I calibrate every instrument in my observatory, and I can sense the interference in my bones.

Her vibration cracks through me like a fault.

Every time I catch the soft echo of her voice, or feel her gaze across a room, my ribs tighten, my sternum caving until breathing alone aches.

It has to be enough.

I watch her stride beneath one of the stone archways. She pulls out her phone and absently presses her foot to the column behind her, posed effortlessly at ease, her knees slightly parted. So tantalizingly seductive I almost feel ashamed for looking.

Almost.

Something dark and dangerous stirs beneath my skin. Seeing her in the darkened walkway by herself, vulnerable, as if she's issuing a dare. The thought scratches at some deep itch just enough to inflame it.

It's getting harder to find relief. Chasing hits of adrenaline, speeding my bike until the rush bleeds the turmoil from my veins, numbing the residual aches in my bones. And still, the hollow inside me deepens, this insidious hunger growing harder to satisfy.

Because fuck, this isn't healthy. Pining after a woman who reminds me—with every aching breath—how dangerously close I am to losing control.

As if to reinforce that thought, I catch sight of Prescott approaching from the side. My spine stiffens as he steps into her space, leaning in far too close—and the sudden, intrusive urge to disembowel him with his own calipers grips me.

"That fucking prick," I mutter.

"Even the most insufferable pricks don't deserve to have their equipment sabotaged."

Leo's irritated grumble further coils the fury in my gut. "Some equipment is just inadequate," I say. At his exasperated sigh, a smirk tips the corner of my mouth.

I sense him drawing near the window, and my annoyance flares. Leo's the only one allowed in this part of the observatory, and that's only because he's the president—and I haven't figured out a way to do away with him.

Yet.

I lower the monocular, but not before he catches on to what I'm observing below.

"You know, a little professional rivalry is typically healthy," he remarks from over my shoulder. "But this is not, my friend."

Hit with the fierce desire to strangle him with Prescott's entrails, I drop the instrument onto the metal table with a resounding *clang* and step away. "The magnets were misaligned and the timing of the beam was off," I say, offering some explanation. "It wasn't safe."

"Then you should've simply overwritten the program for beam alignment and magnet currents," he says with infuriating logic, "correct any anomalies. *Not* kill the unveiling."

Correct any anomalies.

I scrub the back of my head, blinking hard to force the swelling pressure to recede. "When the system detects an anomaly, it calls for a complete shutdown," I say, but I'm no longer talking to him.

My gaze snaps to the screen in the corner. I tap my fingers against my thigh in time with its continuous flicker—*one, one, two, three, five*—my thoughts drifting as the algorithm continues its search.

Leo watches me closely, a concerned draw to his brows. "Rye…" He says my name questioningly.

"Yeah," I say, giving my head a shake. "It was petty. Won't happen again." I tell him this so he'll leave.

"It can't happen again," he stresses, a warning there. He proceeds to pick up the monocular and gaze at the scene unfolding below, letting a beat stretch before he says, "Prescott seems to like Dr. Holbrook. He had a meeting with her after the disastrous unveiling." He lets his baiting remark hang between us. "In fact, he said he finds her sessions *quite* stimulating."

Dark filaments edge into my vision.

"He'd find a seminar on orbital debris stimulating," I say, annoyingly aware of the possessiveness in my voice.

"Well, can't blame him with a celestial body like that floating around campus." He chuckles at his own crude joke.

My jaw clenches, and I snatch the scope from his thick hand. "You're not here to shoot the shit, Leo. What do you want," I demand, unable to curb the lethal edge in my tone.

"Right." He drops his hands into his pockets. "I'm here to make you an offer in the hope that we can get back on track. I'm ready to grant your terms." He clears his throat. "Because I do understand the obstacles you face, if working entirely alone will help you make progress in your research, I'll relocate the team to the RC section."

I cock an eyebrow, waiting for the catch.

He rocks back on his heels. "All that's required is a single evaluation with Dr. Holbrook." He holds up a hand. "Just one. That's all I'm asking, Rye. No, it's not mandatory, but it will go a long way to appease those who have concerns."

At the mere suggestion of being alone with her, a dark current thrashes against my skull. Something deep within claws, gnashing its teeth. While dabbling in a little light stalking can be a somewhat masochistic pastime, it's ultimately harmless. But placing her directly within reach—

That's more than dangerous.

Leo expels an audible breath. "You do owe me this," he says.

A knowing smirk pulls at my mouth. And there it is, cashing in on a debt he thinks I owe him. But for a single evaluation... That's not nearly a high enough ask to balance the scales. I've known my old colleague too long not to suspect an ulterior motive.

At my silent refusal, he curses under his breath. "Christ's sake. Whatever you think, I am trying to help. I don't even ask that you prepare your own course material. Your damn TA handles all that, down to grading papers. I practically let you get away with murder."

I cock an eyebrow.

"You've become rash and impulsive," he continues, undeterred. "Do you realize what the faculty and students are saying about you? That you're unhinged."

I release a dry laugh. "Is that the trending word of the day?"

He bristles, struck right in his fragile ego. He doesn't like to be reminded that he's aging, becoming obsolete.

Hell, we all are.

But here's what Leo can't seem to grasp. Our empathy, our vaunted humanity, is a weakness holding us back from achieving what is otherwise impossible within a single lifetime.

Leo sighs heavily. "They just want a clearance on record," he says.

I shake my head, annoyance mounting. "Fuck, I already gave you that two years ago—"

"Yes, but after the most recent incident," he interrupts, "you have to appreciate my position here. It's risk mitigation." His voice softens a fraction as he says, "It'll be handled internally. I am looking out for you, Rye. Just trying to keep you here."

I glance at the brass orrery mounted beneath the platform, feeling that urgent tug with each mechanical orbit. The solar eclipse is only two months away, and I've been here all this time, waiting.

"Fine," I relent, the bitter concession ground between my teeth. "One evaluation."

Leo nods, looking relieved. "All right. Good." He heads for the staircase, pausing at the landing to glance back. Shadows deepen the lines around his eyes. "It's been six years," he says quietly, his tone tinged with regret. "We've avoided it all this time, but… What happened to Emma—it was tragic. Horribly unfair and tragic. But it wasn't your fault. There was nothing you could've done to prevent it."

The dome tilts around me, pitching me off balance. Old breaks throb with a sudden flare of pain as a faded memory ripples through. The panic in her voice. The crushing helplessness. The vicious twist of guilt as my body lay broken, useless beneath the stars.

I struggle to anchor myself, fighting back the dark tide roaring in my ears.

Leo exhales an exasperated breath. "What I'm saying is, you can't punish yourself forever. Moving on doesn't mean forgetting."

"Forgetting," I repeat in a bitter tone as I flex my fingers, aggravating the phantom ache of shattered bones. A painful reminder that refuses to *let* me forget.

He lingers for a moment longer, then gives a solemn nod before he descends the stairs, leaving me alone with my loathing.

And I'm thrust back to the day he extended a lifeline, offering me the chance to head my own Department of Physics and Astronomy at Stonehurst.

Leonard Banner knew me before I became a blight on the field, mocked for my theories, reputation smeared. Hell, he was even the one who encouraged me into the dark regions of my research, eyes alight with ambition.

Well, technically, that was more spite than Leo.

Nothing fuels the drive to succeed quite like spite.

Still, beneath my cold resolve, some shred of sentiment must remain, because I decide maybe I won't strangle him with Prescott's entrails. Just leave them lying around for him to trip over.

As if pulled by a gravitational force, I return to the panoramic glass, finding Collins still engaged with Eugene-fucking-Prescott.

The breeze picks up, carrying a soft chorus of thunderous waves. Collins shivers, and I wonder if it's from the gusty autumn air or the predatory gaze she senses lingering on her skin.

Every day, I sense the shadow darkening my mind a little deeper. Drawing me further into the clutches of some sinister influence. Like the woman silhouetted in the archway, unknowingly inviting danger, I've attracted something menacing and overpowering.

I curl my hand into a fist against the windowpane, assaulted by the echo of her near-touch that first day. It rings against my skull with a deafening tune, an infection seeping into my bloodstream the more I worry it.

On impulse, I sink my hand into my pocket and touch the brass instrument there, feeling the coolness of it as the breeze drifts past the open shutter to douse some of the heat gathered beneath my flesh.

Collins looks up as though she can, in fact, sense the predator in her midst. She says something dismissive to Prescott, and he gives her the full, arrogant wattage of his smile before he reaches out and clasps her hand.

My nostrils flare, my focus drilling to a pinpoint on their

joined hands. A violence rips through my insides at the sight of his skin touching hers, my breath caught in the aching cavity of my chest until she breaks away and disappears into the depths of the colonnade to release me.

I expel a tense breath, rubbing the back of my neck.

"Fuck, this really isn't healthy," I mutter, bracing my palm against the window as I stare out over the campus.

Over the spires, starlings fly in rhythmic formation. Intricately timed murmurations roll like waves, each movement an echo of the ocean, traced across a twilight sky. Their pattern unfolds in flawless spirals and waveforms, as intimately related as the golden ratio and the Fibonacci sequence.

As if triggered, my fingers tap a compulsive count against the glass, innate as breath, easing the tension crawling beneath my flesh. Twelve beats to maintain some sense of balance and control.

From up here on the bluff, my observatory perched just below the highest spires, I feel like a god watching over his creation.

And Stonehurst *is* my creation.

A forgotten relic of academia, the university was in ruins before I restored Stonehurst Observatory, reinventing the astronomy department to become one of the most sought-after by investors.

In truth, we were both in a state of decay, this dormant carcass on the verge of collapse, my shambles of a career crumbling like ruins into the sea. Both neglected, forgotten. Destined to rot.

Once your name is touted to achieve extraordinary things and you fail—immensely—you're swept aside, buried. Cast into the farthest reaches of oblivion itself.

While I do owe Leo for that lifeline, I've repaid my dues and then some. Besides, I had little choice in coming here. And his charity was hardly selfless.

Desperation can push us to take extreme risks.

My old colleague once cared more about breakthrough and discovery than impressing donors.

Now that Stonehurst is being recognized in a prestigious light, funding and acolytes pouring in, fresh blood infusing the dusty veins of the halls, he'd sell me out just to secure another wing for his institute.

His risk paid off.

Now I'm too great of a liability.

Jaw set tight, I turn to face the Hand of God, the name a nod to Feynman and his number obsession. At the center of the dome is the 14-inch Clark refractor telescope, gifted to the university over fifty years ago.

The tube of brass and precision-cut glass points toward the open shutter, supported by a balance of gears and counterweights of my own design. I pull myself onto the aluminum ladder and adjust the mount's controls, comforted by the familiar turn of gears. A process I don't have to repeat incessantly until it feels *right*.

Before I came here, the telescope was destined to be donated to a museum, Leo having nearly drained the department's funds for the RC telescope. Yet I did more than restore the Clark—I enhanced it beyond its capabilities.

My hand glides over the tube, further chasing back the heated thoughts Collins stirred awake. This is the one place—the *only* place—where I find any peace from the intruding thoughts.

As if to mock me, an image flashes of her sitting on the bench this morning, her pretty teal eyes staring into mine as she licked her finger to turn a page in her book.

Feeling unstable, I spear a hand into my disheveled hair. A dark laugh escapes, nearly shocking me. No matter how advanced we strive to become, no matter how dedicated to our evolution, we're still just these primitive, carnal beasts.

Honestly, I shouldn't be surprised by this development. If you deprive yourself long enough of any sustenance, your body will find a way to get what it needs—by any means necessary.

A dark current thrums along my spine as I descend the ladder and seat myself behind the console. Sliding my glasses into place, I toggle through my coded application and adjust the telescope's position. A calming hum resounds throughout the room before the telescope locks into place.

As the sun dips below the horizon, I try to reclaim that rare peace. Hours bleed away until darkness tints the windows, the reflection of lamplight killing the view. My neck stiff, eyes blurry from monitor glare, I rub the scar below my hairline, bracing for the migraine already pulsing at my skull.

Frustration flares hot, and I shove away from the computer. Before I register what I've done, the chair sails across the room, crashing into the wall with a loud clang.

"Dammit."

I tear off my glasses and drag both hands down my face. I then look up, searching for the stars beyond the darkened glass.

This, right here, is why the research team has to be relocated. Intrusive thoughts used to be just that—thoughts.

One second I imagined Prescott a broken heap on the ground —the next he was sprawled on the lab floor beneath me.

With a harsh exhale, I glove my hands and stalk toward the safety gate. Gripping the metal rungs, I scale the ladder and haul myself onto the catwalk and shove the door open, stepping onto the narrow observation deck that wraps the dome.

Inhaling a deep breath, I infuse my lungs with a cool, cleansing hit of salty ocean air and evergreens, dousing the fire in my chest.

The stars burn against a blanket of black sky. I can feel the kinetic pull, that dark energy capable of ripping atoms apart, a threat to my bones and organs, barely held together by that elusive matter.

On the misty shore below, waves crash against jutting rocks in a hypnotic, punishing rhythm. Crash and recede. Pounding the beach with the same relentless demand as the throb assaulting my head.

I reach into my pocket and retrieve the astrolabe, its compact design crafted to mirror the star-taker once used by ancient astronomers to decipher the secrets of the stars and planets.

A heavy pulse builds in my veins as my thumb sweeps the engraved ecliptic plate, tracing the calibrated dial. On instinct, my thumb moves to swivel the sighting vane on the rule—only to remember it's no longer there. Jaw tight, I tap my thumb against the rete to offset the unease.

I turn my gaze toward the night, immediately pinpointing Orion. Three brilliant stars mark the belt—Alnitak, Alnilam, Mintaka—guiding my gaze toward a dimmer cluster of stars on the sword, where the nebula glows faintly, a wisp of white bleeding into the dark.

While the swirling hues of blue and green and gold aren't visible to the naked eye, I've long since memorized its cloud of dust and starlight.

The same beautiful colors found in her eyes.

"Fuck."

Moving on doesn't mean forgetting.

My ribs strain beneath the crushing pressure of Leo's words. Every day, the implications of my research war with the consuming gravity of memories. Fighting to hold onto them—to let go.

The cruel paradox that defines more than my work.

I lower the instrument, gripping it so fiercely the edges dare to bite past leather before I shove it into my pocket.

Then I'm clutching the iron rail, muscles tensed around bone and sinew. It's just a thought—*what if I jump*—then I'm suddenly climbing over, my back pressed to the railing, my fingertips curled around the rough metal lip. The only solid thing preventing me from tumbling down.

Most people never act on their intrusive thoughts.

Most people allow fear to hold them back from doing the unspeakable.

Such unspeakable things haunt my waking world the way nightmares torment the damned.

I lean farther out, letting gravity grip me, the tips of my fingers giving an inch. Adrenaline floods the chambers of my heart, static frenzy setting my blood ablaze.

The rush is exhilarating. The possibility of letting go. Of surrender. Of gravity claiming me all at once with the bloody slip of my fingers. Sent crashing to the rocks.

Returned to stardust.

Through the howl of wind and roaring waves, a sound slices through the dark. Awareness prickles the back of my neck. I strain to see past the cliffside, my vision obscured by the dense night mist—until the sound comes again.

It's unmistakable this time. A cry for help.

Not just any cry.

Hers.

Without fear to hold me back, I do the unspeakable.

And jump.

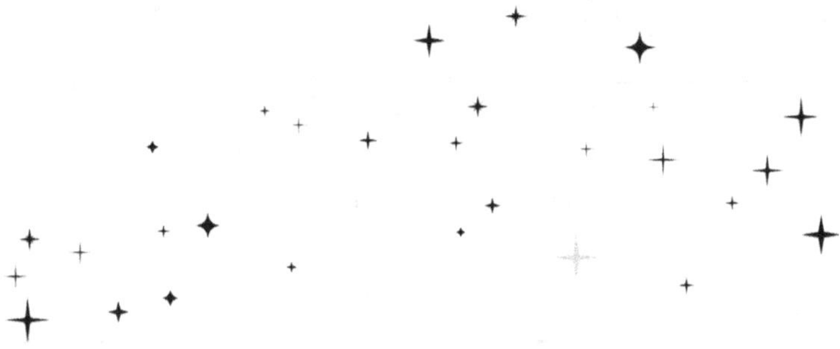

The network of neuronal cells in the human brain and the cosmic network of galaxies.

Although the relevant physical interactions in the above two systems are completely different, their observation through microscopic and telescopic techniques have captured a tantalizing similar morphology, to the point that it has often been noted that the cosmic web and the web of neurons look alike.

— FRANCO VAZZA & ALBERTO FELETTI, *THE QUANTITATIVE COMPARISON BETWEEN THE NEURONAL NETWORK AND THE COSMIC WEB*

7

CHEMICAL ATTRACTION

Second contact (C2): The moment the moon completely covers the sun in a solar eclipse, initiating the beginning of totality.

ORION

Halfway down, I catch hold of the maintenance line, the sudden jolt wrenching my muscles. My hands slip along the rope, friction burning my palms through the heated leather before I secure a firm grip.

I sway in the open air, the metal ring bolted to the exterior of the observatory groaning under my weight. Muscles strained, palms on fire, I glare across at the ladder running along the wall. In hindsight, a much *saner* option.

"Fuck."

Destination unavoidable, I savor the last hit of adrenaline before I release the rope, dropping the remaining fifteen feet. I grunt as my hands and knees take the brunt of the impact, the sand about as soft as a slab of concrete. A jolt of pain shoots up my leg from the old fracture.

Despite my body aching in protest, the faint sound of Collins's voice spurs me toward the sloping edge of the cliff, where the drop-off isn't as drastic.

Searching out a crevice, I wedge my boot into the rock face and begin to scale down the incline. A loose rock dislodges beneath my hand, and I latch onto a jutting stone before my feet find purchase on a large shoreline boulder.

The tide has come in, filling the narrow clefts between the sea stacks. The raging surf crashes against the slate stones, sending a wild ocean spray over Collins as she clings to one of the boulders.

"Hold on—" I shout, my voice cut low by the savage bursts of waves that continuously batter the rocks.

Bracing myself for the icy bite, I drop into one of the deep crags, sucking in a sharp breath as the briny water reaches my thighs. I fight the current through the hollows, the swelling tide nearly toppling me over, until I reach her and heave myself onto the jagged edge of the boulder.

Across the gray-washed dark, lit only by the stars glinting silver off caps of foam, my eyes connect with hers.

And my lungs seize, speared through by the same unnerving sensation I feel every time I see her. Bathed in mist and eerie light, her dark hair wild from the spray, clothes soaked and molded to her curves—fuck, she's so beautiful it's painful.

"What are you doing here?" she demands, just as a wave crashes over us. She hunkers low on the rock before once again spearing me with those unearthly teal eyes, their intensity heightened by the fear I find cresting there.

"That's what I should ask you." A blaze of anger lights up my sternum, so sudden, I grit my teeth against the impact. "Why the hell are you out here putting yourself in danger?"

Shock parts her mouth, and she frantically pushes her damp hair away from her face. "It was a warm evening. I went for a walk," she says evenly.

Her feet are bare, shoes lost. She's not wearing a jacket, just a flimsy white blouse and that same tight skirt. I situate myself on the rock as another hit of anger sharpens my voice. "Alone?"

"What—you're angry with me? How was I supposed to know a crazy-high tide would come in within a matter of seconds?"

I dig my gloved fingers against the coarse surface of the rock, and my palm flares with a satisfying hit of pain. I could blame my heated response on the adrenaline still pouring through my veins, but I suddenly realize how fragile she is.

And that fucking near-transparent blouse clinging to her chest isn't helping.

"Spring tide," I say in a more controlled tone. As her mouth purses in confusion, I point toward the black sky. "Extreme high tides come with a new moon." I glance at my watch, muttering a curse as I try to blink away the blurriness. "I think it's close to ten. The tide will start to recede after midnight."

"Wait… We're going to be stranded out here for two hours?" She curls her slight body against the raised edge of the boulder and pulls her legs beneath her, wrapping an arm around her waist as a fierce shiver racks her body.

Some foreign emotion cracks open inside my rib cage. The same gravity that dropped me over forty feet on impulse now crushes me beneath its pulverizing weight.

I scrape my fingers through my damp hair, and a spike of alarm blazes through me. I ball my hands into fists before inspecting the injury. The sodden leather damn near shredded, salt water like fire against the rope burn, I'm relieved when I see only my palms sustained any damage.

God damn. I jumped off the observation deck for her—without any thought.

By the time I crawl across the uneven stone toward her, she's unable to control the tremors attacking her muscles. Wearing only my oxford shirt, I have nothing to offer for warmth.

"You're going to tell me something I don't want to hear," she says, her voice a quivering rasp.

I turn my face skyward, gauging the depth of darkness. This rock will be submerged in less than an hour.

As another violent spray sends shards of water down on us, I hold up my hand as a useless shield. "Come on," I tell her. "I'll help you wade through."

Collins flattens her palm to the space beneath her collarbone, real fear blanching her features beneath the pale starlight. "I can't…I'm sorry."

"You can. It's not yet that deep."

Stubbornly, she shakes her head.

"I thought fire signs were more daring and adventurous," I say to bait her.

Her pretty gaze narrows on me, an accusation banked there within the hidden striations of gold.

"Your ink," I explain, letting my eyes fall to her covered wrist. "I connected the dots on the constellation pattern. Either you or someone close to you is a Sagittarius, I assume."

Her unsure stare holds mine a moment longer before she looks down and slips her sleeve up, exposing the starry points across her inner wrist. "I don't have anyone close."

When she looks up, something frail and unguarded flashes behind those lustrous eyes, and it clenches the muscle beneath my ribs, dripping a kind of sadness that can't be captured, stolen.

Kept.

She covers her wrist. "But I guess I just clash with water. I can't swim." Her soft voice is snatched by the deafening wind. "The tide came in so fast, pushing me up toward the rocks. I thought I could hike through them back to the pier…"

I frown, not needing the rest of her explanation. It's a slow crawl through the shoreline rocks, much too slow to escape a high surge. Especially if you're fearful of water.

Despite my impaired eyesight, the raw vulnerability of the situation makes it impossible for her to mask the tremulous shame etched across her beautiful face. The desire to pull her into me is so intense, I fear my impulsive thoughts more than the dangers of any tidal swell.

This close to her—alone in the dark—the fiendish cravings should be clawing at my skull. Yet her proximity quiets the noise banging inside my head just enough to maintain a level of control.

It's fucking maddening.

I don't press her. Some things are best left obscured by the dark. Instead, I lean back against the rock and shift my body closer, offering what little heat I can to replace the warmth leached from her trembling body.

"A tidal surge can catch anyone off-guard," I eventually say, attempting to ease her.

"Right." She nods shakily. "So I should be wary of the new moon, then." Her gaze tracks over my profile.

I scrub the back of my head. "All phases of the moon influence the tide, but I think it'd sound odd to say you should be wary of celestial alignment." At her prolonged silence, I clear the ache from my throat. "There's enhanced gravitational pull on the oceans when the Earth, moon, and sun align."

She subtly arches an eyebrow. "Yes, that would sound odd, Dr. Night. But you still said it."

I chuckle, surprising myself. "It might be easier to download a tide app." I look her over, noting she doesn't have her phone.

"I like to disconnect after work," she answers my unspoken question. "Wait. Where's yours—"

"I don't have one. At all." Hope falls from her features, replaced by a questioning look. I release a heavy breath. "Distractions. Germs." I wiggle my gloved fingers for emphasis.

"You could get one of those old flip phones. No touchscreens."

I drag the ridge of my teeth over my bottom lip, thoroughly amused by her. "Distractions," I reiterate.

As the crash of waves fills the stretch of silence, my hope of boring her past a panicked state is ruined as she holds my gaze, her wide eyes sheened with starlight. A captivating phenomenon that lures me closer, caught in her blink pattern—one, one-two, one, two—

"What else should I know?" she asks, disturbing my obsessive thoughts. "I should probably learn how to traverse this deathtrap around here."

I lick my lips, tasting the salt and a warm current of vanilla and amber mixed with her relief. "Tides change every six hours." I pull my leg up and rest my arm over my knee. "There are two high and low tides every twenty-four."

Her smile is more breathtaking than the gusting wind. "Maybe it's just smarter for me not to roam the beach."

"Can't live in fear."

"And that's how one winds up stranded on a rock."

"With a devastatingly attractive astrophysicist," I say, bringing a slight flush to her skin, and I can't help the smile twitching at my lips.

The breathy sound of her laugh unfurls heat in the center of my chest. "God, you have no filter," she says.

I grin, shrugging. "We're not trapped. Yet."

Worry pinches her eyes, and she turns her attention to the churning water, the ocean covered by a veil of endless dark. "Yet," she whispers. "But the tide will keep rising before it recedes."

The intense wind guides my face back to hers. "Yes."

A breath slips past her trembling lips, the softest brush across mine. "I'm not sure the truth is what I need right now."

The gravity of her gaze condenses the atmosphere between us, the echo of her words crashing against my chest more powerfully than the waves trying to shatter this rock.

"What do you need?" I dare to ask.

Her arm curls tighter around her middle as she stares up at me. "A distraction."

An ache lodges at the base of my throat, and I decide I can give her this. "What would you tell a patient caught in a similar situation?"

She releases another light laugh. "Clever. But I think I'd warn them not to get marooned on rocks with devastatingly attractive astrophysicists to begin with."

She pulls a smile from me too easily. "Is there a better way to get you alone, then?"

Something flashes in her eyes, but before I'm able to analyze it, a wave breaks over us with a harsh spray, and Collins buries herself into my side.

The feel of her hair grazing my cheek stokes the fiery itch beneath my skin, and a hit of alarm spikes my adrenals. In an effort to distract myself as much as her, I cast a glance at the starry canvas above. "If the moon were full, we could see it reach its zenith, giving us a better calculation for the outgoing tide."

"All this from studying rocks in space," she says absently, but not at all incredulous.

"Admittedly, I have the advantage of watching the ocean for years."

"For some reason, I doubt you need the advantage." She peeks up at me, her smile sweet but knowing. "Don't try to be humble, Dr. Night. It doesn't suit you."

There's a flutter in my chest. "Noted, Dr. Holbrook."

"You can use my name."

"You caved on that stipulation." The corner of my mouth kicks up.

"Life in peril has a way of doing that," she says, her starry eyes hung on mine.

As the ocean rises around us, I keep her locked in my gaze, feeling unmoored by the rhythmic crash of waves and the sharp, howling wind. The thundering drum of my pulse. The spray misting the atmosphere, ethereal and hazy. Beneath it all, I can sense the violent, uneven thump of her heart, a rising chorus of chords and beats that twine around me, through me, rushing the deeply pronounced crags of my soul more furiously than the ocean between the hollow veins of the rocks.

At the atomic level, chemical attraction is an absolute, a rule. The process to form bonds is a law woven through the very fabric of the universe. The fusion which fuels the stars.

There is no refuting the science. Instant chemical attraction not only exists, on a nuclear scale, it's strong enough to power a hypernova.

I just never believed I'd experience it outside the lens of my telescope.

An ache sears my throat as I realize, here beside her, falling into the captivating depth of her eyes, I'm utterly susceptible.

This attraction burns.

Breaking the charged connection, I swallow, returning my gaze to the dark expanse. There is one advantage I can take—one I should be shamefully opposed to.

But the dark tide rising within me makes its own demands.

As my eyes track back to her, maddeningly beautiful in her disheveled, vulnerable state, obsession licks through me, coiling around me like the dark tendrils that twist tighter and tighter every day.

"Why are you here, Collins?"

Her body tenses next to mine. "I told you, I went for a walk—"

"At Stonehurst."

It's unfair on my part, cornering her like this on a rock in the middle of thrashing waves where she can't escape, where she's too fearful to raise a defensive wall.

But fear has a way of stripping our defenses. Making us honest.

She pushes upright and tucks her arms close to her chest, shielding herself against the next hostile spray off a breaker. "I was brought in to help mediate," she explains simply. "Dr. Banner wants to assure you're being given the attention you need—"

"Don't." My jaw sets hard. "The truth."

She licks the water from her lips, the sensual act a threat to obliterate my resolve. "You're quick to anger, Dr. Night."

"I'm quick to detect bullshit, Dr. Holbrook," I fire back.

The shadowy night presses in, heavy and tangling with the electric pulse vibrating between us.

She adjusts, sitting straighter. "I'm here to conduct a risk assessment," she finally says. "But my objective is to help you, Dr. Night."

Something in the way she says this makes me want to believe her.

I nod once. "You can help by telling me how Leo intends to get rid of me," I say, allowing the darkness to bare a layer of my desperation.

She licks her lips again slowly, sensually, and fucking Christ —whatever barricade I erected crumbles like sediment assaulted by the ruthless storm of waves under her weighted stare.

Firming her shoulders, she says, "I think Dr. Banner wants to have you placed under evaluation. A psychiatric hold."

"*Hmm.*" Now that I believe. It's why he was pushing so hard for me to commit to *just one session.* Hiring a professional who can sign the necessary legal documents to deem me a danger and have me removed, leaving my instruments and research all to the university. That ungrateful bastard. "I confess, that's particularly brilliant on his part."

I have my answer, and yet I'm stalling, searching for an excuse to keep her trapped on this rock. I tap my fingers against the stone in ritual count to ease the restlessness.

"Dr. Banner is concerned for you," she says, her tone softening.

"You were doing so well with your honesty. Don't offer excuses for him."

Collins rubs her arm, chasing away a chill as she nods. "Yeah, you're right. I was appalled when I realized his intentions."

From my peripheral, I study the tightening of her lips, the forced swallow pulsing down the slender column of her throat, my gaze drawn helplessly to the erratic flutter beneath her skin. My tapping speeds, syncing to her accelerating heartbeat—a Euclidean rhythm of rising beats and notes until my chest nearly explodes.

Maybe she's not part of Leo's scheme, but that does little to change the outcome.

What has to be done.

As she shifts her position for comfort, her fitted skirt rides higher up her thighs, weakening my resolve another fraction. If we weren't stranded on the fringe of a surging ocean, I might accuse her of trying to distract me on purpose.

"You should let me conduct the assessment," she says suddenly.

A derisive smirk curves my mouth. "Haven't you already? What was it you called it... Naturalistic Observation?" I tilt my head and *tsk*. "Unless all those lingering glances and blushing smiles when caught watching me was because I am, in fact, so devastatingly attractive."

Her lips part slightly, her blinks coming faster, and I'm

somewhat bothered to realize I'm holding my breath in anticipation of her answer.

When she takes too long to respond, I nod again, firmer. "Sorry, Dr. Holbrook. But given this new knowledge, I feel undergoing an evaluation by you would be unethical."

Her hand curls into a fist against the rock, and a hot coil of tension snaps the air. "That's pretty hypocritical coming from you, considering how unethical your behavior has been."

I cock an eyebrow, amused.

She lifts her chin defiantly. "The inappropriate remarks during our first meeting. All the lurking and smoldering grins, and intimidation tactics—"

"Yes, I can see how offering you an umbrella is diabolical."

She sinks her teeth into her bottom lip, gaze narrowed. "Don't gaslight me, Dr. Night. I see the way you look at me…" She trails off, her insinuation clear.

I scrape a hand over my jaw. "Before I discovered that you came here to sabotage my life's work."

She lifts her chin higher, undeterred. "I see how you're looking at me now."

On impulse, my gaze drops to her exposed thighs, and I take my time roaming back up. A hot ember flares beneath my icy skin at the sight of her nipples peaked against her wet blouse.

Her chest concaves, her breathing shallows, as though she's concentrating on each inhalation beneath my heated stare. When I lock with her gaze, I allow her to read the wicked intent in mine.

Fear has a taste, a scent lingering on the air. Intoxicating to those who feed on it. And right now, it swirls thick and tempting around Collins.

For a single heartbeat, I wonder how difficult it would be to scare her off.

The impulsive thought constricts my chest until my lungs burn. Even if I could, I'm not sure how I can simply let her vanish, not when I can't even tear my eyes away from her. This rock begins to feel unsteady, upending me like a capsized vessel on the deepest, blackest waters.

She shivers, and I feel powerless as I lean in, claiming the space near her lips. "Don't worry, Collins," I say, my words falling across her mouth. "I can't touch you."

Her gaze darts to my gloved hand before she levels me with a meaningful look, and I've never wanted to defy my own words as badly as I do right this fucking second.

After a prolonged beat, where I try to count the gold bands in her iris, memorize the light pattern of freckles across her smooth cheeks, I force myself to draw away.

She tentatively crosses her arms over her chest. "Does that work both ways?"

Her question aims to explore deeper than the surface banter between us, and just the threat of her touch sparks up the column of my spine like a strike of flint.

I flex my jaw. "This isn't a session, doctor."

"It should be."

A groan works free from deep in my throat, and I clench and unclench my hand, the leather strapped tight across my knuckles. The abrasive rub against my inflamed palm feels satisfying.

"The last thing I want to do is sabotage your work," she says, referring to my earlier accusation. "I can promise you that."

I risk another glance into her eyes, startled to find the gravity of truth held there.

Collins tilts her head. "Do you like chess?"

"I don't hate it."

"One game," she offers. "If you meet with me, we don't have to discuss anything in particular. Just play a simple match."

She's a clever little starling, I'll give her that—but none of this feels simple. "That's assuming we make it off this rock."

And sometimes, I can be a real asshole.

"Shit," she mutters. "You're serious." Her blinks come furiously as she glances around, as if only now realizing how high the ocean has risen.

I can't resist being lured in by the pattern, attempting to count the dark fringe of her lashes every time they sweep her high cheeks. There's a symmetry there that quiets the vicious stirring, a temptation to get lost to it.

As the celestial bodies burn in the black sky above, the ocean takes a calming breath, momentarily weary of its assault on the shore.

That weariness is reflected in the woman next to me, in the way her chest struggles to rise with every inhale, her eyes fight to remain open after each slow blink. Though hypothermia isn't a real concern, it's cruel to keep her out here much longer.

Expelling a lengthy sigh, I slip down from the boulder.

She watches me cautiously, panic flaring at the fear of being left alone.

The cold water rises around my waist, and I hold out my hand to her. "Come here."

Another wave crashes, sending a spray across her face, yet she remains frozen. "I really am terrified of water."

"I'll carry you."

Her gaze shifts to my hand held outstretched. There's a weighted beat of hesitation, where she battles to leave the obvious unsaid, before she's inching carefully toward me and slipping her trembling hand into mine.

"Where can I touch?" The unsure, breathy cadence of her question detonates between us the moment my arms wrap around her.

As her weight settles against me, the feel of her soft curves molding seamlessly against my rigid frame—Christ, I swear the adrenaline rushing my heart has enough force to tear my atoms apart.

The darkest of energy at play.

Every vertebra in my spine locks into place, bracing as I wait for the inevitable alarm to rattle my bones before I take my next breath. Jaw clenched tight, I haul her away from the rock, my senses assaulted by the onslaught of sensations rising more furiously than the tide.

"Just link your arms around my neck," I tell her through gritted teeth as I curl her toward my chest.

Feet sinking into the sand, my body planked against the rushing water, I'm struck by the rightness of her in my arms, unable to move. Yet somehow, when her arms gently curl around my shoulders, I take that first step out of the quicksand.

She rests her cheek against my shoulder, and fucking matter ceases to exist. Everywhere her body touches sets off a riot of sparks, a frenzy of heated currents chasing adrenaline through my bloodstream.

All I hear is the harmonic sound of her breath blending with the chorus of waves. The chords of her soft exhales become a tender caress over my neck, her shivers an aesthetic prelude echoed in the hollow of my chest.

The waves lash and batter, breaking against our bodies with each violent swell. We're nearly rocked under, but I keep her bound in my arms, refusing to lose her to the dark waters.

Like navigating a treacherous maze, I wade through the narrow chasms between boulders until we surface clear of the ripping tide.

The darkness howls around us as we cross the shore, my course guided by the pale light cast from the looming structure atop the cliff. I continue to cross the beach, the ocean a muted roar beneath whipping wet wind, mercifully silencing my very dangerous, diverting thoughts.

Even after I hit the loose sand, I keep her clutched against me, convinced we won't reach the pier in her weakened state. Ahead,

I can just make out the *Eventide*—the Zodiac research vessel—bobbing near the tall pilings extending over the cresting waves, and I slow my steps.

"You can put me down," Collins says, and I'm acutely aware of her hand placement. How, if she shifts her wrist even a millimeter higher, her skin will make contact with mine.

My breaths saw through my constricted lungs. "Are you staying at the residence hall?"

I think of her trekking through town in the dark. Wet, alone. Defenseless. And that irrational flame of anger licks through me, hot and violent.

"I can stay in my office," she says. "I have a change of clothes there and a sofa. It should be fine for tonight." She tips her head back, offering a concerned glance. "Dr. Night, are you okay?"

"I'm fine," I bite off the lie as I climb the steps onto the pier. "What unit is yours?"

Astonishment lights her eyes. "You can't carry me all the way there."

"Is that a challenge?" I curl her tighter to my chest and look down into her face, a sly smirk slanting my mouth.

I swear, I would've fought the fucking ocean to carry her across if that's what it took.

"Please don't make this more awkward," she says under her breath. "I'm already embarrassed enough."

Relenting, I lower her bare feet to the weathered planks of the pier.

She slips out of my reach to adjust her clothes, and I take a step back where I can make her out clearly, shamelessly imprinting a visual of her in that havoc-inducing blouse.

"Don't feel embarrassed," I tell her. "If you haven't spent time around the ocean, you can't be expected to predict its behavior."

She swipes the tangled strands of hair from her face, taming the wild tresses over her shoulder. "Predicting behavior is typically what I'm good at, but thank you."

"Oh, don't thank me," I say, forcing her eyes to meet mine. "I'm not chivalrous. Saving damsels in collusion with Leo has a price, and I plan to collect."

She arches a delicate eyebrow. Whatever buoyant relief she may have felt a moment ago vanishes from her expression. "Information I'm sure to regret sharing with you, Dr. Night."

"Call me Orion." I fold my arms over my damp chest. "We can drop formalities, given we escaped near death together."

Despite her exhausted state, a fleeting smile touches her full lips before she levels me with a suspicious look. "Out there—" she nods toward the dark shore "—I'd like to believe that was all just to rile me on purpose."

"You did ask for a distraction," I say, not wanting to give her a complete lie. "It was a choice between boring you with ocean tides, or risking your cute fist smashing my face."

She narrows her eyes, and I send her a wink.

Her beautiful smile hits me right in the chest. "I'm no longer in need of a distraction, thank you." Her teeth begin to chatter, and she hugs her arms around her wet blouse as she moves past. Gripping one hand on the railing, she starts the ascent up the steps of the bluff.

I frown at her slow progress. Catching up to her easily, we reach the landing together, where an iron gate opens to a winding path that leads toward the university grounds.

Collins pauses before the gate, fatigue weighing her shoulders. The breeze whips around her body to steal my breath at the ethereal sight of her framed by the Gothic tracery.

"It's a shame, though," she says, and I cock my head curiously. "Out there on the ocean, with the dark secluding us, a canopy of stars above. You missed a prime opportunity to impress me with tales of the constellations."

"*Hmm...*" I step close. "If I wanted to seduce you, Collins, I wouldn't resort to something as cliché as the stars."

"I said impress, not seduce." She turns, but pauses to say, "What would you use?"

Gaze drifting slowly down her body, I drag my tongue across my bottom lip. "Not words."

A challenge crackles in the condensed air between us, daring me to take another bold step forward, finding it exerts more energy to stay apart from her.

The chemical attraction blazing between us burns hotter than colliding atoms in the heart of a star. A pang of caution flares in my chest, and I know I should stop this—but standing here, clothes soaked, wind freezing my skin to ice, my body is on fire.

Her throat works with a swallow. "Before you confront Dr. Banner, allow me one session," she says, the appeal softening her tone.

Leaning in, I rest my hand on the gate latch. "Ah, but if you can't get inside here"—I tap my temple— "there's no chance you'll find me a danger."

A shiver rocks through her at our proximity. "If you're not a danger, then you have nothing to worry about." Her shimmering gaze searches mine. "So are you, Orion—a danger?"

She shouldn't look at me like that, so enticing—like tempting a starved animal deprived too long of a meal. My fingers grip the latch. Hard. "That depends entirely on what you consider dangerous."

Something destructive fires through my veins. Before I act on impulse, her beautiful smile unfurls, and she says, "Goodnight, Orion."

Hearing my name in her breathy voice… Fuck, the damage is done.

It will never be enough.

I press a measure closer and unlatch the gate, lifting it three times to offset the disturbing urges lashing at my skull. "Just so we're clear," I say, drawing her gaze once more. "I see how you look at me, Collins."

There's the faintest hitch in her breathing. She brings a hand to her chest, and I catch sight of the delicate constellation along her wrist.

Playing with fire.

She makes me feel more than reckless as she gazes up at me, expectant, waiting. I force a hard swallow, lost in those eyes full of dust and starlight.

"Goodnight, Collins," I whisper roughly near her ear and push the gate open, allowing her to escape.

Chest tight, I watch her drift away, the night stealing her from my vision until she's absorbed by the dark.

In astrophysics, anything dark is simply unknown.

And Collins Holbrook is a dark, dark unknown.

The warning banging furiously inside my skull cautions just how fucking hazardous this is, yet it doesn't stop me from wanting to chase this feeling right over the steepest cliff.

Hell, long before she called out, I was already on the edge, barely hanging on by the tips of my fingers.

It's late by the time I return to the observatory. Everything is exactly how I left it, and yet nothing feels the same. Irrevocably altered by one single moment, an event powerful enough to distort space and time.

I set the astrolabe on the desk and peel off a worn glove, abruptly halted as the monitor catches my attention.

The screen has gone dark—all except for a pale line of text. An illuminated name that stalls my breath.

"Goddammit," I breathe, pulse crashing through my veins.

For a long, numb beat, I can only stare, disbelief and dread freezing me in place until an incredulous laugh scrapes free of my throat. Doubt claws at me, questioning chemical attraction and gravity and my own fucking mind. Whether what I felt was even real, or only this ravenous void that devours everything that dares to get too close.

Fury coiling my muscles, I lean in and kill the screen.

Tearing off my other glove, I reclaim the star-taker, its comforting weight settling into my ruined palm. Tempted for the first fucking time not to turn my eyes to the hunter in the sky, I keep my gaze trained down to where Ophiuchus rises.

The thirteenth constellation.

My thumb sweeps the empty groove where the rule should rest on the star-taker, noting the absence with a vicious pang. My grip tightens on the instrument as the echo of her melody fuses with crashing waves and howling winds and the staccato rhythm of her heartbeat.

In search of some order, my fingers tap a rigid count against the brass. Twelve beats in sequence. I start to repeat the compulsion—until the twitch of my ring finger adds a faint tap.

Thirteen.

The undeniable presence of an anomaly, syncing to that fractured cadence.

Brass bites into my flesh, and I invite the pain as blood spills hot into my burning palm.

It's a bittersweet truth of astronomy, that we can gaze into the brilliance of a star, observe its endless beauty, only to realize that its light is a mere echo, reaching us long after the source has burned away.

"Fuck," I curse as the fiery ache consumes.

If all I can think about is kissing Collins whenever she's near, how the hell am I supposed to kill her.

Apophenia (noun): The tendency to perceive meaningful patterns and connections in unrelated or random things, like seeing faces in clouds, or familiar shapes in shadows. A concept coined by psychiatrist Klaus Conrad in 1958.

8

MUSCLE MEMORY

It is only through mystery and madness that the soul is revealed.

— THOMAS MOORE

COLLINS

No one counts the beats of their heart.

As long as the muscle pumps, we don't want to consciously think about the finite number we have left. The moment it will stop.

Hand trembling, I reach into my coat pocket and produce the silver pill case designed to look like a nondescript compact. I open the lid and count the white tablets, the only number I keep track of. I had to stockpile enough of my meds to last several months.

A violent gust of wind whips through the arched walkway as I swallow down a dry pill. The ends of my wind-torn hair snap at my cheek, triggering a burst of anger. The fury bubbles up too quickly to contain, and I smash the case against the stone column, biting down on my lip to hold back the scream trying to claw up my throat.

One. Two—

My body quivers through the attack until the coppery taste of blood hits my tongue, and the fire wanes into smoldering ash in my stomach.

I release the pain with a shaky breath, now dulled to a tight pinch in my sternum. Keeping my hand braced to the stone, I curl my fingers around the case as I wait for the nausea to subside, and vertigo gradually recedes.

Three.

"Shit." That might have been the riskiest, *stupidest* thing I've ever done.

I can practically hear Darby's scowl, see the emphatic shake of his head, gearing up to lecture me.

A broken smile fights onto my face at the thought of him even as the cold penetrates my bones so deep, I fear I'll never be warm again. While I was able to collect a change of clothes and shoes from my office, I had to be fast, not giving myself time to recover.

Dropping the pill case into my bag, I check to make sure Orion is no longer watching. An empty silence haunts the university in the night hours, the dark a physical entity lurking in the corners.

Another gust of wind spurs me out of the colonnade, and I wrap my arms around my midsection as the medicine slowly works through my veins.

Dim streetlamps line the uneven sidewalk, guiding me away from the campus grounds. The distant crash of waves chases me like a taunt, conjuring the sensation of frigid waves rocking my body, and the calm blue-green waters of his eyes that held me steady.

I've interviewed some of the most charming and charismatic

offenders. I've studied the expert manipulations of psychopaths. But after our encounter tonight, Orion is the first to leave me shaken.

The phantom feel of his arms around my body lingers like a brand. I can still hear the heavy beat of his heart pounding through me like a drum, still feel the pulse of it strong against my cheek as he carried me to safety.

Sheltered from danger by the arms of danger himself.

After watching him this past month, I was prepared for the mind games, but not for his emotional intelligence. Orion mirrors better than any psychopath I've studied. The way he tailored his personality to mine, to my fear, knowing just how to put me at ease.

The diverting, flirty winks and smirks, fully aware of his sex appeal. He uses this to his advantage. From anyone else, the unfiltered thoughts would be crude and off-putting.

He's too quick a study, an apex predator, easing into banter effortlessly, making me feel a connection with him.

I can't touch you.

The gravelly timbre of his voice invades my mind, brushing through my body like the heat of his breath over my neck. The way he used those four simple words to disarm me.

Yet as I've seen the result of his violence firsthand, I know I don't need to feel the press of his skin for him to hurt me.

Resting my palm to the valley of my chest, I center my breathing and allow my steps to slow. My fear tonight wasn't a complete deception—I was a good swimmer once—but my vulnerability had to be real.

I can't simply play the victim. I have to bare my throat to the predator, let him sink his teeth into my jugular and taste my fear.

There's power in surrender, in helplessly looking up at the predator, anticipating the bite, letting them believe they have control. Waiting for their fangs to sink deep—

Then they get that first bitter taste of poison.

My veins are primed with it.

As the wind rustles the skeletal branches of the trees, the shadows cast over the town grow deeper, appearing more sinister. Even if I'm used to moving through the world alone, have long since stopped fearing the isolation, the dark still stirs an instinctive dread.

It's where monsters roam. You don't see them coming until they're close enough to wound.

I know Orion could have easily let me drown, or snapped my neck. Appealing to a killer's protective nature is as tricky as it is risky. But for a highly intelligent offender, protective is synonymous with possessive. Orion is territorial by nature, and he's territorial over Stonehurst.

A tragic death at his university would shine a giant spotlight on his habitat, bringing unwanted attention from authorities. The hunter won't risk an investigation. Not when he's this close to completing his ritual.

It's his pattern: Shorehaven. Solar eclipse. And the victim…

I glance around at the quiet town, wondering where his victim is right now. What they're wanted for, what dark deed they're guilty of. Eleven of the twelve celestial constellations have been claimed, leaving only Gemini—the final sign on his chart.

By the time I reach my unit, my hands are numb, my lungs burn from the cold, and I shakily push the key into the deadbolt, practically falling past the threshold.

The only source of light comes from the soft glow of the kitchen appliances. I quickly turn on the lamp, illuminating the space to chase back the dark.

Kicking off my shoes, I wrap myself in a plush blanket on the loveseat, trying to eliminate the chattering of my teeth, unsure if it's from the cold still seeping into my bones or nerves.

"Dammit." I clutch my phone tight, drumming up the courage

to make the call I've been dreading since I first took on this assignment.

With a resigned breath, I set my phone timer, then punch in his personal number, my free hand pressed firmly to my chest. I'm using an app to prevent my number from being traced. If there's no answer after three rings, I have to end the call.

"Who is this?"

Throat tight, I force a swallow. It's been too long since I've heard Darby's voice. "I'm here. I'm with him."

There's a tense pause before he finally says, "Are you safe?"

Relieved, I relax my grip on the phone and glance around my living space. My gaze falls over the few personal effects I've placed around the room to keep me anchored. "Yeah, I'm safe."

His exhale is audible. "Christ, where are you?"

"I can't tell you that. I just wanted you to know I'm okay." And to hear the voice of my friend, to feel like I still have a lifeline.

"But you're not. I can hear it in your voice," he says, his words a sharp lash against my resolve. "Tell me what happened."

I bite the corner of my lip, internally cursing myself. Of course Darby can tell when I'm rattled.

"Hol, if this is our guy, then you've put yourself in serious danger," he continues. "Let me help get you out of there."

I suppress the quick flash of anger and clutch the blanket to my chest. "I know what I'm doing," I assure him. "I've spent months immersed in his world, investigating him—"

"Stalking him."

Indignation flares hot. "I'm the only one who can do this."

Darby didn't get a say when it came to making that call.

"Give me a name," he demands.

"You know I can't tell you that, either. Look—" I sit forward to alleviate the pressure beneath my ribs. "Just…for once, you have to trust me."

"I've always trusted you. Even when this obsession got way out of hand." Another lengthy pause. "You know Laurel would never approve of this. She never supported you working in the field—" He breaks off with a weary sigh.

His words drip like acid in my stomach.

Silence builds between us, my short breaths crackling into the receiver. I swallow past the aching burn in my throat. "I thought about Haylie on the anniversary. I'm sorry I couldn't be there this time."

I imagine Darby spinning the leather bracelet around his wrist, the one his daughter gave him before she was abducted by the monster who extinguished her beautiful light from this world.

Maybe it's cruel of me to use her this way, but if he's going to use Laurel against me, it's my only defense.

"I see you still can't locate your heart," he fires back, anger threading his harsh tone.

The tension in my shoulders deflates. "I deserve that."

As with any defense mechanism, I've built a callus around my heart to protect it, and often, that abrasive layer hurts the ones I care for the most.

"Darby…" I let my voice trail off, expelling an anguished breath. I can't lie to him and claim my motivation isn't entirely selfish. "I don't have much time. But I'm all right. I have to see this through."

"Just remember what I said before, about imposing your will," he says, his tone grave. "Revenge won't change the past."

The warning beep sounds on the timer. A twinge of panic unfurls in my chest. "I'll try to contact you again soon," I promise him. "And, Darby, don't bother trying to trace this call. I used your tech to spoof it."

I end the call.

Exhaustion grips me almost immediately as the adrenaline

leaks from my system. I'm left feeling weak, my muscles sore and achy.

I toss the phone aside and slump back into the sofa, casting a look through the lancet-glass doors. Amid the soaring spires, the observatory glows against the night sky. The domed structure looms over the town like a menacing fortress, concealing his secrets.

The university and I, we want the same thing.

His research.

Fighting the fatigue draining me, I stand and move to the balcony doors. Without thought, I push up onto my toes as I peer through the dingy, double-paned glass.

That's the thing about muscle memory, how over time, our actions become so familiar, so ingrained in us, we perform them with so little effort. It can be a comfort.

It can also be a nightmare.

Our bodies have the ability to retain the memory of a traumatic experience, where the slightest whisper of danger triggers our fight-or-flight response.

Tonight, I didn't merely embrace the alarm sounding through my body—I made it my song. Every threatening, thunderous crash of a wave became a trilling note. Every strike against my bones in fear became a percussive beat that I timed to his powerful heart.

As my gaze wanders over his observatory, I imagine him there within the depths, charting his constellations.

Projecting his next kill.

My hand coasts over my neck, delicately exploring down to the buttons of my sweater. I work one open, then the next, letting my fingertips trail. A shiver tightens my skin as I envision his hands mapping my body the way he maps his star charts.

Touched by the hands of death.

When you've come so close, felt your last breath snatched

from your lungs, your very life teased by the rough hands of death, you almost crave its cruel caress.

You get tired of fearing it.

I wrap my hand around my throat, tightening until the pressure builds. I never take my eyes off his towering haven while I touch the most intimate parts of my body. Remapping my neural pathways. Taking back stolen power.

Excited by the fear I'll invoke in his dark eyes.

As my skirt falls around my feet, I flatten one hand against the glass to brace myself, my other slipping between my thighs. Arousal stirs my blood, muscles gathering tight.

My hunter may be in a cooldown period, but I can feel the impending shift—like the ocean drawing back right before the break, knowing there's nothing that will stop the oncoming wave.

I saw it in the way those beautiful eyes heated with the bluest ember. Orion's hunger is a rising tidal swell.

And I'll be there when he breaks.

I lower my forehead to the cold glass and seal my hand around my neck, dig my blunt nails into my skin, imprinting bruises along my throat. A hit of gratification arches my back, and I moan through the trembling pleasure, my breaths short and raw as I stare into the moonless night.

Every monster harbors a little deviance. I just need to rouse that buried hunger to his controlled surface—the one he doesn't even allow out when it's time to hunt.

The stars burn against the darkness, calling up the memory of Orion hovering close enough I could trace the gray ring around the teal sea of his irises. So breathtaking, like gazing into a cluster of galaxies, an inferno of stars.

If Orion needs a body to use, he can have mine. It stopped belonging to me long ago.

Where I'm most vulnerable, even defenseless, what that weakness does grant me is the elimination of fear. Orion could have strangled me on that rock and I would've had only one regret.

Revenge won't change the past.

No, it won't—but I'm not trying to rewrite history.

If it's the task of the sculptor to discover the statue inside the block of stone, then I'll be the fucking sculptor. I'll chip at Orion's stone until I've carved his secrets free.

"I won't get another chance," I whisper on a broken breath.

I touch myself until my body draws taut, pleasure crashing through me. I grip my throat until my pulse roars in my ears with the rush of blood, until I'm drowning beneath thrashing waves of sensation—

Until the beats of my heart bang strong enough to count.

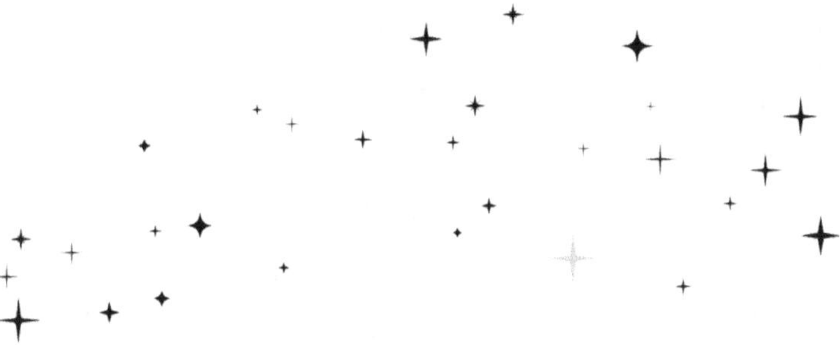

Right now, there are an estimated two thousand active serial killers in the world, with approximately fifty in the US alone. Most are never caught. They either become ill, incapacitated, or are incarcerated for other crimes—but they never stop killing. The compulsion to victimize and steal power never dies.

— COLLINS HOLBROOK

9

ANTIMATTER

The soul came to being at the same time as the sky.

— PLATO

ORION

As the sun falls behind darkened clouds that keep Stonehurst shrouded in a perpetual melancholic gloom, the stream of students begins to dwindle. Clusters of them split off through the colonnade, making their way to the library and professor office hours, while I wait for the one person who will ruin my day.

From where I'm parked, I have a clear view of the West Quad. In the center, a scattering of burnt-orange leaves dusts the ground around a dramatic concrete fountain of Urania.

Every evening like clockwork, Collins crosses through this courtyard. The anticipation to catch a glimpse of her hasn't only derailed my routine for the past two weeks, it's consumed my every waking moment as she incessantly invades my thoughts.

Reflexively, I curl my hand into a fist, inflaming the healing first-degree rope burn. Triggering the pain has become a compulsion to offset the torment of reliving that fragment of time where I lifted her into my arms, experiencing the feel of her body against mine.

The obsessive loops are a consequence of my defective gray matter. A glitch I've learned to coexist with. Yet this is the first time I want to take a surgical saw to my own damn brain and cut her out like an infectious disease to make the compulsive thoughts of her cease.

When I see her emerge from the arched walkway, I'm rewarded with the sweetest hit of relief. Like craving a drug for too torturously long, and finally getting that fix.

"Fuck me," I mutter beneath my breath, scrubbing a hand over my face. She's so beautiful, it physically hurts. She's wearing a sexy, tight skirt, scarf and stockings. My black umbrella swings from her wrist, which sends another shot of satisfaction through me.

I keep waiting for the sight of her to become less startling, like if I subject myself to the torture enough, I'll build up a tolerance—but I'd rather just mainline her straight into my vein.

It's not enough.

Expelling the ache from my lungs, I cradle my helmet against me and crank my Triumph, drowning out the notes of her agonizing tune.

The loud rumble grabs her attention, evident by the little jump of her shoulders, and I can't help the smirk stealing across my face as our eyes clash. I've been caught watching her, and I have no desire to stop.

While I've yet to confront Leo, I have zero intentions of participating in his bullshit assessment scheme.

I was sure Collins received this message when I failed to show in her office. But then there she was once again this afternoon, seated in the back row of my hall, a defiant smile twisting her pretty lips in challenge.

Stopping my fucking heart.

Watching me with those fierce eyes, absently licking those lips as if she's oblivious to the havoc she wreaks. Her mere presence exerting a gravitational pull over me to affect the trajectory of my lectures, my thoughts.

Inescapable.

Balancing my weight on the bike, I shove the helmet over my head and knock the kickstand back, my gaze locked on Collins as she crosses the courtyard amid the stragglers of students.

I squeeze the clutch and shift into first, giving the engine a hard rev before I start to ease out of the spot. From my peripheral, I watch her abandon the sidewalk and stalk my way.

An unwanted warmth unfurls deep inside my chest. Pulse thundering, I kill the engine and lower the kickstand, the vibration of the motorcycle lingering in my veins.

"You never showed for our session," she accuses as she reaches me.

I leave the tinted visor down. "I assumed saving your life earned me enough points to call this farce off."

A trace of guilt touches her eyes before she blinks the emotion away. "And again, thank you," she says. "But I thought we had an understanding. I can only be patient for so long. One way or another, I'm getting the evaluation done, which leaves me no choice but to attend your classes—"

"You're beautiful."

Her mouth parts, and I revel in the way her expression opens, wavering between stunned and offended, as though she's battling which to feel.

"What I mean is…you're a distraction, in my lectures," I say, but my confession lacks the utter truth burning through me. How a fucking quasar now pales compared to the bright bands I glimpse in her eyes. How I've never, not once in my existence, been rendered speechless until I met those beautiful, starry eyes across my lecture hall.

"You really have no filter."

"None," I admit honestly. "When you're sitting in my hall, I have a hard time focusing on anything other than you, Collins. This is a dilemma."

The actual dilemma is the fact that, no matter how many times I rerun the algorithm or recalibrate the predictive modeling, the outcome remains unchanged.

In Shorehaven on November 30th, beneath the shadow of the solar eclipse, I will kill Collins Rayne Holbrook.

And while I'm under no illusion of the monstrous acts I commit in the name of science, being forced to spend time with her beforehand feels especially heinous, like some sick, twisted penance.

The palest blush dusts her cheeks as she tugs her gray scarf high around her neck. "This is highly inappropriate, and sexist. Blaming a woman for your inability to deliver a proper lecture."

Beneath the sweet cadence of her voice is an edge that provokes me, rousing a desperate yearning to slice through this dull pretense between us and name whatever this infuriating feeling is so I claim it.

Smother it.

"You think my lectures are lacking." Amused, I let a crooked smile frame my mouth.

Her only response is a slightly elevated brow.

"I suppose they are when compared to anything beneath a canopy of stars amid crashing waves. Life in peril, and all that."

My ego soars when I earn a pretty smile. "Being charmed amid dangerous conditions by a devastatingly attractive astrophysicist does set the bar rather high."

My whole body is one white-hot flame. "Damn, I've always

been my own worst enemy." I give a shrug. "Regardless, it's more than your physical appearance. It's just you, starling."

She levels me with a vulnerable look that is so damn beautiful, I swear the air crackles with static to back my claim.

"Remove your helmet," she says.

I hold her intense stare through the visor, waiting a painstaking three seconds longer before I relent. Pushing upright, I pry the helmet off and rest it on the fuel tank, then run my gloved palm over my disheveled hair.

She openly inspects the planes of my face, and I feel the press of her gaze as though she reaches out to touch me.

The breeze sends layers of her hair across her eyes to break the connection before she hooks the strands behind her ear, her cuff riding up to reveal the archer across her wrist. "Are you saying these things to make me too uncomfortable to return to your lecture?"

"Are you uncomfortable?"

She doesn't answer right away. "No."

I drape my arms over my helmet. "Then I hardly see any point in stopping."

"You don't?" Her gaze lowers to my gloved hand, and the sharp remark practically impales me. "What's the point in seducing me if you're unable to take it further."

"Fuck, ouch." My hand curls into a tight fist behind my helmet, agitating the burn. "Don't need to spar in a game of chess when you can strike with a gambit like that," I say, letting anger lick my wound.

Her nude lips curl into a gentle smile, and my heart clenches in my chest. "You need to be in my office tomorrow." The way she says *need* digs beneath my skin. "If you don't want me in your lectures, that is."

"Not sure you're in a position to threaten ultimatums."

"Do you feel threatened?"

My tongue coasts across my bottom lip. "You don't want to hear what I'm feeling right this second, Collins."

My words provoke a shiver, and despite my best effort at restraint, my gaze hungrily tracks over her, rousing a buried desire.

I absolutely feel threatened by her.

"Intrusive thoughts are meant to be kept silent, Orion."

"Trust me when I say, I'm holding the worst of them back."

Those teal eyes blaze with intensity as a haunting chord trembles through me, and suddenly, this feels too dangerous.

When observing an event, the observer cannot interfere.

I break the hold of her gaze and grip the handle, leather stretched across my knuckles. "You can tell Leo his scheme failed," I say, jaw tense. "No need to loiter in my lectures any longer, Dr. Holbrook. You're relieved of your obligation."

My words reek of a finality that bears down on my chest with a crushing weight. I pull in the clutch and start the engine, desperate to put distance between us.

She reaches over and turns the ignition off. I follow her arm up until I reach her face. My nostrils flare as I inhale the subtle vanilla scent and a spicy floral note beneath the exhaust fumes.

Her gaze lingers on my gloved hands, and I realize she deliberately avoided touching me. "That's a dangerous thing," I say, my tone dropping a register. "Touching a man's bike."

She pulls away and adjusts her scarf higher, and a flame licks through me at the deviant thought of gripping the fabric and wrapping it tight.

"Yeah, someone once told me words are less effective, or something like that," she says, dragging me from my debased thoughts, and a devious smile curls my lips. "I'm not Banner's puppet. I thought convincing him to agree to your terms would earn *me* enough points for you to trust me."

I make a sound of amusement in the back of my throat. So

Collins is behind Leo relocating the research team. I wonder if she realizes he's only agreeing to her terms for the same reason he's agreeing to mine—to get what he wants in the end.

The sudden thought that Collins might be trying to leverage him stirs something curious within me, and I drum my fingers against my helmet. "You're a Sagittarius and you can't swim. That's all I know about you."

Yet as I say this, my words feel wrong. Even in a void of space, one destructive force recognizes another. Every particle has a twin with an opposite charge. When they meet, they annihilate each other on contact. This process is violent and unstoppable once it begins.

Collins slips the umbrella into her briefcase and crosses her arms. "So you need to know every mundane detail about my life to form a conclusion, Dr. Night?"

"Not every mundane detail," I say, a slow smirk tipping my mouth. "Just your hopes, your dreams. What you most passionately crave out of life."

"Oh, is that all," she remarks with a mocking tilt of her head. "What I want more than anything is for you to let me do my job."

"That's going to be difficult without me."

"Obviously," she mutters. "Which is why the transfer of your colleagues is only temporary during the evaluation period."

I swipe a hand over my mouth to cover a grin. "Your attempt at coercion is sexy."

She firms her posture. "That would violate my ethics."

"And your ethics are incorruptible."

She gives me that wickedly sinful smile that first captivated me, that stole my breath across my lecture hall. "Absolutely."

The dare to discover just how corruptible she is hovers in the charged space between us, a dangerous temptation that crashes against my skull like a thrashing, dark wave.

And once again, I'm questioning why her name lit the screen.

For days straight, I've combed through code, searching for some flaw in the data, some hidden corruption that allowed her name to slip through.

But there's nothing. Collins is different from the others. A fact my algorithm confirmed when it labeled her in bold letters:

ANOMALY.

"I'm impressed," I say. "Coercing me into the assessment by dangling my observatory like bait. Ethically, of course."

She frees a strained breath. "Well, we know how you'd handle the situation. Although punching you might feel satisfying, I'm serious when I say I'd truly like to help you, Orion."

Jesus. Now I'm hung on all the ways I could satisfy her. "You got a little violence in you, Dr. Holbrook."

Ignoring my baiting remark, she says, "Listen, even if you succeed in having me removed, Banner will just bring in another professional—one who might not have your best interests in mind."

"And you do."

"I do," she says quickly. "The discord between you and Dr. Prescott can't remain unresolved. The evaluation could take weeks, or even months. During that time, you'll have your observatory all to yourself. Maybe longer, depending on the outcome." A sly smile twists her lips. "Like I said, I'm completing the eval one way or another. But it is in your best interest to work with me. So, are you going to give me what I need, Dr. Night?"

Fuck, and then some.

With a groan, I release the clutch and sit back on the seat. I've never been so turned on by a lecture. Resigned to my torment, I glance at my wristwatch. "You want to help me."

She nods once. "Yes."

"How about right now?"

Her fine eyebrows draw together. "Now?"

"And it has to be in a place of my choosing."

She catches her lip between her teeth. "Fine."

On impulse, I hold out the helmet to her, a slow smile hitching the corner of my mouth.

A nervous laugh spills past her lips. "Oh, no. That's not happening."

"You agreed," I tell her, a dare edged in my tone.

It's only a flash, but something akin to pain creases her soft features before she flips her hair off her shoulder. "Not to getting on your bike."

"An impasse already?" I lower the helmet. "Shame. I thought you had a little more fire in you, archer."

She rubs her thumb across the starry points along her wrist as a defiant flame ignites the center of her eyes. "There are ways to get me alone other than putting my life in peril, Orion."

As her gaze daringly holds mine, I can feel the matter between us charge, known and unknown forces colliding.

Intoxicating.

"Goddamn, Dr. Holbrook. Maybe I should be worried about being corrupted by you."

With a cute scowl, she locks an arm across her midsection. Beneath her tough exterior, I sense something restless and desperate curling her hand tight around the strap of her case.

"I'm not exactly dressed to straddle the back of that thing," she reasons.

Her words conjure the image of her straddling the seat, her fitted skirt hiked up her thighs, her arms wrapped around my waist—and the sudden, vicious nature of my thoughts turns aggressively heated.

I unsnap the collar of my leather jacket, listlessly untucking my necktie from my suit vest. Then I anchor the helmet to the handlebar and climb off. As I step toward her, I can make out the faint freckles across the bridge of her nose, the warm striations buried in her irises, so bright that, in the drabness of Stonehurst, they sparkle in contrast.

In the time that's passed, the grounds have cleared. Students no longer mill through the quad, the lot nearly empty. The sky has darkened to a deep shade of umber, and the distant, hollow crash of waves drifts on the mist.

Staring down at her, I weigh my options, torn between escaping on my bike and surrendering to the hypnotic lure of her melody, the one quieting the chaos in my head right now.

Decision made, I point toward the courtyard. "There's a bench right over there."

Her perceptive gaze rakes over me. She knows I watch her on that bench every morning. A flash of hesitancy crests behind her eyes, and I wonder if she's suddenly wary of being alone with me in the dark.

Something deviant rears within me at the thought.

"This isn't the way I conduct sessions, just so you know." She pivots in the direction of the fountain, indulging me with the sinful sight of her walking away.

"I'll take that to mean I'm special," I say, helplessly dragged in her wake as I follow after her.

Collins drops her leather briefcase on the dry grass before running her palms along her backside and taking a seat on the concrete. A shiver forces her arms across her chest as she looks up at me expectantly.

"Take a seat." She nods to the bench.

"A psychiatrist who avoids pointless foreplay," I say, landing in the space next to her. "And for the record, I never punched Prescott."

Her eyebrows lift. "Really."

"I tried to push him out of a window."

The relief falls from her features. "That doesn't help your case."

A gust of wind whips through the courtyard, sending a ribbon of hair across her face. I'm entranced as she glides her rounded nails across her lips to clear the strands, drawing my gaze irresistibly to her mouth.

A shadow edges into my thoughts, infecting the moment.

Dull pain throbs behind my eyes, forcing me to press the heel of my hand to my temple. I blink hard, chasing back the pain. "Headaches," I say, answering the unspoken concern creasing her brow.

She offers a light nod. "Because of the accident," she says knowingly.

On reflex, I touch the side of my forehead below my hairline. Even through the leather, I can feel the raised scar.

It's been six years since that night. As a man of science, I don't entertain notions like karma or all-powerful entities that mete out consequences. There are no vengeful gods balancing some cosmic scale. And though many of my disgruntled colleagues may claim my arrogant ass had it coming, the truth of the matter is so tragically, sorely simple.

Pushing dangerous speeds, I took a curve too fast. Flipped my bike several times, resulting in three cracked ribs, a fractured clavicle, shattered wrist, broken radius, and a severe skull fracture. Months spent in the hospital, followed by a grueling year of rehabilitation.

I rotate my left wrist, the residual pain always present. Chasing an adrenaline rush dulls the ache of old breaks some. But nothing kills the guilt.

Even if I'd made it to her while she was still breathing, fucking Leo was right. There was nothing I could've done to help Emma. The undiagnosed subarachnoid hemorrhage was sudden. The brain bleed taking her before the paramedics even arrived. Before we even had a chance.

I wait for a hint of pity to surface in Collins's eyes, but all I see is the iridescent glimmer of her irises picking up the autumn hues all around.

Collins says, "Your university file states there was no long-term damage after the wreck."

No matter how many professionals signed off, the fact remains: I'm damaged goods. The once brilliant astrophysicist who was going to field the research to define dark matter decades ahead of time—in my fucking lifetime—suffered a devastating setback.

"And yet, here I am, confined to this hellscape." My smile's as cutting as my words. Still bleeding bitterness over the loss of my grant, my tenure, and research funding.

My truth hangs abandoned in the gloom, the reality of which blisters like the fiery pinpricks of stars appearing in the evening sky, the atmosphere becoming as transparent as this moment between us.

"It has to be difficult," Collins says delicately. "Haphephobia, or what we call touch aversion, is a challenging condition." She seems to weigh her next words before she continues. "I happen to specialize in obsessive-compulsive disorder."

I groan, dragging a fisted hand over my mouth. "Of course."

"Hey, we're just talking," she says, meeting my dismissive tone with soft assurance. "Orion, please look at me."

I do, moving in a daring inch too close to challenge not only her boundaries, but mine. "It's hard to look anywhere but you," I tell her, my gaze shamelessly roving down her body.

"You're still trying to make me uncomfortable." The faintest catch of her breath gives her away.

"I'd say it's working." The low rasp of my voice scrapes the air between us.

She hesitates, and I read everything I need to know in that single pause. "No, it's not. Because I understand sexually intrusive thoughts are a symptom of the disorder. And while these thoughts are typically obsessional and rarely acted on, they can still be debilitating."

The falling dark does little to hinder her sharp gaze from slicing right through me. Twice now, my little archer has slinked past the weakest area of my defenses to sink her arrow.

"Maybe it would be less painful if you did punch me," I mutter sullenly. Still, I can't take my eyes off her, even as she peers right down to the sick core of me.

Her delicate brows knit together, a frown touching her lips. "Therapy can be painful, but with psychoanalysis and the right medication—"

"I have it under control." I bite off each word as I mentally chew hers, an echo banging through my mind like crashing piano chords. *Control control control.*

I tap in sequence—*one, one, two, three, five, one*—each beat timed with the blink of my eyes, my left foot striking the ground in count. And because there is always the need for symmetry, I repeat the ritual with the right.

Her smile tries for consoling, but she assesses me in that way doctors do.

Sympathetic. *Pitying.*

"I have no doubt you've researched the condition thoroughly," she says. "But it's never as simple as one symptom or one obsession. I fear a mind like yours is being tortured."

"Jesus," I whisper harshly, letting a low chuckle escape. What hearing that word on her lips rouses to the surface, torture doesn't come close.

She arches an eyebrow. "Did I say something amusing?"

"No at all," I say, though keeping my impulses leashed around her is becoming exhausting. My muscles feel stretched, strained too tight over my bones.

If she could only hear the chorus of dark thoughts right now. All I can think about is grabbing that infuriating scarf and dragging her closer, sealing my mouth over hers. Shoving my hand up her skirt to feel how tight she can grip my fingers as she moans softly into my mouth.

I blink hard, fighting the aggressive imagery back into the shadowy trenches of my mind. Frustration liquifies beneath my skin, molten.

"It's been reported your outbursts have been happening more frequently."

"By whom?"

"Everyone," she says, fucking relentless. "Even before the incident with Dr. Prescott and the rumors involving the particle accelerator, you were making your colleagues uncomfortable."

"Working alone remedies that, doesn't it?" I say, teeth gritted against the heat flaring under my clothes.

"Yes, isolating yourself can work…for a time," she says, pressing the matter. "But it will likely only result in increased obsessive thoughts. Ruminating more on fears. Reinforcing compulsive behaviors. Maybe even lead to a detachment from reality."

I smile at this, grabbing the knot at my collar to loosen my tie. "The study of space itself is bleak, lonely. Isolating." I meet and hold her gaze a measure too long before shifting my attention to the fountain.

"Care to elaborate?"

I watch water trickle over Urania, allowing the guiding muse to steer my thoughts. "On the ocean, lonely sailors swore they saw mermaids. Forced to observe in solitude, early astronomers believed they saw angels in space. Whether adrift at sea or the vast cosmic ocean, our obsessions have a tendency to make us a little detached."

She tilts her head. "Do you see hallucinations in space, Orion?"

I look at her, stoic. "As of today, I've only ever seen one angel."

She drops her gaze, her hair falling alongside her face to shield her profile. The urgency to grasp her neck and force those gleaming eyes back on me is a hostile demand slamming through my veins.

"Besides," I say, "can't really blame them for losing their shit. A woman can tempt the sanest man mad."

Her lips curve into the slightest smile. "Sexual deprivation can make a man lose his shit for sure," she retorts, less than clinical.

I run my tongue over my teeth, watching her. "Careful, little archer, that fiery nature of yours is showing." I grin with smug satisfaction.

Her mouth presses into a tight line, those pretty eyes losing some of their spark. "Look," she says. "Banner mentioned you've suffered some loss. I don't know the details, but I do know isolating yourself won't protect you from that pain. If anything, it only prolongs the healing process."

My jaw tightens, anger crashing through me in a fierce wave. "Fucking Leo. He's always so helpful," I say, sarcasm thick.

Collins frowns. "I overstepped," she says apologetically.

I ease out a tense breath. From the start, she's been an anomaly. Being here with her now was supposed to satisfy my curiosity—not allow her to probe my wounds.

"This is why beautiful things are admired from afar," I mutter beneath my breath.

Confusion draws her brows together, regret flickering beneath the defiant fire in her eyes. Though it may burn bright, I recognize a sadness in her fury—delicate hairline fractures where dark filaments slither into the light.

And I decide that it's better if I learn nothing else about her.

"My point is, any great discovery is made alone, Dr.

Holbrook. Working in isolation is not only practical, it's necessary." My point effectively made, I stand to leave.

"Wait—we're not done."

"We're done."

"You're angry," she says, stopping me.

"I'm bored."

"You're lying."

Forced to face her, I stare down, a flame licking through my viscera. "You should understand the nature of my intrusive thoughts enough to know that's unlikely," I seethe the words at her.

She sits forward. "I have a theory about what you want, Orion."

"Not to sound crass, Collins, but you have no fucking idea what—"

"You want to touch me."

It's not framed in a suggestive manner, though the sliver of atmosphere separating us sparks all the same. I swallow, my hand clenching at the idea until it burns. I reach out and grip her scarf, my eyes devouring her as I let the words trapped at the base of my throat scorch: *Alarmingly so.*

The slightest tremble rolls through her, and I can sense an unstable current vibrating just beneath.

"Out there on the shore, you said you can't touch me. Not won't. That's a decisive difference," she says, her voice gentle. "You thought I was worried you might try. But you read me wrong." She swallows. "In fact, that couldn't be further from the truth."

I release her scarf.

"My approach might be a bit frightening," she continues, "but exposure therapy is highly effective for touch aversion. Gradually exposing you to what triggers obsessions. Helping to resist compulsions used to cope."

As I stare down, I'm caught in her blink pattern, and a knot tightens beneath my sternum as I fight to resist *her*.

Fuck, she's like the very embodiment of *poena aeterna* sent to torment me.

I could lean over her, and I do. I could trap her against the bench, and I do. I could collar my hand around her throat, taste her lips…

My jaw clenches until the pressure aches. "It's not that I can't touch you. It's that I shouldn't."

Saying the words aloud flays my chest wide open. Collins should be terrified of me getting my hands on her.

I lean in, my mouth within an inch of hers, and snag the length of her scarf. I bring it to my nose and inhale her seductive scent, then gently unwind the soft material from around her neck. "Just try not to be so damn tempting, angel."

I deliver the warning with a wink as I stuff the garment into my jacket. Before I pull away, my gaze lands on a tender bruise along the warm column of her neck. A dark note pulses through my vessels, and something feral and possessive snaps taut.

The demand to know who put those marks on her claws at my throat. My vision darkens as the savage urge to rip a spine from a body seizes me.

Collins adjusts the collar of her blouse, effectively breaking me free of my violent thoughts. "The only way to overcome touch aversion is to touch." Her voice lowers to a breathy cadence as she adds, "Intimately."

A vicious craving whispers from the shadowy corner of my mind, thrumming painfully against my skull. Blood rushes to my groin, thoughts darkening beyond pitch at the deviant things I could do to her in the dark right now.

The way she slightly draws back, her lips parting, she senses the dangerous shift.

"Did you get what you need from me?" I say, my voice a gruff demand.

She swallows, her bright gaze locked with mine. "Not even close."

A callous smile curls my mouth. Summoning just enough willpower to cage the ruthless urges, I break away, stalking toward my bike with quick strides.

I don't have to look back to know she's still sitting on that bench. Thinking. Breathing. Tearing my structured world apart just by *existing*.

Sometimes, the anomalies can really fuck with your head.

There's another word for obsession:

Crush.

The unknown is so goddamn beautiful and alluring until you're being annihilated in the wake of an antimatter collision.

Once it's begun, the process is violent and unstoppable.

I shove my helmet on and start the engine with a roar, drowning out the lingering notes of her haunting melody. If I could keep her at a distance, maybe I could do this. But after holding her close, knowing how right her body feels against mine, breathing in her addictive scent that burns my throat with the hunger to taste her...

Fuck, I won't survive the next six weeks. Every second I'm forced to be near her, craving her until the moment the sun goes dark, will be goddamn agony.

I twist the throttle hard, and my bike lurches forward.

Maybe it makes me weak, but Collins can't remain at Stonehurst until then. She's giving me no choice.

And yet, stubbornly, even defiantly, the scientist in me wants to test her theory—to see if it's as simple as combing through my mind with a little therapy and a hot fuck.

"Christ," I mutter, gunning the engine harder to escape my thoughts.

Honestly, the outcome would be simple enough to reach. Either I'm on the brink of discovery—

Or I'm nothing more than a killer.

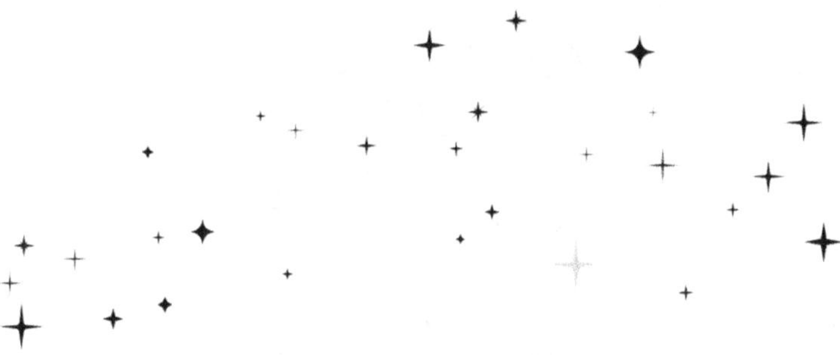

The idea that many stars form with a companion has been suggested before, but the question is: how many? Based on our simple model, we say that nearly all stars form with a companion.

— DR. SARAH SADAVOY, PROFESSOR OF PHYSICS AND ASTRONOMY, QUEEN'S UNIVERSITY

IO

KNIGHT MOVES

Time is nature's way of keeping everything from happening all
at once.

— JOHN ARCHIBALD WHEELER

COLLINS

Laurel once told me the dark side of psychology is far
more nuanced, that we have to be delicate when wading
through the deep waters of the mind.

When I asked her about the light side, she smiled and said,
"What light side?"

When it comes to the mind, there is no region untouched by
shadows—only varying depths of darkness.

Some run too deep to tread.

Delving into psychotherapy to explore a patient's past requires
patience and a tactful, respectful approach. Peeling back layers of
trauma is not unlike a burn victim suddenly recovering feeling in
damaged nerve endings. We need to take care not to shatter the
mind.

But we also have to guard ourselves from being infected by the muck we wade through.

Sensitization can work both ways.

Just try not to be so damn tempting, angel.

Orion's warning echoes through my mind, sparking an enticing thrill at the memory of his rough tone. Confirmation enough that I'm getting under his skin.

Meanwhile, Dr. Eugene Prescott is seated on the beige sofa in my office. Dirty-blond hair neatly trimmed and combed back, clean-shaven and smelling of expensive cologne, he wears his fine academic attire like a statement.

He keeps his phone held at an angle where he can view the screen as I take a seat in the wingback chair across from him. "Banner set you up nice here," he says, giving the office an appraising scan. "Keeping you busy, apparently."

I offer a practiced smile, hearing what's implied beneath. I've been *given* a nice position.

Anything that is given can be taken away.

"I don't care much for decoration." My art prints line the wall, unhung. The shelves are sparsely filled with books that were already here when I arrived.

"I'm sure dealing with Night's absurdity is keeping you plenty occupied," he says with a baiting edge. "So, what can I do to help, Dr. Holbrook?"

"Well first, thank you for always being so cooperative. Especially in regards to this matter."

"Of course." He nods assuredly.

I lace my fingers together over my lap and cross my ankles, not missing the way his eager gaze slips over my legs. If this were a real session, I might call him out in reprimand.

But I'm here to wade around in the muck.

"Let's start with your relationship with Dr. Night," I begin. "How closely have you worked together over the past year?"

He expels a terse breath. "You don't work closely with Night," he states, snide. "Do you know he hardly ever leaves the observatory? I think he even sleeps there. He requires everyone to prep—meaning disinfect every surface and *themselves*—for an hour before entering the facility. And the thing with the gloves... I can't tell you how many projects have been delayed due to his contamination issues."

I reach for a folder on the table and bring it to my lap. "Is that why you went against his directive not to shut down the particle accelerator? Not wanting to face a setback?"

His features harden. He relaxes back into the sofa and rests his ankle across his knee. Taking a new approach, he says, "Look, like I've mentioned before, the science is complicated. You'll just have to trust me on this. I was making the right call."

I part the folder and flip to a page. "From what I understand— and forgive me, I'm not a scientist," I meet his dark eyes briefly with a sweet smile, "but abruptly shutting down the accelerator causes unstable particle decay and can result in high levels of radiation. All that energy needs to be carefully dissipated first, correct?" I look up and tilt my head. "Maybe it's good we're not dealing with worse consequences."

Mouth pinched in a tight smile, he runs a hand down his cobalt tie. "He uploaded malicious software to jeopardize the unveiling and make me look bad, but again—" he raises a hand "—the science is complicated." His gaze slides down my legs, more obvious this time. "I'd be happy to show you the linear accelerator, go over the basics for your evaluation. But I'd need access to the observatory outside of Night to do that, of course."

Message received, I sweeten my smile. "Of course."

I set the file aside and cross my legs, giving him a peek at the slit along my thigh. I don't need Dr. Prescott as an enemy. He's been placed near Orion to keep tabs on him. Which means he's been watching him closely for the past year. There's a chance he could be useful.

"That could be arranged once we—" Without warning, the office door swings open, halting me mid-sentence. "I'm in session," I say, my eyes clashing with the heat in his. "Dr. Night."

Orion darkens the threshold like the night itself, taking up all the air I need to fill my lungs. He closes the door behind him, and the sharp *snick* of the latch firing home sounds loud in the tense stillness.

"Shit. What is he doing here?" Prescott directs an accusatory glare my way before he stands opposite the man dressed in all black.

Orion looks only at me. "You said to be in your office today."

The way he says this, so matter-of-factly, I have to curb a smile. I don't point out that I told him this days ago. "Dr. Prescott, I assure you this is a misunderstanding. Dr. Night's appointment isn't until later." I relay the last part directly to Orion with a slight widening of my eyes.

An arresting smile curves his full lips before he defiantly removes his leather jacket and hangs it on the wall hook. "I think a joint session could be therapeutic. Work out some aggression." His gloved hands fist at his sides as he smirks at Prescott. "Nothing was really resolved the last time we were in a room together, was it, Eugene?"

A flash of fear registers in Prescott's expression. "You know what, it's fine. I have some pressing matters to tend to anyway." He swipes up his phone and heads toward the door, glancing back once to say, "But my offer stands, Dr. Holbrook."

The door shuts, and I level Orion with a severe glare. "I don't understand why you want to make things difficult for me."

A flash of something uninhibited ignites behind the blue-green current of his eyes. He folds his arms over his black oxford, a smug grin slanting his mouth. "Making things easy for you wasn't stipulated in the parameters of your extortion, starling. Besides, you won't get what you need from him. Prescott's a narcissistic sycophant who'd say anything to steal my position."

I uncross and recross my legs, deliberate and slow. "Yet you did try to push him out of a window."

Orion doesn't remove his eyes from mine. "Next time I won't try. What offer?" he demands, dismissing my remark.

I rise from the chair and return the file to my desk, slipping it behind my open laptop before I face him. "To further my eval, I need to see the observatory. Since Dr. Prescott has already been so helpful implementing my protocols, he offered to show me around and explain some of the equipment."

In his own slow and deliberate way, Orion swipes his thumb across his bottom lip, eyes stealing down my body before his gaze solders to mine. "That won't happen."

"He was more than eager to give me what I need," I say, driving the metaphorical knife deeper.

Something dark and menacing surfaces in his expression, and my skin sparks everywhere his heated gaze touches. "If you want to test the theory of whether Prescott can fly, then by all means, take him up on his offer."

His possessive tone coasts down the curve of my spine, inducing a shiver. "You don't sound at all disturbed, Orion."

"And you don't sound at all like a psychiatrist right now, Collins, but here we both are."

"Here we both are." A smile breaks across my mouth. "Do people talk like this?"

"We talk like this."

His intense gaze holds mine captive, his eyes so vibrant and blazing, I'm breathless in the wake of their unhurried descent over my body.

And I study him right back. The way he flexes his long fingers. Shifts his stance. Rolls his head along his shoulders to work out his neck. He's not wearing a tie, the top buttons of his shirt undone. A turbulent ocean rages beneath his stony veneer.

"Dr. Night, you seem…bothered." I smile as I echo the words he once said to me back at him.

"You made damn sure of that." His tense frame practically vibrates. "Unfortunately, I have a curious nature that's not easily pacified."

I arch an eyebrow. "Is this your way of agreeing to therapy," I say questioningly.

He cocks his chin. "And if it is."

"I won't be gentle."

"Fuck, I hope not."

I bite the corner of my lip to hold back a smile. Orion might as well be trying to impress me with his flash pattern. Aggressive. Possessive. A primal alpha male marking my office as he prowls toward the sofa to claim his territory.

He casually folds his tall, leanly cut frame onto the seat, and I have to refrain from touching the place where my heart knocks like percussion against my breastbone. After the sharp pain subsides, I saunter to my chair and sit across from him, cross my legs.

When his direct gaze targets the slit in my skirt, a pulse of heat descends between my thighs. It feels nothing like when Prescott did so just moments ago.

"Tell me the last time you were intimate."

"Intimate," he repeats, his gaze flicking up to touch mine.

"Sexual intimacy," I clarify, just to goad him.

"Fucked."

I try not to blink as I hold his gaze. "Fucked."

He swipes a gloved hand over his jaw. "Since before the accident."

His confession compresses the cool air between us. It's been over six years since Orion last had sex. This knowledge stirs something darkly tempting in my veins, the power of it seductive.

With a careful approach, I ease into the tenuous silence. "The person you lost," I say delicately, "the one Banner alluded to before. Was that her?"

Orion's expression tenses, a shadow drifting across his face. "Dr. Calloway," he says quietly. "Emma." He draws in a controlled breath. "No, it wasn't like that between us. We were close, and...eventually, there might've been something more. But we were partners. Our research was what mattered." His voice dips, a subtle tremor just beneath the rough edge. "I trusted her. She was brilliant. I got most of the credit, of course—unfortunately, that's how most fields work—but Emma was every bit as dedicated as I was." A nostalgic smile pulls at his mouth. "Probably more so."

A current of grief flows through his admission. While Orion may lack the ability to varnish his thoughts, and his confession could be involuntary—it could also be calculated. Yet his regret feels too honest, too raw. The pain I sometimes glimpse through his cracks lingers, like a wave refusing to recede, eroding his stone walls.

After his reaction when I touched on this subject before, I dug deeper into his past. Orion has no social media presence. He keeps himself hidden. The sparse history I was able to uncover during my initial dive didn't reveal everything. Both parents, lost tragically during his college years. A close childhood friend taken by illness. A former mentor whose life ended abruptly. And Emma—his research partner—gone before their endeavors were realized.

Orion Night's existence has been an endless litany of loss.

Drawing in a slow breath, I lean back in my seat, deciding not to push him further on this today.

He breaks the connection further when he turns away,

surveying my office. The walnut bookcases lining the walls. The neutral linen furniture. The one arched window with a partial view of the ocean. A stack of framed, forged credentials lined against a stone wall.

"I haven't had time to decorate," I say in answer to his inquisitive stare.

"So you do enjoy chess," he comments, eyeing the marble chessboard on a side table.

"It's the truth. Have you considered utilizing contraceptives, like a condom, to inspire intimacy?"

A subtle lift touches his lips, his expression amused. "It's not just about physical touch. Sex is a distraction." To emphasize his point, his gaze descends to the slit along my thigh once more.

"On average, how often do sexually intrusive thoughts occur during the day?"

"Thirty-seven."

I measure my breathing. "You've counted."

"I count everything." He rests his hands on his thighs. His fingers tap in time to my firing pulse. "But that was before you. Now, it's between sixty and sixty-seven. On average."

My heartbeat hammers in my neck. His tapping speeds. "Why do you think that is?"

"I spend less time in my observatory," he says, honest. "When I'm there, very little disrupts my focus."

I nod meaningfully. "We need to explore the nature of your—"

"You're going to ask what kind of forbidden thoughts I have," he interrupts, halts tapping. "Whether they're taboo, like incest or bestiality."

I clear my hair from my forehead. "Memorizing a medical journal doesn't mean you understand what to do with that information."

"Agreed." He adjusts his position. "But I think we can cut

through the bullshit and get right to where you explain how driving me crazy will help."

I keep my tone neutral. "You avoided my question."

His nostrils flare. "Deviant sexual nature," he says candidly. "My intrusive thoughts are of a sexually violent nature in particular."

I swallow, and I feel his observant gaze trail the curve of my throat with the action. His left hand clenches into a fist, triggering a visceral response within me.

"It's a unique cluster of symptoms," I say, blocking my thoughts from the dirt trying to creep between the cracks. "Touch aversion in combination with fear of contamination and germs—"

"Mysophobia—"

"And sexual obsessions." I pull in a breath. My vision flickers. "We have a lot of ground to explore before we develop any therapeutic approach."

I stand and stride toward my desk, needing a moment to gather myself.

"*Hmm,*" Orion hums, far too amused. "I thought exposure therapy was the therapeutic approach. How did you put it? To touch…intimately?"

A chord of fear thrums my heart. I saw it in his eyes when he noticed the bruises, the way the marks aroused that buried deviant within him. A tactic meant to stir his hunger—not send him over the edge. Nothing in his previous evaluations, nor the crime scenes, even hinted at sexual sadism disorder.

Rousing his monster means picking at the scabs of my trauma.

I squeeze my eyes shut.

One. Two. Three.

Get a fucking grip.

I release a slow breath. "Given the mind's unparalleled ability to protect its host, touch aversion may be an unconscious way of preventing harm. We first need to understand—"

"I don't follow."

I shuffle a stack of manila folders, giving myself an extra few seconds before I pull his file. "Often, those who experience sexual obsessions are so fearful of acting on their intrusive thoughts, they create even more obsessions as a distraction. It's textbook harm OCD. If you're fearful of causing harm, it's completely rational to develop an aversion to touch." I clutch the folder to my chest and turn toward him. "If you can't touch a person, then logically, you can't hurt them."

His smile is so cutting, it could wound. "That's a lot of psychobabble to say you think I'm dangerous."

"That's not what I said." I brace my palm to the edge of the desk.

Orion sits forward, linking his gloved hands together. "But once you get inside my head, combing around with your little shrink comb, your assessment will state I'm high-risk."

"You continue to ride a motorcycle despite the serious, life-altering accident you suffered," I say. "That is a dangerous risk."

"Statistics state otherwise."

"Maybe, but I think it's something else."

The tension in the air gathers around us, the space between strained with the heavy pause. The demand for me to expound is delivered with the smoldering look he sends me.

"Despite the altercation between you and Dr. Prescott, my main concern isn't that you could be a danger to others." I select my words carefully, treading the rocky waters between us. "But that you may be a danger to yourself."

A gust of wind rattles the windowpane. My belly flutters with the disruption, but I don't flinch, watching Orion intently for the slightest tell.

He gives nothing away, his unyielding gaze fixed on mine.

I clear my hair from my vision. "Do you ever feel the impulse to jump?" I ask him. "That sudden, intrusive urge when you're somewhere high, like your observatory? It's referred to as the call of the void."

He tilts his head, the movement deliberate. "That's normal for most people."

"Yes. But do you ever act on it?" I press.

Something flares behind his eyes. Heated, challenging. "I don't have suicidal ruminations," he states, the corner of his mouth lifting into a wry, humorless smile.

"The sudden urge to jump rarely is," I say, sensing his resistance. I need to back off this topic. "People with harm OCD experience intense, violent thoughts. Unwanted flashes of doing something terrible. Hurting someone. Hurting themselves. The more horrific the thought, the more paralyzing. It's never acted on, but the fear alone makes you feel a loss of control."

His jaw tightens, tendons flexing along his throat. "That's also common," he concedes. "Straddling the line between life and death—literal, metaphorical—reminds us that we have free will. It grants us a certain power in choosing to take the leap and jump, rather than falling. Knowing we can answer the call—" he pauses, a ghost of a smile curling his mouth "—but choosing not to."

Held captive by the intensity of his stare, I measure my breathing. "Then explain it to me, Orion. Why take such risks?"

"It's simple," he says. "I need the danger, the rush. When I'm on my bike and the heart races, the mind quiets. There's no space for obsessive thoughts. To even think."

My pulse quickens in response to his words. "The endorphin rush offers a distraction," I reason, nodding slowly. "How often do you use this tactic?"

"Every chance I get."

"You're addicted to the rush."

"I'm addicted to you."

I grip the folder tighter to my chest. "These impulsive statements intended to deflect won't help here."

"Not deflecting." He pushes back into the cushion of the sofa. "You're beautiful."

"You've said this to me already."

"And I'll say it every time it crosses my mind. You're so goddamn beautiful, I can't think straight. I'm obsessed, and fuck…" His voice lowers to a coarse grate. "Ever since the courtyard, my head's been a mess, Dr. Holbrook."

I swallow hard. "So this is your retaliation against me, for how uncomfortable I made you feel." I search his gaze for the truth.

"Not at all," he says, yet there's a taut thread woven beneath his amused tone.

"Okay, then." I nod once. "You can't say things like that to me while in session."

"I can't help it."

"You have to try."

Our gazes stay locked, silence ringing too loudly in my ears. "If you're under my care, you can't even look at me like that, Dr. Night."

A fierce intensity darkens his eyes. "Maybe your care isn't what I want to be under."

Heat flushes my body. "We need to work on exercises that help you filter what leaves your mouth," I say, steeling my voice against my flaring nerves.

"They're just thoughts. Just words. You said I won't act on them." The way he's watching me, gauging me, like this is a test I can't fail. My spine knots with tension.

I smooth a palm down my skirt. "No, but I'm not sure I can handle sixty-seven instances of your unfiltered thoughts."

He rests his tongue in the corner of his mouth as his gaze lowers to my throat. "I think you can handle a whole lot more."

A sudden chill prickles my skin. Something's off…*very* off. Revealing some of my cracks was supposed to get me closer to him—not expose me to a sadist. I may have pushed him too hard, too fast. I need him unraveled, even a little feral, not imploding.

Casually, I rub my thumb over the constellation along my wrist, willing my pulse to calm. "Besides being inappropriate, you need to understand that for most people, it takes time to feel a certain level of intimacy."

His smile is knowing, and his deep chuckle drops low in my belly. "Time's merely a construct to measure the passing of life." He shrugs against the sofa. "It's delivered to us in little drips, in a stream of lyrics and chords, a song we experience linearly, creating memory." A serious note laces his voice. "I experience our song every time I look at you, Collins. All at once." His eyes blaze. "In a rush."

The molecules of the air crackle with heat. The bruised organ inside my chest flutters. I feel swept into his animated current, dragged by the undertow of his unstable thoughts.

To mask the flicker of unease in my expression, I glance at the file in my hand—two MRI series reports. One dated before the motorcycle accident. The other from a clearance check Banner ordered two years ago.

The report with the structural images states no obvious trauma. No bleeding, no lesions—nothing to explain the changes Orion started exhibiting after the wreck. All cleared and signed off. And yet, there's a subtle shift in functional connectivity, some elevated reactivity in the regions tied to fear and compulsion.

Whatever emerged post-accident rewired something deeper, something psychological. Whether the crash was the catalyst is irrelevant.

He *believes* it was.

And that can be exploited.

"We've strayed off topic," I say, lifting my eyes to him. "You said your observatory is where obsessive thoughts don't invade.

It's your routine that I need to monitor. Observing you there is the only way I can give you a proper assessment—"

He stands abruptly.

Removing his glasses from his shirt pocket, he slips them into place and stalks toward the side table. He rests a finger on one of the black chess pieces, tips it forward. "Did you know the knight is the sneakiest piece on the board," he says randomly.

I frown. "I suppose that's a matter of opinion."

He grins down at the board. "One of my favorite plays is the smothered mate. It's when the king is completely surrounded by his own pieces, nowhere to run. And the knight"—he hooks a finger under the knight and lifts it, moving it in an L-shape—"leaps right over."

He looks up at me. "Checkmate."

I close the file and drop it to the desk. "Are you saying you feel smothered by your colleagues?"

"Interesting you think I'm the king in this scenario." He starts toward me, slowly crossing the distance.

I consider how to maneuver around him. "You still question whether you can trust me."

He stops a few feet away. "I question everything, all the time." His eyes connect with mine past the rims of his glasses. "Like why observing me in my observatory seems to be so important."

"Why wouldn't it be? It's where your time is focused. Typically, getting an academic to show off their work isn't hard," I say, emboldening my tone. "Some would say your secretive nature surrounding your research is somewhat paranoid."

"I would say it's completely paranoid."

I expel a tense breath. "Why do you think you were able to rescue me from the tide, Orion?" I pivot, taking control.

A dark brow lifts behind his glasses. "You're the expert. I'd rather hear your thoughts on why I was able to rescue you, to get close to you." He demonstrates this by drawing even closer.

"Danger," I say simply. "You braved the tide without thought for your own safety. You rushed in impulsively, fueled by the desire to achieve an adrenaline rush. You've admitted you do this every chance you get. Stimulation addiction presents as extremely risky, thrill-seeking behavior."

A crooked smile tips his mouth. "Damn, I thought I was being heroic. You might as well label me a madman."

"That's not the term I would use."

"What would you use?"

"With the way you're behaving right now—" I flatten my backside against the desk's edge to escape his nearness. "I'd say your behavior is…erratic."

He cants his head until nearly all the space between us disappears. Close enough to hear the catch of my breath, where I can taste the scent of ocean and mist clinging to his clothes. It sends a heady buzz through my bloodstream.

His eyes absorb me, trailing down to the violent pulse in my neck. "I'm not the only erratic thing in this room, Dr. Holbrook."

I swallow reflexively, rocked beneath the hunger burning in his eyes. His hair falls across his forehead, and I resist the urge to sweep it aside. An alarm sounds, warning me to tread carefully.

He extends his hand alongside my hip, and I stop breathing, my body frozen as he reaches around and taps the keyboard of my laptop to close out the recording application.

My eyes fall closed, and a breathy curse slips past my lips. I hold back a wince as a pinch of pain tightens beneath my rib cage.

"I trust you have an ethical reason for recording me," he says, his voice a dark rasp, summoning my gaze back to his. "Since your ethics are so incorruptible."

I will my backbone to lock. "I like to keep detailed

documentation. Especially since I'm unable to observe you properly."

His grin is sinful as he places his knuckles on the surface of the desk, caging his body around mine. His attention drifts downward, eyes tracing a purposeful path over my throat. The bruises hidden beneath my hair flare with a throb under his sharp gaze.

Orion's mouth stretches into that beautiful, knowing smile. "You don't need to observe my boring routine, Collins. Do you see where I am right now? I'm not in my observatory. I'm not obsessively tracking star patterns. I'm not chasing an adrenaline rush on my bike. I'm here, with you." His voice is an abrasive brush of friction against my skin. "Being near you is all the danger I need, angel."

My breathing shallows, my gaze drawn to the parted collar of his shirt, where a hint of black ink teases through. Transfixed, I daringly lift my hand.

"Careful," he warns. "Unless you enjoy being smothered, be sure that's the move you want to make."

My throat constricts at the threat, and my hand falls away. "This isn't healthy," I manage to say.

He nods slowly. "Oh, I know. It's a sickness. I fucking dream of what your skin tastes like."

Torrid flames lick over my skin in response, my body torn between fear and desire, the damaged parts of me blurring the line between survival instinct and shameless need.

I shiver under the fiery brand of his gaze. I've dared myself to imagine what it would feel like to press my lips to his, to have his body heavy over mine. While a dormant part of me is curious, may even secretly crave it—his aversion to touch was supposed to offer a barrier of protection.

Me pushing him—not the other way around.

"What I mean is," I say, "it's unhealthy to swap one obsession for another. That's called transference."

He makes a gruff sound. "It's also unhealthy to be so damn tempting to a madman, but here we both are."

Against my will, a wicked smile steals across my face. "Here we both are."

With an unhurried sweep of his tongue, Orion wets his lips, sending a frisson arcing down my spine. The dare hovers like a live wire, crackling in the charged space between us.

Involuntarily, my thighs squeeze together to offset the empty ache. Like a provoked predator, Orion senses my movement, his eyes darkening.

"Fuck." The curse drops from his mouth on a harsh breath. "So what happens now, doctor. Does this exposure therapy mean you'll let me do things like call you baby. Tell you all the filthy ways I've obsessed about you. How every single time I saw you sitting on that bench, all I could fucking think about was bending you over it and spreading you wide, burying my fingers inside you."

A shock of fear spikes my pulse. My breath catches painfully beneath my ribs as the threat of his words constricts my chest. No matter what happens now, escape isn't an option.

My mouth opens to respond, but the words snag behind the tight knot in my throat.

"*Mmm-hmm.*" Orion tilts his head as he studies me, keeping his body a taut line of control. His gaze narrows, a dangerous smirk twisting his lips, like he's won some match between us.

And my stomach dips as I realize I've made a wrong move.

He pulls back a measure. "Your fear has a taste, starling. It's mouthwatering. But as much as I'm tempted to spend the day torturing myself with it—" A devilish smile slants his mouth as he reaches into his pocket and produces a folded slip of paper. "You have something I need, and I told you I'd collect."

For one dreaded, off-kilter heartbeat, I envision the piece of evidence in my pocket—until he says, "Your signature."

Masking my relief, I draw myself up through my spine and accept the document. I only have to scan the top line to recognize it as a copy of the mandatory admittance Banner gave me.

"Orion, I never signed this."

"Your resignation is attached," he says, dismissing my objection. "Effective immediately, Dr. Holbrook."

Trapped between his body and the desk, I suddenly question just who the sneakiest piece on the board is.

Meeting his eyes, I hold up the document between us and tear it down the center, letting the halves float to the floor. "There. That's my move," I say pointedly. "Too bad you already gave yours away."

He licks his lips, cold amusement flickering behind his glasses. "Did I now."

I lift my chin, refusing to flinch. "You lost the ability to intimidate me the moment you gave me your umbrella, Orion."

A knowing grin twists his mouth, challenge sparking in the depths of his eyes as he removes one hand from the desk. He settles his palm along my jawline, fingers pressed to my neck. His glove is a cool kiss to my overheated skin, sending a sinister chill through my flesh as his thumb glides beneath my lower lip.

The distinct scent of leather coils my stomach, dredging a flash of terror to my surface. An icy trickle of fear leaks into my veins.

A predatory intent hones his gaze, the corner of his mouth curving upward with wicked satisfaction. "There it is," he whispers, his dexterous fingers tracing the column of my spine. "That exquisite scent of yours, fear laced with fury."

Past the panic clawing at my chest, a shockwave of desire steals my breath at his possessive tone.

As he straightens, a mocking smile cuts across his face. "The fact is, you were an easy pawn. Perfectly positioned to give me what I needed about Leo's intentions. Now? You're just a distraction. A fucking sexy one—but one I don't have time for."

"I don't believe you."

I don't believe him.

"Here's what you can believe," he says, the gravel in his voice scraping over me in threat. "One of us is afraid I'll act on my intrusive thoughts, and I'm fairly certain it's not me." A menacing smile hitches the edge of his mouth. "So, forgive me if your exposure therapy feels like it'd be an ineffective waste of my limited time, Dr. Holbrook."

For the male species, deprivation of carnal desires can leave them vulnerable, susceptible to a more dangerous predator.

Backed into a corner as I am now, I'm that predator.

Channeling all my fear and fury, I brazenly toss my hair off my shoulder, deliberately revealing the bruises along my throat. It's only a flash, but I see the deviant monster stir beneath his rigidly controlled surface. His gaze heats as it lingers on my throat, and I can sense his fraying restraint.

"Only one way to prove how ineffective." In a defiant move, I brace the heels of my hands on the edge of the desk and lift myself onto the surface, bringing my face within inches of his. "I may or may not be wearing panties, Dr. Night," I say, my bold words a breathy tremble. "How bad do you want to find out? Bad enough to remove your glove and slip your hand beneath my skirt and touch me—or was that all just talk?"

I part my thighs in blatant challenge.

"Jesus—fuck," he mutters coarsely, barely constrained. A crazed spark ignites behind his eyes, and I'm met with six years' worth of raw need, almost wilting under the intensity of it.

"Make your next move," I dare, my voice unsteady with adrenaline.

His nostrils flare, jaw strained until a muscle jumps.

Something volatile and prohibited sweeps over me, claiming. This dark current reaches out, hungrily probing, testing.

Wanting.

With a fierce groan, Orion pushes away from the desk.

My heart thunders as I watch him storm from the office. My body is so primed, I don't even flinch at the slam of the door.

"Check," I mutter to myself.

I'm only given a moment to breathe, to fill my constricted lungs, before the door opens again and he charges right toward me, a blaze torching his eyes. "Oh, shit."

Then he's on me, pushing me down against the desk, his body hovering dangerously over mine. His legs invade between my parted thighs, and I scrape in a breath, anticipating the rough feel of his hand up my skirt—

He presses a gloved finger to my mouth, silencing a desperate sound as it escapes my lips.

"You're the danger," he says, his voice lowered to a guttural pitch. "You have no idea what you're tempting to the surface." His jaw works, the blue-green of his eyes lit with a furious flame, his body prying my thighs apart. "Sign the fucking resignation or not, but you're leaving, Collins. I'm giving you one chance to run as far as you can."

His eyes burn into me, the leather trapping my breath.

Slowly, he drops his finger from my mouth, trailing down my throat, down the center of my chest. Those fiery embers smolder as his eyes track the progression, then his gaze flicks up to trap mine.

Voice lost, all I can do is nod a shaky response.

A shadow falls across his features as he presses something cool into my hand before he draws upward. "Checkmate."

He lifts his chin, his eyes cast down to stay locked with mine as he takes a purposeful step backward. "Forgot my jacket," he mutters as he snags it from the hook and turns, striding through the door.

I wait until I hear the soft click of the latch before I allow myself to drag in a shuddering breath. The aching pressure in my chest releases with a whimper. "Shit. *Shit shit shit.*"

I roll onto my side and slam my laptop shut, anger welling. With trembling fingers, I touch the aching valley between my breasts, searching out the uneven rhythm of my heart before I uncurl my other hand from around the chess piece.

My thumb rubs over the smooth marble of the knight.

As I push myself off the desk, I feel the slick heat slip along my inner thighs, and I should be mortified, ashamed—but those emotions abandoned me long ago.

A surge of fury rises so quickly, I hurl the chess piece across the room. It cracks sharp against the door before hitting the floor.

Fuck. Him.

Orion Night doesn't get to frighten me off.

I reach into my pocket for my pill case, and my fingers brush the brass object there, triggering images of his last crime scene. I may have overlooked something critical in his profile, a sexual deviance I couldn't have uncovered until I got this close. A grave miscalculation on my part. But that just means I have to adjust my strategy.

I've opened a door I can't close.

When it comes to the mind, there is no region untouched by shadows—only varying depths of darkness.

For the sexual sadist, some regions definitely run too deep to tread.

And yet, to overcome what we fear most, we have to be willing to wade into the muck of those dark waters.

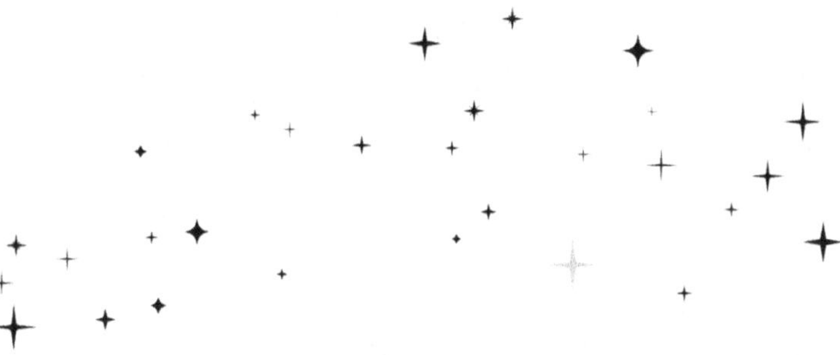

The Fibonacci Sequence turns out to be the key to understanding how nature designs... and is... a part of the same ubiquitous music of the spheres that builds harmony into atoms, molecules, crystals, shells, suns and galaxies and makes the Universe sing.

— GUY MURCHIE, *THE SEVEN MYSTERIES OF LIFE*

II

FROZEN STARS

Music can give you a different way of seeing the universe. It's like finding a pathway into the brain. The notes are made of the stuff of the universe.

— BRIAN MAY, QUEEN GUITARIST &
ASTROPHYSICIST

ORION

When our reality is challenged, it creates a deep, unsettling feeling.

On a fundamental level, we understand that touch is merely the perception of vibration. That at the quantum scale, we never actually touch an object—only interact with the electromagnetic fields at its surface.

And yet, because the sensation feels so intensely real, we can never truly grasp that it's an illusion. It's too disturbing, too unsettling, to challenge our concept of reality. So our mind retreats to what feels safe.

I've existed in this realm of unsettling truths so long that I thought nothing could rattle me anymore. I've learned to accept my irrational fears, because the constant strain of challenging them is fucking exhausting.

And once I did, the desire for touch became an afterthought, lost beneath the ruthless demand of my research. Over time, I forgot what it felt like—the heat, the pressure, the tantalizing friction of skin against skin.

I severed that part of my humanity, discarded like a failed experiment. Obsolete. Irrelevant.

Only now, sitting here on this bench, hand hovering over the ivory keys, locked in this position until my fingers start to cramp and a slow burn builds in my forearm, I'm rattled to my goddamn core.

Since I forced myself out of her office, I haven't been able to *stop* thinking about it. Touching her. Her touch. Our bodies touching. Collins splayed on top of the desk like an offering. Her legs parted for me in invitation, her back arched, blouse torn open as I claw my way through her.

"Fucking Christ," I mutter through gritted teeth.

Letting my demons out to play felt good. Too fucking good. Reining them back in was damn near impossible.

I told her to leave.

Desperation can push us to take extreme risks.

In mine, I raced my Triumph down winding coastal roads, climbing to dangerous speeds as I chased a rush of adrenaline to burn her from my system.

It's not enough.

The dark tide within me is rising—a stirring I feel before every celestial event.

The tide will keep rising before it recedes.

Even after I barricaded myself inside my observatory behind locked doors and shuttered windows, I could still sense her. Like sound waves drawn past the horizon, I'm losing the fight to resist her pull.

I told her to leave—

But there's nowhere she can run to escape me.

I will hunt her.

I will find her.

And when I finally get my hands on her, I will relish in breaking her.

My fingers tremble, hovering just above the keys. Pain sears my muscles, old breaks rebelling as my wrist throbs, but I suffer the burn. If Collins's approach was to push me over the edge, my little archer hit her mark—pushing me right over the threshold of the one place I never enter.

A humorless chuckle escapes, bouncing around the darkened atrium. The bones of the room amplify the aching notes inside my head. Black grilles slice through the glass walls like the ribs of the organ contained within. The glass ceiling above grants a view of the starry night sky. A slash of moonlight spills through an arched pane. Vines crawl along the walls as silver light bleeds across the sandstone, washing the room in a shadowy pale gray.

The doors leading to the observatory are cracked open, allowing a cool ocean breeze to travel through the hollow corridor, but I still can't breathe.

Her scarf drapes the carved music rack of the vintage Blüthner. Scents of amber and vanilla and the sweetest floral note tortuously cling to the fibers, infusing my lungs with white-hot embers. Little pops of satisfying pain to curb the cravings.

With a defeated groan, I finally relent, letting my finger fall to a key.

An A above middle C shatters the silence, resonating at 440 hertz—both foreign and haunting—as the sound echoes off stone and glass.

Overcome, I release an unsteady breath. The note reverberates through my skull, tuning my chaotic thoughts the same way an orchestra tunes its instruments.

My hand spasms from inactivity, and I flex my fingers to restore feeling, pinpricks attacking my nerves. It's a deceptive belief to think we're safe when motionless, unable to cause any ripples.

Remaining frozen inflicts far more pain.

Before Einstein proved his theory of relativity, physicists referred to hypothetical collapsed stars as frozen stars. To the observer, the surface at the moment of collapse appeared frozen in time.

It wasn't until Wheeler defined these cosmic voids as black holes that light was shed on their consuming nature.

They devour everything around them.

While the term black hole might be more accurate, it doesn't evoke the same cosmic beauty as a star frozen in the depths of space, suspended, eternally waiting.

Torrid heat licks through me as my middle finger wanders over the teeth of the piano, my gaze absently trailing the inked designs across the back of my hand. The compulsive need to press the same note with my right hand pulses against my skull. That agonizing desire for symmetry is a demon at war with my will.

Just one of the reasons I haven't attempted to play in all these years. You can't perform a musical piece when you're fixated on pressing keys to feel a rightness versus creating music. It destroys the ability to compose.

Before the wreck, music was a passion.

After, the desire to even touch a piano withered into decay.

When passion is lost, the very spark of our soul that animates us becomes a destructive force. We become these frozen stars, suspended, waiting—fearing the pain from any change.

While this piano is merely a decorative addition for the university, for me, it's an infuriating reminder of that loss every time I walk past the atrium, speared through with a searing rod of resentment.

But tonight, in an effort to expel her torturous melody from my head, I forced my fingers to the keys. I invited the pain. Like a darkening celestial body, she's a star on the brink of collapse. Vibrating at her own frequency, resonating a tune that demands to be captured, composed.

If I could just purge the melancholic notes I hear every time I look into her beautiful, arresting eyes, then maybe her song won't haunt me once she's gone.

When observing an event, the observer cannot interfere. In our universe, it's an unbreakable rule.

Nothing I do will alter the outcome.

Instead, as the warm piano note fades, I flip my wrist over and check my astronomical watch, gauging the alignment markers. The sun and moon dials inch closer—a countdown to the solar eclipse.

Once the sun goes dark, so will I.

I glance at my reflection mirrored in the dark pane of glass, my twin staring back. It's a distorted, disturbing symmetry—the core paradox of my research.

Light and dark. Matter and antimatter. Life and its opposite, coupled in cosmic duality.

At the shadowed boundary of every black hole lies a place where past is preserved, memories trapped beyond the horizon of loss. Echoes detectable at the brink of annihilation, in the final pulse of a fading heartbeat.

My fingers splay wide across the keys, and I hammer down a D minor chord. The dark notes crash through the room with jarring intensity, my resistance splintering against sweet smiles and sultry looks.

Shaken, I pull my hand away and rub the dust between the pads of my fingers, feeling the particles tangle with mine. My vessels constrict, pulse spiking in alarm. The compulsive urge to wash the grime away is surpassed only by the prickling sensation at the back of my neck.

I sense the change in the air, feel the abrasive rustle of fibers against my skin as cold sweat stings my scalp. That's why, even before I hear a sound echo from the observatory, I know someone has invaded my space.

My finger gently depresses the piano key. A stark note rings out, reverberating against the glass, before a sharp *clink* follows in response.

Pushing to my feet, I send the bench scraping across the sandstone in warning. As I slip on my gloves, I stride from the atrium, my steps deliberate.

The corridor grows darker the farther I head toward the observatory, and I catch the familiar scent of vanilla in the air. I breathe in deeply, a smile twisting my mouth as hunger burns low in my stomach.

Like a hunter trailing its prey, I follow, my senses sharpening as I pick up on the clack of heels, the movement whispering through the shadows.

It's been one hundred and fifty-six hours since I last laid eyes on her. One hundred and fifty-six hours of torturous restraint, denying myself even the smallest taste. No lingering gazes on courtyard benches. No heated exchanges in darkened hallways. No stolen glances across lecture halls.

The sight of her now crashes into me with the devastating force of a high-speed particle collision. The impact almost hurts, this energy that can't be contained, its only course is to crack my rib cage.

Restraint shattered, I have her backed against the stone wall, my gloved hand covering her mouth to stifle a scream.

Her startled cry is hot against my palm, the enticing, throaty sound of it traveling right to my groin. Unable to deny myself the sinful feel of her curves, I press my thighs flush with hers to trap her in place, and my cock defiantly twitches.

Her wide eyes stare up at me, and before she can push against my chest, I have her wrist captured and pinned to the wall above her head. She curls her other hand beside her thigh, somehow having the capacity to keep from touching me.

I don't have the same capacity when it comes to her. The fact that I'm stripped of control around her drives a pulse of fury through my veins.

"I told you to leave, Collins," I say, my voice a gruff echo in the hollow corridor. "That means I definitely don't want you sneaking around my observatory."

The darkness is physical, thrumming with an electric chord pulled taut between our bodies. Concealed beneath the shadows, the temptation to do bad things doesn't feel so reckless.

Reining in my impulses, I grit my teeth against that very need and slowly lower my hand from her mouth, just enough for her to drag in a breath. Now that I have her trapped, it's impossible to release her.

I slide my gloved fingers along the delicate curve of her jawline until I reach the back of her neck. Thumb braced to the soft space beneath her chin, I tilt her face up to mine. "Why are you still here."

"Because you need me," she says in a rush of breath. Her strained swallow works the digastric muscle of her jaw against my palm, and it's entirely too arousing.

The heat of her skin reaches me through the sheer fabric of her clothes, and my nostrils flare. "The truth," I demand.

"Jesus, Orion." Her voice cracks softly. "That is the truth. You need me. And I need—" She breaks off. Her gaze searches my face, a hint of vulnerability slipping into hers. "I need this to work. I've spent years studying compulsions in the darkest minds. I came here because of you, because I thought you might be the one person who'd understand this obsessive drive. I just need the ideal patient to prove my approach."

My jaw tightens as I assess her, my gaze drifting lower as I ease my hand aside. Even in the dark, I can make out the faded pattern of bruises lining her throat. A feral anger grips me as I imagine her conducting her *approach* with someone else.

"The ideal patient," I repeat, dry amusement lacing my tone. "And your method involves you spreading your legs on a desk, tempting me to tear my fucking glove off with my teeth and sink inside you. Is that it?"

She releases a shaky breath. "Is that what you wanted to do?"

Her thighs squeeze together, and I make a rough sound. "Fuck me." Helplessly compelled, I skim my gloved fingers along the column of her throat. "Tell me who put thse bruises on you," I demand, voice lowering to a seductive pitch.

Her lips tremble. "That's personal."

"*Mmm.*" Tenderly, I sweep her hair aside, dropping my mouth dangerously close to her ear. "When I find out, I'm going to make it *very* fucking personal, little archer." Pulling back, I align my fingertips with the marks. My hand is too large—but not hers. They're self-inflicted.

"God damn," I mutter harshly. I breathe her in until my lungs ache, letting her arousing scent and fiery defiance sear. "You're also a little twisted, Dr. Holbrook."

She holds my gaze, and as I fall deeper into her, a dark vein threads the golden arc of her teal eyes. "I prefer unafraid. Daring. Challenging convention."

I nod slowly. "Cunning. Manipulative. Torching those incorruptible ethics to the ground."

"What are you going to do about it?" Her eyes search me, and I'm arrested by the way those captivating lashes feather her cheekbones as she settles that branding gaze on my mouth.

A low groan betrays my conflict. "So, working with someone

gifted in their field really meant you needed a deviant with a ruined reputation. That's your ideal patient."

She arches an eyebrow. "You'd rather I lie to you?"

A wild flame lashes through me, every muscle strained as I hold something feral back. Collins flinches with a wince of pain, just a small clench of her features, and I realize how tight my grip has become along the sides of her throat.

I loosen my hold a fraction and turn my head, latching onto where I have her arm pinned, to the inked constellation peeking above the web of my glove. Fixated, I tenderly rub my thumb over her inner wrist.

"Are you experiencing a physical reaction, Orion?" She arches her back, her breasts making contact with my chest and setting off a riot inside my body.

"Collins—" I say her name in warning, my cock straining against the closure of my pants. I swear, if she pushes her hips forward even another inch, I'll come undone right here.

On instinct, I release her and retreat a forceful step back. Her cautious eyes remain fused to mine as I slip my hand into my pocket, seeking the instrument there that demands my attention every bit as much as her consuming stare.

She touches her neck, gingerly feeling the echo of my rough touch. "I know what happened in my office…things got intense." The hesitation in her voice alludes to more than the heated exchange between us.

With a guarded step forward, she continues, "You had a right to question my method. I admit, I expected more resistance from you. And the way I handled it…" She pauses, bites her lip. "That wasn't exactly ethical on my part."

I huff a derisive breath, my gaze descending to the fitted curve of her skirt, traitorously wondering if she's wearing panties right now. No one's ever challenged my goddamn sanity more.

"But then I realized," she presses on, "your anger wasn't

fueled by any threat to have you removed, or even committed. None of that truly threatens you." She swallows, the subtle motion revealing her vulnerability.

Teeth gritted, I resist pressing a hand to my forehead, where the aching pressure builds. Goddammit, I'm trying to show her some mercy here—trying to preserve even a sliver of humanity by not hurting her before I'm forced to.

Everything about Collins is unknown. And a selfish part of me wants it to remain that way.

The liminal space between now and when the sun eclipses thins dangerously with each ticking second.

"I threaten your sense of order, your control. It's the uncertainty you fear." Her voice softens into a gentle coax. "But we don't have to rush this, Orion. We can take it slow."

I swipe a gloved hand across my mouth, stifling a groan. "And what would I get out of this," I demand to know.

Her lips curl in a suggestive taunt, as if the answer should be obvious. "I can help you safely explore those darker, intrusive urges. The ones I know you're becoming exhausted from constantly fighting." She licks her lips, wetting them with a tempting tease. "Satisfy your impulses, find some relief without consequence."

My answering smile is callous. "And when you're not satisfied with the results, you sign your form to have me removed."

She tilts her head, a daring challenge surfacing amid the defiant glint of her eyes. "Then don't leave me unsatisfied."

Fuck. *Playing with fire.*

A blistering heat threads my spine, my jaw locking tight.

Beneath my insatiable hunger lies another, more insidious fear that, once I start touching her, I won't have the strength to stop. Unable to deny the desire to find that perfect symmetry with her body, to touch every inch of her, to discover that rightness over and over until I've driven myself maddeningly past the brink—breaking her by sheer, brutal need.

Hell, I could fuck us both into the grave, surrendering the will to care once I've thoroughly ruined her and whatever remains of my fractured humanity.

She has no idea how dangerous this is.

Reflexively, my grip tightens around the astrolabe in my pocket. "Furthering your research, testing your therapy. This is what you need." The question is achingly familiar, an echo of what I once asked her before, stranded together on a rock. And now, just as then, I cage my breath, waiting.

A well of relief floods her eyes. "Yes," she says simply.

The soft admission ricochets around the hollow of my chest. And I wonder if I can give her this—what she's asking of me. If I can offer her more than a mere distraction. Some form of comfort, pleasure. Make her happy, even. For however fleeting. At least, until the moment she expends her last breath.

If nothing else, I *want* to give her this.

"I don't know why you're fighting it," she says, as if reading my thoughts. "It's not unethical if we both consent."

I can't help the low chuckle that escapes, harsh and humorless. Nothing is more unethical than fucking the woman you will annihilate.

A violent pang resonates deep in my chest, and I drag a hand down my face, defeated. "You don't know what you're consenting to," I mutter beneath my breath.

A tremble rolls through her slight body before she clears her throat. "Communication is important—" She breaks off as I turn abruptly and walk away. "Orion, you can't leave."

"Stop me."

"You're scared you'll hurt me," she says, and it comes out a little breathless.

My steps falter. I hang my head, take a measured breath.

Knowing I'll regret looking at her, I'm torn as I'm forced to turn her way.

She tosses her head, clearing the strands from her eyes. Her teeth scrape over her bottom lip, a nervous tell. I let the silence stretch, forcing her to fill it. "I know you're scared you'll hurt me," she says again, "but I'm not. You won't."

Dammit, she's so achingly beautiful just standing there, daring me to imagine how much pressure to apply as I map her body. To discover the sounds she makes as I test which spots make her shiver and the ones that make her breath catch.

I let my eyes fall over her as I drag my thumb across my bottom lip, at war with my own mind.

I want her.

I can't remember ever wanting anything so badly. My cells ache to consume her the way gravity consumes starlight, extinguishing it all at once in one violent collapse.

And that's what terrifies me.

The shadows encroach, staining my gray matter with a dark residue, creeping in at the edges and corrupting every thought.

"Orion."

With just the use of my name, she pulls me out of my conflicted thoughts. A flash of something hot and aroused courses through her, and I'm drawn to that blazing current of my fire sign, even more curious why she's so desperate to convince me that she's not frightened when I can sense her fear. Beneath those buttons that fasten all the way to the top of her collar. Beneath the brave, fearless mask she wears is something so intoxicating it threatens to strip me of all reason.

Her fear is tangible.

Delectable.

Collins is quivering with it, the same way she was in her office. Even if the violent and deviant facets of my nature intrigue her, they very much terrify her.

With a quick move to conceal her nerves, she swipes the rest of her hair off her shoulder. "I heard a piano earlier, from down the hallway. Was that you?"

A knowing smirk twists my lips at her obvious tactic. Her question is tentative yet devious, prodding me. My sexy archer just doesn't miss.

"Tell me how you got the bruises," I counter with my own demand as I eye her neck. We share a similar hunger, and I want to hear her say it.

She wets her lips, rolls them. Each action slow, her avoidance deliberate, bringing my undivided attention to her mouth. Whatever unknown force she commands, it affects my matter, it affects me, charging the space between us with our own dark electromagnetism.

A hint of a smile touches her lips as she holds her ground. "Some answers are best discovered through arduous research. Wouldn't you agree, Dr. Night? That is, if you're up for the challenge."

Once again, she's tempting the demons to come out and play. And fuck, I'm weary of holding them back.

My muscles corded tight, I'm barely restrained as I say, "And if I do hurt you."

A defiant spark ignites her eyes. "I'll stop you."

Fuck.

The illicit image of Collins fighting me torches whatever shred of restraint I held fast to. I see the fire come to life in her, that fury—and I'm ravenous to taste it.

All this time, I had no idea how frozen I'd become. Empty, desolate. Suspended in a void of darkness. Until the heat of her fiery, consuming nature cracked the confining layer of ice.

I need the danger, the rush.

Now I need her.

Nothing has ever felt more dangerous.

To my own fucking detriment, I take a step forward, then another, gradually lessening the distance to her. The sliver of air separating our bodies animates, molecules begging to be brought together.

I hold her gaze, and something heady passes between us as her seductive melody stirs my atoms into a frenzy, the moment between us magnetic.

The willpower to fight this force goes up in flames.

It's fucking written in the stars. From the moment Collins entered my orbit, there was one thing I understood unequivocally:

She was mine.

She belonged to me.

I take her hand in mine and lead her into the depths of my observatory.

Spacetime is a maddening idea. Imagine the entirety of your life, every moment, event, experience—from your past and the future ahead of you—all composed on the stage of the universe. These are your memories. From your first kiss to your final goodbye, every single memory lost like sand to the tide. Now imagine all of these moments are still out there, the grains waiting, never lost, somewhere in the ocean of spacetime.

— DR. ORION NIGHT, SYMPOSIUM SPEECH
NOV. 30TH

12

EVENT HORIZON

And like a comet burn'd That fires the length of Ophiuchus huge In th' arctic sky, and from his horrid hair Shakes pestilence and war.

— JOHN MILTON, *PARADISE LOST*

ORION

The only light in the otherwise darkened telescope room comes from the backlit viewing table. It washes over the scattered instruments and screens, casting a soft white halo around Collins as she curiously wanders toward the table.

She's more inside the room than I am, infusing every atom with her scent—the sweet notes I can detect and the ones I can't. She stares down at the glass slides, her gaze slipping over images of constellations and nebulae projected on the table surface, illuminated like an angel.

"Are you really interested in a tour?" The deep sound of my voice breaks the quiet.

I want her to say no. The coating chamber, where lenses are

treated with reflective materials, is farther down the corridor in the space where the team that once occupied these stations is now sequestered with the RC telescope—and it's not sanitary.

Collins peeks up at me, a mischievous slant to her nude lips. "Not really. I just wanted to get you alone in here."

I swipe a hand over my mouth to cover my smile. "You used Prescott against me."

"Yes," she confesses, shameless. "How does that make you feel?"

Like I desperately want to discover what gets under her skin the way she slinks right under mine. "Impressed," I say instead. "And admittedly, a little wary of your therapeutic approach."

"We can implement a safeword," she suggests. "If you need one."

Something starved and untamed claws at me from the inside, tearing its way through to get to her. She needs to understand that if this goes too far, it won't be me who needs protection. And there's nothing that will stop me once that line is crossed, let alone any word.

"I'll take my chances," I tell her.

A sexy smile graces her lips, and I'm reminded that, just moments before, I held her throat in my hand. She followed me in here knowing the debased and violent nature of my thoughts. Despite the fear I see glinting in her beautiful eyes, she followed me in here alone, regardless.

An itch flares, my mind uselessly trying to scratch at the infesting, forbidden thoughts of having her all to myself.

Where no one else knows she is.

I unconsciously tap my fingers against my thigh, keeping count.

"So where's this diabolical particle accelerator?" she asks.

A smile tips my mouth. "In the lab."

She nods. "This is the control room," she says, and I nod,

because it's mostly correct. "This isn't where you work, though." Her perceptive gaze darts to the spiral staircase that leads to the observatory dome.

I stuff my hands into my pockets, letting my silence sink us further into this moment. Her fragrant scent overtakes the cool, sterile air. Her fingers touch objects, leaving remnants of herself behind. I'm giving myself time to adjust, but she presses against my restraint just by breathing.

"This is as far as most people get." I give her an honest answer.

Drawn to her, I take a few steps toward the table, but halt to stare down at a glass plate on the floor. When I glance at her, a blush tinges high on her cheeks.

"I dropped it," she says, confirming the clinking sound I heard earlier from the atrium.

I pick up the plate, my thumb gliding over the Orion constellation before I place it on the table where it belongs.

"Do you always wear gloves, even alone?"

Employing patience, I entertain her questions. If indulging her curiosity makes her happy, I can do that. "Most of the time."

"Due to fear of contamination," she says decisively.

I consider how to explain this to her. "That, and when I wear them, I'm not as burdened by the neurotic need to adjust what I touch until it feels right. It's a barrier, something to dull the senses, so I can focus on a task without succumbing to my need for balance."

Collins studies me closely. "That's a form of OCD-related magical thinking," she says, analyzing. "It's not rational, but you've tricked your mind enough to allow you to have this workaround."

I nod slowly in agreement. "I'm aware of that."

"Tell me about your recovery. How long after the accident was it before you started your research again?"

While Collins is doing her best to define and label me, I don't think about it in terms that can be explained by a medical journal, with identifying numbers and buzz terminology.

Before the accident, I was one way. I'd spend hours in the Lick Observatory, writing code for telescope systems, running simulations, analyzing galaxy data. I was a machine, hardwired and driven.

After the motorcycle wreck, I became something else entirely.

My tainted gray matter whispers, *monster*.

"There was a before and after," I tell her simply. "I spent two months in the hospital. While there, fibers began to irritate me. I could literally feel every particle of my clothes against my skin. The germs in the air—I could see them. Taste them. Sense them crawling into my lungs."

"Before and after," she repeats softly, a trace of something meaningful in her expression. "What else."

I run my tongue over my teeth, thoroughly amused by her. "After eleven months in recovery, I was cleared to return to work."

After so many years, the memory is somewhat fuzzy to pull forth. But as I hold her gaze, finding those golden stars hidden there, it becomes easier to recall the moment I walked into the observatory. The welcome I received.

And I do remember how empty the space felt, Emma's absence creating a giant void, a black hole itself. Her research lost with her. When I touched any surface, I could feel the contaminating elements. I could see the microbes, flaring black and pulsing at the corner of my vision. I could hear my pupils dilate, my heart race.

Paralyzing.

The worst part was the way it made my mind feel, discombobulated. Detached.

"My first day back, I spent two hours in the clean room and

four locked in my office," I admit with a chagrined smile as humiliation attacks my ego.

A crease of concern deepens between her brows, and I rub the back of my neck. "It wasn't long after that I was put on 'academic leave' and was 'redirected to focus on personal research'. Academic bullshit that was intended to maintain my sense of dignity, but ultimately meant I wouldn't be returning to my role."

She folds her arms across her chest. "But you did. You started focusing on your own research."

My jaw hardens. "And I refuse to let anyone take it from me."

A thick silence builds, heavy beneath the hum of instruments and the ventilation system that insulates us in the dim room. Collins shifts her attention, her gaze landing on the cylinder. She steps closer, extending a hand toward the glass.

"Careful," I warn.

She withdraws abruptly. "Is it dangerous?"

"No, not dangerous." By now, she should realize exactly where the danger lies. "But it's expensive. Leo might have a coronary if anything happens to it."

She raises a delicate eyebrow, prompting me on.

I expel a slow breath, giving in to her further. "It's a sonic black hole," I explain. "Because escape velocity exceeds the speed of light, nothing can escape a black hole. Here, the circulating water in the cylinder simulates that point of no return, creating an acoustic horizon, where the swirling fluid exceeds the speed of sound. Sound waves are trapped in the vortex, unable to move against the current past this point." I find and hold her eyes. "The way matter and light cross the horizon of a stellar-mass black hole. Beyond that boundary, escape becomes impossible."

I let my gloved fingers rest against the glass. "I record the frequency downshift, the way the trapped sound waves stretch as they approach the horizon. It lets me sonify time dilation. A glimpse at what spacetime does to information at the boundary."

The faint tremor of spiraling water vibrates beneath my hand. Echoes held at the threshold of loss.

A thoughtful expression softens her features. "So the sound stays caught in motion," she says, far too insightful as she watches the swirling vortex. "Like a melody pulled into a riptide, eternally echoing deep under the surface where no one can hear."

I nod once with a hard swallow, throat tight.

"And this relates to your research—how?" she asks.

"I try to hear that lost melody."

The broken cadence of hers fills the tense space between our heartbeats.

I ease a fraction closer, voice lowering to an intimate pitch. "Black holes consume everything," I tell her, "but general relativity and quantum theory can't both be right if information just vanishes. I believe the imprint remains, encoded in the spacetime curvature, preserved beyond the horizon. An echo of existence, suspended somewhere liminal between oblivion and eternity."

Her lips part, her breath catching in awe—or dread. "And you're trying to retrieve these echoes."

I nod slowly, letting a whisper of the truth hang between us.

She blinks, shakes her head. "I think that's too much for me to comprehend, Orion."

My pulse drums as I close the distance another step. "It is for most," I admit. "But imagine if our memories were never lost. If they survive beyond us."

Something flashes behind her eyes, a painful echo of her own. There before it's gone. "Sometimes it's healthier to let them go. The mind isn't meant to retain everything. We forget for a reason, we're supposed to. So we can move on."

I study her in silence. The way she rigidly holds her shoulders. The way her voice cracks on *forget*.

"*Hmm,* maybe," I concede, tone measured. I want to tell her that we're tethered to those painful memories, forgotten or otherwise. "But for now, it's only observation," I say instead.

She tilts her head, a strand of hair feathering her cheek. "Are you observing something in particular right now?"

The weight of my stare should frighten her. "I am."

"Show me."

The way she says it—so fearless, unflinching—stirs my blood hot with a vicious temptation. The glow of the viewing table bathes her, casting faint light over the constellation inked along her wrist, the archer's arrow trained on me.

Like an event horizon surrounding the singularity of a black hole, once Collins and I cross this threshold together, we enter a point of no return.

My gaze narrows on her, predatory. "What if I can't let you go after you know my secrets," I say as I maneuver around the table.

She watches me, mirroring my steps, moving forward until we're on a slow collision course. "Don't worry. I'm good at keeping secrets."

My pulse slams through my veins. An electric charge arcs between us. My little fire sign is fucking determined to incinerate me right on the spot with the seductive way she licks her lips, the sinful gleam igniting her beautiful eyes.

Fire is such a destructive force.

Accepting my torturous fate, I say, "Never claim I didn't warn you." Then I lead her toward the spiral stairs and anchor my hand to the rail, letting her ascend first.

Once she reaches the dome, she stalls on the landing, her gaze sweeping across the instruments. "Orion. This isn't what I was expecting."

A reluctant smile tugs at my mouth. I clasp the back of my neck, my chest tight at the awe in her voice. "You were expecting a madman's laboratory," I say, moving toward the central console.

She doesn't remark, her attention drifting over the brass

orrery, watching the orbit of each planet and moon. Then she glances at the armillary spheres near the blackboard covered in tensor equations. Archaic relics contrasted against modern equipment.

"You really are determined to preserve the past," she says absently.

Having her in my space should trigger every single compulsion, yet it's curiously arousing. I flex my fingers, tempted to remove my gloves, let her sink into my skin. A warning spike of adrenaline crashes through my veins. The gloves are also necessary to prevent observer interference. I hike the cuff of my glove higher instead.

Leaning over the controls, I input the coordinates, and the telescope emits a hum. From the edge of my vision, I see Collins flinch at the sudden sound. She spins toward the telescope as it repositions and locks into place.

"This is where you conduct your research?" she questions.

"Most of it." I collect the aluminum ladder and wheel it around, bracing my foot on the bottom step before I extend my hand to her.

Her gaze drops to my gloved palm. "Have you always been left-handed?"

A deep chuckle escapes. "Have you always been this inquisitive? Hurry up before it's gone."

Sliding her palms down the length of her black skirt, she casts a look up at the Hand of God and takes a wary step closer. Collins places her hand in mine, allowing me to bring her onto the ladder.

"Wait—" She uses her free hand to slip off her heels, tossing her shoes to the concrete floor. "All right, Dr. Night. Where do you want me?"

Jesus, the filthy thoughts she provokes with those simple words. I want to cage her on this ladder and prowl over her body like the starved beast she makes me. Let her use me as her willing test puppet and torture me with whatever sadistic, experimental therapy she wants.

I swallow and nod toward the eyepiece. "All the way up."

A flicker of a smile teases her lips before she turns and braces her hands on the guardrails. I wait until she's in position before I climb the steps, coming up behind her. I bracket my forearms on either side of her hips, my hands safely secured to the bars.

"Just place your eye right up against the lens," I instruct, nodding to the custom eyepiece attached to the optical tube.

Collins leans over the rail and looks directly into the lens. "I'm not sure what I'm supposed to see." She adjusts her position to lean farther out, and the sinful sight of her bent over the bar wreaks havoc on my composure.

"Oh, my god," she breathes. "This is... I don't have words. What is it?"

Easing closer to her side, I study her profile, taking in her awed expression. Wanting to keep it there as long as possible. "The constellation Ophiuchus," I say, voice lowered to a gruff whisper. "Its position near the core of the Milky Way makes it ideal for observing the Rho Ophiuchi cloud complex, one of the most captivating interplays between bright and dark nebulae."

"I don't know what any of that is," she says, intently focused.

A slight smile curves my lips. "It's a stellar nursery where new stars are born from the gas and dust of dying ones, creating the glowing cloud you see. What you're observing is the fusion of destruction and creation happening all at once."

The rise and fall of her chest quickens, and I hear the small hitch in her breath. Her gaze flicks my way briefly. "Are you dumbing it down for me, Dr. Night?"

I lick my lips, fighting back a full smile. "As for my research..." My voice trails as I lean in to adjust the scope, guiding her to the shadowed edges of the nebula. "Those faint rings around stars are diffraction patterns. Interference caused by the telescope's aperture bending starlight. Some of my work involves gravitational lensing, where massive celestial objects curve spacetime, bending the path of distant light. This visual is the closest example I can offer you right now."

I pause, the ache beneath my sternum deepening as I watch her stare into the heart of her constellation. "It's how we glimpse the memory of light," I say, my thoughts consumed, "what's hidden in the darkness behind stars."

Slowly, Collins pulls away from the eyepiece and lifts her gaze to mine, and I read too much in the starry depths of her eyes. "Ophiuchus," she whispers reverently. "It's beautiful. Are you going to look?"

I let my ravenous gaze fall down her body, shamelessly lingering as I take my time roaming back up to trace her divine features. An angel in my scope. "I'm already observing something beautiful."

Her hand comes to rest at the center of her chest. "I thought if you wanted to seduce me, you wouldn't need to use words."

"Are you seduced?"

A blush sweeps high on her cheeks. "That depends on intent."

I draw in closer, towering over her now. "Collins, I've stared into the vastness of space. I've witnessed phenomena I can only attempt to explain. Yet I've never encountered anything as beautiful, or as terrifying, as you." My chest blazes with the confession. "That's simply the unfiltered truth."

A hint of vulnerability opens her expression. "I have a confession," she says, her voice breathy. "It wasn't just about my therapy work…why I came to find you tonight."

My grip tightens around the rail, a swallow working the tendons of my throat. "I know."

The atmosphere of the dome charges, the scent of ocean drifting through the open shutter where the night burns with stars above us, offering a mere glimpse of infinity.

The current between us pulls too dangerously strong—a tidal force I can no longer resist. Soon, there will be no escaping the irresistible pull of her gravity.

Silence strains the moment until I'm forced to break it. "I'm leaving soon," I say, dispersing a layer of tension. "I have to travel to a dark-sky preserve to gather data before the solar eclipse."

Confusion knits her brows at my abrupt shift. It's just a glance, but her gaze darts to the mechanical solar system, where the rotations mark the countdown to the celestial event.

"You're leaving Stonehurst," she says slowly, weighing the words.

I scrub a hand through my hair. "Just for a day or so—a few days before the eclipse," I confirm, dropping down a step to widen the space between us. "The moment of totality offers a rare chance to observe the corona, to measure the heat and motion as the friction ignites until it flares brighter, hotter."

Almost as if in response, those elusive golden rings I glimpse amid her eyes blaze, striking something deep in my chest.

She swipes a hand across her forehead. "Too much information, Dr. Night."

I let a smile form. "Simply put, Dr. Holbrook, I'm heavily focused on black-hole accretion signatures—observing changes in luminosity through anomalies." My gaze holds hers, a hard knot lodging at the base of my throat.

Something entirely too dangerous sparks behind that burning gaze, and I crave to know how painful it would be to touch it.

She bites the flesh of her lip before she says, "We should probably get down from here."

Collins turns to start down the ladder, and I repress every intrusive thought as I move down another rung. "Shit," she mutters as she misses a step, losing her grasp on the railing.

I reach up in time to catch her, my hands closing around her thighs. The moment suspends, stretched taut between each shallow breath. I can't tear myself away—my gaze fixed to where my gloved fingers bunch the hem of her skirt, risen just high enough to reveal the lace edge of her thigh-highs. The sliver of exposed skin right above.

Daringly, I raise my eyes to meet hers.

The air condenses between us. I feel a tremble coast through her, but she doesn't move. Doesn't remove my grip, doesn't lower her skirt. "You said you shouldn't touch me," she breathes.

"I shouldn't." My voice is rough, scraping raw against the tension. Like a summons, my gaze falls to the faint pattern of bruises lining her throat, lured to the basest pit of my soul.

"But you want to," she says, the softest whisper to lure me closer.

Jaw clenched, I ease upward, my palm dragging the hem of her skirt along with me. She tips her head back, eyes locked to my predatory gaze, never breaking contact as I shift over her. Her thighs part instinctively to allow me room, and I'm one fucking second away from losing the last tether of my willpower.

"I want to," I hear myself confess. In compulsive, rhythmic count, I press my gloved fingers into her hip.

She licks her lips, and I'm helplessly drawn in by that lurid act, ensnared by the torrid mix of carnal need and apprehension swirling behind those vibrant eyes. Right beneath the apparent arousal, fear brims in shimmering waves.

Something nefarious coils the base of my spine at the sight. Right now, tasting her sweet scent, her skin humming at a frequency that demands a connection, I'm barely restrained.

Deliberate, controlled, I withdraw my left hand from her and grip my necktie. I pull the knot loose, slipping the silky material free from the collar. She tracks the movement, pupils dilating as the sharp sound cleaves the charged silence.

I drag the fabric along her throat, over the rapid flutter of her pulse, slowly guiding the tie around to cradle the nape of her neck. Then I wind the slack around my gloved hand, drawing her toward me. She shivers at the creak of leather.

"Tell me the truth," I say, my uttered words falling across her parted lips. "How scared are you."

This close, her swallow is audible. "Enough," she whispers.

A low sound vibrates in my throat. "Good."

Before I release her, she circles a hand around the tie. "But I'm more scared of pushing you too far."

A smirk carves my face. "I have six years' worth of pent-up sexual frustration, and you're worried you'll break me."

I've spent a lifetime trying to reach the bounds of the universe. I've pursued it maddeningly, passionately, never tiring.

There is no limit.

With Collins, the only terrifying certainty I need to contend with is that I won't stop even after I've found hers.

A sultry smile curves her mouth. "I think you'll find I'm not that breakable, Dr. Night."

"Fuck," I mutter darkly. A savage pang of hunger twists low in my gut at her reckless dare. The black waters surge, violently battering the crumbling walls of my restraint.

A delicate balance has to be maintained. To give her this—this fleeting pleasure, this stolen moment—without surrendering to the depraved hunger that craves to annihilate her.

My gaze drops to the enticing bruises, the marks of her own hidden deviance, and a vile part of me wants to devour all of her just so the agonizing torture of maintaining this impossible balance mercifully ends.

As I find her starry eyes once more, I'm falling at the speed of light. Time slows, reality fractures, the entire universe bending around us.

Captivated as I toe the edge of the horizon.

Collins relinquishes her grip on the tie, the small act one of surrender. The light I glimpse within her begins to dim, and I'm suddenly desperate to chase it, to catch sight of it once more before it's swallowed whole.

The life of a star is a constant fight against gravity.

But eventually, gravity wins. Its force can't be escaped. And once the star collapses, it consumes everything around it.

That's its nature.

Fear can be a catastrophic deterrent of our desires. Behind that fear I see warring within her is something fierce—*want*. Heady, unadulterated *need*. She craves something desperately. Maybe even bad enough to rival my own maddening pursuit.

She tips her head back farther, baring the enticing column of her throat, and my pulse riots. "No safewords," she whispers, eyes locked with mine. "I trust you."

Goddamn. That trust sings in her eyes, golden striations blazing like coronal flares despite the trembling waves of fear cresting over her—and that might be what finally wrecks me.

Whatever twisted entanglement responsible for our collision, it no longer matters. Whether it was my doing or hers that brought us to this point of no return.

There's no escape—for either of us.

And yet, maybe it's possible that here, with her melody infusing my head, in the one place where I maintain some sliver of control, I can test the boundary.

The thought burns to ash as she arches her hips. All it takes is the slightest brush of her body against my erection, and my restraint snaps.

"Fuck it." I lower myself over her and lock my forearm around the small of her back, hauling her off the ladder. She instinctively locks her legs around my hips, annihilating the last of my control. "Let's test the fuck out of your therapeutic approach, Dr. Holbrook."

There is geometry in the humming of the strings, there is music in the spacing of the spheres. Each celestial body, in fact each and every atom, produces a particular sound on account of its movement, its rhythm or vibration. All these sounds and vibrations form a universal harmony. The stars in the heavens sing a music, if only we had ears to hear.

— PYTHAGORAS

13

MUSIC OF THE SPHERES

Third contact (C3): The instant when the sun's bright disk reappears from behind the moon, marking the end of totality and the sudden return of daylight.

ORION

A line array system is tucked into a secluded section of the observatory. Kept out of sight, out of mind. When I transitioned to Stonehurst, I stacked the PA speakers and subwoofers upright along a wall, leaving them to collect dust.

This is where I carry Collins, to this hidden sector of myself, planting her back against the mesh grille of the speakers. A coarse groan escapes my clenched teeth on impact. The abrasive feel of her pressed hard against me damn near flays my sternum.

Her broken breath coasts across my mouth as she stares into me, a trickle of fear leaking into her glassy eyes. "What are we doing."

"This." My composure all but stripped, I greedily grind between the seam of her thighs, working another groan free as I savor the breathy moan she offers in return. Releasing her thigh, I bring my hand to her face and cup her jaw. My gloved thumb drags down the center of her lips to part them open. "Fuck, Collins."

She about killed me when she spread her legs on the desk. Now I'm one breath away from begging her to finish me off. An infuriating hunger burns through me, torching any remaining fight as I crave to know the taste of her on my tongue. Past the lust-fueled haze, the questioning doubt banked behind her eyes spears me through.

I release a harsh curse. "You have no goddamn idea how you torture me when you look at me like that."

She presses her cheek more firmly into my palm, as if she can tear through the barrier between us. "I want to feel you."

My eyes seal shut, neck corded and jaw locked against the need to unleash every ounce of agony racking my muscles. When I dare to look at her again, my gaze falls heavy on the black tie still draped around her neck. I drop my hand and touch the silk blade, my mind tunneling to base thoughts.

I push in close to her ear, voice strained. "And I want you fucking desperate, your thighs shaking, as you break for me, Collins."

Her faint whimper sends a hot pulse to my groin. "You can have my body however you want, Orion," she says, "but only if you remove your gloves."

Releasing a searing breath, I stroke the contour of her cheek tenderly, pulling back a measure to let her bare feet lower to the concrete floor. With a growl, I seize her waist and spin her, pinning her chest to the speaker. I trap her wrists, bringing her hands up on either side of her head, where I brace them.

"Answer me one thing," I say, collecting her hair in a loose grasp. As I guide the layers over her shoulder, my finger hooks the neck of the tie. I bring it around, letting the silk blades drape down the center of her back. "Is this request based on my exposure therapy, or because my gloves frighten you?"

Her pause hangs heavy in the air. "What would be your response if I said the latter?"

An amused smile curls my mouth. "That I want to make you come so fucking hard, you forget even your own name, angel."

Her thighs squeeze together, and my groin throbs in response. "Quite the ego," she says on a shaky breath.

"You have no idea what I can accomplish when I set my mind to it." I press up against her backside and settle my mouth near the curve of her ear. "Don't move," I tell her, the gravel in my tone eliciting a shiver.

I stalk to the control panel and hit the switch to close the shutter. A metallic groan fills the chamber as we're sealed in darkness. I power on the sound system, and Collins gasps as a soft drone resonates from the low-frequency subs.

I adjust the range, tuning the output. Satisfied, I remove my glove and hit Play on the touchscreen. The speakers emit a deep, low hum, slowly rising and filling the darkened chamber with an unearthly, ambient ring. The sound starts with an eerie prelude, gradually building into a rhythmic pulse until the sound rattles my chest and vibrates the floor.

"Orion—"

"If you move, Collins, I'll be forced to restrain you." The deviant in me salivates over the thought of chasing her down as she flees the observatory.

When she says nothing more, I remove my watch and pull off my other glove. I only hesitate a moment before shedding my dress shirt. The cool air strokes my skin and I fucking swear, I can't see her tremble, but I can feel it. The arousing sensation rolls along my flesh like the ripple of sound waves.

There's something my little anomaly keeps hidden, afraid to let me glimpse this part of her. To strip a layer of her defenses, I'm willing to strip one of my own. I drape my shirt over the monitor, snuffing out the last of the light.

The rhythmic sound increases in intensity, guiding me toward the speakers. I stop within an inch of her body, my chest vibrating with each labored breath.

"You can't touch me," I say, my chin near the top of her head. "That's the only rule. No matter what happens." I sense her movement. "Words, Collins," I demand.

"I won't touch you," she rushes out.

Jaw flexed, I push in closer, where the fibers of her clothes whisper across my bare chest. Cautiously, I reach around her waist and tug her blouse free of her skirt.

"I have a rule," she states, trying to conceal the quake in her voice. My fingers halt. "The lights stay off."

I lick my lips, relishing this curious peek beneath her walls. She'd rather drown in her fear, afraid of the smothering dark, than let me see her.

Gathering the hem of her shirt in a tight grip, I wrench the delicate fabric apart, popping the buttons open. Her sharp intake of air tenses my abdominal muscles.

"You don't touch me, I won't look at you."

Her relief is palpable, allowing me to part the blouse farther and expose her to cool air. As I've visually mapped her body, felt her against my chest, I know she's not wearing a bra. Without instruction, she presses into the speaker to shield herself.

The faintest moan sounds above the ambient music, evocative and thrilling, as stimulation courses along her nerves.

"In the corridor, when you asked if it was me you heard playing piano..." My voice drifts over the building pulse of sound. "I used to compose my own music," I say, resigned to give her this much.

Her back expands with a deep inhale. "Used to?" she questions, still trying to analyze me.

I make a thoughtful sound as I let my bare fingers trace the curve of her back, the thin material of her shirt the only barrier between her skin and mine. Her heated flesh infuses the fibers, and I can almost summon the texture of her soft skin, what she'd feel like beneath my touch.

Muscles drawn tight, I envision the light bruises marking her neck, see her hand clutched to her throat, caught in the throes of autoerotic asphyxiation as she deprives her lungs of air. My cock jumps at the explicit image that I have of her, how her pretty features contort as she brings herself to the brink. Her forbidden desires too intimate, too shocking, to explore any other way but alone.

Something depraved wants to tease those secrets out of hiding. To discover what filthy things she imagines when she's lost in that space.

"You're listening to my music now," I whisper over her ear as I clutch the blades of the necktie in each hand.

From Pythagoras' *Music of the Spheres* to Kepler's *Harmonices Mundi*; Holst's *The Planets* to NASA's cosmic data —music and astronomy have always been intertwined. Bound together on a cosmic scale.

"It's called sonification," I explain in a low voice. "Celestial data translated into music. The orbital resonances of planets and stellar oscillations scaled to an audible range, then mapped into piano notes."

There's more to it than this; matching ratios of orbits to musical intervals, aligning astronomical frequencies into pitch and rhythm. Fine-tuning the harmonics. Each celestial body holds a unique resonance, its own sound. And when these bodies are given a symphony, it's an immersive experience.

One I intend to use to shatter her.

"It's a little terrifying," she admits, and for a moment, I'm unsure if she's referring to the music or the tension gathering in the tie around her neck.

I relax my grip. "*Hmm.* Beautiful and terrifying all at once." If I'm never able to capture her melody, regretfully, this may be the closest I come. "It's the sound of two black holes colliding, merging. As they spiral closer, their gravitational waves build, frequency climbing like notes rising in pitch. And even though their waves pass through each other without touching, barely leaving an imprint," a noticeable ache flares in the core of my chest, "we can still detect their subtle vibrations."

She silently absorbs the melancholic song before she says, "That sounds almost romantic."

A deep pang resonates within me, knowing the romance is just as deceptive as touch. Vibrations interact with the electromagnetic fields at the atomic level only. And yet, despite how completely irrational it is, I'm furious over the fucking sound waves for being able to touch her where I can't.

"Spacetime is like a fabric," I tell her as my fingers deliberately trail the fabric of her shirt along her spine. "Ripples are sent through it, allowing us to experience this breathtaking moment of collision."

Collins trembles beneath my shifting touch. My hands explore the alluring flare of her hips, my fingers inching up her skirt until I have the hem bunched above her thighs. The lacy feel of her stockings sends an arousing pulse to my cock.

"Spread your legs," I demand in a low rasp. A slight shiver travels through her, and I hungrily absorb the recoil as she tentatively parts her thighs.

I uncurl my fingers from her skirt and roam my hand down, grazing over her thigh, intoxicated by the seductive catch of her breath as I coast lower to cup the innermost curve of her knee.

A reactive flame ignites my chest at the faintest taste of her skin. I'm so close to touching her, sensing the warmth of her flesh through the material, the danger of it burns through my veins.

I drag her knee up, spreading her thighs along the speakers. Then I anchor my knee under her leg to trap her in place.

Collins audibly gasps as the sound amplifies, encouraging my hips to press her right up against the metal mesh, where she feels the vibration most intimately.

The science of it can be an erotic sensory experience. Electrical signals cause the cone inside the speakers to vibrate, creating compressions in the air. As the vibrations intensify, the cone moves in and out rapidly, beating harder, faster, simulating sound patterns.

"Tell me you feel that," I insist, my tone coarse.

Her breathing deepens, the enticing rub of her back against my bare chest a torturous friction. "Yes," she breathes. "The vibration from the speaker…" She trails off with a hard shiver and tenses. "Oh, god."

I leash the terrible impulse to give the necktie a hard yank. "You're so fucking bad for me, starling." The confession slips past my strained defenses. "But Christ—I want you."

She rocks her hips in need of further friction, and I'm tethered to her lewd movements, viscerally ensnared by every sexy roll.

"Motherfuck," I groan as I grind obscenely against her with my own needy response.

Ethereal sounds suspend us in the dark, intensifying this heightened moment. And I'm lost to her—the way her nails scrape across the metal grille as she curls her fingers, currents licking over her body. The desperate, erotic thrusts of her hips that is a goddamn infliction, almost unbearable. How each breathy moan builds, more raw than the next as her body crashes against mine in a tantalizing wave.

She releases a throaty sound that racks my muscles, and the

dark waters of my mind rise, forcing me to dig my fingers into her bunched skirt to keep from ruthlessly impaling her.

"The sensory deprivation—" her voice breaks with a rattle of fear "—everything feels more intense."

Jaw clenched hard, I grit back the need to show her just how intense I can make it.

When one of our senses is deprived, the others go into overdrive. It triggers our primal instincts, urging us to either fight or run from the hidden danger in the dark.

And I'm desperate to unwrap my anomaly, to tear her open and discover what hidden danger haunts her dark corners.

There's a monster in her past, and I want to wrestle with it.

"The adrenaline rush amplifies our other senses," I say in a gruff whisper over her ear. A heated curse falls from my mouth when her only response is to rub herself over the speaker. "Fuck, you really want to destroy me."

So damn tempted to hook my finger beneath her panties and tear them away, I have to brace my hand on the speaker cabinet above her. Fingers tapping in time with the rhythm, I'm barely restraining the vicious craving to shove her to her knees. Flip this tower over and force her to ride the speaker in the most salacious, filthy way.

My cock throbs at the prospect, and I'm only deterred by the fact that I wouldn't be able to watch her through the dark.

My rampaging heart chases the escalating rise of hers, where —for a prolonged note—we beat in unison, an unbroken, resonant legato. Drawn into the pulse of her heart against my chest, its rhythm infuses the currents washing through me.

Like a beautiful symphony, we move in tandem, two celestial bodies tidal locking and creating a sound so transcendent it's unsettling. Mingled with her soft cries, it's more divine than a heaven chord ringing into eternity.

When she breaks, it will be a goddamn religious experience.

Every subtle movement between our bodies is slow and measured. Her inhalations timed to mine, her rib cage stitched to my bones, where every shudder pulls at my sinew. Frustrating and painful and gratifying.

The pulses in the music build, the bass hitting strong, drawing a cry as she tenses against the speakers. Tremors thrum through her body to mine, and my heart chases the frantic beat of hers.

She's close—but I don't want her close.

I want her ruined.

"Touch me," she says, her plea a dare to unravel me. "Orion, please."

"Jesus—ah, fuck." Hearing my name pleaded in her desperate, breathy voice torches my control. The dark tide batters my skull, and I'm quickly losing the battle to rein in these intrusive cravings. "I want to pin your body to this wall, Collins. Trap you right here, where I can do the most unspeakable things to you."

And some sick part of me whispers from the depths, taunting that I make all my victims immobile.

Her soft moan curls around the base of my spine. "Touch me, and I'll let you."

A violent anger tears through me, loathing this inadequacy within me that I can't give her what she needs.

In shameless demonstration, I thrust the rock-hard evidence of my frustration against her ass, and her breathy, "Oh, fuck," drops right to my cock.

If she begs me to fuck her, I'll have little choice but to mercilessly ravish her up against this speaker. And there's a difference between *fucking* and the depraved, vile acts I want to commit against her body.

Her beautiful light draws the darkest side of my nature—the sinister force craving nothing more than to snuff it out.

"Goddammit." I squeeze my eyes shut against the violent

images. Yet there is no escape from the vicious, wild chaos that thrashes in the void.

Her broken cries stoke a fire already raging dangerously out of control. The temptation to touch her, to taste her—*god-fucking-dammit.*

The aching demand in my cock begs to lower my zipper and take her while she whispers the last of her warm breath across my mouth. To witness the desperate look on her face as she comes apart under me, her tender melody unraveled beneath my rough fingers. To see the pain etched in her contorted features as her skin pales, circulation all but cut off.

Restraint lost, I seize the blades of the tie, my body crushed against hers. "Tell me to stop."

Her throaty moan is an arousing stroke down my sternum as she shakes her head defiantly.

"Words, Collins."

"No. Don't stop," she forces out on a strangled breath.

The fire erupts, and before I can leash the destructive impulse, I have the blades wound tight around my fists, eating the slack until I hear the sharp catch of her breath.

"Sweet fuck—" I grind into her, rewarded with the seductive sound of her choked moan as she arches her spine. The music swells into a pulsating rhythm, matching the fury between our bodies fighting to get closer, to burn with friction.

This savage need scrapes at my skull to be unleashed. Every wicked and sick need frays another thread of my control. The urge to mark her—to sink my teeth into her flesh, to draw blood just to watch the red bead and trail across her skin—is a demon roaring into the hollow abyss of me.

And for a single heartbeat, I let the lie coil through me—that this is the only way I'll build any immunity to her. That I'll find the strength to resist the sinister force when the void calls.

As her whimper cracks the air, I fight the feverish desire to collar her throat with my bare hand, desperate to feel the frantic flutter of her pulse beneath my fingertips the instant she breaks.

"*Ah...Christ*," I rasp harshly, choking up on the tie. "When you destroy me, I want you to revel in the ruin, angel."

Abandoning all resistance, I let the darkness have me as I pull the tie taut.

The Law of Totality (Holism): The fundamental principle that the combined whole is inherently more than the mere sum of its individual parts. It is the foundation and core of Gestalt psychology, explaining our innate drive to find meaning and structure amid chaos, to treat the whole person, not simply isolate the symptom.

14

GRAVITATIONAL WAVES

Our little terraqueous globe is the madhouse of those hundred thousand millions of worlds.

— VOLTAIRE

COLLINS

The ligature cinches tighter, cutting off my airway. Panic tears through my tenuous grasp on reality, sinking me further into a subspace I can never fully escape.

The ambient sounds surge around us, terrifying, and yet strangely beautiful. A low, heavy bass pounds through my bones. High notes spike my nerves. Each rhythmic beat swells and fades, the reverb off the stone shaping my own personal chamber of fear, driving a painful pulse through my heart.

The dark observatory bleeds away. The briny scent of ocean is replaced by the earthy smell of dirt, the grainy texture of it gritting between my teeth. Dread courses through my bloodstream like tar, thick and toxic.

Keeping my palms fused to the vibrating wall of speakers, I struggle to drag in a breath. The dark too smothering, the scent of the vinyl canvas too potent.

It's not real.

One. Two—

I clench my eyes shut against the climbing anxiety, unable to count myself out of this hell.

A cruel portal to the past opens around me, and I'm submerged further, feeling the horrifying sensation of clothes ripped away, the hard floor pressed into my shoulder blades as heavy weight bears down. Splinters collect beneath my nails as I scrape and claw, teeth gnashing until copper spills across my tongue.

Sharp pain spears my breastbone.

My body freezes, palpitations thrashing my sternum to match the thundering chorus until I'm fading beneath the loss of oxygen. Then mercifully, the tie slips loose.

On reflex, I drag in a deep, staggering breath.

Orion's heavy exhale fans across the top of my head. "Tell me to stop," he demands for the second time. His voice sounds worn, an almost desperate quality to the rough tone, as though he's fighting to hold himself back.

And losing.

Lightheaded, I rest my forehead to the cool mesh, the vibration of sound oddly soothing against my skull. His music is one of his secrets; a part of him he doesn't share.

Yet he shared it with me.

Determined, I lift my head, taking measured breaths to regulate my erratic heart rate. A pinch of pain tightens beneath my ribs. But the movement, coupled with the intense rattle, stimulates my nipples, and despite my body's protest, a hot current licks my skin.

"Collins—" He makes a demand with my name, raw fury

bleeding into his tone. The abrasive caress of it drags between my spread thighs like an intimate touch, eliciting a torrent of flames.

And something wicked ignites from my depths.

I draw in a steadying breath, filling my lungs with the stubborn, resentful rage that fuels my next words. "Orion. I'm not scared of a little breath play and creepy music." To deliver my point, I arch my back and grind lewdly into the speaker, a moan torn from my inflamed throat as the current of sound waves strokes my clit.

He curses on a fierce groan, his body locking tense around mine. Through the dark encasing us, I imagine the flex of his cut muscles. His body corded tight with frustrated need. "All that fire in you, goddamn. You want to fight me, little archer?"

Just the suggestion stirs something heady in my blood. An ember flares hot from deep inside, a kindled flame to lash out—to fight back this time.

The threat of being overpowered. Trapped. Caught between fight or flight.

My breath shallows at the danger, and I swallow hard, the silk tie shifting against my throat.

Our bodies have the ability to retain the memory of a traumatic experience, where the slightest whisper of danger triggers our fight-or-flight response. And my body—

I freeze.

If I don't move—don't even breathe—it will be over soon.

"*Mmm.* There it is," Orion rasps, as attuned to my body as the music. "That delectable taste of fear and fury. God-damn, you do crave a little struggle. The way I could ruin you—" He tugs the necktie, pressure edging threat against my skin. "Fuck. Don't fight, Collins. I'm not sure what I'm capable of."

Raw honesty frays his voice, his restraint wearing dangerously thin as he battles his compulsion toward harm.

Every organized killer has a trigger. Some incitement that will spiral them over the brink. Uncovering Orion's is a delicate dance; exploiting his suppressed sexual violence without shattering his weakening impulse control.

The art of manipulation isn't about force—it's the subtle pull of the thread until it snaps.

I seal my eyes shut, knowing with terrifying certainty that, once the monster is unleashed, there's no locking him back up.

"Even if I beg you to stop," I whisper, licking my dry lips, "don't hold back."

"Christ, Collins," he says, his voice a harsh caress, "you have no idea what you're asking of me." The evidence of his arousal presses hard against my backside. "The things I want to do to you for making me want you this badly—unholy, punishing things."

His unfiltered words fall across my shoulder like a brand, an accusation. "Like when I tell you how wet I am," I say, my defiance prodding those dark urges. "Unless you want to feel for yourself—"

He makes a tortured sound from the base of his throat, raw and guttural. The vibration drags along my back, sending an electric shiver up my spinal column. His entire body coils tighter around mine, hips pressing with an involuntary thrust against my lower back. "Don't tempt me, angel," he growls into my shoulder.

My skin flushes, wet heat pooling low as an illicit thrill trickles through my veins. A smile steals across my lips in the dark. Gaining leverage over Orion is more seductively arousing than the stimulation strumming over my nerves.

Triggering this deviant violence within him is reckless. But he's built a fortress around himself in this observatory. Here, his walls are just as high as the towering spires of Stonehurst.

He's secluded, controlled. Structured.

Yet I've seen what lurks beneath those cold blocks of stone. Out there where he hunts, when the urge can no longer be contained. I know the wild carnage he's capable of—and I'm tired of carving at his stone.

I want his walls to come crashing down.

A deep sound rumbles through his chest before tension grips the tie, and I brace myself. I latch onto the fading ember of rage buried beneath my fear, fanning it into a blaze with my next stolen breath.

I've been stealing every single one since that fatal moment.

A fierce growl is the only warning I'm given before the tie jerks taut.

My head snaps back, and I strain to hold my place against the vibrating speakers as he sadistically strangles my throat. He chokes up on the tie with both hands, sealing off the last drop of air from my lungs as the intensity of sound grows in strength.

I curl my hand into a fist against the thumping speaker. Feel the shell crack in my palm. The dirt creeping in. The canvas clogging my airway.

With the next wave of sound, my eyes slam shut against the burst of pleasure, stars sparking behind my lids. The unearthly, rhythmic beat crashes through me, relentless. Bass hits over and over until my body tightens, desire turning molten between my hips.

And I'm lost beneath the onslaught.

He loosens his grip, allowing me a thin ribbon of air. "Fucking hell, you're beautiful," he says, his gruff tone raking over me. "I hate that I can't look into your starry eyes as you come apart."

An ache blooms in the hollow of my chest. It's been longer than six years for me since I've been intimately close with anyone. The fact that it's Orion who's taking me to the brink more than terrifies me.

"Hold on, fire. Don't move your hands from that speaker."

That's the last warning I'm given before the soft drone of music tapers away, and the only sound is the heavy rise and fall of our mingled breaths—

Then an explosion of sound.

The burst of music is a white-hot pulse through my body. Currents of sensation course through me, and an arousing frisson covers my skin. My senses come alive, wanting to experience the ruthless feel of his touch.

Touched by the hands of death.

When you've come so close, you almost crave its cruel caress.

And some part of me craves this from Orion. For him to claw at the callus, unfeeling parts of me. To sink his fangs into my flesh. Siphon the poison from my veins.

To have his mouth seal over mine and swallow the last of my breath—

He straps the necktie tighter, and whatever's left of the fear falls away. I'm exhausted by the struggle. The constant dread.

The fight against the inevitable.

As the music crescendos, the rise is relentless, an unyielding swell that makes me shiver under its furious climb—and the climb feels impossible.

The frantic bursts are a jagged rattle behind my sternum. The caged muscle hammers painfully against valves, the erratic tempo striking against my ribs. Adrenaline pours into the constricted chambers, speeding my heart beyond its limit. My vision flickers as blood-oxygen falters, cells starved.

"Fuck, you're shaking." Orion's voice is ravaged with the same agony tearing through me. The tie falls away. But my lungs stay locked, refusing to draw air. I collapse against his chest.

"Dammit." His body heat envelops me, solid, bracing. "Collins—say something."

At my weak nod, his voice turns guttural. "Words, Collins."

"I'm just…lightheaded."

He exhales a rough breath, my body shifting with the strenuous movement. "Collins, listen to my voice. I'm going to count. I want you to breathe."

His hand rests firmly along my thigh. Pressing against the fabric of my skirt, his fingers tap out a rhythm, matching the rising notes. "Counting isn't just compulsion," he murmurs, "it's entrainment. Beats naturally synchronizing when close enough. Orbiting stars pulsing in time, two heartbeats aligning. Pulses matching." His smooth timbre induces a shiver. "One rhythm captures the other until both move as one."

Each beat is a painful plea for air. But after a moment, I'm able to model my breath to his, breathing with his count.

"That's my girl." His chest expands with a deep inhale. The hard lines of his muscles press along my back, encouraging my next shallow breath. As he exhales, his fingers drum a steady beat against my thigh.

"That's it. Breathe with me, baby," he commands, tender. "In for four…hold two…out four. Lock onto my rhythm."

Supporting my weight, he hums, inducing a low current that arcs between our bodies. "One breath at a time. One beat."

As I strain to match him, letting his cadence draw mine, I sync my broken breath to the force of his. My pulse aligns beat by beat —and his strong, rhythmic heartbeat at my spine claims my pulse.

"That's it," he whispers, a desperate edge threaded through his praise. "God, that's perfect. You're fucking perfect, Collins."

The reverence in his deep voice unfurls a hot ache of desire low in my belly, stoked by the subtle, controlled shift of his hips against mine.

As the music builds, a rising tide sweeps through my cells. And I'm being dragged below, into some euphoric surrender. Piano chords flow like currents in the deep, caressing through muscle and bone, these stirring notes that whisper of roaring waves and night, of Orion's violent, turbulent nature.

"Are you with me?" The rough timbre of his demand drags like friction over my skin.

"Yes," I breathe out.

"Good." His voice drops to a gritty rasp, fingers never faltering their count. "Because fuck, angel—I'm seconds from losing my mind."

His heartbeat is a soothing percussion at my spine, timed to the crashing pulses from the speaker. The heated brush of his breath steals along the sensitive slope of my shoulder, and I shiver at the intimate caress.

"I know exactly what you need," he murmurs. "I want to hear you shatter, baby. You have to trust me."

Before I can reason, his hips press me hard into the vibrating speaker, holding me immobile between his unyielding body and the penetrating wave of sound. With slow, controlled thrusts, he rocks against me, each movement timed to the press of his fingers against my thigh.

He sets an infuriating pace. The grind of his erection against my backside is torturous, each tantalizing lick of friction teasing me apart.

"Oh, god...Orion." I can't move—caught between the abrasive rub of his body and the relentless pulse of the music. His hips continue to push into mine with a maddeningly slow, possessive prod that hits each beat.

His tie anchors at my throat, held with just enough tension to heighten every sensation, amplify every cascading pulse through me. The restraint I feel trembling through the silk blades does something devastating to my heart.

With a final rock of his hips into mine, he traps me against the mesh, where the endless rise of bursting sound creates a wall of intense bass hits.

A euphoria infuses my cells, giving my body no choice but to surrender to the rush. Tendrils of desire curl through me as his body crushes against mine with a solid, comforting weight.

Flames lick low between my thighs. A penetrating throb hits deep in my core, the ache so consuming, I start to break before the climax even rips through me.

A fever burns through my flesh as I needily grind back against him. I'm tethered to the steady rhythm of his fingers, to the slight, evocative thrust of his hips, as mine cant reflexively into the solid length of him behind me.

Orion groans, low and tortured. "Jesus—fuck, Collins." My name gritted through the fury of his need sends a shot of arousal into my system.

The feel of him pressed against me, the undeniable proof of how close he is to shattering his ruthless control, ignites a primal hunger. A violent tremble grips me as I gasp for air, my lungs just as starved for that sweet relief.

The moment Orion loosens the tie, my orgasm crashes with breathtaking intensity.

"Oh. Fucking. God." I toss my head back as pleasure overtakes me. Orion's body bands tight around mine, holding me immobile against him as I fall apart. The climax spirals through me so intensely, I hear as much as feel the last violent pound of bass. The punch of the final note rocks through my bones, rhythmic aftershocks flutter over my nerves.

Then I'm suddenly weightless, adrift in an ocean of sensation. The canvas disappears, the dirt with it, leaving only soft waves licking over my skin.

The sparking vibrations slowly fade, leaving us in a charged silence broken only by the labored sound of our breath. I push back slightly, just enough to feel the hard length of him—still erect.

"Don't move," he says, issued in a low, guttural warning.

My breath catches, and I hold still, my exposed skin drinking the cool air, my neck throbbing with the lingering leash of the tie. I lick my lips, tasting salt, and I remove a shaky hand from the speaker and wipe numb fingers across my cheek, smearing the trace of tears over my damp skin.

Orion's strained breaths slow, his body gradually relaxing around mine. As he lowers his leg to release me, my thighs come together, and I'm unable to suppress the quiet moan at the tender ache.

"Fuck," he mutters, muscles racked with shivers as he draws away. His warmth vanishes instantly, leaving a chill in his place.

The dome shutter begins to groan open. Faint starlight filters into the observatory. Harsh reality creeps back, driving all that was depraved and sacred into the shadows once more.

In a panicked rush, I tug my blouse closed and quickly fasten the buttons. "I assume this wasn't what you intended when you composed your music," I say to break a layer of tension.

His rough chuckle thrums across my sensitized nerves, provoking a low flutter in my belly, yet it sounds forced.

I sense his proximity like a sparking current, raising fine hairs along my skin. I turn to face him, and he's now standing beneath the pale ray of moonlight, shirt and gloves back in place.

God, he's devastating. After everything that transpired between us, I should feel self-conscious, vulnerable. Yet as he prowls closer, all I feel is hunted. Ruined.

Endangered.

He hooks a gloved finger around the center of the tie draping my neck, slipping it free like a ribbon, the silk blades whispering against my damp skin. Then, stepping close, he says in a low voice, "Completely unintended." He gathers my hair in one hand, stealing every last bit of my breath as he secures it gently in a ponytail with his tie.

My pulse tangles in my veins as he draws back, just enough to settle his hands at the base of my neck. His palms roam up the curve of my throat, thumbs gliding over my skin. And I realize he's searching for marks, inspecting for damage. His gloved hands far too gentle where, just moments ago, they strangled with brutal demand.

I swallow, emotion knotted tight beneath my ribs at the feel of his tender evaluation. He notices, tilting his head above me. "But seeing that look on your face right now," he says, his tone lowering into a rough cadence, "completely intended."

A fever burns through my skin.

"You're breathtaking when you're flushed," he says, unable to curb the satisfaction in his smirk. It lasts only a flicker before a shadow descends over his features, a hint of anger sharpening his expression.

He halts, his hands folding around my neck possessively. "You had me worried."

"I'm fine. More than fine," I assure him, bringing a sinful curl to his mouth. "But you didn't—"

"I got what I wanted," he interrupts, answering why he didn't find release. "Seeing that look on your face—fuck. It's more than enough."

A flush forces my gaze to drop, landing at his parted collar, to where the inked script along his neck hints to secrets below. Tentatively, I rest my palm against the solid plane of his chest, fingertips grazing the parted edges of his shirt—a silent dare, a test.

"Stay here while I turn the system off," he says, his muscles tensing beneath my palm before he steps back. My hand falls away. "Then I'll walk you to your place."

I offer a quiet nod. Folding my arms around my waist, I use the few seconds alone to bring out my case and swallow down a pill, then search his private habitat. My gaze drifts over the monitors, the console, looking for a camera. "Should you erase the recorded feed?"

"No cameras here. I don't trust them. Someone could hack the feed. They'd be fucking stupid to try, but it's a risk I won't take. You don't have to worry about privacy."

"Good to know." A gleam catches my eye, my breath snatched by the sight as a trail of dark red streaks down the speaker. The metal mesh is caved in, crushed beneath the violent impact of a fist. The smeared imprint evidence of a losing battle.

Throat raw, I swallow past the ache as I swipe my fingertips through the stained surface. Orion's blood coats my fingers, and I realize that, to stop himself from hurting me, he caused himself pain.

I look his way, heart twisting at how easily he could've unleashed that violence—yet he held back.

I've barely scraped the surface of the violence he's capable of.

He stalks toward me, and whatever was raw and intimate just moments ago is shaved away under sharp moonlight, bringing a weight of reality. I'm left painfully aware of how fragile, how vulnerable I allowed myself to become in his arms.

Gathering courage, I meet the volatile current of his eyes. "You removed your gloves," I say. "You were close to giving yourself permission to touch me. You wanted to make a connection."

Something prohibited claims his gaze. "That's where your analysis is wrong, doctor." His voice drops into a deep timbre. "I removed them to stop myself from tearing into you. It can never go that far again."

He cups my face, fingers braced to the nape of my neck as he tips my head back, positioning his mouth near my ear. "I hope you got what you needed, because this won't happen again, starling."

"Orion—"

"I hurt you," he says, voice like gravel as he releases me. "I came damn close to doing worse."

I draw in a steadying breath. "I trust you."

"You shouldn't." He moves so close I can taste the heady scent of blood on his skin. His thumb traces over my inner wrist, his soft touch in direct contrast to his coarse warning. "Don't ever let me touch you, Collins."

The golden ratio refers to a unique relationship between two numbers, symbolized using ϕ (*phi*). The same golden ratio that appears as a rectangle in human constructs often is expressed in nature forms as an elegant spiral. The chambered nautilus expresses this principle as it outgrows its old "living quarters" and sequentially builds roomier ones in a spiral pattern whose dimensions are determined by the golden ratio.

— GEOPHYSICAL INSTITUTE, UNIVERSITY
OF ALASKA FAIRBANKS

15
WANING

That's us... a lonely speck in the great enveloping cosmic dark.

— CARL SAGAN, *PALE BLUE DOT*

COLLINS

I have a bad heart.

The organ in my chest is broken. It's black and bruised and callused, suffering a wound that has never repaired. And while time seems to heal some wounds, apparently its passage fails to mend mitral valve damage.

The very blood that keeps the muscle pumping flows in reverse, traveling the wrong way. Making it bad.

Some things just are.

A frigid wind breaks across the soaring spires, sending the briny scent of ocean through the West Quad. Dead leaves crunch beneath my boots as I push past the exertion in my body and the students, fighting the fatigue settling deep in my bones. It's the kind of weary that makes me almost regret how far I let things go with Orion.

My heart hasn't felt the same since.

As one day slips into another, Orion says, "I want you alone, angel." The muscle flutters as I tell him, "Yes." Another day passes, and I ask him, "So what's your star sign?" He chuckles, then murmurs in an amused tone, "You're adorable, starling," and my heart skips a beat.

One week bleeds into the next, and tender moments are stolen as Orion plays piano, a melody so achingly beautiful, I swear the organ in my chest stops beating altogether as the notes shape and unspool beneath his fingers, and captivated, I rise onto the tips of my toes for the first time since before.

Then one night, when he leads me to the university theater, the lights go out, plunging us into absolute darkness. Before panic drags me under, his arms circle me from behind, and the ceiling illuminates with an explosion of stars, transforming the theater into a shimmering planetarium.

And my heart bursts.

We lie side by side on the stone floor, gazing at the cosmos in the starlit dark, and Orion says, "Finally, a use for that fucking VR simulator." I look over at him. "You're seducing me with the stars, Dr. Night." His smile is too striking as he whispers, "It's not cliché when every time I gaze at you, I want to immortalize you in the heavens with them, angel," and I hear the crack, a deep, internal fault line through my heart.

One. Two. Three.

The stern tone of Laurel's voice echoes through my thoughts, always forcing me to look in the mirror, *see what's truly there.*

I convinced myself I could undo Orion while maintaining control. Yet manipulation requires a degree of belief in your lies. The deeper you sink into that deception, the more you risk falling victim to your own tactics. Losing yourself to the curated feelings.

In that observatory dome, I didn't just lower my defenses; I dropped them into the deepest chasm of the ocean. I tore my trauma wide and let it bleed, trusting a killer in my most vulnerable state.

For one fractured heartbeat, as he tightened that ligature around my throat, it wasn't my life I feared he'd take. With his strong arms holding me immobile as I fell apart, like the music beneath his fingers, I felt the desire to let it all go—the pain, the anger. The burden.

And yet, the firefly doesn't allow the male to bleed the toxins from her veins.

Revenge lives in my blood.

As more days pass, I've started to notice Orion's agitation. The increasing mood swings. The darkness deepening the gray ring around his irises, dulling the vivid blue-green waters.

The closer the eclipse draws, the more withdrawn he becomes.

Beyond the heated glances and charged near-touches in shadowy corridors, he's spent the past few days locked in his observatory with his research. I could push him into a session, but he's volatile, unstable. And with Banner content for the time being, it's safer to wait until the last moment.

Lips buried in my scarf for warmth, I cross underneath the arches of the colonnade as birds take flight overhead, my hurried steps echoing against the stone. I'm almost to the entrance when Prescott appears from my periphery.

"Collins," he calls out.

Straightening my backbone, I turn his way and force a smile. My teeth chatter too hard to correct him on the informal use of my name. "Dr. Prescott, how was your day?"

The rigid set to his jaw clashes with his smile. "You never took me up on my offer," he says, disregarding the pleasantry.

"Oh." I touch my forehead, then give a soft laugh. "Time has really gotten away from me. There's so much going on with the upcoming symposium—"

"We need to talk," he cuts me short with a sharp look. "You know, I've been here for a year now. I've put in a lot of time, a lot of hard work."

Something in the way he says this feels off, and my senses go on high alert. "No one's discrediting that."

"Look, you need to be careful around Night." A pensiveness settles in his gaze. "The fact is, he's dangerous. I worry you're not safe."

There's an anxious quality to his tone that gives me pause. Pushing past the unnerving feeling, I tell him, "I assure you, I've worked with far more challenging individuals."

A smug smile pulls into place. "That's unfortunate." He pushes in too close, towering over me. "Here's the thing. By having me removed from the observatory, you're interfering with my progress. But for your own safety, I think it's best if you leave."

My grip tightens instinctively around the umbrella handle, a defensive reflex. This is the second attempt from a man to cow me into leaving.

"Thank you for your concern," I say evenly, adjusting my briefcase in my other hand, "but I'm perfectly capable of managing myself."

Ending our conversation right here, I turn to leave. He takes hold of my upper arm, drawing me to a stop. "Collins, I need you to stop the sessions with Dr. Night."

Alarm rings through my bones. My sudden shortness of breath clips my words, too many of them rushing out in my panic. "It's harmful to abruptly end sessions with a patient working through loss…especially when it's someone close in the same field—"

"Who are you talking about—?" he cuts in, his dark brows drawing together. "Ah, you mean Dr. Calloway." He releases a derisive breath. "Jesus, she died years ago. Their engagement was well over by then."

My mouth parts. The sandstone beneath my feet shifts, unsteady. "Please remove your hand from me," I manage to say.

I twist my arm in an attempt to break his grip just as a loud rumble disrupts the altercation.

Prescott's hand falls away. His reaction is delayed as he jumps back just in time to evade the wheel coming into contact with his leg. "What the hell—?"

The roar of the motorcycle is deafening in the covered colonnade. Orion drops his booted feet on either side of his bike and kills the engine. Helmet visor shielding his face, he straightens on the seat. "Sorry. Lost control for a moment."

Heat blooms in the center of my chest. I've spent days trying to figure out how to crack his defenses, and all it took was one threat from Prescott asserting his dominance.

The lowering sun reflects off his black visor as he briefly turns his head in my direction, and I feel his thorough inspection cover every inch of me.

"Not a problem, Night." Prescott drops his hands into his coat pockets, his annoyance evident in the curl of his upper lip. "But you should be more careful. Someone could get hurt."

Orion lifts the visor and stares dead at him. "That warning goes both ways." The steely tone of his voice provokes a shiver. There's a crazed gleam to his eyes I've never seen, and the danger there shallows my breath.

Prescott nods curtly, then glances my way once imploringly, before he stalks off amid the lingering threat. I watch him for a moment longer, still unsettled.

"You actually should remove the bike from the walkway," I say, giving Orion my full attention. "Dr. Banner won't be too impressed by this display."

Unconcerned, Orion removes his helmet, and I'm met with

the fierce current of his ocean-teal eyes, drawn helplessly into their depths. He's windblown, as wild and unpredictable as the ocean itself, always looking as though he's made of night and waves.

Amused, he crooks an eyebrow. "Are you impressed?"

I bite the corner of my lip, fighting the urge to smile. Whatever disturbed spark I glimpsed there a moment ago has dissipated, replaced by a heated ember, like stars igniting amid those dark depths.

"You've been avoiding me," I say.

"I have," he admits, not denying the allegation. "But you make it fucking impossible to do so for long."

My mouth twists. "I'm not letting you out of our arrangement."

He cocks his head. "Every time I save you, I find myself deeper in trouble, Dr. Holbrook."

I inhale an aching breath, releasing it with a slight quiver that has nothing to do with the chilly afternoon. Ever observant, Orion notices. He rakes his fingers through his disheveled hair before throwing his leg over. Leaning against the seat, he extends the helmet toward me. "I'll keep you warm."

I hold the fierce challenge in his gaze. In psychology, the law of figure-ground shifts our focus in order to offer new perspectives. Such as the "faces or vases" illusion, where distinguishing the object from its background reveals an entirely different image.

The more Orion focuses on me as his object of obsession, the more the surrounding threats blur, dissolving into the abstract image. He doesn't perceive the danger.

It's the figure—the object itself—that controls the illusion.

And yet, as the powerful current in his eyes threatens to drag me past the boundary of safety, I sense the object of my desire shifting just as dangerously.

I can't lose focus.

Fortifying my defenses, I step forward and take hold of the helmet.

The captivating smile that breaks across his face clenches my heart, right before he gives the helmet a hard tug, pulling me toward him and eliminating the remaining distance between us.

Standing between his parted legs, I unconsciously brace my hand to his thigh, and he doesn't tense at my touch.

He reaches down, sliding the umbrella strap from my wrist. He looks it over, gloved thumb sweeping the black steel handle as he says, "This is a nice umbrella," before he secures it in his pack.

My lips twitch. "It's a little arrogant to complement your own tastes, Dr. Night."

There's the briefest draw to his features, then it's swept away as his gaze lowers, eyeing my briefcase. "But that won't fit."

I let the briefcase slip from my hand, dropping unceremoniously to the stone with a thump that barely registers over the crashing pulse in my ears.

With a sure touch, Orion smooths my hair back, and I don't recoil at the cool feel of his gloves before he carefully slips the helmet over my head. "Fuck, that's sexy."

The helmet sits heavy. I'm hit with his heady scent of ocean and man. "What about you?"

"I don't need one."

"Right. Statistics," I say, situating the helmet for comfort.

"No, you change that," he says, something hesitant buried in his eyes. "My dark little anomaly, altering too many variables to know the precise outcome."

Brows knit, I study his guarded expression. "You're doing a terrible job of making me feel safe."

His deep chuckle hits my stomach with a flutter. "I promise, nothing bad will happen to you on my bike." He expertly fastens the strap under my chin, securing the helmet. "Still, I won't take any chances with you."

A soft murmur vibrates through my chest.

I believe him.

He glances at my discarded briefcase, brows hiked, and I shrug. "There's nothing important in there," I say, earning another heart-stopping grin.

He removes his leather jacket and drapes it around my shoulders, tucking my scarf inside. His jacket covers my wool coat easily, and I slip my arms into the sleeves as he draws the zipper up.

I'm only given a second to appreciate the warmth before he seizes my waist and effortlessly lifts me, placing me on the seat. Keeping his gaze on my parted legs, he skims his gloved hands down my hips. His descent doesn't stop until he reaches my knees, where he inches my skirt hem up painfully slow, causing my breath to stall as he pushes the material to the middle of my thighs.

"Damn, not sure how I'm supposed to keep my eyes on the road."

Emboldened, I inch my skirt even higher and swing my leg over the seat. "Just don't look back."

An ache sinks deep in my core at the way he watches me shift forward on the cushioned leather, my skirt barely covering my slip of panties until I bring the length of my coat closure forward.

He drags a hand over his jaw. Mutters something unintelligible as he shamelessly reaches down to adjust the bulge in his black slacks. A tender pinch tightens in my sex at the sight.

"Hands back here." Orion instructs me to grab hold of the metal brace behind the seat. As he mounts the bike, I have to bite my bottom lip to stifle the sound that wants to escape at the heavy feel of him settling between my thighs.

A fiery current arcs over my skin, urging me to wrap my arms around his waist. Between the oversized jacket and his body heat, I'm burning up.

The engine rumbles to life, and any reservations over how dangerous this is fall silent beneath the roaring growl.

"Shit," I whisper. I swear, he changed some chemistry in my brain, because the vibration immediately makes my thighs clench. Through his dress shirt, I feel his abs tense beneath my palms.

"Hold on," he calls over the sound of the engine. "And, Collins, do not drop those hands."

A shot of liquid fire courses through my veins at the suggestion. Forced to rest the helmet against his shoulder blade, I tighten my hold around him, feeling every cut flex of his abdominal muscles when the bike takes off.

Cruising at a steady speed, Orion circles the university, then steers onto the main street of the downtown area. All the decorative effort that has already gone into preparing for the upcoming symposium solidifies into a heavy mass in my chest with the unwanted reminder of time.

As Orion turns down a narrow street, he reaches back and clasps my thigh, holding me secure and igniting a flurry of heat low in my belly.

Once we clear the town limits, all thoughts of looming eclipses and victims are forgotten as Orion picks up speed. Wind whips past, making me grateful I wore my knee-high boots that help guard against the chill. For the first time since I drew new breath, I'm present in the moment, unconcerned about the destination.

Soon, we're winding down a coastal road, the brisk wind streaming around our bodies as the view of the ocean unfolds alongside us. At sunset, it's beautiful. Silver clouds dust the sky in a soft, hazy glow above the mist, hued in vibrant pinks and oranges. The distant edges fade to a deep blue over the stretch of endless waves.

Orion accelerates, and the jolting speed of the bike stirs my blood with a hit of adrenaline, thrilling, intoxicating.

Euphoric.

I flatten my hand over his chest, absorbing the thundering rhythm of his heart as it crashes against my palm. He releases one of the handles to bring his gloved hand to mine, covering it and holding it there before he gives it a strong pulse, urging me to hold tighter.

The road ahead curves around a high bluff. We follow along the narrow stretch, the climbing rock face rising high on one side, the ocean on the other. Adrenaline burns through the chambers of my heart, and I can no longer feel the bite of wind, the cold air—

My own heartbeat.

The sudden realization sends a tremor of alarm through me, and I strain to feel the struggling pulse that's become the tempo of my life. Only the faster Orion pushes the bike, the less I'm able to think of anything other than the way his thumb soothingly traces my inner wrist, softly tapping a beat against my pulse point.

Before long, he returns his hand to the clutch, downshifting smoothly as he veers onto a stretch of sandy trail leading through dune grass and rocks. He eases the throttle, slowing enough to maneuver over the loose sand.

For a brief moment, the muffled sound of my breathing inside the helmet pulls me into another space—one thick with the scent of overturned dirt and suffocating vinyl. Anxiety claws up my chest, claustrophobia pressing in from all sides. I'm desperate to lift the visor, to drag in a lungful of fresh air.

As if sensing my unease, Orion guns the engine, driving the panic from my mind. He coasts across the damp sand, easing us closer to the water, chasing the shoreline across the unbroken stretch of beach.

This time, when he grasps my thigh, it has nothing to do with safety. His thumb drags slowly back and forth, sparking a blazing path along my skin. The firm press of him between my thighs, coupled with the vibration, sends a hot flush of arousal through me.

I'm not sure at what point my hand drifts down, but the moment I graze his erection straining against his pants, an intense ache pulses low. Daringly, I explore further, moving below his belt. His stomach muscles tense, and the motorcycle jerks slightly before he regains control.

Something reckless and heady thrums through my veins, and I boldly press the heel of my palm to the hard length of him. His hips shift upward in response, and that one movement is so damn erotic, my thighs squeeze against his legs.

He downshifts abruptly, and my heart stutters with the lurch of the bike. Then we're slowing, coming to a stop. His sharp inhale expands his back, igniting friction along the length of my front.

Dropping his feet to the packed sand, he revs the engine hard, digging the back tire down and anchoring the bike in place. He kills the engine, and the sudden silence rings in my ears, followed by the hollow, rhythmic crash of waves.

Orion uses both hands to reach back and tap my thighs. "Push back."

The coarse grate of his tone scrapes over my senses. Before I even get to the edge of the seat, he twists around. One arm wraps my lower back, his other hand captures my thigh, urgently hauling me onto his lap. Forced to straddle him, I grab hold of his shoulders, adjusting until I feel the undeniable hard press of him beneath me.

His forearm bands tighter around the small of my back. "Christ, Collins. Do you want me to fuck you on this bike." There's no question implied in his gruff tone. It's a certainty, a warning.

I reach up to unbuckle the strap, but Orion grabs the bottom of the helmet and presses his forehead against the visor. "Don't," he breathes. "It hurts how badly I want to kiss you."

A small sound escapes my throat. "I wouldn't stop you," I whisper, reinforcing my words with a purposeful roll of my hips.

He curses under his breath and pulls back enough to flip my visor up. His teal eyes spear mine with so much want I'm breathless. The desperation behind that look says what he's unwilling—that he's stopping himself.

I release a breath before reinforcing what I've told him repeatedly since that night in the observatory. "You didn't hurt me, Orion."

"And I won't." His throat works with a hard swallow, pain etched around the lines of his squinted eyes.

A tense silence locks us in this moment.

Then slowly, he unbuckles the chin strap, gently removing the helmet before tossing it to the sand like an afterthought. His hands slip beneath the leather jacket in search of my hips, gripping possessively.

"I just want to keep you right here," he says, and an ache forms in my throat at the earnestness I hear in his voice.

I briefly close my eyes.

Focus on the object.

The light tug of my scarf draws my gaze back on him as he slides the sheer fabric down to expose my neck. His gloved fingers trace the faint bruises that linger from his tie. He's done this often, assessing the fading marks he placed there.

I hold my breath, watching the subtle shift in his expression before he closes himself off. A shadow flickers across his eyes, and I read the fear there—fear of what might happen if he goes too far. If he loses control.

I press him, daring to ask, "How often do you allow yourself release?"

"Jesus." He exhales a harsh breath. "Not today, Dr. Holbrook," he says, his tone adamant.

"You don't get to avoid this, Dr. Night," I counter, feeling less steady than my voice alleges. "You choose the locations of our sessions, but we're still here for that purpose, aren't we?"

He releases the scarf, scraping a gloved hand over his windblown hair. "Never," he confesses. My mouth parts, and he raises an eyebrow. "You think I'm lying."

"No." I shake my head quickly. "Just…with the frequency of your intrusive thoughts, I was expecting a different answer."

His tongue drags over his lips, eyes heating with so much intensity they rival the breathtaking depth of colors washing up on shore.

A dangerous current churns beneath that beauty.

This is how it feels to be swept into the ocean of his eyes, caught in that blue-green undertow, pulled deeper into an endless eddy.

A groan resonates from deep in his chest, the rough vibration of it a lick of friction between my thighs. "That wouldn't be satisfying, Collins." He brushes my wild strands behind my ears, hands settling on either side of my face. "I've woken up fucking my bed after dreaming of you, goddamn out of my mind, and still forced myself to stop. Knowing any cheap pleasure would never compare to the real thing with you."

A feverish blush burns through my skin at his admission. It should be crass, but Orion's inability to filter his thoughts makes his honesty vulnerable—and far too arousing.

"Maybe you're ready to try exposure therapy again," I say, easing back a fraction. His hands fall away, finding placement on my knees, where his fingers curl and tuck intimately into the hollows beneath. "But more gradually this time. Just a small—"

"One taste would never be enough," he says, voice pitched

beneath the crash of waves. "I'd only crave you more, and it might just drive me mad, angel."

The caged muscle in my chest batters frantically. Out of habit, I flatten my hand over my breastbone. Orion studies me too closely, a curious draw to his features.

He lifts a hand, fingers skimming my jawline, tenderly trailing down the contour of my throat, the tantalizing feel in conflict with the cruel caress of leather. The hunger in his gaze burns into mine as he coasts farther to the collar of my blouse, his hand halted right above mine.

As he begins to unfasten the top button, a spike of dread accelerates my pulse.

I reflexively pull back, body tensing.

He wets his lips, pressing them together. His hair drifts over his forehead in the misty wind, a question banked there in the intensity of his eyes.

"The gloves," he says knowingly, and I simply nod, allowing the excuse.

"*Hmm.*" His hands slip to my thighs, fingers splaying. "Maybe I'm not the only one who would benefit from a little exposure therapy."

Orion drags his palms up my bare thighs, the clash between rough leather and his tender touch unnerving. It unsettles my senses, anxiety tangling with anticipation as his grip firms.

His thumbs come to rest at the sensitive joints of my thighs, and I scrape in a tight breath, inadvertently rocking against him. He mutters a harsh curse under his breath as his gloved thumb edges the lace seam of my panties.

My tremble of fear excites him. I can feel him beneath me, growing impossibly hard, the instinctive lift of his hips driving the ache deeper.

"Fuck," he swears, and in one desperate move, he hauls my knee up higher along his hip, fingers digging into my thigh.

216

"Orion—" I say his name on an escaped breath, my hands dropping to his forearms.

"I need to feel you come," he says, the low, abrasive tone of his voice delivered in demand. Not want—*need*. "Nothing would give me more pleasure than watching you unravel on my fingers."

The fierce desire in his gaze steals my breath, and any refusal. With a shaky exhale, I remove my hands, the subtle lift of their weight giving him permission.

He reaches his free hand around my waist as he cautiously hooks a finger at the seat of my panties. Cold air drifts between my thighs, making my arousal apparent.

His eyes fuse to mine, holding me as bound as his hand braced at my back. His finger slowly slips beneath the thin barrier of material, then the coarse feel of leather is touching me. He circles the pad around my center, and a shock of alarm snatches the air from my lungs.

My stomach tenses, my hands grab hold of his biceps, bracing myself—

"Breathe, Collins."

At his coaxing words, I draw in a sharp breath, release it slowly—and then he's pushing inside me, stealing my next, my muscles tensing at the sudden intrusion.

An unrestrained groan rumbles from the back of his throat as he inserts his gloved finger deeper, his thumb pressed to the tender flesh of my pelvis. "Oh, god—damn." It's a heated avowal falling from his lips as he stills inside me. I feel his tremor of restraint the same way I felt the tension vibrate through the blades of his tie collared around my neck.

"I'm fine," I say to reassure him, urging him on with a slight rock of my hips, and something starved and reckless ignites behind his eyes.

"Fuck. I'm not, angel." It's the only warning I'm given before the hand at my back slides to my nape, fingers splaying into my hair and arching my body toward him. Then he drags out and pushes in deeper, setting off a spark of heat through my skin.

I try to control my breathing as his strokes deepen, becoming unguarded, heightening the fear wanting to swallow me at the coarse leather touching so intimately. My teeth sink into my bottom lip, and that action strips another measure of his control. Raw hunger darkens his eyes as he inserts another finger. Filling, testing, fraying my nerves apart.

"Goddammit, Collins, you'd be so fucking tight around me —" He breaks off, his eyes slamming shut as an agonized current of want arcs from him to me. He's fucking me with his fingers, stretching me around him. Slipping out only to sink in deeper, harder. Working the low, achy heat into a throb.

His rhythmic insertions ignite a flame in my chest, threading lust through every nerve ending. Heat suffocates me beneath his jacket, and I yank at the scarf to loosen it. My nipples tighten against the shifting material of my blouse, turning my breaths erratic. Orion's predatory gaze hones on the bruises, his hips grinding upward in search of relief.

"Tell me how that feels," he demands. "Tell me what you like." His thumb scrapes over my clit, making my breath stutter and sending a searing shockwave of arousal up my spine.

"It's intense—but don't stop," I gasp between words. "God, Orion—take off your glove. Let me feel you."

"Fuck, angel. Don't tempt me." Whatever restraint he held fractures. The small noise that escapes my mouth undoes him, and a feral growl rips from his throat as he strokes mercilessly deeper.

"I want you…" It's a whisper coming from my trembling lips, and I'm shaken to find I mean it. In this suspended moment of heat and sensation, I want Orion in a way I never thought possible again.

"You have me," he answers on a claiming thrust, the coarse

rasp of his groan just as abrasive against my skin. Every lurid sound is friction across my nerves. Skillful fingers I've watched meticulously balance instruments, move masterfully over piano keys, now curl expertly inside me, finding that deep, desperate ache.

My inner muscles clamp around him, throbbing with urgent pulses. My thighs tremble, clenching against his waist. God, he's laying claim to me out in the open, marking me like one of his scenes beneath an endless sky, so exposed. And if he wanted to break me like one of his victims, I'm helpless to stop him.

My eyes squeeze closed, trying to block out the terror that flickers at the edges, the phantom sensation of pressure and painful, tearing penetration—

"Open your eyes," Orion commands, tone measured, controlled. "Look at me. Stay with me." On instinct, I obey, anchoring to those heated teal currents. "Breathe, Collins. That's it, baby. You can take it for me—fuck." His rough moan of approval liquifies my muscles.

Body strung tight, I arch into him, shamelessly rolling my hips atop him. With a violent curse, he drops his mouth to the swell of my breast, teeth nipping at my blouse as if trying to tear through. He catches the fabric, his teeth coming away with a button. He spits it out, eyes feral with hunger. And that look—so raw, unbridled—makes my pulse stagger.

A trickle of fear leaks into the building pleasure, striking a shiver against my bones. There's something menacing in his eyes, getting off on the fear in mine. Fueling this primal need in him until he's fucking his fingers into me with merciless, possessive strokes, his thumb skillfully swirling my clit. The stimulation stirs charged pulses through my veins, leaving my body trembling under his relentless touch.

My thighs burn as he circles my center, then thrusts deep,

wrenching a strangled cry from my throat. A crackling heat sparks beneath my flesh, and I can feel how wet I am, slick and coating his fingers as they plunge in broken, desperate rhythm to my tripping heartbeat.

And I'm crashing too fast, my heart thrumming my ribs. An aching pressure gathers at the base of my spine, urging me to plant my hands on the support bar behind me, gripping as I arch backward, my hips rocking in eager search for release as I tighten around him.

"God, fuck—you're so fucking perfect. That's it…" His groan escapes rough through gritted teeth. "Fuck my fingers until you come, angel." His voice breaks into a guttural sound. "I want to feel how tight and wet this cunt gets for me."

"God…you have…no filter…" I gasp around a moan.

"None," he growls, fisting his hand in my hair and tugging my head back. "You want to hear my filthy thoughts of you, starling? The way I want to ruin you so goddamn thoroughly you forget every man who ever touched you. How I want to make you come so fucking hard, you only remember the way I wreck this sweet pussy. You belong to me. Only me."

His filthy words awaken something darkly forbidden within me, each one a brand seared into my skin—a promise I desperately want. *To forget.*

"Oh, fuck…oh, god." My hips buck, rolling with the thunderous waves breaking against the shore, fusing with the hunger churning darker in the ocean of his eyes. "Orion, god— more. Fuck, please don't stop."

And that's all it takes.

"Ah—Jesus—fuck, Collins." A coarse groan tears free of his chest as he bands his arm around my back, pinning me to him as he drives his fingers in relentless desire to make me fall apart, pushing me toward release with each punishing stroke.

His mouth coasts dangerously close to mine, swallowing my

ragged cries. "God damn, I have never seen anything sexier in my fucking life than you," he whispers over my mouth.

He brings me right to the precipice, easing me breathlessly toward the brink. My orgasm teases on the fringe, just out of reach, my body one frantic heartbeat away from shattering.

"I want you to come for me, angel," Orion demands roughly. "Right now. Come on my fingers."

Mist off the water rolls in with the tide, dusk draping us in a veil of seclusion that allows Orion to claim me with fervent words and purposeful thrusts, teasing me apart until I'm shaking, coming utterly undone in his hold.

The tighter he grips me, the more I crave the restraint, allowing me this effortless surrender. In the same way he held me immobile against the speaker, the dark unknown pressing in, safe within the cage of his arms. Taking away the war between fight and flight where everything was simply—

"Oh, my *god.*"

—feeling.

And he senses exactly what I need, his arm binding around my body. The plea falls from my mouth, breathless and unguarded, "Hold me tighter."

His eyes capture mine, a fierce devotion there that clenches my heart, before his hold tightens, and every rhythmic stroke hits harder, my pulse speeding, the ache bruising deep beneath my ribs. But the pain feels alive.

His thumb drags rough leather against my clit, friction sparking with each pass, unspooling me apart like his music until that exquisite ache pulls low in my back, igniting my inner thighs and along the fusion of my pelvis where his thumb braces, rocking me harder as my body shamelessly moves into his touch.

His sinful strokes quicken, urging me toward my breaking point. An intense burst of pleasure unfurls and my climax shatters through me, the pleasure unbearable.

Orion groans in satisfaction as I clench tight around him, unrelenting as he continues to work me past the point of pleasure, until he's claimed every pulsing aftershock.

Our heavy breaths fall mingled between us, charging our silence with crashing waves and staccato heartbeats.

Orion doesn't move right away, keeping his fingers seated just inside me, as if trying to memorize the sensation of me through the leather, and a guarded expression moves across his face.

I lick my lips, and his gaze ravenously tracks the path of my tongue, a torn sound emanating from his throat before he pulls free, stealing a hitched breath from my lungs.

He pushes his fingertip past my parted lips, easing the slick leather over my tongue. Those flames of his eyes intensify as he swirls his finger, his agonized look of lust and hunger burning through me as I taste the heady mix of us together—desire and leather.

He makes a tortured sound, a low rumble that scrapes across my skin as his hand falls away. I catch a glimpse of the fading anguish in his gaze before he tightens his hold on my hips.

"God—fuck," he groans, pulling me down hard as he grinds up against my center. "You feel so fucking perfect against me, it scares me how good. Just the goddamn perfect symmetry of us… that I could get so lost in you, starling."

Orion pulls his jacket closed around me against the ocean wind and drops his forehead to my chest, his ragged breaths dropping heavy.

And my heart constricts painfully.

We stay like this, locked in embrace, waves breaking against the shore as the tide recedes farther out. His fingers tap a rhythmic beat against the small of my back, a soothing cadence that resonates along my spine. Wind lashes against our trembling bodies as adrenaline slowly ebbs, leaving me torn, words caught beneath the ache in my throat.

I swallow hard, unable to collect my thoughts enough to voice any. I don't tell him the mess he's left me. I don't confess how utterly, irrevocably ruined he's made me.

"Your heart is thundering," he says suddenly. Then, as he pulls back, his gaze moves over my face, bright eyes glittering with satisfaction as though I need to say none of it.

His arms tighten around me, holding me close as he shifts backward. He throws his leg over the seat, effortlessly dropping to the ground, keeping me secure against him a staggered heartbeat longer, my legs still clinging to his hips, before he sets my booted feet on the sandy earth.

As I stare up at him, he gifts me with his captivating smile. "You have a little gold in your eyes," he remarks.

I drop my head, blinking rapidly to avoid his gaze as the awe in his voice cracks a piece deep inside. "Why am I the only one you let get this close to you," I ask, masking the tremor in my voice with a shiver.

Orion tips my face up to his, gloved fingers coming to rest alongside my neck. "Because you quiet the chaos in my head," he confesses, raw vulnerability edged in his tone.

I focus my breathing, hoping he can't feel my shallow pulse through his gloves. The intensity of his gaze forces me to duck my head again, wishing for the barrier of his glasses—some shield between his eyes and mine. I tuck my windblown hair behind my ear, only for the wind to send strands back across my face.

"Which, I might add—" a lighter note threads his timbre "—works exceptionally well when I draw those lovely sounds from your mouth."

A tendril of heat curls through me as a wry smile pulls at my lips. With a disarming wink, he finally releases me and stalks toward the lapping water, leaving me with an ache burrowing beneath my ribs. I hug my arms around myself, pulling his jacket tighter for warmth.

With his back to me, Orion stares silently out over the ocean, watching the last shafts of sunlight sink below the darkening horizon.

Pelicans fly low, their black silhouettes dotting the sky above the rolling ocean. There's a crunch beneath my boot and I glance down, bending to pick up a broken piece of spiral shell.

As I palm the jagged shard, I'm taken back to another night, another ocean. Feeling another rising violence as a roaring tide crashed against the shore, stars glittering coldly above. Desperation constricts my chest just as it did then, standing at the edge of a crime scene that would forever alter my life.

I sweep my thumb across my wrist.

One. Two. Three.

A few steps away, Orion brings his hands together and slowly removes the black leather glove from his left hand, and I drop the broken shell, forgotten, as the action draws me closer.

I've glimpsed his hands before, as he played piano, as he adjusted his telescope, but only from a safe distance—and I halt now, torn between my burning curiosity and the implication he might not realize what he's doing.

Only I can't tear my eyes away, tracing the intricate ink covering the back of his hand, the shaded lines and fine artwork. There's a sparrow, or—

My breath snags in my chest as I recall his endearment.

Starling.

A flush of warmth spreads through me, my pulse quick as a pang reverberates through my chest.

I clear the ache from my throat, my gaze moving over star patterns and planets layered within the design, scrawled letters and glyphs I don't recognize. Then my eyes catch on the fading bruise discoloring his knuckles—a remnant of his fist destroying the speaker.

Orion lowers to his haunches, the waves lapping the gray sand near the toes of his boots. Leisurely, he skims his bare fingertips over the surface of the receding water.

"You've never explained to me what it's like for you," I say, keeping myself at a distance.

He glances over his shoulder, the fading rays of light softening the contours of his face. If he's letting me in another measure, I want to get even closer.

"What it's like for me," he echoes, seemingly understanding that I'm referring to his aversion.

He pulls in a breath. "It's like, when you stare into a beam of sunlight and notice all the dust particles floating in the air, and for one brief moment, dread grips you. Because suddenly, you realize this matter is everywhere, all around, all the time. You breathe it. It fills your lungs, suffocates you." His gaze searches the misty horizon. "But then the light shifts, and you slip back into the shadow. Relieved, because you don't have to exist in that constant awareness."

He rises, turning to face me, his gaze dark, haunted. "I never escape that moment."

A sharp pain catches beneath my breastbone, a reminder of my own inescapable prison. My voice softens. "Living in that constant state of awareness must be exhausting."

Though striking, his smile is strained, defeated almost. "Some days," he says roughly. "Then on another, a sexy-as-hell therapist gets herself stranded on a shoreline boulder, and when you look into her eyes, you hear the most beautiful, melancholic song. For that brief moment, the harsh light dampens, and you can breathe."

Pressure builds behind my eyes. I blink quickly to clear the moisture, blaming the salty wind. Mercifully, Orion casts his gaze back toward the deepening skyline, and I push my hand into his jacket pocket in search of something to wipe my face—

And my fingers connect with something solid.

Turning my back to the wind, I withdraw the circular object. As soon as I see the brass device with spinning dials and plates, I instinctively know this is where the piece I found came from.

Blood roaring as loud as the wind in my ears, I dig out my phone and snap a picture before I quickly wipe the brass of any prints or residue, and drop the instrument back into his pocket.

When I face Orion again, he's scooping ocean water into his bare palm. Rising slowly, he turns my way. "Hold out your hand."

A flutter of nervous energy quickens my pulse as I edge closer, unconcerned by the water washing over my boots. "What are you doing," I ask, pushing the leather sleeve up as I extend my hand toward him.

Orion positions his hand above mine, close enough I can feel the charged heat of his skin. He tilts his palm until water spills, bridging the fragile space between us as seawater drips from his hand to mine.

A strained smile curves his mouth. "Water isn't just a substance," he says, "it's a quantum dance. Molecules vibrating, seeking connection." His eyes trap mine. "Stay still."

Carefully, he skates his fingertips just above the beaded water along my knuckles, trailing upward along the backs of my fingers, evoking a current across my nerves without ever making contact.

"It feels like you're touching me," I say, voice a little breathless.

"No distance can prevent the energy exchange between our bodies." A blaze captures me in the heated depths of his gaze. "Saline is a conductor. Charged particles allow electricity to flow between us." His voice lowers into a rasp. "Movement, heat, friction—stimulating nerves. That's all touch is really."

A frisson covers my skin, at the near touch, at the fierceness in his voice. I'm holding my breath, struck by the contrast of our hands—the size of his compared to mine. The roughness I can see and nearly feel as his long fingers ghost over my skin.

And here, saline and molecules form a bond. An anchor. That impossible connection I've been seeking to create.

As my gaze trails the beautiful ink across his hand, I desperately want to ask the meaning—but stop myself. Not because I don't want to know him that much deeper. But because if I do, it will only make what I have to do that much harder.

His fingertips hover closer, tension radiating as though daring himself to close the last sliver of distance. In this gap of charged space, every nerve hums with anticipation, yearning, drawn toward the moment our skin might collide.

My hand begins to tremble, and as the water runs dry, Orion's hand falls away. The near touch of him fading like the last embers of burnt sunlight beyond the horizon.

"I just needed to know what it's like," he admits, gravel roughing his tone. The unspoken *just once* lingers beneath the misty air, summoning a blade of pain between the costal cartilage of my ribs.

The desire to reach out and touch him becomes an unbearable ache in the center of my chest.

He brushes his thumb absently across his knuckles, and I'm once again drawn to the shadowed bruises. The wind tosses his hair, exposing the deep scar along his forehead. A stark reminder of the pain I sometimes see between his splintered cracks.

All the subtle details that make him *him*.

Achingly real. Beautiful. Dangerous.

Sometimes, it's impossible to fathom how Orion kills so ruthlessly and methodically—hunting his victims, dismantling their skulls. In tender moments like this, the man and monster blur, and I can glimpse a shade of who he once was.

His before—

And what could have existed for us in ours.

Before I took my last breath. Before he stole his first.

What Prescott said drifts back to me, threading tightly through my chest as a low rumble rolls over the water, making me question just how deep Orion's wounds cut.

He casts a glance toward the looming clouds. "We should head back."

"We should," I agree quietly. "Before we're caught in the storm."

I drop my gaze, arms folding across my waist, letting his leather jacket shelter me from the elements, suddenly feeling too fragile against the storm he stirs all around and within.

As the stars blink into the deepening night and a waning moon takes the sky, he strides away from the water's edge, fighting his glove back into place. Some part of me mourns the loss of his skin, the closeness of his almost-touch.

The law of figure-ground is what's used to separate the object from its blurred background in order to focus on what's vital.

My gaze falls down his striking figure set against a bruised sky of gray storm clouds and waning light, trying to keep him in focus amid the blurring backdrop, the sun slipping beneath the hazy offing.

There's a charge to a building storm, a breath held, pressure mounting. Waiting for the crack where the taut thread snaps.

Before I meet him at the bike, I scoop a handful of sand with the fragments of shell, letting the coarse grains sift through my fingers like escaping time. Its passage marked by the scars it leaves behind.

Time is cruel. But memory can be crueler.

And by his own science, in the only tense that matters—the now—Orion is ruled by obsession. Even as he fights that darker pull, the monster will always win.

I've witnessed that fallout.

There's no amount of time that will lessen the desire for vengeance. Revenge lives in my blood—the very blood that flows wrong, through the hardened ventricle of a bad heart.

If I lose that heart to Orion, the wound will be deep, but—

It's black and bruised and callused, anyway.

The arrhythmic beat of the broken muscle drowns out any guilt over what I'm about to do. Soon, Orion will leave Stonehurst. His research unguarded.

By the time he returns, I'll be gone.

The largest void in the known universe is the Boötes Void. 330 million light-years of near-total emptiness. The Great Nothing. A cosmic anomaly so immense, it defies logic. Where there should be galaxies by the thousands, there are but a sparse few, scattered like dying embers across a limitless dark. A cold reminder that the universe itself holds the power of erasure—that oblivion is not merely a concept, but a place, a void.

— DR. ORION NIGHT, ASTROPHYSICS
LECTURE

16

DARK SKIES

Stars, hide your fires; Let not light see my black and deep desires.

— MACBETH

ORION

If you knew the exact time of your death, how would you spend your last moments?

Would the answer change if you were given months? Weeks? Days?

Hours—?

Would you savor the time left, cherishing the light that remains, or try to defy that dark fate?

For everything beautiful in the universe, there exists a terrifying symmetry. What is luminous and breathtakingly full of wonder is mirrored by its opposite. Shadows that are desolate and horrifying, brimming with destruction and decay.

I've been riding inland for almost two hours, battered by

wind. The salty coastal air has thinned to the crisp scent of leaves and earthy soil.

If I keep riding, just keep going, could I outrun our dark fate?

I push my Triumph past a sane speed, the roar of the engine failing to drown out the storm inside my head, shadows coiling tighter to mock my defiance.

The road narrows as I take a sharp curve, winding through forests dense with amber and gold. Those hidden hues of her eyes.

The sky grows darker.

By the time I reach the clearing, the skyline is untouched by urban lights, the stars carved into a black canvas.

For the first time since I began the hunt, I accept I have no control. My arrival at the dark-sky preserve of Blue Hills is as inevitable as every annihilation. With the approach of each cosmic event, more of my willpower erodes.

I roll to a stop along a stretch of thin pines, muscles stiff as I drop my feet and cut the engine. Silence rings in my muffled ears, the isolation as stark as the unfiltered view.

Right on time, a twig snaps.

My blood rushes hot in my veins as I remove my helmet and meet his eyes. He stands frozen, shovel halted mid-dig, the blade buried in the earth.

"Who the fuck are you?" he demands, his grip on the handle bleaching his knuckles beneath the pale starlight.

I dismount my bike, boots crunching dead leaves. I don't bother with an explanation, having already tried that before. It only causes more panic, more confusion and pleading.

And it changes nothing.

Instead, I sling my pack off the bike and slip the astrolabe from the inner pocket of my leather jacket. Like muscle memory, my gloved thumb sweeps the ecliptic plate, tracing the empty space where the rule should lie like a phantom limb.

Without that one piece, I can't accurately sight the position.

I tap a thirteen-beat count against the brass, the golden sequence triggering a memory of those golden stars in her eyes, and it quiets the roar inside my skull.

I huff out a resigned breath and lift my gaze skyward, finding the hunter's belt. There's a twinge beneath my ribs, something residual left over. Sprawled broken on the asphalt, scraped raw. The wisp of a memory that slips away before I can fully grasp it, a wave of anger rising in its void.

Letting it smolder to ash, I shift my gaze. Between Castor and Pollux, the twin stars of Gemini, a comet burns faint green—a pale halo fanning across the night.

"Beautiful," I whisper, breath fogging the chilly air. "Some of the most impressive spectral emissions I've observed, but—" I push the star-taker into my pocket, eyes narrowing lethally on Cassian Bevins. "You didn't come here to gaze at a comet."

"I asked you who the fuck—"

The dart in his thigh cuts him short. His body jolts in shock, the shovel slips from his grip as he stumbles back. The dual-chamber dart first releases a small dose of sedative before the paralytic kicks in.

He collapses to the forest floor.

I drop the tranq pistol back into my pack, rolling my shoulders to further work out the stiffness. For one brief second, I catch a trace of her scent—sweet, floral, maddening—and my throat constricts at the memory of her pressed against me on the bike. Her soft breath warming my neck.

The climbing, Euclidean rhythm of her pulse as I counted every heartbeat as she fell apart above me.

I came so close to touching her. Aching to link my fingers through hers, hold on tight. Willing to endure the violent loss of control that comes from a bare touch at the boundary.

Yet the instant her skin met mine, the void would open its jaws, ravenous to consume.

And I'd be powerless to stop it.

Just as I am right now, moving toward Annihilation Twelve.

To test my resistance, I tap my gloved fingers to the lingering echo of her hypnotic tune, desperate to be lost in her blink pattern, the rising cadence of her pulse. I picture her beautiful smile, her softly escaping moans, as her notes reverberate through my mind.

Yet it's not enough to calm the vicious stirring, to dull the relentless pounding against my temples. The impending moment buzzes in my blood, vessels hot and constricting with the rush of adrenaline.

The dark waters churn and thrash.

My fingers seek the scar along my forehead as something acidic scorches my veins, the familiar pain compelling my steps forward until the roar quiets to a whisper and then—

She's gone.

I drop my pack to the ground, sparing a glance at the discarded body near the shallow hole dug for a grave.

I cock an eyebrow in amusement. "You could've at least sealed Julian in plastic. Do you know how many animals will dig your brother up out here?" I tilt my head. "I have to assume you wanted to get caught, Cassian."

The brothers are wanted in a dozen jurisdictions for serial rape. The duo stays moving, changing names, hiding in cities. Leaving just enough of a signature pattern to pick up their trail.

Starting to rouse, he can only groan in response. The neuromuscular blocker temporarily paralyzes him, locking his muscles without affecting his mind. A small but effective dose so his diaphragm still draws air. Awake, aware, but unable to move.

I release a low hum, slipping my glasses into place before I set to work. Over the next fifteen minutes, both Cassian and his twin are positioned on their backs, limbs impaled to the earth, clothes cut away, hands bound together at the center in mirror alignment to the Gemini constellation.

Symmetry.

Beautiful and terrifying.

For centuries, we've aligned stones and structures with the stars. In worship, in sought guidance. In ritual.

While geometry is the language of the universe, ritual is the control over its disorder.

Ninety-nine percent science, one percent magical thinking—a slim margin I can allow, just to quiet the neurosis. Similar to the way gloves shield against observer interference. And the ritual parallels the violence of that single catastrophic moment when control was lost, recreating the exact cosmic conditions from that night—conditions I've been compulsively chasing since my wreck beneath the Orion constellation.

I retrieve the star-taker, feeling its familiar, balanced weight. Hidden behind the antique aesthetic are quantum sensors and a quartz resonator, designed to record neural signals. And since bone interferes with signal, I need direct contact.

Touch.

Right at the boundary.

That requires boring a small hole through the skull with a cranial drill, just large enough to place the microelectrode a couple millimeters deep at the edge of the cortex, where neurons emit their last patterns before collapse.

The final echo before death.

According to the algorithm, Bevins's projected Entanglement Entropy at Death will be 75.7% resonance. Which simply means a strong, coherent echo that's clear enough to retrieve.

Fuck, I can imagine the horrified expression on Leo's face. If he were here, he'd be appalled for about five-point-two seconds before he saw the data. Then he'd crack Cassian's skull open himself to get to it.

At every moment, faint ripples from violent cosmic events are passing through the universe, through space and time.

Through us.

Unseen, unfelt—yet can be timed to rare celestial alignments. Like a comet nearing perihelion, its volatile ices erupting in a sudden, radiant outburst.

Like the one happening above us now.

These outbursts are erratic, nearly impossible to predict. Yet my algorithm pinpointed the precise instant this cometary flare would intersect gravitational waves from a distant tidal disruption event—a star torn apart by the merciless gravity of a black hole, its stellar heart shredded into a luminous ring of gas and plasma, then devoured by shadow.

A brilliant event, beautiful, and devastating.

I draw a slow breath at the drag of my pulse, my fingertips tapping out the broken cadence of hers.

As the ripples wash over us, Cassian's unique neural signature forms a shadow, a horizon.

The darker the psyche, the louder the echo at the boundary.

Later, when I feed this data into the sonic black hole, I'll try not to let the ache consume as I recall how Collins watched the vortex, how her eyes lit as I explained how trapped sound waves warp and stretch, pulling hidden notes within reach.

I scrape a hand through my hair, anxious to get back to my sub-level lab and run the signal through the quantum array. If the entanglement entropy climbs, something survived at the shadowed edge.

"All that's left is to wait," I say as I crouch next to Cassian. His eyes are open, sheened with tears he can't blink away, his chest rising with shallow breaths. I sigh and cast my gaze skyward. "Let's just watch the comet for a while."

I mean, what's the life of one homicidal, serial-raping brother worth in the quest to define one of the greatest mysteries of the universe?

What is her *life worth?*

Dark filaments choke my mind, fury blazing through my viscera at the intrusive thought. It's become its own obsession, the incessant thought of taking her life. Like standing at the edge of my observation deck, staring down at crashing waves, the thought of jumping so consuming that surrender feels inevitable.

Just to make it *stop.*

Jaw clenched, I reach for my monocular and focus on the comet's coma, a striking halo streaking through the night.

Like a falling angel.

"Fuck." I toss the scope aside. Collins may be able to string enough psych jargon together to craft a diagnosis that explains my evolution into a deviant, serial-killing psychopath. But I wonder if that will bring her any sort of comfort in her final moments, to offer some excuse.

Or if the horror of what I am will only make her despise me all the more.

In truth, I wasn't born with this deficient lack of empathy. Although I experience a rush of endorphins every time the oscillating blade slices into bone, the high is a consequence of the act, not the attraction to it.

My transformation wasn't immediate. It took time, a process. The first kill was a brutal battle with my conscience. I can still taste the bile at the back of my throat as I drilled through the skull.

The second, I gave in a bit more easily. My resistance a degree weaker. My revulsion a fraction more desensitized.

The shadow a shade darker.

By the third, I understood my morality wasn't just being eroded—it was being overwritten. Replaced by something violent, insidious.

Wrong.

These psychological voids have a pull, a force with its own gravity. At the moment of death, of conscious collapse, something passes through me. Call it awareness... consciousness... Memories. But these gravitational echoes leave a stain, a residue.

Killers. Rapists. The most vile dregs of humanity. How can I not be tainted?

Where I used to fear pain, my neuropathways worn to avoid it, a deep fault has cracked. Connections crossed, rewired. Pain brings pleasure.

And inflicting it is fucking orgasmic.

"Since we have all this time," I say, reaching into my pack. I remove my gloves before I uncap a syringe and plunge the needle into the crook of his arm. "Let's talk, Cassian."

He gasps in a cool shot of air as the stimulant hits his bloodstream. "Oh, fuck... You fucking—"

I trap his mouth with the syringe. "Don't waste the breath you've got." Slowly, I lower the barrel.

"Hell. At least...cover my dick, man."

My gaze wanders to the flaccid dick in question. His exposed skin is blotchy, covered in dirt and blood from where his arms and legs have been skewered to the earth.

"You're minutes away from death, and that's your concern."

Tears leak into his filthy hair. A sob shudders through his chest. From the collarbone down, he's immobile.

I make all my victims immobile.

The way I'll make her—

A flash of Collins pinned helplessly beneath me surfaces, and I slam my eyes shut against the intrusive assault, forcing it back into the dark, thrashing abyss.

"The thing is," I say through gritted teeth, "you might be able to help me figure something out." I rarely have the chance to question them, and I never want more of the vile details than necessary.

He swallows, Adam's apple hitching with effort. "Figure out that you're sick?"

I let the corner of my mouth turn up. "There's nothing I can do to stop what's going to happen," I tell him honestly. "You're going to die. I can't prevent that."

"Shit…" he stutters out.

"But before you do, I'm going to take that drill"—I tic my chin toward the compact cranial drill next to his head—"and open your skull."

He whimpers, and I drape my arm over my knee, counting the staggered rise and fall of his chest. I hold up a clear vial, flicking my finger against the glass to call his attention.

"You'll be awake to feel everything." I pause, waiting to feel even a small measure of remorse. I shrug. "This right here is a potent pain reliever. I can administer it before I start burring into your skull. And you might be telling yourself it will be quick. But I promise, time is relative, and pain slows time considerably. Fractions of a second can stretch out like eternity."

"Jesus, I'll pay you," he says, clipped breath fogging the air. "I have money."

I stare down at him, knowing what he sees, the void in my eyes. "I don't need money."

He manages a hard blink. "What the hell, then?"

I drag a hand over my jaw. "Answers."

I stab the needle into the vial and fill the barrel before setting the syringe aside. "Tell me the truth, Cassian. Don't lie. I want to know the exact moment you made the choice to kill your own flesh and blood, someone you loved." I swallow the raw ache. "Tell me every fucking detail."

After a minute of him uselessly groveling and slinging threats, he finally relents. There's this phenomena that happens when a person accepts their death, that the end is unavoidable. A kind of detachment from reality.

Cassian divulges his sordid history in this calm state of detachment. Devoid of emotion, he recounts his brother's murder like he's reading from a manual. Maybe he believes this confession will cleanse his soul. Pardon his heinous sins in death.

I should tell him I'm no fucking priest. In the end, I'm not surprised by how uninspired his reason was. Two brothers, partners in sick, twisted crime, stalking the same woman. One takes her for himself, the other devolves into a deplorable state of jealousy and rage.

Repulsion twists my mouth. "A woman can tempt the sanest man mad," I whisper roughly as the memory of her beside me on the bench is dredged from the depths of my mind, a vision of her eyes glimmering with early stars.

Looking up, I drag in a tight breath, reaching for the awe I once felt at seeing the Milky Way stretched across an expanse of dark sky.

"You know," I say, voice lowering, "the myth of the Gemini twins was one of sacrifice. Two brothers who loved each other so deeply that when one died, the other begged the gods, offering his own life in exchange. That's why they were placed among the heavens." My gaze traces that collection of stars. "So they'd never be separated again."

Yet here, beneath the constellation, Cassian's hand clasped to Julian's cold, lifeless grip, I find no symmetry. Only violence and ruin.

And he's answered none of my questions.

I've spent all this time gazing at her, observing her like a distant star, dreading the moment she'll go dark. For the fucking instant her light will flicker out, and she'll collapse into a void before my eyes.

A flame of fury licks through me, and I shove to my feet. "I know I'm sick," I say as I start to pace. "It's a sickness. A twisted, consuming sickness, falling for the woman you have no control over killing."

"Christ, man. You have it bad—"

"At least give me a goddamn clue," I grind out, choking back a bitter laugh, teetering on the verge of manic. "She's a star." My gaze lifts toward the night sky. "A fucking star. Brilliant and beautiful, and god, so fucking terrifying. I wasn't expecting her."

And I didn't just search her background—I scoured it. Fed every shred of data through my algorithm, trying to find a single damnable act that would mark her like this vile piece of filth at my feet.

There's nothing—nothing but the hidden fury I sometimes catch burning behind her eyes. The fragile pain she guards so fiercely, desperate not to let it crack through.

My dark anomaly.

Hit with a spicy floral fragrance, I come to an abrupt halt. My gaze lowers to the flower near my boot, finally able to name the elusive, seductive scent that clings to her skin. Dropping to my haunches, I pluck the snapdragon from the earth, bring its silky pink petals to my nose.

A groan wrenches free, muscles strained against the turmoil clawing under my sinew. It's an agitation I can't bear, the simmer before the eruption.

"I can't lose her," I mutter, voice drained as I drop down near Cassian.

"Naw, you want to kill her." A dark flicker catches behind his dead eyes. "I can see it, that same crazed look Julian got when the need became too much." Breath labored, a knowing smile struggles to tip his mouth. "Some girls, they like the fight. They want it, hiding a little darkness in them." He licks his dry lips, becoming revoltingly aroused by his own victims.

Rage kindles and snaps, a vehement denial on the cusp of my

tongue—but his words strike like a punch to my gut, provoking the memory of Collins as I held her pinned against the speaker. Her muscles gathering tight, nails raking for purchase. Her desire to fight swelling beneath her surface like a wave.

That same fierce undercurrent I've glimpsed swirling behind her captivating eyes. A dark vein of fury lit, sparked, like a sharp note rising in her tune, before the sudden crash. Banged like a D minor.

My fingers curl around the brittle stem of the flower. As if he can read my deviant thoughts, Cassian's smile stretches. "Oh yeah, you think about it all the time. Strangling her pretty throat, hearing her cries. Her warm blood flowing over your hands as you take her raw—"

Making him bloody is barely a formed thought before my fist meets the hard bone of his jaw.

"You understand nothing," I seethe, more snarl than rebuke. The pink petals crushed in my palm, I cast the flower away, cleaving a piece of my insides with it.

His chuckle is mocking, getting the reaction he wanted. His tongue collects the blood from his bottom lip. "I understand you won't be able to help yourself. The temptation will drive you mad. I lied a little—" his dark eyes gleam—"for the reason I killed my brother. He was out of control, getting sloppy. I couldn't allow that, for him to get us caught. I need to do what I do, man. There's no other feeling like it. Nothing else compares. That's how I know you'll give in, no matter how hard you fight it." A glint of smug satisfaction lights his gaze. "And you'll savor it."

My nostrils flare, a flood of wrath ripping through my bloodstream. I flex my fingers, welcoming the painful throb. Red smears my bare knuckles. Bruises still shadow my skin from when I had to all but demolish the speaker to stop from losing control—from violently taking her.

"But hey, listen. I can help you." He says this like we're conspirators, pals. Like he's bestowing the secret of his trade. "I can teach you how to be careful, to control it. Even how to make peace with it."

Beneath the roar of bloodlust, Cassian's muttered words taper off. I can no longer hear his scratchy voice past the rising torrent in my head, a tidal surge that drowns out everything but the snapping sinew and bone. A shadow edges into my vision, deepening until the deafening, empty chaos of the void pulses black.

"Because I know"—he won't shut up—"how good it's going to feel—"

"Enough." My tone is a lethal command. The wet feel of his blood on my skin—sinking into me, infecting—rattles with a deranged anger through my bones. Rage clutches my throat, igniting the vicious need to draw more.

As a tremble of fear breaks across his sweaty face, dark amusement curls my mouth. "Fuck, I didn't realize you were so damn insightful, Cassian."

I bring out the astrolabe. My bare thumb traces the grooved plate, the missing rule strumming a panged chord against my ribs. The compulsion to check my astronomical watch grips me, but I can feel the approach in my marrow. I'm fine-tuned.

"It's time," I say, voice hollow.

Neck tendons strained, I reach for the drill, bypassing the syringe.

"Wait—" Cassian's eyes track me, wide, frantic. "Hey— fucking wait. You said you'd give me the stuff for pain."

Relinquishing a tense breath, I clutch the handle and depress the button. The whine of the spinning bit starts his protests all over again.

"You lied," he shouts, breath ragged. "You fucking lied."

"Did I." Casually, I set the tool on the steel case and grab the syringe, moving to hover over the corpse. I lift Julian's limp wrist and stick the needle into his arm. "I didn't say who I'd administer it to." I tap his brother's cold cheek. "Guess that makes us both liars."

I don't usually take sadistic pleasure in the ritual. But right now, there's an insidious impulse gnawing inside me—a visceral need to punish, to inflict immeasurable pain to somehow offset this gaping ache ripping a hole through my goddamn chest.

Staring down into Cassian's glassy eyes, his blown pupils reflecting the faint glow of stars, I let the empty syringe fall to the earth. Wondering, when the time comes, if I'll be coherent enough to ease her pain. Whether she'll suffer less at my hands than the universe's.

My only solace is that, after tonight, maybe I'll finally be too far gone to care. Sunk beyond even the reach of her haunting notes.

And you'll savor it.

The echo of his words summons something despairing from my depths—something dense and final that settles in the core of my chest. Molars gnashed, I fist my hand, dry blood cracking against skin, and whatever lies at the shadowed boundary of me thirsts for more.

The tide will keep rising before it recedes.

I take hold of the bone saw.

Time fractures, a lost interlude filled with the whir of steel screaming against bone. The sound is a shrill discord crashing off boulders and pines, drowning the last of his cries. Bone dust chokes the air. Blood spatters my skin.

Before long, I'm bathed in it.

Like a melody pulled into a riptide, eternally echoing deep under the surface where no one can hear.

It's her refrain, caught on an endless loop beneath pounding dark waves, that reaches me below the abyss. Where it will become both my refuge and my torment.

For what I'm bound to do, I hope it destroys me in the end.

I don't resurface tonight. As silence rings in my ears, I stand frozen, gaze cast on the endless dark sky. My drill lies untouched, forgotten. The astrolabe abandoned.

The echoes lost.

Above, the comet suddenly brightens. A teal halo flares in a luminous outburst between the Gemini twins, crossing the path of gravitational waves from an ancient, violent event.

When a star dies, its core collapses under its own gravity. Once it burns through its nuclear fuel, the heart becomes so heavy, so dense, it's crushed, unleashing a stellar explosion.

The more beautiful and radiant the star, the darker its annihilation.

In its final beats, a star's life is beautiful, brilliant. Immensely powerful. It's also destructive, violently imploding as its energy is cut short before it darkens into a black hole.

A cataclysm beautiful in its devastation.

Light swallowed by shadow.

I know the exact month, the day, hour, minute—the goddamn second her heart will stop beating.

And I know there is nothing I can do to stop it.

Her light will burn out.

And so of larger—Darknesses—
Those Evenings of the Brain—
When not a Moon disclose a sign—
Or Star—come out—within—

— EMILY DICKINSON, *WE GROW
ACCUSTOMED TO THE DARK*

17

DARK ADAPTATION

The eyes may be confused in two ways—by a change from light to darkness or from darkness to light; and the same thing happens to the soul.

— PLATO

COLLINS

Each steady blink of the cursor mocks my faltering pulse. A distressing hitch catches beneath my rib cage, and I press my palm hard to my chest as the realization crashes into me, dread sinking further with each flashing line of code. So cloying, so deep, it seeps past the callused leaflets and hardened muscle.

Years spent inside ViCAP, training on one of the most elite database systems, and yet, this was too easy. I shouldn't have been able to crack Orion's security protocols this quickly.

Once I realized the server was air-gapped, I should've backed out of the system and erased my tracks. Waited for him to return and try another tactic. My male apparently has a whole other habitat, and I've spent precious months gaining access to the wrong one.

A setback—but there's another way in.

That's not what chokes my heart with dread, however. To anyone else, the data flickering on the backlit screen might look like an intricate star chart. The lines of right ascension, the degrees of declination. The celestial coordinates measured down to the hour, minute, second—

I recognize the pattern.

And I've made a grave error.

"Shit," I whisper harshly.

With numb fingers, I grab my phone and bring up the image of the brass instrument. I didn't fully comprehend what the device was at the time. But now, staring at the highlighted node on the screen, comparing it to the star chart, and then the dialed coordinates on the astrolabe in the image—

I drop my phone to the desk surface, spearing shaky fingers into my hair before I plunge deeper in search of the dark-sky data.

Before I even set foot inside Stonehurst, I knew my hunter was different. I knew once he found what he was searching for, I would lose him. He's unlike other predators of his kind.

He has an expiration date.

And his pattern all came down to where he'd strike next.

Shorehaven. Gemini. Solar eclipse.

I zoom in on the data—and my heart stutters.

Blue Hills Preserve. Gemini. Comet outburst & Tidal disruption event (TDE).

"No," I whisper. Panic drives me to my feet, and a surge of dizziness slams into me. I grip the edge of the desk to steady myself.

Twelve.

Twelve constellations. Twelve celestial events. The final one *had* to be the eclipse.

I fumble for my phone and pause, thumbs hovering over the display—*one, two, three.*

"Goddammit, why don't you have a phone, Orion."

My breathing shallows, chest constricting under the pressure. I reach into my pocket for my silver case, and it slips from my fingers. Pills scatter across the floor.

"Dammit."

Fury lights up my body as I drop to my knees and pluck a pill from the floor, forcing it down.

There's still time.

I tell myself this, even as my heart fails to find a stable rhythm. I tell myself this, even as my gaze is drawn to the brass orrery above, the bladed arcs slicing through an orbital countdown.

As I gather the pills, stuffing them and the case into my pocket, my fingers brush the slender piece of brass buried there.

I found him once.

Perched on my knees, I draw in an aching breath and open a browser window on my phone. I search up the address to the dark-sky preserve. *An hour and a half away.* With a tight swallow, I lift my gaze to the darkened sky beyond the windows.

A fusion of rage and despair tangles in my chest until, in a burst of anger, I hurl my phone at the orrery. It ricochets, disappearing somewhere over the platform. Fire licks the walls of my throat as I bite back a scream.

Get the fuck up.

On shaky legs, I shove the telescope ladder toward the wall and hurriedly climb onto the catwalk. After I recover my cracked phone, I pull in a ragged breath and fling the balcony door open, letting a hit of cool night air fill my stinging lungs.

Just a moment—I just need a moment.

One. Two. Three. Breathe.

I exhale a long, foggy breath as I take in the stretch of starry sky. From up here, it is beautiful. Vast. Endless. I can see why Orion spends time here, gazing out over the ocean and sky, like viewing a clean slate.

I brush my thumb over my wrist, counting each faint beat as I let my gaze pick out the three stars along the hunter's belt, knowing Orion has stood right here. His hands braced to this iron, connecting us by time and space.

When I warned Orion he was a danger to himself, it wasn't exactly a manipulation. Despite ultimately going against my own objective, my evaluation was an honest one.

Orion's psychological profile is complex, layered with obsessive methodology. Regardless of the number of offenders I've studied, he defies classification. Driven by grandiose delusions of purpose, he maps death like a symbolic ritual, aligned with cosmic symmetry.

He isn't merely a serial murderer—he's an existential killer.

Hunting his victims right along with his own annihilation.

Gemini, the constellation of twins, technically counts as more than one victim. The person he's chosen—

And Orion himself.

Born May 21st, his sun sign straddles the cusp, aligning with Gemini. Once he completes his ritual, he'll end the cycle suicide by proxy.

I understood this as I first walked the shadowed corridors of this institute, feeling the chilling presence grip my soul like the Grim Reaper.

And I had a plan.

Fingers curled around the railing, I let a bitter laugh slip free. Did I honestly believe it would be that simple? Get the information I needed. Send Darby the evidence and have him intercept Orion before his next kill. Then just vanish.

In death, she will have her revenge.

Revenge won't change the past.

For the first time since I stood on that beach and knew I could find him, uncertainty churns in my chest. Each ticking second frays another thread of my resolve, raging a war within as I desperately cling to that revenge. Without this purpose, Collins doesn't even exist.

I can't lose Orion.

I clutch the rail until the rough edge bites into my palms. Desperation flares hot in the pit of my stomach, and with it comes the brutal strike—the phantom sensation of cold steel. The scent of damp earth. The screech of insects. Forest trees overtake the salty air, the roar of the ocean overwhelmed by my roaring blood.

Gasping, I lift my gaze once more to the constellation. Orion, cast into the abyss of night, defiantly burning amid the endless dark.

"I can find you," I whisper, pleading there's enough time to intervene.

Swallowing hard, I light my cracked phone screen, preparing to make the call to Darby—

And my gaze catches shadowed movement past the hazy cliffside.

Waves crash against the rocks below. The tide pushes against the dark shore. And there, bathed in the silvery moonlight, his familiar silhouette stands stark against the night.

A strangled sound escapes my throat. Relief seeps into me like the mist, slowly filling me with a mix of relief and dread.

My breath trembles. "Orion…"

Then I'm moving, my heart barely managing to keep up. My pulse suspends, not wanting to waste a beat. I escape the dome, time hanging motionless and speeding as I search the quickest path to him.

Standing torn at the edge of the cliff, I waver between the pier in the distance, and the steep descent down the rocky slope.

Pressing my palm to the aching hollow beneath my left breast, I feel the frantic kick of my heart.

"Fuck it."

I kick off my ankle boots and slip over the edge, toes feeling for purchase along the narrow stone shelves. Rough rock scrapes against my bare feet, fingers digging into toothed edges as I cling to the jagged wall, lowering myself inch by inch toward the shore.

Icy water seeps up through the hard sand, mercifully numbing the raw soles of my feet as I weave an unsteady path between slate sea stacks. Arms tucked around myself, I brace my trembling body against the whipping wind, coming to a sudden stop.

Orion stands off to my right, as motionless as the stones surrounding him, his gaze cast out over the gray, rolling waves.

For a brief second, I let a tendril of relief curl through me. "Orion," I call his name, my teeth chattering. He doesn't respond.

Something in the way he's just standing there tightens a band of apprehension around my chest. My gaze drops to his boots sunk into the wet sand, the foamy tide washing over them before retreating.

I tilt my head back, anxiety pouring through my veins as I gauge the nearly half-lit moon hung in the black sky.

Muttering a curse beneath my breath, I lift the hem of my skirt and creep closer. "Orion, what does a half-moon mean for the tide—"

My voice dies as I come around to face him, breath seizing at the devastating sight before me.

Dark red streaks his skin, spattered in brutality across his face. His gray thermal is stained and torn, hair caked in gore. Bathed in blood and violence, the light has vanished from his eyes, those blue-green waters churning with turmoil. Something fierce and cold stirs beneath their surface, as wild and desolate as an ocean abyss.

"Orion." His name escapes on an unsteady whisper. A question, a plea—a helpless echo of the horror crashing through me.

I draw another hesitant step closer. Beneath the salt and mist and his own heady scent, I taste the sharp note of iron. In this slant of moonlight, with the ocean spray misting his skin, the crystallized blood glints along his jaw and throat as though he's been anointed by the violence of the stars themselves.

Beautiful, and devastating.

Whatever happened tonight, however he got himself here in this state—this isn't the calculated Reaper standing before me now. This is something untamed, primal. Merciless.

The hunter.

I'm terrified. But not of the blood, or even of him. It's the vacantness of his eyes, the empty dissociation shadowing their depths.

The fear that he's lost.

The tide rushes in, and with it all my fear, flooding every hollow crevice of this rocky basin and fissure within me.

I can't lose Orion—

I *need* him.

The frigid water soaking my skirt hem, I rise onto my toes, trying to make eye contact. "Orion... Orion, come back to me." My voice breaks. "I need you to come back to me."

Desperation lifts my hand toward his face, trembling fingers hovering close. When he doesn't react, I curl my fingers into my palm, nails biting until it hurts. "Dammit."

Blood flecks his cheekbones. There's a thin smear at the corner of his mouth. For Orion, this level of contamination would do more than simply trigger him; it would send him into a full-blown spiral.

His scenes are contained. They're ritualistic artistry. Never this chaotic, displaying this level of dysregulation, this absolute loss of control. So utterly…broken.

As foamy water rushes around my ankles, I follow the path of carnage to his hand. Stained with dried blood, he clenches the brass astrolabe, his grip fierce.

The sight of it stirs the memory of another fraught moment as we stood before the ocean, drenched in fading light and breathless anticipation. When the space between our skin was charged with a silent dare, challenging Orion to defy his aversion and touch me in the only way he could.

Slowly, I lower my hand into the cold tide and scoop water into my palm. I grasp his sleeve, carefully guiding his hand not fisted around the instrument between us. A second of hesitation, then I let the water trickle onto his skin.

The salt water and blood run together across the back of his hand, the soft moonlight revealing the dark ink hidden beneath. I lift my gaze to his, watching him closely as I daringly hover the tips of my fingers just above.

Clear beads glide over his bloodstained skin, dissolving the crystalized blood like stars fading from the night.

Breath held, I try not to move, recreating the moment he touched me through the same conductive friction of saline and subtle pressure, forming an anchor. Connecting us.

For an eternal heartbeat, there's no response. Then gradually, his pupils dilate, a low flame lit in the depths of his eyes. His gaze finds our hands. My retreating fingers. And then, me.

Recognition flickers, breaking through the vacant haze. The flame blazes, sparking a filament of warmth amid the cold darkness. His breath shudders out, a fractured sound. "Collins."

A weight settles within my chest. The rough caress of his voice abrades more than the air between us, the familiar sound resonating past the callus around my heart, turning it porous.

"I'm here, Orion," I say gently. "I'm right here."

I lick the salt from my lips, and his gaze hones, following the path of my tongue and rousing a fire beneath my flesh no frigid wind or freezing water could extinguish.

"You are, starling," he says, a trace of reverence bleeding into his rough tone of voice.

The cadence of the endearment moves in time with my pulse, strumming weak heartstrings, awakening dormant chords buried too deep.

A wave crashes against my legs, sending me off balance. I instinctively reach out and grasp Orion's shirt, curling my fingers into the bloody fabric. I turn my hand over. Blood tinges my fingers. I rub the tips together, feeling the gritty texture, and an unsettling guilt thickens my throat.

"The tide's getting higher," I say, unable to mask the tremor rolling through me as the water clings heavy to the hem of my skirt. "We can't stay here."

My gaze darts anxiously toward the university before I look up at him, the blood streaked across his face, soaked into his clothes. Indecision battles inside me, knowing I can't risk anyone seeing him like this.

"Come on," I urge him, giving his thermal a tug. "You have to rinse off in the ocean." Fighting my fear, I take a backward step, drawing him with me as the cold slices through my bones. "God, it's freezing."

Icy waves lap against my calves, and my body stiffens, halted by cold and fear. Desperate, I drag my skirt up, trying to tear at the wet material, needing something—anything—to wipe him clean as a wave crashes into me, nearly knocking me over.

"Fuck," I gasp out, frustration clawing at my chest. I smack at the water, panic stinging hot behind my eyes. "Shit, Orion. It's fucking cold."

He looks down, his movements oddly calm as he slips the

instrument into his pocket. "You get used to it," he says, voice distant beneath the roar.

A weary smile touches the corner of his mouth before he leans into the oncoming wave and lifts me into his arms. My body curls against his, feeling the cautious tension in his hold, aware of my hand placement.

As he begins to wade us deeper, panic seizes me. "Wait—no." I glance around, out over the gray, tossing waves. "We can't see anything. Please, Orion, it's too dark—"

"It always is at first," he cuts in, "but we adapt."

He's speaking to something beyond the dark, icy waters. Beyond even the blood staining us both.

"We adapt to the dark," I question, searching his unreadable eyes.

"It's a process," he murmurs, shifting me higher against his chest.

Out in the ocean, enclosed by this utter darkness, fear should be tearing me apart. But something happens when his arms embrace me, caging my body against his, just as he did amid the music in his observatory. My pulse steadies, modeling its rhythm to the strong, even beat of his heart beneath my palm.

"Our eyes naturally seek the light," he continues quietly, securing me tighter. "Even indirect, there's light to be found in the deepest shadow. Dark adaptation is the gradual shift, the slow recalibration of our senses, until what once seemed too dark, too unknown, no longer frightens us. It becomes familiar."

As the water rises around his hips, he holds me safely above the surface, our bodies intimately close within the danger. Freeing one of his hands, he wipes his face, smearing the blood along his jaw.

"That helps to know, Dr. Night."

The subtle lift at the corner of his mouth tugs at my heart.

And it's here, deep in the night, that we're able to

acknowledge darker truths we'd never dare own in the brightness of day. Not when the sunlight reveals the scars and flaws too starkly, exposing what we aren't ready to confront.

Beneath starlight, immersed in the cold shadows, we can rationalize almost anything.

The blood. The torn clothes. The death undoubtedly caused by his hands. The secrets we both harbor, hidden below layers of denial and deception.

Feeling the soft contours of my body give effortlessly against the hard lines of his, all I can do is cling tighter to his steady strength, his warmth, where I should feel anything but comfort. Yet Orion embodies it all—the night, the darkness, the calm refuge.

"Don't worry," he says, his voice rising above the crashing waves. "I won't lose you to the dark waters. Not tonight."

"I'm not afraid," I tell him, my hand held to his chest.

The ocean reaches around us higher, rocking us gently in the current. After a moment, I no longer feel the burn of frigid water. I watch as he lifts his hand once more, clearing another trail of blood from his face.

"Orion, what happened tonight," I dare to ask.

The tendons along his throat work, silent conflict banked behind those eyes of dark teal waters as they meet mine. "I hurt someone," he confesses.

I hold his gaze, unrelenting. "Is it possible they deserved it."

Because I know, if they were chosen by Orion, they committed a far worse offense. Some monsters can only be hunted by darker ones.

A muscle tenses along his jaw as something reverent and pained passes over his expression. "You are such a beautiful anomaly."

And I'm suddenly weightless, lost within the starry ocean of his gaze instead of the dark waters.

As my eyes fully adapt to the night, pale moonlight glimmers across the waves, and the endless stretch of ocean becomes serene, beautiful even in its terror. The sea is cast in silver and deep teal, a reflection of his eyes, turbulent and clouded by a storm.

I become brave and shift in his arms, lifting myself slightly to wrap my legs around his hips. Orion helps me, bracing his forearms around the lower curve of my back to anchor me against him.

I drag the hem of my skirt up and, carefully, gently, wipe the remnants of blood from his neck, his jaw, his cheek. He remains utterly still amid the rolling waves, his gaze unwavering, trusting. With cautious pressure, I brush his lips, breath stalling as I draw the fabric across the smear of red, erasing the evidence of violence.

He moves a fraction closer, head tilting, gaze falling to my mouth—and the hunger to close the final space between us becomes a painful ache. But I pull back, not wanting to push him further, even as his eyes beg for relief from this agonizing, tortuous distance.

Releasing a slow breath, he eases a hand between us, settling just below the hollow of my clavicle, and I stop breathing entirely. Hands of a killer, tense with the sexual violence he craves, capable of the brutality and destruction and, undeniably now, the carnage he delivered tonight—those same hands rest tender on me, holding me as if I might shatter under the weight of his touch.

That's why, in the same way Orion restrains himself, refusing to cross that boundary, fearing he'll hurt me…I can't hurt him. Not when he's this vulnerable. Even here, wading the cold shallows beneath the stars rather than the muck, I have to tread lightly, careful not to shatter his mind.

His gaze skims my features, droplets of water running down

his. "Are you still cold," he asks, his breath a warm brush across my lips, making me shiver.

I drag in a trembling breath, scared to breathe too deeply, for him to feel what's barely hidden beneath the sheer material. I shake my head. "No," I say, "but we should probably go in."

He licks his lips, tasting the salt water, making me irrationally envious over the water that gets to taste him back.

His hand slips away, leaving my chest cold from the loss of his warmth. Delicately, he touches a wet lock of my hair, guiding it behind my ear in a way that avoids touching me, but it's the closest he's come without his gloves, and a murmur echoes through my chest.

If Orion is broken, his cracks reveal something startlingly beautiful beneath—and I bear some of the blame for those cracks. I helped carve them deeper. I watched the fault lines widen.

But if his ritual is really complete, then maybe there's a chance I can help him while still getting what I came here for.

I still have some time.

Taking the risk, I ask, "Orion, what happened tonight…" I hesitate, and a furrow forms between his brows. "Will it happen again?"

He inhales deeply, his chest expanding against me. "No," he answers simply.

A tremble of relief washes through me, and I relinquish the aching breath from my lungs. Just one word. But it's enough.

The hunter is done.

To ensure this, I have to see the dark-sky preserve. I need to assess the carnage myself. I don't know exactly what spiraled him tonight, but in his current state, I can only imagine the mayhem of the crime scene. The potential trace evidence left on the victim— far too close to Shorehaven.

Protecting Orion protects me, us.

The artist should never impose their will on the stone.

And yet, since the start, I've been doing just that. Something Darby warned me against so many months ago. And maybe it's time to stop. Maybe the firefly doesn't need to lure and trap. Maybe she can be selective of her counterpart, finding that one rare male she can trust. Finding another way into his habitat by forming a real bond, a connection, attracted by a mutual desire. To work together. And maybe, for me, this was always my way in.

Because maybe—we're not two different species at all.

"Take me in, Orion," I whisper across his lips, voice soft, imploring his protective instinct. "Take me in and make me warm."

With a shaky exhale, he nods once, his arms banding possessively tighter as he begins to wade us back toward shore. "The sun will be rising soon."

I cast one last glance over the water, a solemn ache blooming in my chest at how something so terrifying in the dark can be made beautiful by the simple act of illumination. If dark adaptation is the incremental descent into darkness, then perhaps it's what we allow, what we accept. Until eventually, inevitably, we no longer fear the dark.

We become part of it.

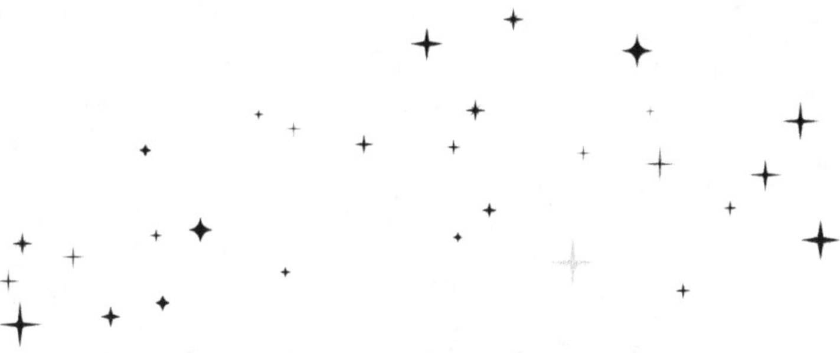

yours is the light by which my spirit's born:
yours is the darkness of my soul's return
you are my sun, my moon, and all my stars.

— E.E. CUMMINGS

18

MEMENTO MORI

Any moment might be our last. Everything is more beautiful because we're doomed.

— HOMER

ORION

I know exactly how they will die.

I know when, where, and how death will claim them.

A heart attack. A sudden stroke. A fatal embolism. Timed down to the very second their life expires.

There's never anything I can do to prevent it. It's unavoidable, predetermined—a truth that flies arrogantly in the face of beliefs and modern medicine.

A model that narrows chaos to a second, marking the date and time of death. Based on physiology, habits, scraped data—all collapsed to a single point.

My first victim suffered an aneurysm. Well, almost my first. There were three I tried to prevent before the void started eating away, numbing my morality. Making each subsequent attempt a little easier, less conflicted.

Just like Cassian Bevins, whose malignant tumor was a ticking bomb, silently counting down to a fatal hemorrhage. Had I not splashed his brain matter all over the clearing, then twenty-two seconds after I opened his cranium to harvest the echoes, the mass would've ruptured.

The ruthless tide crashes against the dark shores of my thoughts, the compulsion to check my astronomical watch churning higher until I push back my cuff. Soon, the moon's umbral shadow will move across Shorehaven, plunging us into a totality of darkness.

At the heart of the most brilliant star lies the deepest shadow. It calls to the hunter. Once the sun goes dark—

So will I.

"Every time I pass this painting, I get chills."

The soft current of her voice draws me around, the melodic cadence of her tune flowing over my skin to conjure my own electric, full-body shiver in response.

Collins stands to my left, arms folded across her chest, an umbrella anchored to her wrist, her attention fixed on the painting mounted near the arched entrance of the library.

I let my hungry gaze fall down her body, lingering on the suggestive slit in her tight skirt. Three days deprived of her presence, and I'm starved for the sight of her.

Suppressing a low groan, I drag a gloved hand over my mouth. "Why is that," I ask her.

She offers a slight shrug, her gaze never straying from Cézanne's *Pyramid of Skulls*. "It's just rather creepy."

A smile twitches at my lips. *"Hmm."* Amused, I adjust my glasses, openly, shamelessly, drinking her in. She's wearing her hair down in loose waves, the same way as the other night, and I'm suddenly reminded of the friction of her near-touch.

The faint creak of leather betrays my restraint as my hand clenches into a fist, resisting the urge to grip those silky dark waves.

While doctor-patient confidentiality ensures your therapist keeps even your darkest secrets, finding their patient in such a state—covered in blood, completely detached—would've easily negated the clause, justifying a signature on her form for involuntary commitment.

It's possible Collins saw it as an opportunity to observe me, as I was quite literally dropped into the deep end of exposure therapy. My little therapist does have a twisted curious side.

And yet, as I held her close in the rolling waves, dying a little at the desire to kiss her breathless, her melancholic song preventing me from going fully under, I saw the ripple of fear in her. The trepidation that, whatever I'd done in those lost hours of the night, she'd have to shoulder the guilt.

For that, it was necessary to feed her the lie. Ultimately, it was easier for her to believe that my compulsive, risk-seeking behavior landed me in a bar fight. Covered in another man's blood, my contamination OCD triggered a spiraling, dissociative blackout.

She didn't even question if I left the person breathing. *"Aren't you going to ask about the blood,"* I said to her as I wrapped her in a blanket after escaping the beach.

"Was there anything that would've changed the outcome?" My silence was answer enough. *"Then it was out of your control."*

The dark light that shone in her eyes then as she gazed up at me is here between us now, the fury I sometimes see ablaze there.

Secluded in the dim corridor, the rain steadily pelting the stained-glass windows, I cross toward her, lured by the heat of that fire and the arousing tease of her skin. "It's meant to evoke feelings of discomfort," I say, referring to the art. "It's *memento mori*. Latin for: remember, you must die."

She turns my way, hitting me with those expressive eyes. "You find it necessary to confront such morbid, existential thoughts today?" She arches a fine eyebrow. "Should I be concerned about your speech?"

A crooked smile tips my mouth. Unable to keep my hands off her any longer, I reach out and tug the cuff of her blazer, drawing her closer. I ghost my thumb across the pattern of stars along her delicate wrist, inciting a shiver.

What's necessary was staying away until now, even when it became a special brand of torture. With every passing second, the craving for her increased, the desperate need to seal my hands around her waking me in the night, becoming more beast than man as I fought the vicious demand lashing at my bones.

"Not today." I force myself to release her. "Awareness of our ephemeral condition keeps us modest. This particular piece always grounds me. Figured I needed the reminder." I shift my gaze to the oil painting, tracing the calculated play of light, the way the shadows emphasize the reliefs and cavities of the skulls. "Really, it's a deception. Death being a non-event makes it no less real. An event defined only by the absence of life. Like a horizon we can't see or touch, yet we know the boundary is there by what's lost."

Collins studies my profile, a slight divot creasing between her brows. "Does this mean you have something prepared for the investors on your research?" she asks, doing her best to keep me grounded herself, but I catch the hard swallow slip along her throat.

I lower my mouth close to her ear. "The fragrance you wear smells like snapdragons." I inhale a punishing lungful of her seductive scent. "Did you know that when the petals die, they look like skulls?" I straighten, casting a purposeful glance at the painting. "I'm simply saying, if we can't escape the reminder that's everywhere, at all times, we might as well embrace it."

I haven't been able to escape her—not once—since she crashed into my orbit.

Her mouth parts, her concerned eyes searching my face before dropping to the trace of ink escaping the collar of my unbuttoned oxford. "Is that why you've inked those words on yourself?" she asks. "Your way of embracing what you feel is out of your control?"

"Clever starling." A wry smile slants my lips. "I'll show you mine, if you show me yours." I make a move to touch the top button of her blouse, and she pulls away.

"Orion, please," she whispers, "talk to me."

My jaw tightens, teeth grinding under the restraint. Another reason I had to stay away; I have absolutely no control over the dark tide of urges surging inside me. The vicious swell grows stronger as the hour looms closer. Her nearness might quiet the distortion, but right now, this close, it also provokes these wicked impulses.

"God, it's fucking maddening," I mutter under my breath, and she eases another inch closer, a fearful desperation filling her eyes.

Maybe she's worried about who she brought back on that shore. Whether she should have simply let me devolve into dissociative oblivion.

She raises a hand toward me. "Orion—"

"Ah, *memento mori*," Leo interrupts, emerging from around the corner. Collins quickly withdraws. "In pursuit of our greatness, we must remain humble. Nothing is as sobering to the ego as our mortality. Right, Rye?"

Frustration singes my muscles as I face him. "It definitely kills a mood."

He recoils slightly from the affront, though nothing can

dampen his mood completely. Clearing his throat, he says, "Well, I hope the weather clears soon." He casts a nervous glance toward the arched windows just as a rumble of thunder sounds. "The rain will not make for ideal viewing conditions."

As forecasted, a storm has washed ashore, dragging a torrent of chaos into Shorehaven. Battering winds and heavy rain have forced residents—along with the thousands who've flocked here to observe the solar eclipse—to seek shelter indoors.

Collins lifts her chin, hand now gripped around the handle of her umbrella. "Do you think we'll have clear skies by noon, Dr. Night?"

I remove my glasses, sliding them into the breast pocket of my suit jacket. "Unfortunately."

A frown darkens her pretty features, the tension practically tangible.

Leo glances between us, then pins me with a look. "I just wanted to confirm that your speech kicks off at eleven-fifteen." He makes a production of checking his wristwatch. "Just a half hour from now—"

"I'll be there," I assure him, my response curt as an anxious coil winds around my spine.

He nods once, taking the hint. "Right. I have to say, I've been impressed this past month, Rye. I know the donors are looking forward to your update as much as I am," he adds, layering a subtle threat there.

"I have no doubt the symposium will impress everyone, Dr. Banner," Collins says, dispersing some of the tense atmosphere with a sweet smile. "Which, I should probably get ready for myself."

Yet, even as Leo steps away, Collins remains, wary eyes narrowed on me and brimming with the same fearful uncertainty I witnessed amid the rocking ocean waves.

She senses some danger, and for a fractured heartbeat, part of me wants to confirm her fear—to show her the fiend and send her fleeing.

But another part of me wants her more.

"I have something to show you first." I slip my hand into hers, threading our fingers together to prevent her escape.

She sends me a sideways glance, unease etched in her drawn features. "Do you really, or are you just trying to get me alone, Dr. Night."

The dark filaments stir, a devious lash against my fraying control. "If I admit to the latter, will you run?" I tighten my hold on her, her umbrella swaying between us.

She makes an amused, breathy sound that strokes my skin, dangerously arousing. "Unlikely." The slow sweep of her tongue across her lips is torturous. "But only if you tell me why Banner calls you Rye."

I suppress a smirk as I guide her down the shadowy corridor, the sound of the storm enveloping us. "I chose Orion for myself," I tell her honestly, seeing no reason to keep secrets at this point. "After the accident, I wanted a new start."

As we approach the observatory, my thumb settles over her inner wrist, brushing the stars inked there. I tap a soft rhythm against her pulse, each measured beat of my obsessive count syncing to the accelerating tempo of her heartbeat. My cadence, attuned to her melody.

Pausing just inside the entrance, I turn her way. "My legal name was Ryan before I changed it, but old habits die hard with Leo. He still uses his nickname for me."

A spark of realization ignites within her eyes, a single glimmer of gold captured like a lone star. She blinks twice, breaking the spell, and then a beautiful smile unfurls across her lips.

I tilt my head. "What is it?"

She shakes hers gently. "Nothing." Her free hand settles on

my bicep, her warmth bleeding through the fabric of my sleeve. "Somehow, I just expected something more complicated. But I like this more."

Control strained beyond its threshold, I pull her inside the facility.

Once I have her trapped in the dome, rain battering the sealed shutter overhead, the darkly lit interior bathing her in the softest glow, the last of my resistance snaps. And in the seconds it takes to strip her of her jacket, I have her backed against the telescope pier, my gloved fingers speared into her hair.

I swipe my gloved thumb across her nude lips, hunger stirring the frenzied energy in my veins. I tilt her face up toward mine, a low growl emanating from deep in my throat.

"Every time I have you close, I can't help but count the beats of your heart." I edge another fraction closer, my free hand drawing her skirt higher as my knee presses her thighs apart. "Like how right now, your pulse is speeding past one-thirty, the beat climbing until your heart skips."

Collins swallows, the broken cadence of her heartbeat accelerating wildly against my palm in defiance. She licks her lips slowly, seductively, a daring taunt. "Are you going to kiss me, Orion."

My nostrils flare, the ravenous hollow inside waking. It takes all my fucking willpower not to collar her throat and seal my lips over hers, let gravity have its way.

When gazing into a nebula, you find these dark lanes—dense bands of cosmic, light-blocking dust, creating dark paths within the luminous cloud. Staring into the depths of her eyes, those shimmering blue-green hues that reflect dust and starlight, I find those dark lanes there. Veils of shadow that obscure her light.

I graze the leather along the delicate skin beneath her eye, across the faint scatter of freckles. My voice lowers into an unyielding demand. "Remove your contacts, Collins."

Her breath catches audibly, an involuntary sound that sends another surge of heat through my blood. For a brief moment, uncertainty and fear tangle within her. Then she reaches up, breaking my hold.

Her fingertips slip between her lashes, carefully removing one lens, then the other. She blinks to clear her vision, and when her unfiltered gaze connects with mine, it steals the air right from my lungs.

"There," she says, rolling the lenses between her fingers before discarding them to the floor. "Does that satisfy your curiosity, Dr. Night?"

She blinks again—once, twice—long lashes fluttering in a mesmerizing pattern to pull me deeper. I'm lost to the slate-gray depths, flecked with gold like the sky between dusk and twilight. In the liminal space around her pupil, a vein of shadow is spun through the molten light like a coronal flare.

A ragged breath escapes my aching lungs. "Very," I say, my voice a gruff rasp as I capture her face, possessively tipping her head back as my lips defy the remaining span of air daring to keep us apart.

"Did I say you were beautiful," I murmur, my body all but fused to hers. "I meant you devastate me, Collins."

I study her like a fine work of art. The interplay of frail light and shadow washing her skin, captivated by the delicate contours, the intricate reliefs of her beauty. Nothing on this planet nor beyond has ever captivated me more.

"Were you happy these past months, even for a moment?" I ask her.

Those fleeting moments before the end—fuck, they're beautiful. Every second spent with her has been breathtaking. I can only hope she's felt even a fraction of what I have. That for her, it's been enough.

She smiles, nodding slightly. "Yes, of course. I've been happy, Orion."

I swallow down the aching chord that threatens to choke me. "Good."

I know intimately the sounds she makes when she breaks with pleasure. The way her thighs tremble, the slow, erotic tilt of her hips, the degree her spine arches in surrender. I know the exact amount of tension to place at her throat to bring her to the brink, and how fragile she feels when she shatters in my arms. I know how seamlessly her body molds to mine when we lie on the floor beneath artificial stars, the breathy awe in her voice as she gazes on them. I know the fury and sorrow she holds at bay. The quiet desperation in the curl of her fingers when she begins to lose the fight against both.

I've memorized every moment, all of them, great and small. Every stolen second, every shared breath, every radiant smile, every wince of pain, every devastating frown—

every every every

—and I can't be without them.

Without *her*.

Those lustrous eyes gaze up at me in anticipation, her lips parting, making my chest cave under the unbearable, torturous need for her. A rough groan escapes as I drag my thumb down the center of her mouth, knowing once I taste her, I won't ever stop.

Like the ravenous void I've become, I'll consume until there's nothing left.

"But I did warn you, starling," I whisper coarsely as I circle my fingers around her wrist and guide her arm toward the brass RA wheel, "that you should be fearful of celestial alignment."

I flatten her wrist against the spoke and snap the cuff in place, locking her to the pier.

A flicker of confusion draws her features tight, twisting a sharp blade beneath my sternum.

"Orion, what—is this some game?" She yanks her wrist against the restraint. "We don't have time for this. You're going to miss your speech."

I force myself to take a measured step backward. "I won't leave you for long," I assure her, retreating another painful step. "Just until it's over."

"Until what's over?" she demands, testing the cuff again. "You can't leave me like this. What are you talking about?"

"The eclipse."

On reflex, she looks up at the sealed shutter. "I don't understand—"

"This is the only way I can keep you alive, Collins."

Her gaze falls back to mine, real fear breaking across her beautiful face. "Orion, please," she breathes, her blinks coming faster. "You're scaring me."

The drum of rain grows louder in the tense silence between us. Collins jerks her wrist against the right ascension wheel, the harsh *clank* a strike against my bones. I fist my hands, tendons aflame as I fight the urges stretching my control.

"Whatever's happening, you know I can help you. Just like the other night on the beach." She licks her lips, desperation flaring behind her slate eyes. "But you have to talk to me. So we can figure out how—"

"I've tried," I say, throat raw, another weak thread of control fraying. "So many fucking times, in so many fucking ways. And, theoretically, I'm not sure this time will end any different." A bitter, self-deprecating laugh cracks as I drag a hand down my face. "Fuck, Collins. You've consumed my every thought, become my every obsession. My research—something that's been my sole fixation—no longer even matters."

She stills, those intense eyes fused to mine, her chest rising and falling in rhythmic motion of the sea. "Your research," she says slowly, unable to conceal the panic bleeding into her words.

"I swear," I whisper harshly, "I'd destroy it all without hesitation if that would change anything, but—" I check my wristwatch, the creeping dials nearing position. "But when the celestial bodies align in syzygy, I can't be anywhere near you." I rake a hand through my hair, meeting her stricken gaze. "You just have to trust me."

"Trust…that I won't die." The conflicted fear banked behind the turbulent swirl of gold and gray in her eyes doesn't just devastate—it obliterates me. A crushing reminder of my limitations, of my failures. That the light I've been so utterly captivated by came from a star already gone, reaching me too late. A *memento mori* of the cruelest kind.

Yet death takes many forms. Even if I manage to keep her breathing, I've already lost her.

A chord of anguish thrums through my constricted veins. Fury strains my muscles as I shove a hand into my pocket and swipe my gloved thumb over the worn brass of the astrolabe, unable to smother the licking flames of regret.

I've contaminated everything.

And standing here before her, confronted with that undeniable truth, I know there's no coming back from this. But I can live with that. I can accept this consequence, so long as she's breathing.

It's not enough.

"It has to be enough," I say through gritted teeth.

My jaw tightens, my thumb tracing the empty space on the star-taker, the missing piece like an open wound that won't close.

I withdraw the instrument, gripping until the edges bite through leather. I let the snap of pain ground me as rage builds thick at the base of my throat. With a guttural roar, I hurl it across the observatory.

Chest heaving, I tap a compulsive count against my thigh in a desperate hunt for symmetry, for balance—for any goddamn pattern that will unlock another outcome.

"Orion." The low utterance of my name slices through the battering tide, coaxing my tortured gaze back to hers. "Do you actually want to harm me?"

"No." It leaves my mouth on a fractured breath.

A wave of relief breaks across her pretty features. "I know you don't," she says, and with a tight swallow, she reinforces her words. "I know you don't, because you've never wanted to see me hurt. You stopped yourself from letting that happen right here in this dome." Her gaze briefly flicks to the speaker cabinet in the far corner. "You fought that compulsion once. You can fight it again. You can stop this from happening—"

"It can't be stopped," I say, my voice breaking with finality. If Collins leaves this observatory before third contact of the eclipse and our paths cross, there is only loss.

Loss of control.

Loss of symmetry.

Loss of *her*.

Right now, when I look into her eyes, I see her—her light. It's distant but there. And though the void within aches to claim her, a sliver of control remains. Just enough to let me walk out of this observatory.

"You're an anomaly," I say, barely audible. "The only way I can prevent this is if I'm nowhere near you."

I know exactly how they will die. I know when, where, and how death will claim them—

But she didn't come to me the way they did, soaked in darkness, devoid. She's an anomaly for this reason.

She has no pathology. No record of violence. No dark psyche. And yet, the algorithm drew her name—

Because there had to be someone.

The gravitational pull of this event is too strong, demanding an alignment. A local mind in the right place, at the right time.

All these years spent waiting for a name to emerge, and the system chose hers. Someone with no past indiscretions. No incurable medical diagnosis. She was chosen not because of her—but because of her proximity to *me*.

Which means the missing variable isn't within her at all.

It's within me. My contamination.

If I subtract myself—no ritual, no observation, no touch—the wave never collapses.

There's a chance.

As long as I'm not near her, as long as I defy this sinister force, her light might never go dark.

Like a brilliant, tidal-locked star falling dangerously close to the orbit of a black hole—this force that tears apart everything it loves, devouring every fragment of beauty caught within its grasp—if I deny this hunger, if I remove myself completely, there is no tidal disruption. No violent annihilation. No fiery light extinguished.

"Orion, I don't understand what that means."

"It means, you were always mine," I say to her. "You belong to me, with me. Mine to protect. If your death isn't observed...it suspends."

"Oh, god..." she whispers, as if some connection has fallen into place. "I need you to hear me," she says sternly. "I understand celestial events affect you. That you feel compelled by them, that you think you have no control."

I tilt my head. "How would you know this?"

She pushes on, easing closer until she's yanked to a stop by the restraint. "I'm your therapist," she says. "You just have to trust me." Collins watches me with guarded eyes, that beautiful slate flaying me open. "Haven't I given you every reason to? Please, Orion. Just...let me help you."

"Fuck, angel. But I wish you could," I say on a ragged breath.

"This isn't right. It doesn't make sense," she tries again, desperation edging into her voice as she yanks against the cuff, drawing my gaze to the constellation along her wrist.

I press the heel of my palm to my forehead, trying to ease the pressure against my skull.

"You know me," she whispers. "Orion, you know *me*. My hopes, my passion—remember? Please remember." Her smile is shattering. "I'm a Sagittarius who can't swim—"

"Technically, you're not," I say, taking a daring step toward her. My thumb brushes the faint stars scattered across her wrist. Desire burns the back of my throat with the aching need to taste her just once. "You were born under Ophiuchus, the Serpent Bearer."

Her face pales, and she shakes her head slowly. "No. There's no Ophiuchus zodiac sign—"

"It's a constellation," I correct her. "The thirteenth along the ecliptic, hidden among brighter stars. Astronomically accurate, not zodiacal. Over the centuries, the sky has shifted. The day you were born, the sun was in Ophiuchus." My gloved knuckles skim over her cheek, reverent. "But you still have so much fire in you, little archer."

"Then don't extinguish it." She presses into my touch. A tense silence envelopes us as the soft patter of rain outside the dome fades, leaving only the rhythm of our heartbeats.

"Your eyes are so dark, Orion," she murmurs, searching me. "You look like you haven't slept in days, and that can worsen compulsions. Obsessive beliefs can become indistinguishable from delusions." Her free hand covers mine along her cheek, voice breaking. "That's all this is, a delusion driven by fear."

My jaw tightens, a fierce pain rupturing through my chest. "God, I hope you're fucking right. I hope I'm insane. And—" I move in closer, towering above her as I reach for the duct tape on the pier "—I hope you'll forgive me one day, angel."

"Orion, no—please." She twists, turning her face away, fighting with one hand. "There's something I need to tell you. You have to listen—"

Her fingers claw at my shirt, and I groan, denying myself the deviant pleasure of feeling her nails rake my skin. I close my hand around her jaw, forcing her face toward mine. With clenched teeth, I tear a strip of tape free and seal it over her mouth.

"I promise," I whisper hoarsely, pressing a tender kiss to the tape, savoring the warmth and delicate curve of her lips beneath. "I'll come back for you."

I grasp her wrist, my jaw set hard as I unlatch the handcuff from the pier. She thrashes wildly against my hold as I draw her hands together and clasp each cuff around her wrists, binding them on either side of the RA wheel, the final *click* a harsh crack through my resolve.

Slowly, I draw back, my gaze locking with hers—tearful, blazing. Alive. Those eyes I'm determined to keep lit with her beautiful, fiery light.

Even if I have to hurl myself from the highest cliff to keep her heart beating—

I will take that leap.

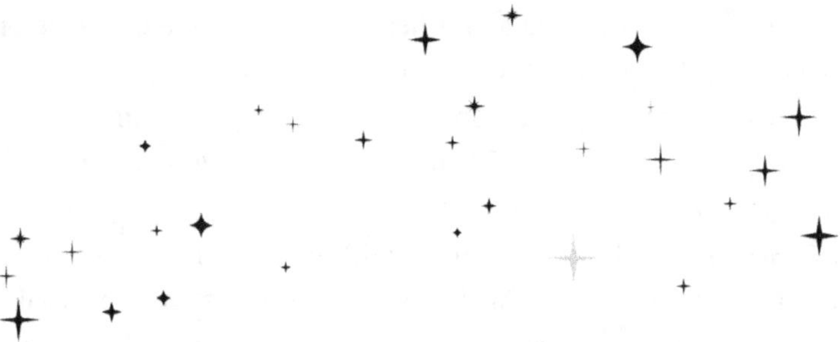

The Ψ (*psi*) symbol stands as a connection between the study of the inner world and the outer universe. In psychology, it represents *psuche* (the mind). In physics, it symbolizes the wave function; the mathematical description of a particle's quantum state. The same Greek letter encompasses both the study of the mind and the fundamental building blocks of the cosmos.

19

SYZYGY

The conjunction of the king and queen, the supreme *syzygy*, is a union of opposites par excellence.

— CARL JUNG, *PSYCHOLOGY AND ALCHEMY*

COLLINS

We shouldn't be so fragile that one moment out of the whole of our existence should alter us. But that's the cruel reality every victim of a crime comes to realize, just how delicately fragile we truly are when caught in the fury of a storm—

And that storm is furious.

I clamp my eyes closed, shutting out the dirt trying to creep in. A tide rises in my lungs. Panic snags my breath, and I force a trembling breath through my nose over the tape, easing the sharp pressure beneath my ribs.

One. Two. Three.

Despite my desperation to hold purchase in the present, time bends, folding around me in a suffocating clutch. With one harsh twist of the knife between ribs, skin splits. Pectoral muscle parts. The blade slices through cartilage, tearing past muscle and sac, until steel kisses the wall of my heart.

Like the frail exoskeleton of a seashell, my breastplate cracks.

My vision tunnels under the intrusive memory. Pinpricks assault my fingers, my hands turning cold above the metal cuffs. My chest seizes with palpitations, a dizzy rush flooding my head as the damaged valve catches, the leaflet refusing to move. My heartbeat falters. Too fast, uneven—then skips. Blood rushes backward in a sickening *whoosh* as my lungs fail to pull air.

I make a failed attempt to reach for my pocket, only to recall my pill case is in my jacket. *Dammit.*

Stilling my body, I focus my breathing. Taking slow breaths in and out, I count—*four in. Hold for two. Four out.* I manage to find a rhythm, slowly stabilizing my heart rate.

And then, I open my eyes and stare into the low-lit depths of Orion's observatory. Rain lashes the windows and slams the dome, drumming with the same force as the heavy pulse in my ears. The torrent rages with the same silent wrath swelling within me.

Time is always against me. Another cruel reality.

I've been caught in the fury of a storm since my life ended beneath the hands of a monster driven by obsession. Since my heart stopped beating, damaged by the edge of his blade.

And I fucking swore I'd never again be so fragile. That I would never again be a victim.

Muffled by tape, a desperate sound escapes, something between a laugh and a sob at the fucking irony.

With a furious burst, I yank at the restraints locking my wrists. The loud clang echoes through the chamber to mock me. Orion isn't even technically a Gemini. My whole damn profile was off because of a *shift in the sky*. And I completely overlooked a thirteenth constellation.

I draw in another shaky breath to stem the fury, and a flash of light guides my gaze across the dark. Awkwardly using my shoulder, I clear the tangle of strands from my eyes. My jacket lies on the floor, right where Orion left it discarded. And underneath—my phone lighting up with a call.

Frantic, I extend my leg, straining to reach the hem with my toe. Years of punishing discipline rush back. Yet despite all my rigorous practice, my muscles burn from neglect, falling short.

I slump against the telescope pier, wrists throbbing. Calming myself further, I mentally comb through everything that happened before, desperately searching for any way out of this.

...when the celestial bodies align in syzygy, I can't be anywhere near you.

Orion's words come back to me, ominous and damning. *Syzygy. Alignment.* His fixation on symmetry was a blatant warning.

I should've recognized the pattern.

The law of symmetry was right there, a rule written in his fucking stars. We don't simply crave balance and harmony—

We *need* it.

Just as celestial bodies align during an eclipse, our minds seek that same balance, unifying opposite aspects. Jungian psychology, the unity of opposites. Conscious and unconscious. Masculine and feminine. Shadow and self. What that innate desire for symmetry drives us toward: completeness.

For every good, there's a bad.

For every truth, a delusion.

For every prey, a predator.

And my hunter...

He needed his victim.

A hot surge of anger floods the constricted chamber of my

heart. Orion failed to complete his ritual with his last victim. He wouldn't just be compelled to finish it—he'd *need* to. The compulsion too strong to deny.

Any feelings he harbors for me simply became warped, entangling me deeper into his fixation.

From the first moment I laid eyes on Orion, I recognized the break in him. And I manipulated it, employing dark psychological tactics to infiltrate his habitat. My methods worked so damn well, in fact, I infiltrated straight into his obsession—as his fucking *victim*.

God, I really did *not* see that coming. Especially when I spent the past few days focused on trying to help him. I just thought we had enough time.

But Orion is driven by his need to complete the pattern, to fill the void. He can't stop searching for what's lost, what's missing—

Shit.

At the thought, I twist my body, angling my cuffed wrists enough that I can dig my fingers into my skirt pocket, groping for the object hidden there.

Pinching the slender brass between my fingertips, I painstakingly pick at the left cuff lock. Thankful I had the patience to learn how. *Thank you, Darby.*

When the locking mechanism clicks, I slide my wrist free, not giving myself a moment to brace before I tear the tape away from my mouth. I stifle a cry and immediately drag in a full breath to fill my lungs before I pick the second cuff, slipping it off my wrist.

One second where I savor the relief, then I make a dash toward my phone. I toss my umbrella and jacket aside and grab the device, my heart clenching as I light the cracked screen.

One missed call from Darby.

A torrent of rage and panic batters my resolve. *No—not yet.*

I claw my fingers through my tangle of hair, facing the bank of windows. The storm has subsided to a misty rain, leaving behind a bruised sky in its aftermath. Dark clouds block most of the sun, one thin blade of light bleeding through.

Determined, I flip the phone over to pop out the SIM card. If Darby has this number, then he's already tracking me. I halt as the screen illuminates again, his number displayed across the screen. Dread clamps my ribs like a vise.

Indecision weighs on my shoulders as I stare at the phone, taking measured steps toward one of the panoramic windows. Resigned, I accept the call and bring the phone to my ear.

The line is quiet until: "Hol."

I blink slowly, hearing all that's said in just the single syllable of my name, beneath the somber tone of Darby's voice.

"Hol, are you with him right now?"

I swallow, steeling myself for the lie. "Yes."

His heavy exhale sounds across the line, some combination of relief and frustration. "I need you to stay where you are," he instructs. "I'm going to be the one…" He trails off, leaving a tense beat of hesitation. "This is done. It's over. But I'm going to be the one to bring you in and conduct the interview, all right."

My gaze wanders past the cliffside, out over the rocky outcroppings and rolling ocean in search of the horizon. It's a faint, misty line. Nearly indistinguishable as the gray waters blend with the steel sky.

"How?" I ask, but I don't really need Darby to detail the way he found me. If he had a starting location, it would then be simple enough to gain access to business and university registries. Run names through an anagram generator until there's a hit.

Time is always against me.

He was never supposed to have a starting location. Which means—

"There was another victim," he says, releasing a tense breath.

"Two, actually. Roughly an hour and a half away from you. At first, I wasn't convinced it was the same perpetrator. But I just had a gut feeling."

There's another tentative pause, and I know he's keeping me talking, keeping me on the line—because I know these tactics. I even know his next move. My gaze falls over the long stretch of pier in the distance. With a sudden flutter, my pulse spikes. Destination decided, I'm moving before Darby gets to his next bullet point.

"Look," he says, and now I'm the one letting him fill the silence as I keep him talking, just long enough to pull a trace on my movement. "I'm not sure I want to know. I don't want to ask, but..."

As I round the telescope, I come to a halt and swoop down, my hand closing around the steel handle of the umbrella. I stand and test its solid heft. Heavy enough to cause some damage should I need a weapon.

A pang lances my chest at the thought of having to use Orion's own umbrella against him—but the disturbed look I saw amid the current of his eyes leaves me little choice.

I'll come back for you.

That's my fear.

"The victims were found mutilated," Darby says, disrupting my thoughts. "Dug up by an animal from where the bodies had been recently buried. It was obvious the scene was tampered with, masking the MO. Which is not like our guy."

I can sense his aversion, can hear his disgust. And while his mortification should bother me more, I'm already descending the spiral staircase, heart thundering with each defiant step. Adrenaline winds my veins as I grip the umbrella at my side.

Before I escape the observatory, I quickly search the main control room, finding the key hanging from a chain along a panel. I push through the heavy arched doors, inhaling a deep breath of mist-laden air. A gust of wind bites into my sweat-slicked skin. Urgency propels me across the damp grounds, my heart thrashing against my ribs, struggling to keep pace as I race toward the trail ahead.

"Hollyn, tell me it wasn't you." Darby's voice breaks through the line. "Fucking hell, tell me you weren't the one who bashed in the skulls."

My steps falter. One missed foot placement, and my heart slips a beat. My grip tightens around the handle, palm burning against the cold steel as I push forward.

Maybe I'm the one with the distorted reality, and I was always intended to be his victim. Maybe Orion sees the truth of me—the defective, callused organ I've carried since the moment I clawed back to this life.

Darby isn't wrong to question me. It's his job. He can't overlook the evidence, or ignore all he knows about the woman with a bad heart. The fact it's hardened and wrong. He can't discount his instincts, honed by his many years in intelligence.

Once it was safe to leave Orion the other night, I went to Blue Hills—and found two bodies instead of one. It didn't fit the pattern, but I told myself I could've been wrong, or that Orion's dissociative spiral was triggered by an intruder, resulting in the utter carnage I saw there.

But either way, after everything, I couldn't let him be discovered.

I used a rock to cave in the skulls he left behind in his fugue state. I bashed them until the remains were unrecognizable. I buried the bodies. I concealed the scene. Hid his kills. Destroyed all evidence.

The Gothic iron gate swings inward with a creak. The wind lashes my clothes as I grasp the railing and hurry down the steps. "You're good, Darby," I say, my feet hitting the weathered planks of the pier. "The best. But even you couldn't have gotten this close without inside help."

There had to be some informant.

"That's fair," he mutters, sounding distracted. "I just wish you could've trusted me."

"I always have."

Midway down the landing, the weight of what I'm about to do draws me to a stop. I take a moment to catch my breath. For now, I just need to keep my distance from Orion. At least until the eclipse is over. Not let him *kill* me before I get through to him. And I have to prevent Darby from getting to him first.

I have to make sure no other predators smother his light. I have to protect him.

He's mine.

"I am sorry it came to this, Darby," I say into the line, the wind stirring the loose strands of my hair.

Darby sighs. "I know, Hol," he says, and I try not to feel gutted by the disappointment I hear in his voice before I end the call.

With a reflective glance over my shoulder, I take in the towering structure of Stonehurst. Its soaring spires cast against the gray sky, the domed observatory I once believed held the secrets I so desperately wanted. Yet those secrets were locked inside the man, hidden behind his walls of stone.

It's my fault Orion fixated on me. By the time I recognized the hollow, despondent look in his eyes on the shore, saw the vacancy and dissociation after his last kill, it was already too late.

Correcting course now might even be too late, but I have to try.

Each determined step brings me closer to the *Eventide*—the docked rigid-hull Zodiac the university uses for research purposes. The craft knocks against the pilings, the tidal swell rising higher with each powerful wave.

I press the heel of my palm beneath my left breast, willing the sharp pain away before I link the umbrella cord around my wrist and power down my phone. Then I ease toward the side of the vessel, setting my device on the edge.

I grab the mooring line. The serrated wind cuts through the sheer material of my blouse, salt spray stings my legs. I'm wind-torn and near drenched by the time I finally loosen the knot.

An unsettling prickle crawls up the nape of my neck, and I glance up toward the windows of the observatory. My pulse quickens as I question if Darby is there within—if he's already tracked me this far.

I wrench the knot loose, urgency rushing my movements. Darby can chase my phone out into the open sea. All I need is for the boat to drift far enough offshore, leading him away from Orion. Giving me enough time to find Orion first, to reason with him, and—

"Dr. Holbrook!"

Startled, the coarse rope slips from my hands. "Shit," I hiss. I reach for the line, knocking my phone into the hull of the boat. Heart pounding, I shove my annoyance down and turn toward Banner.

His quick strides close the distance between us, his features drawn in confusion. "Dr. Holbrook, did you not get my calls?" Impatient, he waves a hand. "Never mind. Orion abruptly left in the middle of his speech. He just—walked out." He gives his head an incredulous shake. "Tell me you know where he is."

Dammit, Orion.

Dread threads my spine as my gaze darts back to the observatory. Fear that Darby has already apprehended Orion strangles my throat. "I'm sorry, Dr. Banner. But I don't."

Banner frowns, his attention shifting from me to the research vessel, to the unknotted rope, before his gaze narrows back on me. Wariness settles in the furrow of his brow. "What exactly are you doing out here?"

Desperation curls my hand tight around the handle of the umbrella, fingers numb against the icy pommel. "Actually, I thought Orion might be here." Thinking quickly, I add, "I saw him leave. I thought he might take the *Eventide* out to view the eclipse."

He tilts his head, unconvinced. "In these conditions?" As if to make his point, a spray of frigid water crashes over the pier, the tide rushing in furiously. "No, there's an advisory keeping crafts out of the water. Not even Rye would be reckless enough to risk the storm surge."

"Of course, you're right." I nod with a forced smile. "We should head back, then. See if Dr. Night has already returned to the symposium."

A chiming ring breaks into the moment, and Banner fishes his phone from his jacket pocket. I glimpse the number flashing on the screen, my pulse roaring louder than the crashing waves.

"Don't answer that," I warn him.

His thumb hovers above the screen, his gaze locked hard on me. "What's going on?"

I clench my teeth, anxiety flaring beneath my skin. Banner needs to go—*now*. If Darby is calling his line, that means he's closing in.

Banner silences the call. "You know, it seemed like you were starting to make progress with him," he says, lowering the phone. "However, I fear that I no longer have a choice. As soon as the event concludes, I'll be making the arrangements to have Dr. Night admitted for a formal evaluation. Dr. Holbrook, I'm afraid your services at Stonehurst are no longer desired."

Like the fury of the swelling tide, a surge of rage cracks my composure. A bitter flame ignites low in my stomach as I grip the handle, the steel biting cold into my palm.

"Right," I say, eyes narrowing. "Now you want to get him proper help. I'm curious, though." I tilt my head in accusation. "Were you really trying to protect Orion before, or just keep him cleared for your own benefit? Was I hired to help, or just to alleviate your conscience?"

Anger flushes across his pale features. But it's there again, that betraying flash of guilt. Honestly, I wasn't entirely sure about him until now.

"I promise you, I don't know what you're implying," Banner says.

A derisive, knowing smile touches my lips. "Of course not, Dr. Banner," I manage to say, swallowing my fury. I take a step toward him, steadying my voice. "We should get out of this weather, though. And I am concerned about Dr. Night. We should find him."

Banner's nod is firm, resigned to my suggestion until his phone lights with another call. Suspicion hardens his expression as he lifts the phone. Pressure builds behind my ribs, desperation coiling my muscles until the tension snaps, giving over to a kind of bleak resignation.

Against the howling wind and deafening roar of waves, the sound of Laurel's voice reaches me, just as urgent in my memory as in that pivotal moment: *"How far are you willing to go?"*

And as I surrender, the relief washing through me is almost weightless. "I'm sorry, but I really can't allow you to take that call, Dr. Banner."

Adrenaline fires hot through my viscera as I snatch the phone from his hand and toss it into the Zodiac.

"Dr. Holbrook, what the hell—?" Out of reflex, he grabs my arm.

A viscous jolt of alarm slams through me. And suddenly, I'm no longer standing on a pier. Bright stage lights burn into my flared eyes, tears frozen in horror, refusing to fall.

My heart rate slows right along with time, trapping me in a moment of fear.

In a wide arc, I swing the umbrella down, connecting the steel pommel with the side of Banner's head.

Broken free of his hold, I yank backward, nearly toppling over. He groans, bringing a hand to his head as he sways, his other bracing against the side of the boat. His phone vibrates from the hull, and he makes a desperate move to retrieve it.

"I'm so sorry," I whisper, barely audible. It's like watching it happen from outside of myself, still trapped in another timeline, caught in a single, static frame—a distant scene playing out in a theater, a girl's life being stolen, torn away, unable to stop it.

Banner slumps against the gunwale, his groan lost beneath the next furious wave breaking against the pier. He reaches a shaky hand toward his phone—

And I can't let him find out about Orion.

I *need* him.

I slash downward once more. The impact steals the air from my lungs. The steel handle collides with the back of his skull, the blunt force vibrating through my bones. Warmth splatters my face. My fingers slick with blood.

Banner's body sags against the gunwale of the boat.

My vision flickers. The world narrows to the sound of the raging ocean, the creak of the rope. The dull thud in my temple. My heart rams my rib cage, and I release a sharp wince as the umbrella clatters to the pier.

Adrenaline floods my bloodstream, burning through my arteries. Throat raw, I swallow, leaning down to press my fingers to his limp wrist.

He's unresponsive.

I exhale a foggy breath in the mist. Trembling, I turn into the sobering gust of wind, feeling the icy spray needle my face. I swipe at my cheek, smearing briny water and blood.

Then I stare down the length of the pier, chest heaving. Waiting to see Darby appear.

"Go," I urge myself. "*Move.*" I force my frozen body into motion.

I grab the bloodied umbrella and toss it and the mooring line into the Zodiac. Climbing over the edge, I grab hold of Banner's arms. Muscles aching with exertion, I grunt and lift. "I'm also sorry for stealing your car the other night," I mutter as I drag his lifeless weight in with me. "But I didn't have much of a choice then, either."

Staring down at his still body, I release a shaky breath. This time, I can't bring back what I've taken.

A pool of dark red swirls along the bottom next to his head, his neck crooked in an unnatural angle.

Before the blood reaches my phone, I kick it aside, then bring my heel down on the screen, crushing the device beneath my boot.

For a breath of a moment, I seal my eyes shut, just long enough to calm the frantic pulse in my ears. Fighting the rock of the vessel, I dig the key from my pocket and shove it into the ignition. A spike of anxiety grips me at the rumble of the engine.

With shaky hands, I circle my fingers around the throttle, slowly guiding the boat away from the pier. Water churns fierce under the hull, the salty spray whipping my hair across my face.

Keeping at a steady speed, I cut across the rocky waves, steering out past the sea stacks. The jagged slate peaks merge with the overcast sky. The hull thumps against each breaker, but I don't let off the throttle, my gaze aimed ahead.

Before I'm out too far, I pitch my shattered phone over the side of the craft.

When the town goes dark during the eclipse, I'll do the same with Banner. Let the receding tide carry his body out. It's a strange irony, a body buried in the ocean. That something as fleeting as a life should make a grave out of something so vast and endless.

As I steer the *Eventide* over choppy waters, I'm caught in the rolling current, haunted by the phantom feel of Orion's solid arms holding me amid the waves, the unknown all around us.

I should've been terrified.

His embrace was more unknown, more dangerous, than anything lurking in the dark ocean depths. A fact made devastatingly clear the instant I chose to trust him—and he shattered that trust.

And I should be terrified right now. Alone. Surrounded by a ruthless ocean. And yet, I'm strangely calm. Where I'm most vulnerable, even defenseless, what that weakness does grant me is the elimination of fear.

Acceptance can cauterize any fear. All the pain, all the struggle, every consuming desire for revenge—

It's as simple as letting go.

As the waves swell dangerously, tossing the boat, I ease the throttle back. A rough breaker jerks the bow sideways. My grip slips from the wheel.

"God—dammit." By the time I regain control, it's too late to correct course.

In the moments before a violent impact, it's surreal how clear the world becomes. Details sharpen, senses heighten. The ocean the exact shade of Orion's eyes when set in the deepest teal. The misty horizon like the dark gray ring around his irises. So fucking beautiful, like staring into a cluster of galaxies.

Silver glitters across the water, the beauty so vibrant—like the seconds before a knife cracks skin and slices past ribs. How clear and sparkling the lights shone above the stage. They should've looked just as vibrant when I danced beneath them. Those seconds of my final performance savored, rather than the terror before it all went dark.

"Shit—"

I wrench the wheel, trying to maneuver away from the rock. The metallic scrape reverberates through my cells as the craft tilts, pitching me off balance. My shoulder slams hard against the side. Another wave punches the hull. Water floods past the breach.

All around, water churns in a furious vortex as rip currents build, gripping the boat and dragging it down. I feel the violent force of that gravity, only recalling too late what Orion told me about enhanced gravitational pull on the oceans when the earth, moon, and sun align.

I turn my face skyward, witnessing the first touch of shadow darken the sun. A gust of wind snatches the bitter laugh from my lips as the biting water rushes around my legs.

And for a suspended heartbeat, the bright shards scattered across the water become reflected stars. Stage lights that once glimmered. Fireflies tossed by the wind, fragile yet resilient against the elements and the oppressive darkness.

We shouldn't be so fragile, altered by one cruel moment—but once caught in the fury of a storm, our resilience is as frail as a shell cracked in a ruthless clutch.

I brace against the inevitable, the ache in my heart a fierce reminder of the fleetingness of it all.

My breath seizes as the ocean sucks in a breath and draws back—right before a giant wave rises up like a claw.

I watch it crash over the vessel.

That one defining moment may have fractured my life, but I'm the one who let it become a pattern. My own symmetry of trauma and violence.

The world now so clear, so bright, upends.

And the boat capsizes.

Though my soul may set in darkness, it will rise in perfect light;
I have loved the stars too fondly to be fearful of the night.

— SARAH WILLIAMS, *THE OLD ASTRONOMER*
TO HIS PUPIL

20

TOTALITY

What doesn't transmit light creates its own darkness.

— MARCUS AURELIUS

ORION

I once swore I'd fight an ocean for her.

The instant my arms closed around Collins, I knew I'd fight the dark, violent waters of the tide to carry her ashore.

The wind whips around me, rising into a roaring chorus as waves crash furiously against the jagged cliffside below. Even as the rain breaks and the sky clears, the misty air remains charged with a storm.

I hold the brass object between my thumb and forefinger, feel the balanced weight of it. Its sudden appearance in my observatory stirs an unease, an implication that makes me question my own mind.

There's a cost to loving anything too fiercely. That only after losing what we love most can we truly realize its value.

It's a cruel paradox.

With an aching breath, I lift my gaze toward the horizon.

Out there in the vast ocean is my violence. I recognized its fury before the ripples could reach me, before the vibrations could be felt. Like gravitational waves passing silently through one another, we were never supposed to collide.

That's the law of physics.

And yet, near the shadow of the horizon, laws are bent, warped. Altered.

My thoughts rage like the restless sea stretched endless before me, cast in tossing black waters that absorb the fading light. Two worlds layered one on top of the other.

In the distance, that faint seam of horizon threads the space where the ocean touches sky, blurring the boundary between the two.

Overhead, first contact is being made as the moon kisses the disk of the sun, initiating the countdown to occultation.

The waves push and pull against the shoreline as I stand fixed on the rocky ledge, the towering spires of Stonehurst looming from behind. I clench the brass in my hand, my fingers as numb with cold as my body with indecision.

Soon, a blazing corona will circle a black sun, the moment of totality eclipsing the beach.

And me.

Right here, trapped in this space between, I feel that push and pull on a cellular level as gravity mercilessly dominates my atoms. An inevitability that has tormented me since she first entered my orbit.

As crosses form on the shallow waters, the tide displays the mark of danger. Rip currents strong enough to swallow us whole are building. The gravitational pull churns the tide higher, pulling harder at the ocean.

I recognize the pattern because the science of what I do depends on it. Inherently, we are designed to recognize these patterns. It's coded in our DNA. To escape predation, to identify danger.

I should have recognized the danger in her.

My gaze tracks over the pier, where blood pools dark on the weathered wood. Salt water surges up, splashing between the planks to wash the evidence of her violence away, yet the stain remains.

Fuck, all this time, I've been fixated on the wrong celestial event. It was never the sun going dark—it was her. With every escaping second, the eclipse was taking place within Collins, the shadow slowly devouring her light. I sensed the fury there, the violence, that undercurrent of turmoil simmering just beneath her surface. Until finally spilling free, bloodying the waters.

Her totality is here.

With fire lashing my sternum, I remove the star-taker from my pocket and fit the piece into place, and her melodic tune sings through me, an intoxicating, haunting refrain.

Nothing is as perfectly measured as the symmetry of a reverberating tune. A sound caught forever in motion, like a melody pulled into a riptide, eternally echoing deep under the surface where no one can hear.

Yet I hear it.

Her echoes that come to me as harmony, the staccato cadence of her pulse, a tender, melancholic rhythm of heartbeats that I could always hear.

Raising the sighting vane, I look across the churning waves and align the astrolabe. Sunlight filters through the aperture, striking my palm as I confirm the measurements—the exact position of Ophiuchus.

And right beneath her constellation, a faint trail illuminates the way.

I lower the star-taker, letting it slip from my fingers.

I've suffered this moment on an endless loop. Altering

variables, simulating outcomes, searching for the one where I don't lose her. Dreading the second when I can no longer defy this sinister influence.

Standing at the precipice, I step closer to the edge of the cliff. The waves roar, crashing higher, spitting up against the rocks. Something vicious stirs in my blood as I strip away my jacket and wrench off my tie, allowing the serrated wind to sink its teeth into my skin.

When observing an event, the observer cannot interfere.

I've known the exact month, day, hour, minute—down to the goddamn second her heart would stop beating.

And I've known there'd be nothing I could do to stop it from happening.

I can't save her.

When a star begins to die, there's no preventing its collapse. Stellar death is an intense, violent event. Those fleeting moments before the end are breathtakingly beautiful, the destruction inevitable.

It leaves an impression in the void, an echo felt long after its heart goes dark.

And her absence will leave a cavernous abyss.

As the markers on my astronomical watch align closer, the sky falls darker, and a discordant chord bangs through my vessels. Gravity becomes secondary to this deeper, darker pull within.

The void whispers, the seductive urge to jump. To surrender. To succumb to forces beyond control.

And I answer its call.

With the next frigid gust, I pull in a shuddering breath. My foot slips along the rocky incline as I look down into the turbulent waters below.

There's no fear of falling in space, only the silent terror of becoming adrift. Frozen, motionless.

Yet there's a paradoxical truth to the danger of that all-consuming force—a force that can simply be removed just by falling.

Removing resistance.

I once swore I'd fight an ocean for her—a battle now waged against the dark, violent waters of my mind.

Loving Collins was never a jump. Not even a leap.

The instant I saw her, I was already in freefall, experiencing that brief moment of terrifying, exhilarating weightlessness just before the plummet, stretched into infinity.

I close my eyes—

And step off the cliff.

The wind screams in my ears, a rush stealing my breath as adrenaline floods my bloodstream. For a fleeting moment, I surrender to the freefall, right before the ocean swallows me.

Plunged into an icy grave, all light vanishes. The freezing water is a brutal shock to my system. Salt water fills my mouth as a ruthless wave twists my body, wrenching me under.

Disoriented, I claw in every direction until I break the surface. Dragging in a sharp breath, I fill my burning lungs. Every molecule of my body wants to freeze, to let the undercurrent drag my motionless form to the bottom.

With an obstinate will born of sheer stubborn determination, I thrust one arm in front of the other, carving a path through the vicious crosscurrent.

The turbulent waves batter me, but I latch onto that faint beat, the fading cadence of her heart. Fighting the pull, I stroke hard, muscles igniting in fire. Between the heaving waves, the craft comes into view.

I push harder, cutting through the swelling current toward the capsized Zodiac rocking against the jagged sea stacks. Amid the undulating breakers, I catch a glimpse of her—an angel in my scope. Her surf-beaten body clings to the edge of a rock.

Time dilates, feeling as though the seconds it takes to reach her are never-ending, stretched by an impossible distance I can't close. Each warped strike of a second is a slice through the cavity of my chest as I slowly watch her slip beneath the surface.

"Fuck. Collins—" I shout her name, my throat raw, voice drowned by the thunderous crash of waves. A savage desperation tears through me, obliterating any fear.

Slammed under by the next crash of a wave, I surface gasping, dragging in another painful breath to fill my lungs before I dive below. I swim deeper, arms slicing through salt and kelp. I fight the riptide, hands scraping through the murky depth in search.

And then I feel her.

First contact—a spark of warmth breaking through the icy water and saline, conducting an electric arc between us. Breaching every barrier, my fingers touch hers.

The yielding softness of her skin sends a visceral shockwave through me, surging with heat to ignite my frozen bones. Arms weightless above her head, Collins drifts suspended in the deep, swallowed by the crushing darkness of the ocean void. I link my fingers through hers, teeth gritted against the crosscurrent as I drag her higher.

My left hand finds the curve of her cheek, guiding her face toward mine as I strain to see through the stirred silt and murk. My forehead presses to hers, fingers threading into her silky hair, savoring this isolated moment of serene calm, before I wrap my arm around her and kick us to the surface.

"Collins." My voice cracks as I cough up water. With a fierce groan, I haul her closer. Exertion scorching my muscles, I search her for signs of life.

Tossed by the waves, I tread water, clearing strands of her matted hair from her face. My thumb brushes over a tender bruise along her pale cheek, anger igniting hot. "Starling—"

I smother the flame of panic as I press my fingers against her throat, relief stripping a ragged breath free at the shallow flutter of her pulse.

"Fuck," I swear, casting a defiant glance up at the sky. The shadow has grown, taking a dark bite out of the sun.

Before the rip current drags us back under, I shift her back against my chest, anchoring my arm across her sternum. Her head rests on my shoulder, and I tilt her face upward, keeping her airway clear of the surf.

"Just stay with me, angel," I rasp near her ear, my low plea lost beneath the tossing waves.

As my legs kick below the surface, my free arm slices through the choppy water with determined, rhythmic strokes. Ignoring the burn in my muscles, my existence narrows to this one impossible act.

Waves thrash and crash around us, the ruthless currents striving to tear her body away from mine. Breath scraping my lungs, I grip her tighter, bones aflame from the effort. But I propel us forward, each stroke driven by utter defiance. As a breaker barrels over us, I'm thrust beneath the surface, the dark covering my vision, assaulted by what lurks in my own violent waters.

Jaw clenched, I fight the intrusive images back into the abyss, tightening my hold on Collins. The weight of her against my chest sends fresh adrenaline surging. With a furious roar, I claw my way back to the surface of my shore.

I hold on to her, refusing to lose her to the dark waters.

An eternity passes before my boots scrape the sand. I stagger ashore, legs buckling beneath the weight of my exhaustion and her limp body. I collapse to my knees, laying Collins along the hard sand.

Lungs searing, vision blurred, I press my fingertips alongside her neck, waiting to count her beats, her blinks, her breaths. Waiting to hear her soft notes.

My throat constricts. Hand unsteady, I clear the sand from her pale blue lips, her skin like ice beneath my bare touch. Her blouse has come undone at the top, and I settle my palm at the hollow beneath her collarbone, between the swell of her breasts. Breath caged, I lean in, waiting to feel the faintest brush of her breath. My chest goes as still as hers—

She gasps in air, and with my own shuddering breath, I turn her face. A cough rattles her chest as seawater spills from her lips. With my other hand, I grasp the nape of her neck, bracing her while she clears the water from her lungs. Her eyelashes flutter, eyes blinking open to reveal a slate sky, gold waking in the depths like early stars.

I swallow hard, my throat aflame with salt, as her gaze slowly focuses on me. A shiver clings to her body, lips trembling, before a slow smile graces her mouth.

"You're touching me," she whispers.

A rush of air escapes my raw lungs. My hand moves lower, fingers reverently covering the scar that splits the valley of her chest. "You're letting me touch you."

Emotion wells behind her eyes. She reaches up, fingertips gentle against my cheek, her touch an electric, humming current. She wanders lower, exploring my jaw, my neck. Descending even lower as she tenderly trails her fingers over the planes of my chest, tracing the designs inked into my skin.

And I'm just as reverent, mapping the last of the light along her cheekbone with my thumb, memorizing the soft feel of her skin. But the moment is broken too soon, the awe in her gaze stolen by a flicker of panic as memory begins to flood back— everything that happened before.

The dark lanes in her eyes deepen, dimming the gold. And yet, as I fall deeper into those shadowed corridors, a subtle brilliance emerges. Once your eyes adapt to the darkness, you find the hidden light there, like uncovering a distant cluster of stars within the void.

Her fingers curl urgently into my damp shirt. Her throat pulses with a hard swallow. "Orion—"

"I'm going to kiss you, Collins," I say, my voice scraping the air between us. I hold her gaze, letting the fiery ache consume. I graze my beaten knuckles over her bruised cheek, still so shaken at the soft feel of her.

Above us, the sky darkens, the eclipse nearing totality. Shadows stretch across rocks, color bleeding away and plunging the shore into a surreal, silver dusk.

Everything stills. The ocean falls to a hush, as if holding its breath in anticipation for second contact. An unnatural silence envelops the shore, the universe pausing for this one moment.

And within this breathless dark, she's so fucking beautiful. A frozen star bathed in twilight, ruinous and devastating.

I brush my thumb across her lips, aching to taste them. Her fingers curl over mine, lacing our hands together in response, and my entire body ignites. I surrender to the hunger burning through my veins, desperate to give her these fleeting seconds.

Billions of light-years away, two black holes merged in a violent collision, their gravitational waves sent rippling through the fabric of space and time to eventually reach us here, now— resonating in the space between our pounding hearts as I slant my mouth over hers.

The impact is cataclysmic.

The instant her lips part against mine, I'm pulled into her. I tunnel my fingers into her wet hair, cradling the back of her head against the sand as I crush my mouth harder to hers, deepening the kiss.

A groan is torn from my throat as my tongue sweeps hers, tentative for a moment before she moans, then I'm a rising tide of molten need. She inhales deeply, stealing my breath to reclaim her own, and I hungrily, greedily steal it right back. Our bodies move on instinct, bridging a divide we've held in place far too long.

Her leg slips through the slit in her skirt to curl around my hip, boot heel digging into my thigh, pulling me closer as another surge of icy tide washes over our calves. I drag her body half beneath mine, falling heavy over her with the surrender to gravity. And we align—heart to heart, pulse to pulse—two tidally locked stars, flaring in a single beat.

Sensation and need build to a crescendo. A symphony rising higher, louder.

Something primal breaks loose at the gentle vibration in her throat, and I angle my head, bracing my palm along her jawline, my thumb sweeping her skin as I savor her, fierce and ravenous, tasting salt and life and sweet, intoxicating want.

"God—fuck," I groan over her mouth, my restraint stretched unbearably thin as the soft contour of her body meets with mine, perfect in our symmetry.

"You came back for me," she whispers against my mouth. Her hand in my hair tugs, urging me even closer. It takes every shred of my control to resist, to bury the darker desires clawing at my skull.

"I will, always."

The moment the eclipse reaches totality, I feel it down in my marrow, fine-tuned. This obsessive fear of losing control, of losing her, tightens my grip.

A dull throb pounds at my temples, and I push back against the pain being this close to her brings. I'd cross an entire goddamn ocean for her. Fight the destructive waters of my mind. Fuck, to keep her just like this, I'd let the pain burn me alive.

As the moon covers the sun, devouring the last traces of light, the shadow claws forward, urging my hand higher, to seal tighter. Black filaments invade, compelling me toward this monstrous act —to claim her final moments beneath the rising constellation of stars.

My fingers tremble at her throat, balanced precariously

between tenderness and threat. Collins gasps against my mouth, her breath shallow and quick. Fire lashes against my bones as the dark tide surges, the violent impulse to take her last breath.

As my hand collars her throat, I kiss her harder.

As my body strains against the painful urge, I clutch her tighter.

As the insidious force all but strangles me, I breathe her in deeper.

And as a crown of fire ignites the dark sun, casting a blazing halo around shadow, my muscles coil brutally tight, bones locked in a vise as I desperately deny the ritual. Fighting the compulsion to capture her echoes at the brink of annihilation, in the final pulse of her fading heartbeat.

When the system detects an anomaly, it calls for a complete shutdown.

This crucial moment of retrieval, to recover that lost unit of time, slips away like the last grains of sand from my grasp.

Gone.

And still, I hold on tight—so tight she winces, and a breath shudders out of me as I force myself to loosen my grip.

Darkness pours across the shore, draping us in the umbral shadow of totality. I capture her mouth in another fervent kiss. My tongue skims her lower lip, tender, tasting—

Her breath catches sharp, her body clenching in pain. "Orion," she whispers over my lips, her voice going breathy. "Something's wrong." She flinches. "My heart—"

Dread is a monster ripping open my chest. "I'm right here," I say, hand pressed fiercely to her chest. "I'm not letting go."

Above, the sky darkens in mirror of the void thrashing within me. Desperate, I press my forehead to hers, eyes fastened shut against the suffocating agony. Fingers dug into the hard sand, I clutch the dip of her lower back, arching her body into me.

"Don't worry," I tell her, jaw tense. "I'll come for you. I won't lose you to the dark waters." I pull back and kiss her forehead, her cheek. "Not ever, Collins. I will never let go."

My left hand remains centered in the delicate slope of her chest, feeling each jagged inhale and exhale, counting every precious, irregular beat of her heart before her rhythm slips...

...falling silent beneath my palm.

And her heart stops.

I fall back on my heels, my face turning skyward. Chest heaving, I drive a hand through my hair, caught between the breathtaking solar eclipse and the violent reckoning tearing through me.

In the eerie stillness of totality, details are luridly vivid. Collins, lying unnaturally still, her skin pale and ethereal beneath the uncanny glow. Colors drained away, shadows clawing across her motionless body on the gray sand.

Every cell of my being revolts, terror tightening like a mass beneath my ribs as I haul her body against mine. I clutch her to my chest, thumb brushing the stars along her wrist, the absence of her pulse tearing a broken sound from my throat.

The loss of her is annihilating.

This moment suspends, a moment that feels infinite, stretched like the endless fury of the ocean as it tears through me.

A storm in time.

Collapsing into a single, unbearable point—a singularity where everything stands still, as frozen as her heart.

And in the same breathless beat, I'm laying her flat along the sand, positioning myself over her. With an enraged groan, I wrench the astronomical watch from my wrist and cast it to the rocks.

I've known the exact month, day, hour, minute—the goddamn *second* her heart would stop. And I've known there would be nothing I could do to prevent it from happening. I couldn't intervene. Couldn't fucking save her.

But this time—

"I can bring you back."

I tear her drenched shirt open, removing all barriers, a touch at the boundary, and have the heel of my palm braced to her chest.

She didn't come to me the way they did, soaked in darkness, devoid. She's an anomaly for this reason.

My anomaly.

Without hesitation, I begin compressions, my hands centered atop the cruel scar that becomes my guide. "Come back to me," I command, pressing down in furious demand. "Come on, starling. Collins, I know you have some fight. You have to fucking fight."

Tilting her chin up, I seal my mouth over hers and force my breath into her lungs. Then, keeping a merciless rhythm, I count each second, each compression, each breath.

Time narrows, the eclipse holding the sky in suspended darkness. Quickly, I check for her pulse before forcing another breath into her. Each compression is a defiant plea. Each breath I breathe into her is an intimate demand to reignite her fire.

I work her heart, pumping with a determination that borders on madness. Terrified I'll break her, desperate enough to risk it. The window to revive her shrinks, close to collapse.

Her echoes held at the threshold of loss.

Mouth hovering above hers, I whisper, "Collins, it's entrainment. Remember? Two heartbeats aligning. Pulses matching. I need you to catch my beat, baby."

I drive down, compressing in a relentless rhythm. My heart clenches at the give and recoil of bone beneath my hand.

The sand hard under my knees, an ache tearing through the hollow cavern inside my chest, my voice is a ragged whisper across her still lips as I count, modeling the pulse. "One—two—three—four—five—"

At thirty, I tip her chin. Seal my mouth over hers. Breathe for her.

Palms braced over her sternum, I whisper fiercely, "Breathe." Muscles rigid, I start to tremble. My voice cracks. "Fuck. Come on, angel. In for four...hold two...out four. Lock onto my heartbeat."

Between compressions, my fingers tap out a cadence—her pulse; her melody—over the cage of her ribs. The beat of her fucking heart I've memorized.

Forehead touching hers, I say, "One rhythm. One pulse. Find your way back to me—"

Beneath my palm, it's faint and arrhythmic but it's there—a flutter.

My own heart seizes, muscles frozen in an infuriating, painful grip of hope. With a trembling hand, I apply another gentle compression to her chest, coaxing her weak heartbeat to strengthen.

"That's it," I whisper roughly against her parted lips. "That's my girl. Breathe with me, baby."

Her chest rises with a shallow gasp, life flooding back into her lungs. Relief slams through me as her heartbeat climbs beneath my touch, and I never stop drumming a steady beat across her chest.

Her breath is a soft brush of warmth across my lips, and I draw it in like the sweetest relief. Pressing my forehead to hers, I whisper in my own broken breath, "Stay with me, angel." I swallow, my throat tight with salt and desperation. "I need you to stay with me."

Overhead, the corona flares around the eclipsed sun. Shadow swallows us, the chill sinking deep into our entwined bodies. My breath holds, lungs burning, until the moon starts its slow retreat into third contact—and her heartbeat steadies.

Her pulse stabilizes under my hand, rhythm aligning to mine. Two separate beats locking, a syncopation of pulses fusing into one beneath the waning shadow.

As I lift away, her eyelids flutter, opening to reveal those slate depths threaded by blazing striations of gold. Like a second corona igniting, its fiery filaments reflected in her eyes that flare with heat and life.

With a strenuous exhale, I lower my lips to the pulse in her throat, tasting of salt and life and *her*.

The moon shifts, shadow receding farther. Light bleeds across the shore. Warmth floods me as her breath meets mine on a shallow exhale.

"There you are," I say, the anguish slowly ebbing like the tide. "There's my fire."

Her chest rises beneath my palm, and she coughs weakly. Her cold fingers find mine still splayed across her bare chest and she grips them, a sob catching in her throat.

"Take me in," she whispers, her breath breaking. "Make me warm, Orion. Take me somewhere safe."

Tenderly, I cup her cheek, powerless to deny her anything. Shifting onto my knees, I gather her into my arms and lift her from the sand. Just as I did once before, I cradle her close against my chest. Only this time, the threat isn't in touching her.

As the shadow of totality retreats, a new, sinister fear seeps cold into the marrow of my bones.

I hold Collins tighter, desperate to keep her close, to keep her fragile melody playing as my fingers obsessively tap against her bare thigh, keeping pace with the arrhythmic beat of her heart.

"You know once I show you my secrets," I say, voice low in warning, "I can never let you go."

Collins cups my face, forcing my gaze on her. "Then show me everything."

The black holes collide in complete darkness. None of the energy exploding from the collision comes out as light.

— DR. JANNA LEVIN, *BLACK HOLE BLUES AND OTHER SONGS FROM OUTER SPACE*

21

SOUND OF SPACE

The eternal silence of these infinite spaces frightens me.

— BLAISE PASCAL

ORION

There's a quote often cited by musicians that says: *the music is not in the notes, but in the silence between.*

It's been debated who first said this—whether Mozart, Debussy—because, I think, the truth of it transcends any single voice. For musicians, artists, those who hear beyond the notes and chords, the melody itself, there's a profound understanding that the contrast, the tension—the emotional heart —lies in those quiet spaces between.

It's the breath held.

The heartbeat suspended.

The anticipation for the next note.

Awaiting the shattering rise—

The inevitable fall.

That we shouldn't rush to fill the silence. Because it's in those quiet moments where we find these critical beats needed to experience a piece as a whole.

When her heart stopped beating, when I could no longer hear the sweet, melancholic refrain of her tune, fearing I'd never experience the next note—that single, devastating silence laid me bare.

And it's in this fraught silence now, the anticipation thrumming through my veins, that I carry Collins toward the towering university.

There's a hidden sub-level beneath the observatory, an abandoned sector sealed off decades ago. The place where my darkest secrets are kept. This is where I take her, to this shadowed and haunted part of myself. Waiting, with bated breath, to hear the next notes, to finally unravel the whole piece.

The corridor is mercifully empty. Everyone still in attendance at the symposium. A taut stillness presses in as I carry her past the facility threshold and into the low-lit seclusion of the telescope room.

Her arms drape around my neck, her skin like fire against mine. The softness of her held against the hard lines of me, my muscles strained as her mouth tucks close to the hollow of my throat, driving every sane and rational thought from my head—compelling me to move faster toward the unmarked wall.

My molars grind until my jaw aches as I'm forced to release her—freezing, shivering—reluctantly lowering her feet to the floor. "Just for a moment," I say, voice gruff.

I peel open the front of my damp shirt and press my palm to the concealed, embedded panel. The scanner activates, reading the intricate celestial map inked across my sternum, an encryption of constellations and astronomical coordinates I tattooed myself. It's a code I alter every month to ensure I'm the only one who can gain access.

Until now.

The lock disengages with a hiss, and the heavy door parts open.

If Collins is wary, she doesn't let it show. What she said on the shore still infects my mind: *somewhere safe*. This secret sanctuary is the only refuge I have to offer her. Secluded, protected. Untouched by outsiders and contamination. And right now, I'm desperately hoping it's safe enough to keep the intrusive urges held at bay.

She's fearful of something, but it's not me lifting her back into my arms, or the muted click of the door sealing behind us as I descend the spiral staircase into the dark depths.

I curl her closer, trying to banish the chill from her body. The relief I still feel at war with the creeping unease simmering just beneath.

Soon, concrete encloses us, the air of the lower level colder, denser, infused with the hum of equipment. Dim lighting spills across the floor, revealing the obsessive order of my private space. Minimalistic furniture arranged in precise angles. Stone walls covered in rows of star charts and spectral maps. In the adjoining lab, the computing array housed with metallic racks. Screens calculating quantum entanglement entropy and waveform simulations.

I pause only briefly to grab a bottled water, my only desire to get her hydrated and warm. I twist off the cap for her. "Drink this," I say, heading straight to the bathroom.

The light flicks on as soon as I enter the enclosed room, and I feel her flinch. "Dim light," I command, and the sconce along the concrete wall lowers into a soft glow.

I free a hand to reach into the shower, holding her protectively with one arm as I lift the nozzle and adjust the temperature. When I'm finally forced to release her completely, she stands close, one arm wrapped around her waist, barely holding her torn, soaked blouse together. Her other hand trembles slightly as she brings the water to her lips, taking slow sips, eyes downcast beneath heavy lashes.

My gaze drops to the bruises encircling her wrists. The evidence of her struggle and my damning failure to protect her. Self-loathing is a vicious, building fire beneath my flesh, seeking an outlet. I'm shaking with it.

I refuse to look directly at her, aware that the instant I do, this tenuous tether that's kept me from coming undone will snap. The boundary has been crossed. There's no return, no escape. There's only the agony that flays me deeper every second I'm not touching her.

A light *clink* sounds as she sets her silver case on the concrete counter, the one she's clung to since the beach. Somehow, managing not to lose it to the rip currents, as though her life depends on it. After watching her slip a single tablet onto her tongue, and the visible relief that quickly followed, I loathe that it might.

I rake an unsteady hand through my wet hair, fingers still numb from the cold—but not numb enough to dampen the lingering feel of her. I submerge my hand in the rain of water to test the warmth, and the words leave my mouth unfiltered. "You can't swim, or…" I trail off, the question implied.

Her silence strains my fraying composure, muscles corded tight until I hear her draw a breath.

"It's not that I can't. It's that I shouldn't," she says, throwing similar words I once said to her right back at me, her hollow tone scraping something raw inside my chest. A bite of anger firms my jaw. "It's the exertion," she adds, nearly inaudible.

My throat closes, and a coarse acknowledgement works free with a grunt.

Regardless of what my algorithm predicted, I didn't think she'd charge straight toward the fucking ocean. Since she led me to believe she feared the water, I thought—

My head drops, eyes squeezing shut against the building pressure. I didn't know exactly how she'd end up in that location. But out of all the possibilities, that's not how I imagined it. With the visceral fear eroding my reason, clearly, I wasn't thinking at fucking all.

"Cold shock," she explains, breaking into my tangled thoughts. "Water temperatures in the sixties…it causes—"

"Increased blood pressure. Incapacitation. Rapid heart rate." I thrust the glass door open a little too forcefully, the abrupt *bang* making her flinch. I turn and reach for her, grasping her by the slim dip of her waist and lifting her easily. Her hands brace against my biceps as I step us both into the shower under the warm spray, before retreating a safe distance.

She shivers, running a hand over her arm, blinking against the steady stream as briny seawater rinses away. An immediate flush of color returns to her skin, where I can make out the pattern of light freckles high on her cheeks, and it loosens the knot lodged in my throat.

My gaze sweeps the soft planes of her beautiful face, down the column of her neck, inspecting every scrape and bruise that mars her—until I land on the vulnerable hollow beneath her collarbone, where an incision scar runs between her breasts.

It's a jagged, pale line that stretches the seam of her sternum, curving the costal cartilage and spanning the joint between ribs. Seventeen delicate points of connection, mapping pain like the stars of the Hydra constellation.

A surge of fury cracks beneath my chest, so sharp and sudden, I'm forced to look away. I want those hidden truths she guards, but some resistant part of me dreads knowing them more.

The contacts she wears—the ones that conceal the solar storm of fury burning at the edges of her gray irises. Her hair— the lighter strands apparent at her roots. All the details the algorithm never revealed—her condition, her apparent medical procedure. Either something happened in her past and wasn't reported, or—

"Shit." Collins bends awkwardly, reaching down to remove her boot. I exhale a rough breath and wordlessly drop to my knees before her, grasping the zipper. She braces her hands on my shoulders, fingers noticeably trembling as I ease the first boot off. As I remove the second, a small wince escapes her, the sound cutting right through me.

"How much pain are you in." My voice cracks as I set her boots aside, rising to grip the counter hard enough the edge bites into my palm. No glove to dull the sensation.

After a hesitant beat, she says, "There's some sternal soreness, like I got punched." My knuckles bleach, her words like a fucking punch to me. "Deep breaths sharpen the pain, but I'm okay. There's no fracture." She takes a slow, measured breath to prove her point. "But I'm used to the pain. You know, we just…adapt." Her fingers curl into her wet blouse, rivulets tracing a path down her skin. "I've suffered worse."

What she leaves unsaid detonates in the air between us.

"It's a sternotomy scar," I say, my statement a demand for more.

Her fingers trace the raised seam of her chest. "Mitral regurgitation," she confirms quietly. "I had a valve repair…a while ago. But I still have symptoms."

Her clinical tone strikes a match inside my chest. She struggles to take a deeper breath, her features etched by unmistakable discomfort. Anger surges hot, and I reach for her pill case.

"Those aren't for pain," she says, halting my movement. At my narrowed gaze, she says, "Beta-blockers and amiodarone to slow my heart rate and keep it stable. Nitroglycerin for emergencies. When blood flows…wrong."

I lower my hand, then drive it through my hair, rage clawing at my scalp.

"It's happened before," she continues, "and it can again, Orion. Sometimes a valve leaflet catches. It's manageable, but… Nothing could've changed the outcome."

Changed the outcome.

Her shallow cough threads my spine taut. Anger lashes hot across my skin. Everything in me wants to tear the room apart for a pulse-ox. Call in a trauma bay. Demand a chest film, an ECG— all the actions a sane man takes to prove he hasn't broken the woman he loves.

"We should get you—" I stop, jaw hinged tight. "A doctor. Just in case."

"No hospital. Please." A tremor fractures her plea. "I just need to get warm. Stabilized. Let the medicine work. There's nothing more that can be done, anyway."

I start to grab the med kit from the lab and stop cold, muscles locking. The thought of her out of my sight for even a fraction of an arrhythmic heartbeat is a cavernous pit of fear opening beneath me. My fingers stutter an anxious *one, one, two, three, five, one* against my thigh.

I know precisely how long she was under. Exactly how long I lost her. I counted every terrifying second.

I hate that it makes me feel useless. I loathe even more that I question her.

What I want to demand is trapped behind the knot in my throat. And if I look straight into her starry eyes, there will be no holding it back. Every answer I want from her, every confession I owe her, is suspended like the silence between two notes.

Instead, I listen to the rattling sound of her breaths, uselessly counting each rise and fall.

How the hell do I demand anything from her when there's no

way to explain this place without damning myself further. Admitting that I've imagined what crushing her heart would feel like. Obsessed over tasting her last breath as it trembled against my lips.

I blink hard, forcing the intrusive thought down deep as I attempt to bury my rage. Bowing my head, I turn to leave.

"How did you know, Orion." Her whispered question is laced with the same fearful apprehension constricting my chest.

The knot thickens into an ache at the base of my throat. Keeping my back to her, I release a tense breath. "You wouldn't believe me."

"Try me."

I lift my head, staring into the shadowed depths of the room across from me. "I've known since the night I carried you from that rock," I say, letting that single truth hang in the gathering steam. Then, swallowing the anguish, I turn and meet her imploring eyes with fierce conviction. "I've known, and I've been fighting a fucking rising tide of desperation not to lose you."

Something guarded and uncertain flickers behind her eyes. "You've known this whole time."

"Yes," I admit, utterly miserable.

Her swallow slips along her throat. "How?"

A harsh, incredulous breath escapes me. She wants to know how I knew she'd nearly drown in the rip current. How I knew her body would wash ashore, that her heart would stop beneath the shadow of the solar eclipse.

How I knew the exact moment to pull her from the sea, breathe life back into her lungs, restart the faltering rhythm of her heart—defying the goddamn universe itself to bring her back.

Yet the *hows* are all too impossible to unravel in this singular thread of time, and such a confession would demand an equal measure of truth from her in return—a demand that reflects so vehemently in my fierce stare it forces her lashes to lower, dropping her gaze.

That fleeting glimpse of shame washing over her face with the trailing beads of water scores the length of me. My chest ignites as I take one determined step toward her.

Her fingers cling tighter to her soaked blouse. "I don't know what to say—"

Her words have barely left her lips before I'm inside the shower and towering over her, leaving only a sliver of charged space between our bodies. The violent fury I've struggled to restrain erupts before I can cage it.

"Collins. *Fuck*." My hand slams against the humid tiles above her head, the harsh sound of my breath filling the tight confines.

She doesn't recoil, eyes fixed on the droplets of water cascading down my bare chest, refusing to meet the anguish burning through my gaze.

My hand curls into a fist along the wall, knuckles splitting chafed skin. My breath comes hard and shallow. I close my eyes, voice ravaged by the fear still tearing me apart. "What I knew or even how is irrelevant at this point. What I thought I could control…" I trail off with a bitter, gruff laugh as I fight back the loathing. "You knew."

The accusation breaks between us. Anger and agony clash within me, shredding my hard-fought composure. "You knew what you'd risk. Why the fuck would you do that, angel?"

She swallows, reflexively bringing her hand to the center of her chest as she buries a wince. The same guarded action I've watched her do countless times, and it carves through me like a rusted blade.

"Right. Because you handled that so well. *Not* terrifying me at all with your cryptic, insane ramble." Her voice shakes, rising. "Jesus, Orion. What did you expect me to do? Just wait there— cuffed to your telescope—for you to come back, and then…what?"

I drag a hand down my face, wiping away water and regret in

one stroke. Furious at all the ways I've failed her. "You're right,"
I say roughly, feeling just as desperate as I did in that moment. "I
handled that poorly."

Her breathless laugh is brittle. "You think?" A beat of tense
silence follows before she looks up, searching my face. "What the
hell even happened? Was it some residual setback from the other
night on the beach—?"

"No." I shake my head, dropping my hand.

"But you were afraid you'd harm me."

The way she whispers it, the fearful tremble she's trying to
conceal, is another brutal punch to my gut. "I never wanted to—"

"But you were scared you might." There's a hitch to her
voice, just audible above the raining water. "Are you still afraid
you will now?"

A groan tears loose from my throat. "No. You do not get to
steal my anger right now." My eyes descend to her chest, the air
in my lungs leaden as I take hold of the wet fabric and wrench it
apart, revealing the surgical scar.

My gaze catalogues other, fainter scars along her ribs. The one
brutal mark above her left breast. And I'm a fucking sick bastard,
I know, unashamed as I hungrily rake my gaze over her breasts,
her body, a torturous mix of turmoil and arousal flooding my
bloodstream.

I swallow hard, forcing my gaze to meet hers. "You should've
told me about this, Collins."

Every ragged breath she takes carves deeper into my chest
wall. Even in the dim light, the shiny scars winding her body are
visible. Some surgical, some not. Evidence she's been hurt
—sadistically.

And the knowledge that I ever allowed this void within me
to harbor even a shadow of desire to cause her harm twists
my gut.

Yet I know, standing before her now—furious, helpless—I

would've flung myself from the highest fucking cliff to my death first.

"If I had told you, would that have changed anything?" She pulls in a taut breath, preparing to lash back further, but her ire fades just as quickly when she reads my eyes. "Orion, I couldn't—"

"Tell me now," I demand.

She glances away, pressing her back against the tiles. "It doesn't matter. It's in the past," she says, the edge draining from her tone. "I can't live in fear. Isn't that what you once told me? Oh, and that I want the fight." She shakes her head slowly, a cold laugh slipping free. "You have no idea how much fight I do *not* have left."

Her words hit like a blow to my abdomen, winding me. I see it now, veiled beneath the suffused gold, within those deep, dark lanes—the darkness behind the stars in her eyes. All she's hidden in that void. The truth of her pain shatters through me, decimating.

"Nothing matters anymore," she says on a broken whisper, gathering her soaked blouse closed as though she can shield herself from me, and a rising wave of fury licks my bones. "Not after what I've done."

Leo.

Her dejection is as thick as the steamy vapor enclosing us, and I wish—of all the memories lost—that this was the one I could fucking banish from her mind. She took a life. And where I've taken many, she believes she took an innocent one. The torment claws at her, the guilt threatening to drag her under.

Yet it doesn't matter if she took one life or a hundred. If she came to the misty ends of the world to take mine, I'd let her—if it could erase even an ounce of that pain from her eyes.

I will not let her drown in this.

The instant I saw Leo grab her arm, time folded, and suddenly it was Prescott's hand gripping her in the colonnade. And just as I witnessed her anger rise during that moment, I watched it swell into a tidal wave on the pier. I wasn't supposed to observe, yet I couldn't look away as I watched her fury brew, the umbrella clutched tight. Watched the reactive flame ignite—right before she swung it as a weapon.

Now, her heartache flares as bright as the gold threading her slate irises, and it god damn terrifies me—that this could be where I could lose her. Not to the ocean. Not to a lost heartbeat. But here, dragged under by her grief and guilt. A void that consumes everything.

These are the treacherous, dark waters where she could slip beyond my reach.

Tenderly, I claim her waist, tethering myself to her. I hold her tight, refusing to let her drift away. If she needs someone to take her wrath, someone to punish to keep her fighting, breathing—

I decide I can give her this.

I can take it. All of it. The pain, the fury. The fear crashing through her like the cold, dark tide.

I can be what she needs.

"It does matter," I tell her, impatience bleeding into my tone. "You should've told me." I catch the hem of her shirt, prying the material open once more and possessively splaying my hand over the length of her scar. "You should've made me aware before you asked that of me in the observatory, knowing what could happen." The memory is a visceral assault of her body collapsing against mine, breath and heartbeat faltering. "How could you tempt me to strangle you, knowing—"

"You wouldn't even touch me," she interrupts, chest rising against my palm. "You wanted to. Yet you couldn't, wouldn't. *Shouldn't.*" Her tone turns mocking. "This entire time, you've been suffering these violent thoughts of me, and if you'd known about this—" She breaks off, lips trembling. "Would you have ever allowed yourself to even look at me?"

At my intense silence, she nods knowingly. Then she tentatively lifts her hand to my chest, fingertips tracing the ink scored across my skin, the lines of the constellation—her constellation. Her eyes spear mine in haunting revelation. "Your mind must've truly been a tortured place."

"And what if I had hurt you…or worse?" A fierce ache scalds my throat, and I swallow painfully as the warmth of her skin seeps into my palm. "How tortured do you think my fucked-up brain would be then?"

"God, Orion. If you think I'm so broken, why even bring me back?" Her accusation slices through me, deep and anguished. "Why drag me back to this? The constant pain, the relentless struggle, and the—" She draws a shuddering breath, eyes blazing. "Do you even understand how fucking exhausting it is? Why not just let me go?"

The raw misery behind her demand levels me. As the fire fades behind her eyes, fury coils beneath my ribs—at her scars, at the answers they hold, at the terror of what they mean. And I'm viscerally enraged that, right this moment, I have no one to kill.

We stand beneath the fall of water, each drop a catalyst. Her hand braced on my chest, mine fused to hers, the silence between heartbeats stretching. Waiting for the next note, the next shattering revelation.

This space between us spans as eternal and infinite as the darkest void of space, terrifying in its utter silence.

And yet, even in the deepest reaches of these cold, dark places there is friction, vibration, heat—collision that births stars.

Her pulse, my breath. The shared current of touch. What's needed to eliminate the distance and fear across this chasm of silence.

Her eyes burn with those heated bands of gold, bright enough to ignite my blood. A storm of desperation and desire churns within her eyes of dust and starlight. They beg something of me.

And god-*damn*, it reduces me to a wretched, base creature. I grasp the waistband of her skirt with my right hand, pulling her flush against me. "Fuck," I hiss, immediately relinquishing my grip. With a harsh exhale, I slap my hand against the tile and lean over her, letting the broken cadence of her heartbeat against my palm ground me.

"You can't look at me like that," I say near her ear, voice roughened by need. My thumb brushes a tender sweep across her skin. "You have no idea what you're asking of me. I can't deny you anything—so please…fuck, angel. Don't ask this of me."

Her head tips back, throat bared defiantly as her shimmering gaze meets mine, fierce and unyielding. "I know exactly what I'm asking," she insists, though this time, her lips quiver with the challenge. A contradiction that rends my composure. "And I'm not that breakable."

Her beautiful breasts rise with her quick breath as her hand slips down the wet plane of my chest, across my tense abdomen, slender fingers hooking beneath my waistband.

"Jesus—fuck, Collins. Don't make me fuck you up against this shower wall." Tendons corded in fire, I brace my hands on either side of her, caging her in and holding myself back in the same desperate move. "Don't make me risk hurting you."

I close my eyes against the intoxicating vision of her beneath me as her fingertips find the leather belt, making every muscle in my abdomen tighten. She needs proof—proof that I can see past the scars, beyond the broken places. To prove her accusation false.

With one word from her, I'll surrender to this insatiable hunger. Becoming something more vile and depraved, even as I've just stolen her from the brink of death. Only there's a crushing vise locking my ribs, the fear that this is where she exists, perpetually balancing on this hazardous edge.

She works the buckle loose, and I capture her arm, driving it above her head. Anchoring her to the tile, I press my fingers to the pulse point of her wrist, synching my internal count to each racing beat.

And fuck—

I'm ruined.

Just the feel of her restrained beneath me shatters any illusion I had of redemption.

"If you look at me like I am…" Her voice breaks as she tenses against my hold. "Like I'm just something damaged, something broken." A sob catches in her throat as her fingers curl into a fist against my chest before she brings it down in a weak strike. "I have a bad heart, but I'm not…"

The anger fractures inside me, stripping away another layer of my defenses. Gently, I cover her fist with my hand, holding her there. I find her gaze, letting her anguish tear through me. All her pain, her exhaustion, her resignation.

"I have a bad heart, but I'm not broken," she says, her voice faltering as she slips along the shower.

I drop to my knees and catch her, bracing her between my body and the wall. Framing the back of her head, I cradle it against the tile, my other cupping her waist as I look up into her face. "I know you're not, baby. Fuck." I press my forehead to her stomach, breathing her in deeply. "You're not broken. You're mine," I murmur the words fiercely. "Your heart isn't bad. It belongs to me." Pulling back just enough, I press a kiss to the soft space beneath her navel. "You're not broken. You're mine. Your heart isn't bad," I utter this to her as my lips leave tender, desperate kisses as I trail upward, mapping a line of devotion along her body.

I continue to whisper these words, branding them into her

skin, imprinting each one like a vow over every scar. "You're mine." I kiss the pale line cleaving her breasts, dropping fervent kisses across her collarbone, her throat, her jaw, until I'm towering above her, killing the distance between us as I tip her head back.

"You are *mine*," I murmur against her trembling lips. "And I will never let you go. Never lose you. I will always bring you back."

She shakes her head lightly, eyes shimmering with aching vulnerability in the steamy low light. "How can you say any of this when…" Her voice frays softly. "I've been standing under the spray, half-naked, and you've barely looked at me. Ever since you saw the scar, you don't—" Her throat tightens visibly. "You don't look at me the same."

"Goddammit." I grip her wrist and bring her hand to the front of my soaked pants, pressing her palm right against my aching, rock-hard erection straining beneath the zipper. "Does this fucking feel like I don't want you?"

Her swallow is audible, her gaze flashing bright and needy as she meets mine, and god-fucking-dammit, I'm helpless as I surrender to her entirely.

"Use me," I tell her, voice worn with desperation. "I don't fucking care. If it means I get to taste even a drop of you—that I get to see your mouth go slack with pleasure, those beautiful eyes glaze with satisfaction…then just use me, angel."

I grasp the high slit of her drenched skirt and drag it aside, my bare palm seizing the soft curve of her hip. I let my fingers taste the tempting, silky feel of her skin, making me goddamn feral, before I tear the thin fabric of her panties away.

"Spread your legs." I issue the demand even as my thigh presses between hers, parting her open to me.

Her hands find leverage on my shoulders, blunt nails digging into muscle as I grip her hips, guiding her soaked heat into a slow grind against my thigh. My left hand grasps the nape of her neck, fingers threading into her wet hair as I bring my mouth to her ear. "Just don't tempt me to do something worse…something I can't take back."

Controlling the motion of her hips, I rock her body in a slow, torturous rhythm, my jaw clenched against the sensual feel of her.

She shivers against my caged arms, her breathy moans dissolving into the saline rinsing between us, charged and electrified, becoming a flowing current. We're locked here, held captive within this quantum dance. Molecules vibrating, frantically seeking connection. An energy exchange between our bodies that demands more movement, heat, friction.

Touch.

A torn sound vibrates from her throat, and *fuck*—I know it's not enough.

"It has to be enough," I grit out, an involuntary, ardent demand falling from my mouth, and her answering whimper drops right to my groin as she drives a weak fist against my chest —as if trying to push me away and pull me closer in the same, bruising motion. Her fury and pain and need all collide, fragmenting beautifully into raw, surrendering hunger.

I grasp her face, thumb sweeping her jawline as I stare down at her, our lips separated by a breath. Her fingers dig into the drenched fabric of my open shirt, the smallest gesture pulling me inexorably closer. Her touch drifts, fingertips tracing across my chest, tracking the stars of her constellation.

"I was always yours," she whispers against my mouth. Beneath the steam, heat unfurls, almost unbearable. "And you're mine," she breathes. "You're mine, Orion."

"I am yours," I rasp, working her harder against me. "You have all of me." One final claim before I slant my mouth over hers, capturing her lips in an unyielding kiss. A soft, needy whimper escapes her as I grasp the back of her knee, dragging her body flush against mine. She arches off the tile, rolling her hips in desperate search for friction and making me utterly mindless with the need to feel her, taste her—

Take her.

With painstaking restraint, I remove the temptation, placing my palm to the center of her chest. Her heart pounds beneath my touch, and I lightly drum my fingers there, keeping time with her beats, matching the cadence of her pulse. Holding the count— holding myself—painfully, maddeningly back.

Warm water streams between our exposed skin, rivulets sensually infusing our kiss with heat as I deepen it. Her hand moves over mine, boldly guiding me from the incision scar to the curve of her breast, where I'm helpless to do anything but cup her perfectly within my palm.

I relinquish a harsh groan against her lips, muscles tensing as my thumb skims her peaked nipple, sending a shockwave of arousal through me as my fingertips tenderly caress the softness of her, feeling the swell of flesh where two small, circular scars mark her skin.

With a shuddering moan, she arches into my touch, spine bowing against the wall, hips moving in aching, torturous rolls, pressing her hard against my erection as her body pleads for more.

"Goddamn, angel, I want you," I say, my voice a dark, possessive growl. "You're so fucking beautiful, it physically pains me. I want every part of you, Collins. You belong to me. *With* me." My grip tightens, drawing her impossibly closer. "You feel so fucking perfect against me, it terrifies me, starling. Once I discover how right it feels to be inside you…I'll be utterly lost."

"I won't let that happen," she says, eyes shining with a mix of desire and resolve. "Just...Orion, please. I need to feel all of you."

Something lethal flares in my gaze, and I allow her to see it. "Once I start, I won't stop. And I won't be gentle."

"Fuck, I hope not," she whispers, delivering my smug words right back to me, a challenge that unfurls a dangerous current within me.

"Tell me this is what you need," I beg of her, the grate of my voice scraping the steamy air between us. I hold impossibly still, muscles locked. Teeth gritted hard as my restraint frays.

Her breath turns ragged, wet lashes glinting with each tremulous blink. "I need—" Her voice breaks on the fragile confession. "Hold me tight. I don't know if I can...otherwise."

"Fuck."

I know exactly what she's asking—and it incinerates the last weak tether to any morality.

There's a monster in her past, and I want to wrestle with it.

A fiendish craving rears from my depths, a primal beast all but feral to fuck that fear right out of her.

"Even if you want me to stop," I whisper gutturally, pressing my forehead to hers, "I won't be able to. You're going to have to fight me off, little archer."

I can't keep holding back these dark urges. She's going to have to fight—

And she can't stop fighting. Not ever.

Water rains over us, the steady rhythm sealing us within this tense moment as our racing hearts crash together, waiting. Daring.

Her chest rises and falls against mine. "I trust you," she finally says. "It's what I need."

And it's permission enough.

Those simple words eviscerate my control. "Fucking Christ," I mutter rough against her mouth. Something dangerous and final breaks loose inside me, and I grind hard between her thighs. Her breath catches, eyes fluttering shut as she licks the beads of water from her parted lips, wrenching a low groan from my throat. "Shit, you're in so much danger, angel. Hold tight to me—"

Her arms link around my neck just as I shove away from the tile. Hooking her legs around my hips, she clings to me as I snatch the pill case from the counter.

I haul her to the darkened recess of my room. Everything she leaves unspoken, what we both leave unsaid, remains suspended —abandoned in the steam and shadow.

As I lower Collins to the mattress, the pill case slips from my fingers, landing with a soft click to the blanket. Hovering above her, I hold eye contact, making sure she knows exactly who's about to fuck her.

"Dammit," I whisper hoarsely, my thumb brushing the rapid pulse of her throat. "I fucking hate that I can't make this gentle for you."

Her swallow drags against my palm, her stare unwavering. "You don't have to be anything else for me. That's never what I wanted."

Her confession slices deep. She's not the one who's broken. Dangerous cracks spider across my surface. If she sees the breaks, she doesn't shy away.

My love is woven deep with violence, absence and loss. And still, she holds the intensity of my eyes with stark conviction.

Slowly, I strip off my wet shirt, discarding it somewhere behind me as her wrists remain locked around my neck, as if fearful of losing connection. Her gaze moves over the complex ink lining my body. Across my chest, along my abs, over my arms. Trailing lower, following the shaded lines along the taut diagonal muscles slipping below my waistband.

Her music echoes through me as I hold my place above her. Her pulse an aching staccato that vibrates between her breaths,

Euclidean harmonies resonating sweet notes beneath her skin, and I endeavor to learn every hidden melody of her body, measure by exquisite measure.

I reach behind my neck and circle my fingers around her slender wrist. She reflexively twists, testing resistance. I firm my grip, fingertips finding the frantic beat of her pulse.

Counting beats. Counting breaths. Counting in ritual so neither stops.

My gaze fuses to hers, a demand issued by my fierce stare. Her last chance to stop me as I continue to count, seconds stretching, the thrum of my own heart a painful scrape against cartilage, costing me another measure of sanity—

"Stop counting, Orion. Just fuck me."

"God damn." A groan tears loose, raw and guttural. "I'm going to do so much more than fuck you, angel," I say, my lips pressing a bruising vow against hers. My hand drags down the length of her side, thumb charting every delicate rib beneath her skin. "You're going to let me worship you. But first"—my voice roughens—"I'm going to reduce you to a beautiful, filthy mess right here beneath me. And you're going to take it. Every debased thing I do to this divine body."

This is what she desires from me, *needs* from me—and god help me, I'm powerless to deny her.

Even as her shiver tears at my feeble restraint, I keep count. Fingertips compulsively tapping against her skin, marking pulse points as her melody thrums in my veins. An intoxicating rhythm falling somewhere between the golden symmetry of phi, the spiraled perfection of Fibonacci, and the untamed tempo of her heartbeat—

Where each breathless pause stretches into an empty, terrifying infinity. A space suspended between dread and awe, hope and devastation. Waiting in excruciating silence for that next critical beat to strike.

And yet, we can't rush to fill this silence, no matter how agonizing. It's the tension before a note is struck, the breath held right before release.

And the exquisite relief when her heart beats once more against mine.

Fourth contact is an ending, and a beginning. The moment when we return from shadow to sunlight, forever changed by what we have witnessed.

— DR. KATE RUSSO, PSYCHOLOGIST AND
ECLIPSE CHASER

22

COLLISION

In music, a heartbeat tempo is a musical pace that aligns with a pulse.

ORION

There's a moment where anticipation fractures into surrender, where desire collapses into defeat. A reckless instant suspended in freefall, powerless against gravity. That dangerous edge where longing ignites into madness.

It's the destruction of the boundary.

At this terrifying brink, hunger sears so viciously, so ravenously, that pain itself becomes a necessary shackle.

Until restraint snaps, and you fall willingly, helplessly, into ruin.

Staring down at the ethereal angel in my bed, my gaze roaming over her beautiful, alluring body, I'm past the point of famished. I'm a goddamn frenzy of atoms, hellbent on annihilation.

With one last reverent sweep of my thumb over her cheek, I

savor her softness. Trailing my knuckles across the tender bruise, my touch is a careful brush against her abraded skin. This is where gentle dissolves into rough. Where the tremble in my strained muscles from holding resistance gives, and sinew and tendons harden into steady force.

It's a surrender so pleasurable, it's almost orgasmic.

Collins blinks up at me through her captivating lashes, her mouth parted in invitation, as my hand settles at her throat. The shocked breath that slips past her lips urges my palm close to her jaw, fingers firm against the delicate column.

I glide my tongue over my bottom lip, tasting her delectable scent in the air before I lower my mouth to hers. I lick into her mouth, goddamn feral as I taste her slowly, thoroughly, before I deepen the kiss.

"Spread your legs." The demand is delivered in a deep timbre against her mouth, and her pulse flares in wild revolt against my fingertips.

Her hesitation brings a dark, crooked smile to my lips. I let my body fall heavy over hers, securing my grip around her neck.

She swallows hard, the flutter beneath my fingers quickening.

"Have it your way, angel." My legs invade between her knees, the soaked fabric of her skirt a restrictive barrier that only heightens my desire to shred it. In an urgent move, I wrench the wet material up her thighs and force her legs apart.

A flash of fear ignites behind her darkened eyes, and fuck, it's as intoxicating as her scent. "I can practically taste your arousal," I say, my voice all friction and groan.

My elbow digs into the mattress as I let her feel my weight. Hips flexing in painful need to be inside her, I drop a tender kiss to the slope of her shoulder, tongue delving out to further torture myself.

This next part I make quick for her. Shoving my hand between us, I yank open the buttons of her skirt. She releases a clipped curse, and the breathy sound of it winds hot through my muscles as her fingers curl into the blanket. I skim my fingers beneath the waistband, and the reactive flutter of her abdomen unleashes a guttural groan.

I brush my lips across the joint of her shoulder and neck, scraping my teeth over her pulse, before I fist my hand around the band, and—pushing back—drag her skirt down her hips.

Dim light streaming from the other room bathes her in a contrast of shadow and light, revealing the sexy contours of her body. And I visually trace every intimate curve. A shiver racks my spine, and the motion elicits the softest gasp from her.

I drag my hand over my mouth as I hungrily take her in. "Fuck, you are so beautiful, I don't know where to begin."

My heated gaze absorbs the delicate angles and bends of her, admiring the sensual swell of her breasts, the sexy dip of her belly, her curvy thighs and hips—every fucking inch of her body I savor, letting my eyes have her first before I dare give my hands permission.

With an impatient grunt, I flip her onto her stomach. Collins presses her hands into the white blanket, fingers digging in for purchase as I pull her skirt down past the middle of her thighs. I allow myself one lingering gaze at her sinful ass before I grip the collar of her shirt and tow it down her arms, binding it around her forearms.

Then I quickly have my hand around her wrist, bringing it to the small of her back and bracing it between the two slight dimples. I push the flat of my palm beneath her pelvis, angling her ass up to me. "Holy fuck—you have no idea how crazy you're making me."

I'm devolving into a crazed madman at the need to taste all of her at once. It's taking all of my willpower not to tear through her, to ravish her so thoroughly it leaves nothing of either of us behind.

As her breathing escalates, I press hard against the rising pulse in her wrist, my fingers centered over the inked stars that point toward the fiery heart of her.

It will be blinding and swift, the utter immolation of my humanity. For her, I'll incinerate whatever boundary I have left, burn myself to a hollow husk in that radiant fire.

And when the void swallows the last of my soul, these heartbeat stars will be my tether.

The tempo of a pulse falls somewhere between one-twenty and one-thirty beats per minute, and I map her rhythm, scoring the beat of her heart into my bones like notation onto staves.

Jaw flexed tight, I grasp my belt buckle and tear the damp leather free of the loops. She quakes with a whole-body shiver at the sharp sound, sending a wicked thrill coursing through my heated veins. I slip the leather tip along the column of her spine, and she trembles under the threat of it, her pulse spiking against my fingers.

Reluctantly, I drop the belt on the bed next to the silver case, then I grab her ass, callused palms greedily feeling her, relishing the lurid way her hips roll as I slide my thumb between her crease.

"You are so goddamn sexy, starling. Let me hear those throaty whimpers." I skate my thumb down the hot center of her pussy, biting back a savage groan at the feel of how wet she is, so close to undoing me. "Fucking hell, once I feel your hot flesh against me—"

She bucks a little at the intrusion of my thumb, and suddenly I'm desperate to see her writhing against this bed. Her body tenses as I glide the tip of my finger through her slick lips.

"Breathe, Collins."

Her back rises with her deep inhale, splintering a measure of my control. The second she releases a slow exhale, I sink my fingers inside her, jaw clenched at the sight of her ass kicking up from the pressure.

"Oh, Jesus. Fuck—" I bite off the words, teeth gnashed against the gratifying feel of her tight cunt sheathed around me. Skin to fevered skin. Nothing between us. And the erotic sight of her twisting below—*Christ. Hell.*

Her arms bracketed at the small of her back by her shirt, I grip her wrist tighter—for her, for me—to keep us here at this torturous edge a moment longer before I'm fucking us both into oblivion.

Intrusive images from too many bloody and violent scenes claw their way to the surface, and I can't force them back below the dark tide.

As if sensing my struggle, she moves her hips, igniting a feral lust as she clenches around my fingers. I unleash a guttural curse and press my thumb to her sacrum, massaging that erogenous zone at the base of her spine. And god damn, she's so receptive, wet heat floods over my fingers.

Her thighs press against my legs. Unable to squeeze them closed or spread them wider, she's trapped by the band of her skirt. Hushed by the blanket, she makes a helpless sound that attacks my restraint with a vicious craving, encouraging me to sink deeper, rhythmically inserting my fingers. Truly feeling her for the first time. Her heat, her arousal. Her soft, slick flesh.

"This cunt is so goddamn needy and *mine*," I say around a growl. "You need to tell me how this feels," I demand, curling my fingers deep inside.

She releases a throaty moan, and with a tug at the restraint binding her, she nods her head against the mattress.

"Collins, I need you to use words." The edge in my tone cracks on the demand.

"It feels good…perfect," she says. "Orion, you feel perfect. I want more of you."

"Goddamn, you want to destroy me."

Keeping this gradual, maddening pace, I'm slowly torn mad, lost to the arousing sensation of her soaking my fingers. Driven out of my mind with need as she arches her back, grinding against my hand in demand for more.

Seeing her rock her hips so shamelessly strains another thread of control. And having her bound, at my complete mercy… Fuck. Those dark filaments stir and lash, pulling me dangerously close to the brink.

Keeping my hand leashed around her wrist, I count each furious beat of her pulse, waiting a torturous length of time until the cadence of her heartbeat steadies. I keep fucking her with my fingers, priming her to take me. Because the second I do, there will be no more holding back.

Draping my body over hers, I push my fingers deeper, loving the way she writhes beneath me. I'm losing the battle when I remove them to taste her, unleashing a low growl. "Fuck. I could make a meal of your pussy alone."

Harnessing a level of control, I smooth her damp hair away from the side of her face in a tender sweep, dropping my palm to the nape of her neck. I brace her there as I press my mouth to her ear. "Stay just like this."

Her breathing intensifies, her back crashing against my chest. I raise up just enough to lower my zipper, and the severe sound cracks the tense silence.

"Orion—"

My name leaves her lips like a plea. I've barely lowered my pants before she begins to twist away, her body moving across the bed in a brazen act of defiance.

"That will make it so much worse," I warn her, my voice a dark rasp as I push my pants down.

Forearms still bound behind her back, she pushes herself with her knees. The forbidden sight of her struggling to escape soaks my bloodstream with a euphoric rush of adrenaline.

Untamed hunger sparks through my veins, provoking a primal urge from deep within the marrow of my bone, and shadows bleed into my vision. The knowledge that every act to follow is damnable does nothing to stop me.

A violent hunger claws free as I shed the last of my restrictive clothing. "Oh, starling—" I reach across the bed, securing both hands around her ankles. "You had your chance to run. I fucking *told* you to run, baby. There's no escape now."

I forcibly drag her back toward me, and she kicks out, striking my body with a little fight to whet my appetite. I climb onto the bed. And amid the brief struggle, I have her skirt stripped the rest of the way off her legs, her blouse torn away from her arms.

And as I hover above her, chest heaving, my groin aching at the salacious vision of her trapped underneath, she manages to wriggle a hand free. I pin her other wrist to the bed above her head, leaving her that one hand to fight with.

Banding my fingers tight, I tether myself to her pulse as I drag the crown of my cock over the seam of her ass. Then lower, gliding the tip through her arousal, damn near losing my mind at the hot, drenched feel of her.

I straddle her thighs, clamping my free hand to the sexy flare of her hip. She squirms defiantly beneath me, and shit, her throaty little moan ignites a line of fire up my spine. "God—damn, you're begging for a brutal fucking."

"Your unfiltered thoughts are so filthy," she breathes into the blanket with a reactive shiver.

"*Hmm.* Trust me"—a dark groan resonates from the cavern of my chest as I grind lewdly against her ass—"I'm holding the worst of them back."

"Don't."

That one word strikes like a match in my gut, charring my weakened restraint to ash between us. Eyes slamming shut, I battle the destructive urge to answer her demand in the most depraved, ruinous way.

"That's it—" I grunt as I push onto my knees. "I want your eyes on me while I fuck you." I flip her beneath me, spreading her wide and guiding her legs around my hips, where I settle heavy between her slick thighs and—"Fuck," I growl, the ravaged sound torn from my throat.

I hold myself rigidly still against her. Muscles corded, tendons strained, every part of me rebels against my shaky control. "Angel, I'm about to commit every filthy, depraved act against this body. Once I'm deep inside you…" I trail off, letting her feel the threat behind my words with the incessant prod of my cock.

The dread that I will destroy her—body, mind, heart—is a volatile mass behind my ribs. I've gathered enough fragments to form a crude picture of what haunts her past—and it rips through me with visceral rage.

Her eyes are fathomless as she moves her hand instinctively toward the stretch of scarred skin along her chest to cover it. This same action I've watched her do countless times, unaware of the revelation of other scars that I've now glimpsed on her body. I recognize their pattern. I know the size and shape of the toothed blade used to carve them.

An unbearable ache flares in the center of my chest as I dip my head, dropping a kiss to the scar seated beneath the soft underswell of her breast. Her breath hitches, a sound lodged thick in her throat.

"You need to tell me, Collins," I utter against her skin. "Tell me what frightens you." My demand is punctuated by the slow, controlled grind of my hips as I notch the head of my cock right at the tender center of her.

And the fragile space between us shrinks to breath and pulse and heat.

I could fuck her, mercilessly, ruthlessly, in this bed. Swallowed by darkness. Lost beyond all salvageable reason. That stark truth quivers between us, an enticing dare that would take only the slightest thrust of my hips to satisfy.

In this way, she was always meant for me—to be my victim. Helplessly pinned, held immobile. Impaled to this bed—

"It's muscle memory," she says, her voice dragging me back from the abyss of my thoughts, and I blink hard.

Her swallow moves along the delicate line of her throat. "The paralysis is muscle memory," she explains, her voice a breathy murmur. "The touch of leather on my skin. The sharp scent of it. The feel smothering my mouth... The weight bearing down..." Her eyes squeeze shut, forcing back a wave of torment as her exhale trembles out. "I froze. I couldn't fight. I thought...if I just stayed still, it would be over fast." A sob catches between breaths. "But it wasn't over fast—and more than my life was stolen. No matter if my heart still beats, if my lungs still draw breath, I didn't survive. Anytime there's a threat of intimate touch, my body locks me in that hell. I just...freeze."

Rage ignites in my bloodstream, a searing fury that infuses my cells. I could incinerate the entire world, let it burn to cinders around us, just to make certain he was reduced to ash within the flames.

She doesn't need a hero to save her. She needs a monster to fight.

With deliberate movements, I capture her wrist and push it above her head. The motion draws her taut, laying her surgical scar bare, putting the full, sinful beauty of her breasts on display to me. I hold her pinned to the bed as my body drops heavy over hers, aligning us perfect, seamless.

"Fight me," I say, my voice a broken rasp. "Any pain you need to deliver, I won't just take it. I'll relish it, angel."

At her tremulous exhale, I lower my forehead to hers. My thumb makes rhythmic circles over the pattern of stars across her wrist, fusing my pulse to the staccato beat beneath her skin. And just like that moment as I held her against a speaker of sound waves, I feel her body tense beneath me, her muscles gathering tight in preparation for a struggle.

As I ease back to find her gaze, her pupils are blown. Dark, glittering pools of raw emotion. The fear banked there should decimate me. Yet it seeps molten into my vessels, an intoxicating summons to this terrible, wretched desire that, once granted a single taste, will consume.

Irrevocably.

"I want your fight," I say, urgent as I wet my lips. "I'm taking you, Collins. Rough, hard. And you need to fight."

Holding her immobile, my body a bonded cage around hers, I keep her gaze—a silent, severe warning delivered in mine. Because once I cross this boundary, there may be no return. Not all annihilation births creation from dust and starlight. And if something does emerge, it might be something monstrous and lost.

On the shore beneath the shadow, I fought to save her. I held back the insidious, dark urges clawing at my mind. But this—this is reaching into the unknown, into the void itself, and hoping some semblance of humanity survives.

A torn sound escapes her, and she bites into the cushion of her lip as her gaze searches the rigid planes of my face. Within her storming depths, I watch a spark of her fury ignite, that celestial fire that wants to rage.

"You're the only one I trust to..." she whispers, her words failing, "to do—this." Her swallow is audible. "I trust you, Orion."

A primal desire tears loose, and I hungrily claim her mouth, cutting off her pained concession. The sound that emanates from me is barely human as I kiss her until I'm drowning in her, letting my lips linger against hers until our ragged breaths align.

"Hold on, angel." My voice breaks as I lace our fingers together. She grips back, muscles tensing and thighs pressing against my hips.

"Collins, take a breath for me."

With a quick nod, she does, her nails biting into the back of my hand—a fierce counterpoint of pain and pleasure as I thrust inside her.

And we collide, intense and incandescent, like atoms merging in the fiery heart of a star. Fusion at its most elemental, crashing violent and devastating.

"God, you feel so fucking good," I groan against her mouth. Muscles strained, I mutter a gruff curse, utterly wrecked. "Too goddamn perfect—fuck."

For one aching beat, I keep myself deep inside her. Then, gripping her hand, I pull back and thrust again—rougher, deeper —shattering myself against her as she releases the softest cry, an erotic note that undoes the very core of me.

Collins goes rigid beneath me, her heartbeat trapped in fear, nails carving crescents into my knuckles. The tension in her body mirrors my own, and I can sense the panic clutching her, locking her in place.

I release a shuddering breath with my next restrained thrust, a low curse working free. "Being frozen hurts far worse, starling," I whisper over her parted lips, urgently coaxing her as I deepen my strokes, losing myself to the sinfully corrupt feel of claiming her.

For one moment, she's held captive by that fear, then her body comes alive beneath me. Reactive, frantic.

Violent.

Her body crashes against mine.

My fingers laced through hers, my other hand restraining her wrist to the bed, I rear back and slam into her. A guttural curse rips from my throat, my flesh aflame with friction as I bury myself impossibly deeper.

Each building thrust grows more demanding, more punishing as her body thrashes against mine. Her cries fill the air as her hips surge upward in fierce defiance. And god-fucking-dammit—a savage groan scrapes loose as I feel her squirm and buck, an erotic rebellion making me a damned fiend as I press her deeper into submission, dropping my full weight on top of her.

Her eyes fasten shut, the glistening fringe of her lashes so achingly beautiful as I bear down, mercilessly driving inside her, defiling her with each ruthless thrust. Tearing through her—through me.

And I hold her restrained—

So she can fight, so she can rail.

So she can crash against me, wave after battering wave, unleashing her turbulent fury.

I let her storm rage. I let her anger surge.

I take it all.

For a shattered heartbeat, my grip on her wrist relaxes, and she pulls free. She brings her balled fist down on my shoulder. Once. Again. Relentless as she strikes out. With her next blow, her hand slips against my sweat-slicked skin, but she doesn't stop until her strength ebbs, her ragged breath giving way to raking nails, branding me in furious streaks of fire.

"Jesus, fuck—"

The curse grinds past gritted teeth as pain lights a fuse, and my hand slips around her throat, collaring her with enough pressure she can scream, where her breaths don't drag.

But dammit, each breathy cry she releases scratches across my senses in tantalizing rakes, like her nails shredding my flesh right along with my resistance, summoning this twisted desire to squeeze the delicate column of her throat.

"Yes, fuck—" My voice is a gruff demand between thrusts. "That's it, baby. Let me feel those claws."

Her resistance makes her clench around me, gripping tighter, pulling me deeper each time I withdraw to plunge back into her slick heat. Just as I drive forward, losing myself completely, her nails catch my cheek—

A gratifying burn carves a visceral, delicious pain through my body.

For a shocked flicker of a moment, she looks stricken, until her eyes meet mine through the dark—and she's confronted with the depraved fiend that wants to do more than feed on her agony.

"God, you're sick," she bites out, chest heaving, eyes blazing as her anger mounts.

A wicked smile curls the corner of my mouth. "*Mmhm*. I'm sick…" Fisting my hand in her hair at the nape, I tug sharply, tipping her head back as I press my lips to her ear. "I can feel how fucking wet you get every time you try to hurt me." My voice lowers to a dark rasp, every guttural syllable punctuated with a brutal thrust. "Go ahead, fight harder, baby—I promise I'll fuck you through every delicious, punishing hit of pain, until all you can scream is my name."

Her body bucks enticingly beneath mine. "Fuck you—" A litany of vicious obscenities tears free of her. Every vulgar curse, each heated accusation sending a searing trail of pleasure down my spine.

A darkly amused grunt slips past my lips as I slam against her. "Oh, you love the way I fuck you, angel." Her defiant thrash rips a primal growl from my throat. "If you want to hurt me—" I rail into her, once, twice, bruising and unrelenting "—then fucking hurt me."

My next thrust is decimating, wrenching a sexy, unguarded

moan from her. As long as her heart keeps beating that fierce, raging beat, I will stoke the embers of my little fire sign, keeping her flame burning.

Another merciless thrust strips a desperate cry past her sweet lips. "Oh, god…Orion. Don't…" she gasps between each ruthless stroke. "Don't stop."

Her back bows from the mattress in surrender, drawing my heated gaze to the seductive arch of her body. Driven by compulsion, I set a punishing rhythm with my hips, each relentless thrust timed to the feverish beat beneath her skin.

Lowering my mouth to her breast, a possessive groan reverberates from my chest as I lave my tongue over her peaked nipple—teasing, tormenting—before capturing it between my teeth and sucking hard, earning another throaty moan.

"Can't believe you kept these gorgeous fucking tits from me all this time, Collins Holbrook." Accentuating my point, I punish her nipple, teeth grazing over the taut bud. Then I sink a bite into the lush curve of her breast, groaning as my fingers covetously caress the round scars along her side.

A torrid mix of pleasure and pain arches her chest against mine, her heart a frantic staccato pounding into my ribs. The raw scratches left by her nails flare with a satisfying burn at every glide of our bodies as my strokes devolve, turning unguarded.

I press my weight heavier against her, forcing her thighs wider around my hips with bruising insistence, utterly lost beneath the unyielding current of her storm.

And I'm beyond reason, mindless with want to taste and touch and fuck—my body crushing against her struggling body with agonizing need.

This twisted hunger demands everything, feeding like a glutton off her broken cries. A wicked, ravenous fiend savoring her fight as I drag my tongue over the tears streaking her bruised cheek. And god help me—I revel in them. The saline a perfect conductor, intensifying this depravity between us.

Nostrils flared, abdomen flexing, I rut into her with savage force as her hips writhe beneath me. Her blunt nails cut across any flesh she can touch, can wound—my ribs, arms, back. A guttural sound is torn from me as her teeth sink into my shoulder.

The pain lights my senses. Each strike, every scrape and bite, stokes a fire deep within, until I'm completely undone. Desire fuses with this insatiable hunger, turning molten as adrenaline surges up my spine, flooding my veins in a heady rush.

The pleasure is damning.

"Ah, fuck—" I growl. My hips snap rough against hers in relentless fury. My body drives into hers, every thrust dragging us closer to the edge. Stripping her bare. Flaying me open.

Two dark and violent forces spiraling closer, colliding, merging, claiming one another until we're locked in our own inescapable, rending gravity.

Only a damned deviant could take such sadistic pleasure in the way she struggles beneath me. The force as seductive as the pull. The take as intoxicating as the surrender. Craving the searing rake of her nails, the sharp bite of her teeth. Savoring the way she draws my blood—blood she never got to draw before. Every drop quenching a thirst she needs to slake.

And for me—a monster unmasked—it's the only way I can justify my own depraved pleasure. To finally touch something so loved, so desperately desired, right at the boundary, where I'd break it irreparably.

My bare hands explore her with unfiltered reverence. No gloves, no barrier to prevent me from feeling all the nuance of her skin. The lateral scars my lips brush under her jaw, revealing the sharp object that was held there, nicking her with every violent jostle of her body during a struggle. As I drag my tongue over the marks, a feral, primal rage ignites within. Rage is a demon tearing at the cage of my ribs.

I hold her down and fuck into her like she's the only thing tethering me to this plane. I fuck into her like a crazed fiend, like I can punish this phantom from her flesh and annihilate my own in the process.

There is no light in this darkness.

We've crossed the horizon, the point of no return, where any illumination frays to threads and is devoured by shadow.

And what reemerges from such an abyss is selfish and catastrophic. A love violently consumed by its own destructive hunger. An obsession, a sickness—one that will either bind or break us.

Her pulse stutters, faltering in terrifying arrhythmia beneath my touch. My heart stalls with it, caught with the sound of her trapped breath.

Instantly, my hand reaches for the pill case, a desperate panic twisting through me—

"No," Collins breathes, wincing as her gaze captures mine. She grips me harder, trembling fingers threading in my hair. "Don't—don't stop."

Halted, chest painfully constricted, I search her eyes. "Collins—"

"Orion," she fires back, her voice breaking on my name as she rolls her hips in seductive rhythm, stealing my goddamn reason. "Oh, god. Please—don't stop."

"Fuck me." It escapes my mouth, harsh and surrendered, as I let gravity take hold. Falling helplessly into her, willingly drowning beneath the erotic rock of her current.

"Collins, I will break you," I whisper coarsely against her ear. "God—dammit," I growl, my lips finding the faint pulse at her throat. "I can't…" I grind out, my voice gravel. "I don't have the strength to stop."

Pulled deeper, I claim the last vestiges of her fight with a bruising, possessive kiss. Her fight depleted, Collins wilts beneath me, surrendering to my next unrestrained thrust. Her fingers interlock with mine, gripping so tight our knuckles bleach.

My thumb traces her heartbeat in obsessive devotion, following its rise and fall, fearful of losing even one. Letting that faint pulse dictate my pace. Slowing when it falters, speeding when it races. I tidal-lock to her gravity, my rhythm set to the erratic tempo beneath her skin.

One hand anchors hers in place, my other splays over her sternum, feeling her heart surge under my palm. "I've got you, baby," I murmur, lips brushing hers as I attune to her beat. "Never letting go."

And as she begins to unravel beneath me, I move into the spaces, winding through each trembling shudder, following her to the precipice of her pleasure. Burning alive in her fiery collision as she crashes over me, through me. Entrained to her pulse, taking her breath into my starving lungs, like that first relief of breath after breaking the surface.

Her music has never existed solely in the notes, but in the breathless anticipation before, in the charged silence between. The pause preceding a touch, the shivering inhale just before release. That tension suspended on a knife's edge.

She is that devastatingly perfect chord held in aching suspension, waiting for the beautiful, inevitable resolution.

And I feel the exact moment her fury gives way to longing. Her pain to rapture. A euphoric shift that overcomes me, wholly.

I ease my pace, rolling my hips with slow, reverent intention. Entering her in long, languid strokes. Unhurried as I take my time to learn her breath, memorize the way it flutters on a quick inhale. The way it catches and holds as expectation tightens her body. How her chest rises against mine, muscles quivering and taut as she hovers at the brink of shattering.

I savor her like the notes of her melody, immersing myself in every subtle change of her cadence.

When I sense her nearing—muscles winding tighter, breaths turning shallow—I angle myself deeper, slowing my pace to something torturous, shuddering as her warmth clenches around me.

"Ah, god—fuck. Just like that," I groan roughly against her parted lips. "I could live and die right here buried in you."

I press her knees wide, lifting slightly to slip my hand between us. My fingers circle her clit in tantalizing strokes, matching the slow, possessive rock of my hips. "Right or left," I demand.

Her eyes flare open, catching mine in disbelief. "What—are you seriously being this fucking meticulous right now?"

"Always." I rub to the right of that tender bundle of nerves, gauging her body's response, then move deliberately left—and she arches beneath me, head tipping back as a cry catches breathless in her throat.

"Left," I declare with arrogant satisfaction.

And then I'm relentless.

My right hand threads into her damp hair, gripping her close. Holding her captive to every punishing, rhythmic stroke as my fingers work her in tight, controlled spirals.

My mouth hovers just above hers, swallowing each gasp, each moan. Her spine arcs, slick heat pressing against me as I grind deeper, harder—each thrust matched to the unforgiving pace and pressure of my fingers.

"Fuck, that's it, baby," I coax, my mouth brushing hers, voice coarse and demanding. I drag my lips up her jawline, licking a mindless path along her parted mouth. "You're taking me so fucking perfectly." I nip her bottom lip, then kiss her with unrestrained hunger as I draw her closer to the edge. "God damn, you're so wet for me, so fucking perfect. I need you to come, angel. Come for me. I want to feel you break around me. I'm not stopping until I feel every maddening pulse of your body, and you're thoroughly ruined."

As she bites into her lip, I seize her mouth again, tongues tangling as I devour her whimpers, feral in my pursuit.

And when her release crashes through her, it's devastating. Fucking earth-shattering. Her body clenches around me in a tight, shuddering embrace, the fierce rise of her hips tearing me mad.

"God—fucking *damn*, you're gripping me so tight," I rasp, voice wrecked. "So fucking tight and wet as you come for me, baby…just for me." I groan harshly, pushing deep inside her. "Tell me who's fucking you—who's making this sweet pussy come."

"Oh, god…*oh…god,*" she breathes, thighs shaking as they press against me. "You—"

"Say—" I thrust hard "—it. I want to hear my name, Collins. Who do you belong to."

"Orion…*fuck*. Orion." Her voice breaks on my name, spine bowing off the mattress and pulling me mercilessly toward the edge with her.

"That's goddamn right, angel. No one else has claim over you. You're mine."

White-hot tension gathers at the base of my spine as I thrust once more—holding myself there, feeling the teasing pleasure grip. A broken groan tears free against the soft hollow of her throat, the sound guttural and ravaged, reverberating through muscle and bone as I fuck against her tight heat—hard, pulsing— with mindless, unhinged rocks of my hips as I release deep inside her.

Breath ragged, I shiver as Collins drags her nails down my back. A soft moan escapes her, and I surge up, lips finding hers to swallow that delicate sound with a groan. Starved, insatiable, as I kiss her to consume every last tremulous drop of her.

As I reluctantly break away, our breaths collide, mingling in the charged space between, our bodies still shuddering with aftershocks. Bracing myself on my forearms above her, I smooth the damp strands of hair from her flushed cheeks.

And in this shattering aftermath, our gazes find each other through the darkness. A profound, unspoken understanding sparks between us. Her heart pulses against my chest in flawless, echoing harmony.

"God, you're beautiful." The thought slips from my mouth unfiltered.

The strain lining her brow eases as a radiant smile breaks, and it's like fourth contact, when the last lingering shadow finally retreats. The luminous gold threading the slate flares, dispelling the dark.

"You're beautiful," she whispers, her fingers tracing paths over the taut planes of my back. "So painfully beautiful, Orion Night."

Amid the starlit ocean of her eyes, I feel myself become something whole, something of light instead of void beneath her gaze.

Her fingertips drift upward, grazing the inked script across my throat—*memento mori*. Her gentle touch summons a raw ache, arresting my pulse. There's a hesitant snag of breath before she says, "I know what this cost you—"

My lips brush the trembling corner of hers, silencing her with a tender kiss. "Just say you're mine."

A vulnerable window opens inside her, an unguarded depth of emotion laid bare. "I'm yours," she whispers softly. "I've always been yours."

I tighten my grip around her thigh, keeping her bound to me, my other hand cradling the curve at the nape of her neck. Our bodies fused, held tight in this intimate pause. Where the silence falls deeper, pulsing with its own unspoken cadence, filled with everything we haven't yet dared to say.

This tension strung in the quiet spaces between.

It's her breath held.

Her heartbeat suspended.

My anticipation for her next note.

Awaiting our shattering rise—

Our inevitable fall.

And until those next crucial beats unravel, I experience her wholly, savor her thoroughly, my lovely dark note, my haunting refrain. My beautiful, shattering collision of shadow and starlight.

Cassiopeia was a queen in Greek mythology whose hubris angered the gods. As punishment, they placed her among the stars, setting her forever in the night sky as the constellation Cassiopeia.

— HYGINUS, ASTRONOMICA; PSEUDO-ERATOSTHENES, CATASTERISMS

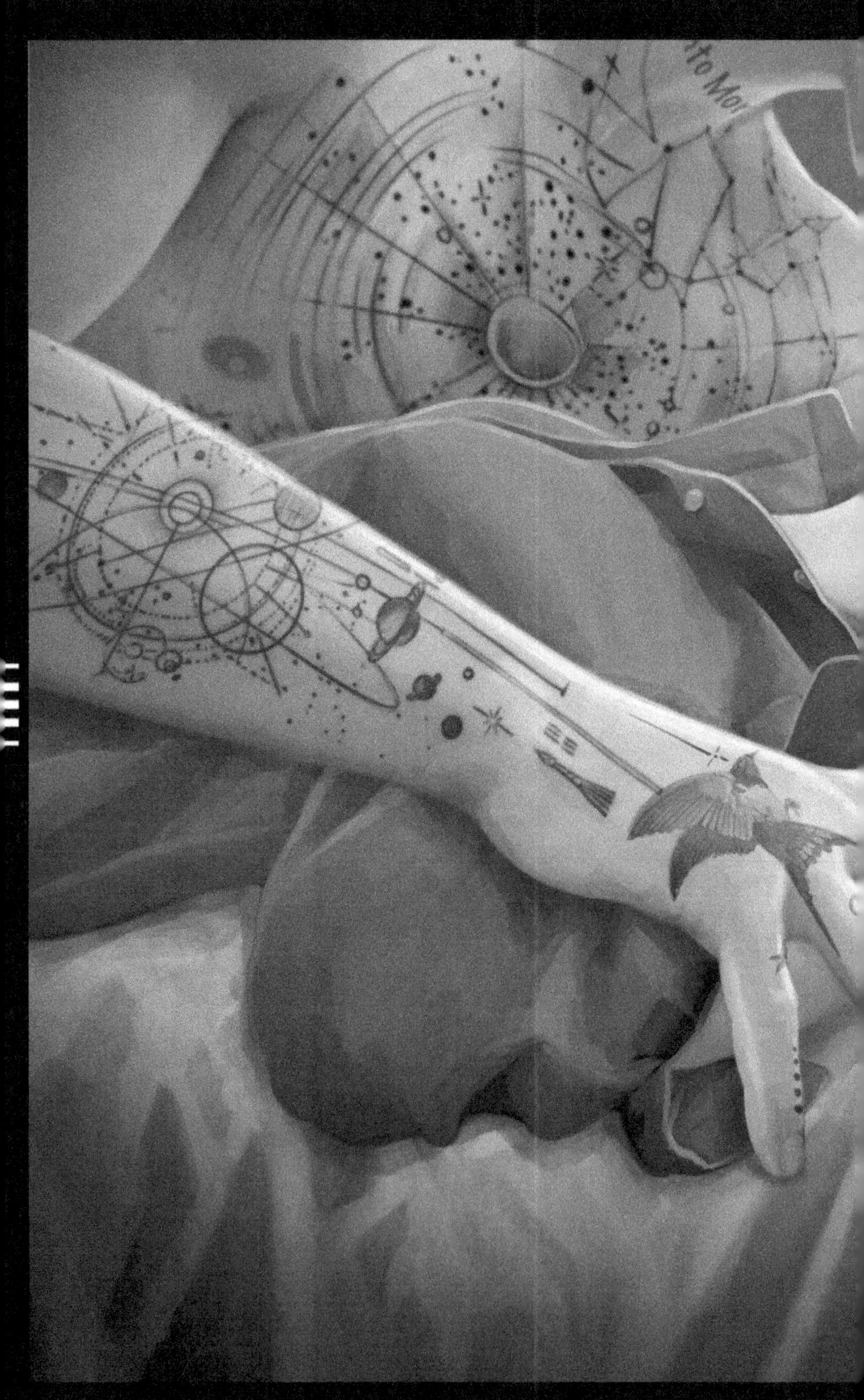

23

CASSIOPEIA'S GAMBIT

I saw the angel in the marble and carved until I set him free.

— MICHELANGELO

COLLINS

The number of heartbeats in a lifetime feels immeasurable. Billions of heartbeats, each one capturing a single frame of a life. So immeasurable, we take them for granted—an infinite number comparable to the stars in the night sky.

And yet, we can feel the terror in a single missed beat.

Fear that the final number has been reached. Our heart unable to catch its next strike, our pulse failing to find its next flutter.

Because there is a number.

And it terrifies me that Orion could know the exact number of mine. That he will count every one, measure my life in intervals of seconds. That I will see those fleeting seconds rushing past in his beautiful teal eyes, waiting for the last crash of a wave, the tide gathering for the final break.

The last breath drawn, never released.

He's stolen so many of my beats already. My heart races for him, skips for him, entrains to the strong pulse in his veins, trying to keep pace. Now he possesses my breath, too.

Even as I try to hold this one in my lungs, a breath too precious to surrender, I can feel it slipping. I try to hold it past the ache, like I can make this one moment last, make time suspend, if I just don't let it slip past my lips.

But when his bare hand—rough and warm without the leather —grazes my hip, it expels in a shaky rush, spent.

Orion has half my body tucked beneath his on the bed, his solid weight and heat a comfort. A thin sheet drapes the upper half of my body. His trim waist is nestled between my thighs, his heartbeat a guiding, steady pulse over my most intimate part. His chin rests on my belly as his fingers strum the curve of my hip, pausing to tap a melody into my skin. So intimate, it steals another trembling breath.

The air down here is cool and filtered, controlled by Orion's obsessive need to regulate his environment. The silence is also a making of his space. We're both too aware of this fragile thing hovering between us. The tension gathering beneath this tentative truce, where—if we keep touching, keep kissing, keep the words from spilling out—we can keep the bubble from breaking.

Down here, there are too many wounds scraped open. Painful breaks that never properly set or healed. Toxins bled out like a bloom of blood in the water.

And somewhere aboveground, Darby is hunting for a wanted serial killer. He's looking for me. There's a body in the ocean. Orion will know soon enough what I've done.

I seal my eyes shut against the thought, and my breath hitches.

His strumming halts. Sliding his hand up the side of my ribs, he takes my forearm and turns it over. His thumb strokes the pattern of stars along my wrist. "Tell me about this," he says, the vibration of his roughened voice a tantalizing drag of friction between my thighs.

I swallow, lifting my free hand to touch his tousled hair, committing the way he feels to memory. Finding it just as difficult to keep my hands off him, yet still cautious.

Those rising stormwaters within him reached a crest. His dark urges fed and sated. At least, for the time being, after balance was found between violence and fear. And now he's tranquil in the aftermath, unafraid to touch, to taste, to map each pulse point of my body, making up for what he's denied himself.

He's wearing an extra pair of wire-rimmed glasses, so there's no concealing the distress in my expression when I say, "It's the last thing I did for myself before everything changed."

Understanding flickers through his eyes, followed by an unguarded flash of something darker. My gaze drifts to the jagged scar that mars his forehead, knowing he does, in some capacity.

"Is he still breathing."

The question cuts through the quiet. My breath lodges in my chest, fingertips stalling mid-caress in his hair. The way he says it, an edge beneath the calm, as if there's an unspoken threat to make it otherwise.

I ease out the breath, fighting to maintain his fierce stare as I try to forget how deep we are down here, surrounded by all this concrete and dirt.

"I think so," I say, offering him the closest thing I can to the truth.

A muscle flexes along his jaw, and I feel his forced swallow against me. His thumb continues to brush my inner wrist, lightly tracing the constellation.

My chest pangs with a dull ache, still sore and vulnerable, and I shift to find a comfortable position, letting the sheet drop lower.

Orion's eyes turn heated, drawing another unstable breath from me. "You did that on purpose," he accuses.

I smile. "Maybe. You're easily distracted."

He releases a low groan as he presses a kiss beneath my navel, and I let my gaze fall to his tattooed hand resting protectively over my sternum.

His body is a celestial tapestry of ink, each mark a secret etched into his skin. Delicate spirals sweep his shoulder, flowing into the constellation Ophiuchus inked over the center of his chest, its stars bleeding toward his heart, where spectral lines and waveform patterns converge into a threaded heartbeat along his ribs. There are musical notes there, like a song scored into his flesh. My gaze follows the scattered stardust down to cones of hourglass-shaped spacetime across his forearm, and farther to quantum bars and intricate symbols mapped into his hip.

I rest my fingers over his, gently tracing the glyphs marked across his knuckles. I pause over the symbol for phi—the golden symmetry he's constantly hunting.

"Why starlings?" I ask, further diverting his thoughts as my thumb brushes the outline of the bird on his hand.

He drags a kiss over my skin, the friction of his breath sparking an ache deep between my hips. "Starlings move in unique patterns," he says, his voice a low rasp. "If you've ever seen them fly above the spires, it's like watching the sky move. Adjusting direction instantly, one small movement creating a ripple effect that travels through the flock, forming waves of motion." His eyes flick up, locking with mine behind his glasses. "A fluid, fascinating murmuration."

My breath shallows as his fingers drift farther up my ribs, his thumb grazing the underswell of my breast where thin scars stitch my skin. His fingertips caress a gentle line across the tube scar along my side.

"Not only breathtaking," he adds in a soft murmur, "their patterns are evasive, defensive. For survival. Synchronizing to confuse predators, like a thousand individual heartbeats moving as one. Making them unpredictable, and impossible to capture."

My breath shivers past my lips. "But why do you call me that."

"*Hmm.*" He hums as he lifts to pull me farther beneath him. "Because you're beautiful," he says, voice rumbling, abraded with need. "Because you have a unique pattern, impossible to predict, evading capture." His hand finds my wrist, his thumb outlining the inked dots as his tone deepens, reverent. "You're a star constellation that points an arrow straight toward the most destructive force, little archer."

My heart flutters wild beneath his touch. "And where's that?"

His gaze lifts, ensnaring mine with an intensity that steals my next breath entirely. "Right to the fiery heart, the center of everything." His eyes darken, deep as night. "Right to the heart of me. And when you look at me, that dark void has shape."

Then he lowers his mouth to mine, kissing me deeply, desperately, attempting to steal every breath as my fingers run over his back, mapping the definition of muscles under the shaded ink. Feeling the scratches I placed there—the evidence of my buried pain turned inside out. One of his hands slides beneath my spine, the other traps my hip, anchoring my body to his.

He tosses his glasses off before his lips brush the hollow of my throat, and then he's entering me with a careful press of his hips. The kind of restraint that feels like worship and threat in the same stroke. He's unhurried, unspooling me maddeningly slow with each controlled thrust.

"…I'll never let you go, starling," he murmurs into my pulse.

I sink into him. I'm undone by him. In this fervent moment between us, this feral hunger stops being anything but love in its most dangerous form.

The room dissolves into sensation. Concrete offers our desperate movements a shattering reverb, resonating beneath the music of touch and caressing skin. Orion moves with harnessed control as he rocks into me with a low sound in his throat that sounds like he's close to losing it.

When I break, it's a quiet surrender. A blazing light blinking out, a flare consumed in the dark. He swallows my cries, folding around me until we're a tangle of parts. In the silence between heartbeats, I hold my breath and he compulsively thrums his fingers, both trying to keep the moment unshattered.

Afterward, our truce tries to hold. Orion presses his mouth to the space below my ribs, fingers drifting along my waist. He kisses the sternotomy scar slicing my sternum like a promise.

For as long as I can, I hold the breath—and I could live in this space where heartbeats are counted for me and time is split into notes instead of days. I could forget what awaits us above.

His voice is an arousing scrape against my skin. "You're mine. My whole universe, angel."

I rest my hand on his chest, fingers fused to the constellation inked there. "I'll always be yours."

He kisses me—deep, fierce, tender—and when he breaks away, I press my lips to his forehead, where the scar slashes his skin, memorizing this one framed heartbeat. For just a little longer, I hold the breath.

And then, inevitably, I let it go.

●│‖φ★

It's the scratch of the printer that must stir him awake. At the sound of his groan, my fingers halt over the keyboard. Alarm claws into my chest with one sharp twinge of guilt, before I bury it and abandon the console.

With cautious steps, I cross the dim quarters toward the alcove where Orion's bed is framed by charts and data readouts. He's stretched out on his back, the hard planes of him softened by sleep and the sedative I took from his lab.

"So you drugged me."

His voice is low and gruff, but absent of any resentment. I swallow past the tightness in my sore throat. "Not heavily," I admit. "I didn't use nearly as much of the paralytic that you do, but the sedative was necessary."

A wary edge carves his features, and I sense his rising unease as the guise falls away.

While he was under, I used his belt to restrain his wrists to the wrought iron frame. He makes a groggy, failed attempt to move his arms, tendons flexing against the leather. A stark reminder that, once he regains full use of his muscles, the belt won't hold him for long—just long enough to offer an escape.

"Restrained by Orion's belt. Fucking ironic." His chest rises and falls on a sluggish, resigned breath. "Damn. You are good at keeping secrets." His gaze pins me. "Did you finally get what you needed from me, then?"

The passive acceptance in his tone punctures my weakened defenses. I resist the urge to touch the ache beneath my left breast. "And then some," I say, my voice unsteady as the joke falls flat between us. "But it wasn't easy. Any of it."

His gaze locked hard on me, I feel the weight of his unspoken demand, and I nod once. "Your biometric lock would've been impossible to bypass, except you gave me the code yourself."

His attention flicks toward the hardware in the corner. Two black racks are stationed there, coax cables woven like veins into a metallic, barrel-shaped cryostat.

"I didn't realize I was that easy." He cocks an eyebrow, adopting an amused countenance.

Taking a deliberate step forward, I say, "Did you know male fireflies pulse in a sequence?" This earns a confused look from him. "Each species uses its own distinctive flash pattern to communicate, to find a mate."

His expression dims, all amusement fading as a crease forms between his brows.

"You use a Temporal Authentication Pattern—a TAP—for your access code. That's clever," I continue, allowing a despondent smile. "It's the Fibonacci sequence with an accent on phi." I tap my fingers lightly against my wrist in demonstration. "You've tapped it into me, Orion. On my wrist, my thigh. Emphasizing the seventh tap with heavier pressure, a firmer touch. Like a firefly's pulse, your own distinctive signal." I pause, watching as he registers this information.

"I've observed your counting ritual so many times, obsessively tapping this sequence over and over. Always twelve taps. I've felt the exact pressure on my skin…and I noticed the moment it altered. One small deviation, an extra tap."

It was after that night on the shore, stranded on a rock together, that his compulsive count changed. The night I must have become his victim, his obsessive thoughts centered on the thirteenth constellation.

And I misread this change. *Catastrophically*. Believing at the time that Orion himself was the final victim in his pattern.

Orion swallows, eyes never leaving mine. As if triggered, his fingers twitch against the belt: *One*—thumb. *One*—index. *Two*—middle. *Three*—ring. *Five*—pinky. Then a final *tap* with his ring finger.

"Ophiuchus," I say in confirmation. "Thirteen taps. It altered your sequence, and therefore your code."

His jaw tenses. "Yes, my entire being warped for one anomaly."

With a controlled exhale, I glance toward the printer tray, bolstering my resolve as I command my legs to move. After I retrieve the printouts, I let my fingers graze over the marble pieces set on the board, selecting one.

I look up at him. "I mimicked your cadence on the touchpad, the plate on your console designed to read the timing and weight of your taps."

His tongue slowly sweeps his bottom lip as his eyes darken. "Clever little starling," he whispers hoarsely.

Throat tight, I force a swallow. "I have a knack for pattern recognition."

"Apparently." The conflicted pull of his features spears me.

Every stolen breath, every stolen touch, every stolen heartbeat between us—

They were always numbered.

Orion makes a deep sound, something between frustration and admiration, as his drowsy gaze coasts over me. I also took the liberty of stealing his clothes, wearing one of his oxford shirts and a pair of slim joggers.

"Fuck," he mutters roughly. "Why do you have to look so goddamn sexy right now."

An unwanted flare of heat burns through my flesh. "It's possible I did drug you too heavily," I say. Tilting my head, I study him closely. "But I have to ask... Did you allow this to happen?"

A storm swirls behind his eyes, hurt tangled with currents of anger that twists my heart into a painful knot. His gaze holds mine intently before lowering to the chess piece clutched in my right hand.

With a weighted exhale, he says, "Chess isn't just about the moves on the board. It's all the moves off it, too. All the subtle actions leading to that critical moment. The way you hold your breath in anticipation when you want something. The fury you try so hard to smother. How your fingers curl into fists when you can't. It's not that I was expecting something specific—" He manages to shift his forearm, the belt strapping his wrists creaks with the movement. "I was just expecting something."

"You read me pretty well, too." My pulse hammers in my neck, fingers tightening around the marble piece. "For what it's worth, you did surprise me. Turning me into your victim." I shake my head lightly. "I honestly wasn't expecting that, Orion. However, you also saved me—"

"And I seem to find myself deeper in trouble every time I do." The corner of his mouth tics upward, failing to mask the dejected resignation behind the hardened planes of his face.

"Well, intentional or not, you played some good moves to divert me," I say.

"*Hmm*, maybe." His voice drops dangerously low, eyes heating as his lips twist into a wicked grin. "But I admit, your move is so much hotter, little starling." He flexes his wrist against the leather, sending me a devastating wink.

"I looked through your code," I say quickly, and the mention of his algorithm immediately captures his full, furious attention. "Orion, I could've never been one of your victims. The moment you fixated on me, you made me one. I tried to find the proof of that, but your code... Truly, it's above my capabilities. But you had to have altered something, some parameter."

"I could never have predicted you. Not enough data points."

"I'm not a set of data points." My shoulders drop in a low shrug. "I'm just a girl with a score to settle."

Reflexively, I fist the cool object in my hand. Despite the anguish ripping me open inside, despite the threat he still poses, I daringly close the final gap between us. Placing the printouts on the edge of the bed, I ease myself down beside him. Close enough that his scent of wild ocean spray sears my throat.

Leaning over him, I reach up and place the chess piece in his open palm, helping him fold his weak fingers around the white queen. "Smothered mate is technically a mating pattern," I say. "It might be the knight's play, but it's the queen's sacrifice that sets the trap."

I press my lips to his ear and whisper, "Checkmate."

His throat works on a swallow. "I knew you could strike with a dirty gambit, but damn, baby. That's brutal."

"You had it coming."

As I straighten, his gaze follows me. "Yeah, I did." A faint smile tugs at his mouth, and my gaze is drawn to the scratches on his cheek where my nails raked his face. "But what was your sacrifice?"

I hold his gaze a measure longer, letting him see the pain of exactly what I've given up. In this game, there are no winners.

A serious note deepens his voice as he demands, "But why risk it? You got inside here, got my access code. What you apparently wanted. Why take it this far. Why fuck me, Collins. Let me do…that." His voice breaks, the candor he usually exhibits catching in his throat, and he releases a clipped breath. "Why risk your heart," he finally says.

I break his gaze, mine wandering over the intricate ink covering his chest. I rise slowly and move over him, straddling his thighs. Palms braced to his stomach, I feel the flex of his abdominal muscles beneath my touch.

"There's power in surrender," I say, meeting his eyes through the dark. "I needed you to let your guard down fully, to trust me completely."

A flash of raw anger ignites in the depths of his teal eyes. "I would've given you anything you asked of me."

Except the truth. The thought lodges like a blade, buried deep. I waited for that truth to come in the shower, for him to let me all the way in.

As I make a move to pull away, urgency tightens his voice.

"At least give me some kind of an answer. Something— anything." A ragged breath escapes him, then: "Your name."

I hesitate only a beat. "Hollyn Elara Cawthorn," I say, a whisper of a name that lances the bruised organ beneath my ribs. "But her story is far too complicated. So I chose this one for myself." A dejected half-smile tugs at my lips. "Something we have in common."

"We have more than one thing in common, angel. The symmetry is uncanny."

More than he knows.

"She died a long time ago, though. Which is why you had to have altered the code, either deliberately or unconsciously. Because, as Collins Rayne Holbrook is a ghost, that name should've never flashed across your screen as one of your victims, Reaper."

A cold flicker of betrayal passes behind his eyes, swift and cutting.

I inhale a fortifying breath, spine straightening. "I was the one who issued the moniker," I tell him honestly. "It's technically frowned upon, but it helped me feel closer to you, connected somehow, giving you a name. I'm a psychopathologist with ViCAP—or I was, before I went rogue. Databases are my special interest."

He licks his lips as his gaze sharpens, shadowed by wary curiosity.

"I also specialize in abnormal psychology and maladaptive behaviors," I add, letting the truth pour free now. "I've conducted over forty interviews with violent offenders. You're number forty- one."

Orion remains so utterly still beneath me, it's unnerving.

"Before I came to Stonehurst, I was hunting an existential killer. One who was using a high-level, algorithmic database to locate untraceable offenders. I had a narrow window to find him.

And damn—" I curl my fingers over his warm skin, reverent as I touch him, feel him "—he was the most sophisticated offender I had ever encountered."

"Is that right," Orion says, a rough groan escaping as my nails graze his skin.

I rock my weight against him, unable to curb a faint smile. "I found him beautiful," I confess, "the brilliance of his mind, the artistry of his scenes. From the very first one, I knew he could help me…if only I could find him. Yet that felt impossible." My palms settle at his hips, thumbs slipping just beneath his waistband, drawing a shiver from his body.

"But then he left me a clue." My voice softens, intimate. "Which, that wasn't like him. He was too meticulous, too organized and exacting to make such a careless mistake. But I was so consumed by my obsession—with him, with his algorithm —that I didn't start to process this fact until recently."

"Shit," Orion mutters, breath ragged. "That's why I couldn't uncover anything substantial on you. Your background was scrubbed. Thought I was losing my goddamn mind."

I arch an eyebrow. "Not completely."

A taunting smile touches his lips. "That feels unprofessional."

"If you wanted professional, perhaps you shouldn't have fucked your therapist."

"I still want to do nothing more." A slow, devious smile twists his mouth, and he drags his teeth over his bottom lip. "Since you're up here…" He bucks his hips beneath me. "Why don't you go ahead and sit on my face, angel."

A dangerous flutter murmurs through my chest, and I steady my voice. "Orion. Please hear me. Your quantum algorithm… I've never encountered anything remotely like it. I doubt anyone has. I'm not even sure you fully comprehend what you've built. Its potential, its implications—" I break off, shaking my head. "What it's capable of."

"Why don't you start by telling me what it's capable of for you," he says, a turbulent storm rising behind his flinty expression.

Seated astride him, I pull a shaky breath into my tight lungs. "I've spent years curating this identity of Collins Holbrook for one objective." I swallow the well of emotion. "Emery Collins. Lyra Rayne. Irene Holbrook. Hollyn Cawthorn." Each name cuts deep, a blade dragged through an open wound. "The names of his known victims. Names that not only haunt me, but remind me every day that I can't stop hunting him."

"The man who hurt you," Orion states.

"The monster who killed me. Who did this"—I touch my chest, tracing the length of the scar that bisects my chest—"he's untraceable, and lacking a victim count impressive enough to warrant federal resources. Not considered high priority. But that's because, I think, he changes his MO. Not even the most advanced tech within ViCAP can track a perpetrator who shifts signature and motive like he does. But," I pause to catch my breath, "I know he's killed more girls than have been identified."

"And you want to catch him, to put him away—"

"No." The word drops heavy between us. "I want to drive the dullest fucking knife through his heart, watch as he chokes on his own rotten blood. And I want to do it on a theater stage, right under blaring lights. Then I want to wrap his lifeless body in scenery canvas, drag him into the blackest part of the forest, weight him down with dirt and river rocks, and submerge him in the muck. Leaving him there to be forgotten. To decay. To rot. For scavengers to pick his bones until nothing of him remains."

The gravity of his gaze holds me bound, those lustrous eyes of oceans and galaxies clashing and seeing down to the broken, shameful truth of my vengeance. Heat flushes my skin, forcing me to look away.

"I don't have to be your opponent," Orion says, his voice

taking on that smooth cadence that melts the hardened parts inside me. "I never did, angel."

My heart stutters as I return my gaze to his. I don't tell him that I realized exactly this while he held me close in the ocean, my dark adapting to his. That maybe I could have found a way to trust him. That in some terrible, beautiful way, our cracks match.

That I realized only too late we're not two different species.

"Right," I say, bitterness edging my voice. "And at what point was I supposed to trust you with this, Orion? Before or after you made me your thirteenth constellation?"

A muscle ticks in his jaw, a brief flicker of guilt surfacing before his features lock into a stony mask. An ache pulses in the charged air between us, thrumming with notes of his own past, painfully sliced into a before and after. And mine, fractured violently between victim and survivor. He dared to make me a victim again, and that betrayal ignites a fresh surge of anger.

"I had a before and after, too," I tell him as I trail the tips of my fingers over the taut ridges of his abdomen, tenderly outlining the swirls of ink. "I'm not the girl I once was. To become what I am, to get this far, I've done things I can't take back. One step too far is still too far, and if I don't finish this, then every sacrifice made becomes meaningless."

Orion's throat works on a strained swallow, the dark tide behind his eyes breaking like a relentless wave finally crashing, receding.

He doesn't press for more, doesn't attempt to deny the painful heart of my confession. When he speaks, his voice is subdued, hollowed by defeat. "Just tell me what I need to do, Collins. Tell me what you need of me."

"You've already given it to me," I say truthfully. "To find him, I needed a predictive modeling system. One advanced enough to track him now. I can't wait for him to make a mistake."

"Make me understand why."

"I'm an endangered species."

"What does that—"

"I'm dying."

The words detonate on impact, shattering the tenuous space between us with the force of a cosmic collision.

"No." Orion's denial is immediate. "That's not possible—"

"—despite all your data points, I assure you it is—"

"I saved you." His voice breaks, an ocean of stubborn refusal cresting behind his fierce gaze. "I altered your outcome. Your heart stopped, but I brought you back—"

A bleak, callous laugh slips free. "You can't revive a dead girl," I say, incredulous. "All you did was bring back the same pain, the same struggle, the same unrelenting hunger for revenge. You didn't rewrite my fate, Orion. You only postponed the inevitable."

He studies me for an endless moment, the tendons of his wrists flexed, a defeat so profound sharpening his beautiful features it wounds. "How long."

Folding my arms across my chest, I turn my face aside, unable to bear the agony carved into his features when I say, "Not long enough."

"*How. Long,*" he demands, restrained fury resonating like a tremor beneath each word.

I force my gaze back to his, meeting the swell of violence there. "A year," I manage. "Maybe two. Possibly only months." My shoulders rise in a helpless shrug. "According to their timeline, my clock already ran out. I'm on borrowed time."

His silence infuses the air. At least he's intelligent enough not to ask the obvious, tired questions. There are no surgeries left. No matches. No alternative treatments. I've exhausted all viable options.

Mercifully, he doesn't make me say it.

"Then why are you still here," he asks, the vehemence in his voice roughened to gravel. "If you came here for one purpose, why didn't you just leave once you got it, Collins?"

I nod slowly, gaze falling to the printouts tucked at his side. "That was always the plan, to vanish before you ever realized anything. It would've made this easier. Knowing nothing about me. Believing I just disappeared. Then I realized something for myself."

I lift a page, holding it before him. "I told you that I didn't understand how you could've made such a blatant mistake at Bethany Beach. Not until I was here, able to observe you. You were never reckless, Orion. Fearless, yes—but too cautious to leave evidence behind. And your impulsive behavior…it didn't align. It's as if with each ritual, each kill, you've been losing pieces of yourself. At first, I thought psychological decompensation, but—"

I angle the printout into his line of sight. A structural MRI with the clearance report attached. The workup Banner requested two years ago—the version that was altered. The proof, undeniable.

"I honestly thought you swapped the paperwork in your file yourself," I continue, measuring his reaction. "That you feared any evidence of deterioration after your wreck would jeopardize your research—your grants, your credibility. An institution wouldn't risk backing a researcher whose cognitive function was deteriorating. It would call into question the integrity of your work."

Orion remains silent, the intensity of his gaze unnerving. Not once does he glance at the damning evidence between us. Then, with a controlled breath, he says, "Go on."

My chest constricts. "I thought this because of what I found." I tap the corner of the page. "This is the clearance workup, Orion. The version that was filed with the university."

I lift the second sheet that displays the same header, same

date, but the readout is different. "And this is the original," I explain. "The one that mentions ventricular enlargement. It recommends a follow-up."

The damage wouldn't have been obvious after his wreck, taking time to build. And unless symptoms were reported, to know where to focus, it's the kind of finding that's easily overlooked.

I lower the pages. "Then I realized who would benefit more from keeping a progressive neurological condition like hydrocephalus hidden. From the board. From the university." I take a slow, steady breath. "Even from you."

Banner's words echo back at me from beneath the colonnade that day: *I've done my best to protect him.*

"Banner was raking in funding off of you," I tell him. "But as you became erratic, difficult to control, especially with violent incidents and large expenditures, he needed a contingency—"

"Leo brought you here to diagnose my condition," he says, his incredulous laugh a bitter sound in his throat. "To get me out of the way. Free of any blame."

"Yes," I answer him, softening my voice. I push my hair over my shoulder as I lower myself closer. His body heat seeps through the shirt, making me shiver. "But this explains what you've been experiencing. Headaches. Blurred vision. Cognitive lapses. Impaired impulse control. Bouts of anger and violent outbursts. Even sadistic urges and compulsions toward deviancy."

A weak smile tips his mouth. "You might as well label me a madman."

An ache burrows deep, and I slide a tender touch over his chest. "As your memories deteriorate, it's like sensing a stranger in your own mind," I confirm. "Often a violent one, allowing a darker, destructive nature to take up residence."

His fingers clench around the chess piece, knuckles paling—

and for a torturous moment, I'm tempted to release him, craving to feel his touch just once more...

I force myself to retreat a safe measure. "Orion, your need for the rush is a way to fight the literal tide swelling inside your skull," I say gently. "It's the intracranial pressure, rising and falling like ocean waves, squeezing away cognition."

The queen drops from his grasp, clattering against the floor. A flutter attacks my chest, my heart banging against my rib cage.

"This is why you're so obsessive about your research," I press on, making him hear me. "Why you've been trying so desperately to retrieve those lost echoes—your memories."

He drags in a breath, tension tight in the line of his jaw. His silence pulls taut between us as my fingertips lift hesitantly, tracing the spiral of inked stars winding along his bicep.

"You've imprinted them onto yourself," I whisper, following the path up his forearm. "Creating a mnemonic map, like a memory palace, coded from celestial charts and symbolic imagery. Recording your memories helps you remember what you feel is important."

It's why it's not obvious that he's losing any important ones. I wonder how often he has to decode them, to modify the ink. If he's left the most painful memories out, willing to let them fade, and an unbidden thought of Emma enters my mind.

"God, you're so fucking clever, starling," he finally says. Though this time, his words hold no amusement.

On impulse, my gaze flicks to the starling inked across his hand, just above the leather belt. My first hint to this terrifying secret of his. It was there on the shore, in the waning light, when the pieces began to slot painfully into place.

I reach up and grasp his hand, interlacing our fingers. I press the tips of mine against the glyphs above his knuckles. His code inked in stark black.

● | ‖ φ ★

One dot. One line. Two parallel lines. Phi. And a five-point star.

Fibonacci mapped into his skin, his tapping ritual counting toward the golden ratio of phi, where he applies a heavier pressure to the seventh tap—a sequence progressing toward symmetry, toward that universal constant.

I brush my thumb over the ink, a hollow burn flaring in my throat. His access code imprinted here in case he forgets it, obsessively tapping it, fearful of losing its rhythm.

Always twelve beats. Until the moment he incorporated one extra with his ring finger—the symbolic heart vein—marking an anomaly.

"An extra tap," I whisper across his lips, glancing again at the starling—the ink darker, newer.

His jaw clenches, a vulnerable truth locked behind his guarded eyes.

"You added the starling to your mnemonic map recently." My gaze traces the shaded feathers. "It's not just an update to your code so you don't forget. Starling…the way you use it as an endearment—it's a memory recall," I say, the ache painful, "so you don't forget me."

He wove me into his most vital memory.

"But the little things, like giving me your umbrella in the rain, you don't remember. Not every moment can be recorded."

"All the big and little things," he whispers roughly, his fingers tensing around mine. "I wanted to remember them all. I thought I did." A melancholic smile ghosts his lips, and seeing it chisels at the hardened wall around my heart.

"For what it's worth, thank you," I tell him softly. "These past few months… Yes, Orion. I was happy."

His voice breaks on a harsh breath. "I don't want to lose you."

The raw emotion behind his words resonates with a dual truth, honing the piercing ache behind my ribs. With one last, lingering touch, my fingers graze the starling, wondering what other pieces of our story he's encoded on himself. What of our time together he didn't want to forget.

I force myself to release his hand. "I'm not who you think I am," I confess. "You should let me go. Let Collins go."

I glance toward the darkened lab, finding the robotic arm stationed in the corner. The automated instrument he uses to tattoo his memories. "Cover this up," I tell him as I draw my hand away from his.

Willing strength into my body, I lift away from him and drop my legs over the side of the bed. As I stand, I place the rest of the printed pages on his chest.

"If left untreated," I say, injecting a clinical tone into my voice to curb the tremor, "your condition will worsen, deteriorating more of your memory. I've printed the treatment you need to receive. Immediately," I stress.

It was never me carving at Orion's stone—it was the relentless water. A ruthless tide eroding him little by little, wearing him away until he's eventually as empty and hollow as the darkest voids of space.

Not long from now, if he doesn't act to correct course, he might not even remember me.

After all the time that's passed, he won't reclaim everything, but he can help prevent further, severe loss. And maybe he'll even remember who Emma truly was to him. At the thought, I glance at the time on one of the mounted monitors, a tight pinch in my chest speeding my pulse.

There's a slight tendon flex along his wrist, and his shoulder shifts, confirming that the paralytic is wearing off.

"You should start to regain full mobility within minutes," I say. "I suggest you use your time wisely instead of chasing after me." My gaze clashes with his, those deep, endless oceans rocking through me. "Not only is it likely someone here suspects you, may even be feeding information to the Feds, but there's an FBI agent here at Stonehurst. I'm not sure if he's alone, or if there are more. But he's looking for you, Orion."

I turn away, ready to abandon this haunted place. Steeling myself, I pick up my boots and head toward the staircase—then pause. "Just out of curiosity," I say, keeping my back to him, "what did you do with the skulls?" I glance over my shoulder. "Trophies—or just a counter-forensic measure?"

A faint, devious smile curls the corner of his mouth. "We have to keep a little mystery, don't we, baby." He sends me a wink.

Fortifying my resolve, I face the staircase—

"Collins."

The subtle command of his voice pulls me to a halt, my pulse racing against every second slipping away.

"This changes nothing," Orion says, his voice firm with conviction.

"Dammit," I mutter.

With wavering steps, I turn and close the distance to him, compelled by a desperate impulse I can't deny. Leaning down, I trace my fingertips across his smooth jaw, guiding him as I press my lips to his.

I kiss Orion slowly, deeply. A kiss infused with aching tenderness and heartbreak and everything left unfinished between us. The fractured chords of my heart align one last time to the strong, steady rhythm of his pulse.

"You were worth the risk," I say against his mouth, giving him the answer to his question. "You were worth risking my heart."

Then, wrenching myself away, I rush from the sub-level, forbidding myself another glance back.

On my way out of the facility, I grab my stashed burner phone, making a snap decision as I eye Orion's gear. As I slip on his leather jacket, an ache flares beneath my breastbone as his familiar scent envelops me. I snatch his keys and force myself toward the arched doors.

The campus is dark and silent, shrouded in predawn mist. Only the gargoyles and stone statues bear witness to my escape as I make my way across the wet pavement.

As I seat myself on Orion's motorcycle, a twinge of longing surfaces, and I try to suppress the phantom feel of him between my thighs, the comforting strength of his arms around me as waves crashed and roared.

Fingers trembling from the cold, I place the call.

Laurel picks up. "Did you find him?"

I draw in a steadying breath, committing to memory the mist and salty scent of ocean and his warm, rich notes. "I found what I needed."

"Good girl," my mentor says.

Orion taught me one other thing about patterns, about how to recognize the more elusive ones. Something I wouldn't have been able to connect without him; this vital piece that I need to hunt my killer. For that, and for so much more, I'm forever indebted to him.

However little time that forever may be.

A foggy breath shudders out, and I press my hand to my chest. I tap his count against my bone, grounding my pulse to his soothing rhythm to stabilize my heartbeat, breathing in box counts of four.

"Tell me what's wrong." An edge of concern threads Laurel's voice.

You're not supposed to get too close to your mark. You're not supposed to fall in love with them.

"Nothing," I assure her. "I'm fine. Just ready for this to finally be done."

Her tone softens. "I know." A weighted pause. "Did you clean up the loose end?"

"Yes."

It's the first lie I've ever told her.

I was also never supposed to leave Orion alive.

But he and I—we're the same species of hunter. We feed on the same toxins.

"Where did you stash the emergency bag?" I ask her as I key the ignition.

"At the Shorehaven port. Locker thirteen."

A bitter, breathless laugh escapes before I silence the sound. "Of course." My throat constricts around a knot. "Headed there now. And…thank you, Laurel. For getting the report for me, and finding the discrepancy in the imaging record."

There's a heavy pause before she says, "You did him a mercy, Hollyn."

I swallow the fiery ache. "I know."

"Just be safe," she says gently.

With a rigid nod she can't see, I end the call.

It was Dr. Laurel Montgomery who pulled the canvas away on that late winter evening as I floated dead for over three minutes under forest branches, who breathed new air into my lungs and gave me new life—helping Hollyn Cawthorn remain dead, so my killer wouldn't see me coming.

She saved me in more ways than one.

By bringing me into the fold. Offering shelter, a home. A purpose, after mine was stolen. A professional ballet dancer whose bright future fractured as violently as her heart—a heart unable ever again to sustain the rigorous demands of a dancer's life.

Then Laurel guided me, maneuvering me into a new role with strategic references. First into the FBI, then ViCAP, granting me access to the most sophisticated databases. Another way to perform, on another stage, choreographing another dance.

One of revenge.

As Laurel once told me: *There's no better way to hunt a predator than from the inside.*

I lower Orion's helmet over my head and buckle the chin strap, no longer fearing the dark, confining space. I turn the key, and the bike rumbles to life. I then mirror every action I watched Orion perform on his bike as I ride off, disappearing from Stonehurst.

Aggressive mimicry is how the female firefly lures males from different species. By mimicking their flash signals, she's able to capture them, consume them. It's more than sating a hunger—it's survival. By eating her prey, she absorbs defensive toxins, protecting herself against predators.

And I've spent every moment since my death feasting on the vilest males of the most predatory species. Building up toxins. Strengthening defenses. Perfecting my survival skills.

Some monsters can only be hunted by darker ones.

As I throttle onto the empty stretch of highway, putting the ocean behind me, I search for that sense of closure I should feel in this moment, the completeness promised by Gestalt's law of closure.

Our minds instinctively fill in the missing pieces to complete a whole, driven by the compulsion to perceive meaning in the fragmented, in the broken. It's why artists leave negative spaces. Why storytellers leave their endings unfinished—

Because the empty places haunt us.

Because absence leaves us hungry, wanting more.

Because we're never truly complete or whole. And nothing ever ends, not really.

My life is defined by a before and after.

Before I took my last breath, and *him.*

The man who killed me.

Now, twice over.

A derisive laugh chokes free. I didn't think he could kill me more, that I had nothing else left to take. But now he's stolen this, too—a second chance at life, with a man I could've loved—

If only my heart wasn't bad.

Yet in death, she will have her revenge.

And this time, I'm taking my killer with me to the fucking grave.

There is no passion in nature so demoniacally impatient, as that of him who, shuddering upon the edge of a precipice, thus meditates a Plunge. To indulge, for a moment, in any attempt at thought, is to be inevitably lost; for reflection but urges us to forbear, and therefore it is, I say, that we cannot. If there be no friendly arm to check us, or if we fail in a sudden effort to prostrate ourselves backward from the abyss, we plunge, and are destroyed.

— EDGAR ALLAN POE, *THE IMP OF THE PERVERSE*

24

L'APPEL DU VIDE

CALL OF THE VOID

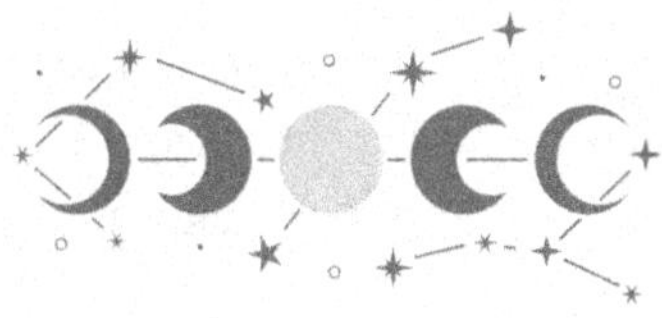

Then I defy you, stars!

— ROMEO

ORION: INTERLUDE

There are more stars in the universe than grains of sand on Earth.

An aphorism that feels too immense, too infinite, to fully comprehend. Which is the intention, to feel that immensity, to recognize our fragile, wondrous existence grasped for a mere breath of a moment.

We can debate the factual accuracy of Sagan's adage—and many have—employing mathematical formulas and astronomical models to prove it, to try to conceive the infinite. Yet even if we could visualize it on a granular level, in an ever-expanding universe continuously birthing new stars, the number remains staggering, humbling.

It's terrifying to realize something exists that you're unable to quantify. Something so vast, so immeasurable and fathomless, it's impossible to count.

A sea of endless stars.

And she is one of them—a single, radiant point of light adrift in an infinite cosmic ocean. A star once bound in a binary, whose companion was torn from their shared orbit, drifting too far away…losing each other over time to the void of darkness.

Yet sound, like memory, can traverse vast distances, reaching across time and space. And hers reached me in drips of melody, fragments of notes, a beautiful, Euclidean rhythm drawing me into her gravity.

The sheer enormity of the cosmos asserts there must be something more that shapes our existence, some elusive agent hidden in the dark sector of the universe.

And she is the unknown force that shapes mine, in the darkest sector of me.

My dark anomaly.

Like a gravitational wave, she was supposed to pass right through me, undetected, unfelt.

Yet she left a cavernous imprint.

A pang of regret resounds through my chest as I scrape my boot along the rocky ledge, smearing a trail of briny seawater and rain. I dig my hand into my pocket and touch the cool marble of the chess piece, a faint, anguished smile tugging at my mouth.

A star's life is a constant struggle against the force of gravity. Fighting a brutal tidal force against an inevitable collapse. Nothing can stop it.

But I'm nothing if not insufferably stubborn.

"Should've been stubborn enough to do away with you sooner," I say aloud, tossing a scathing glance down below.

Fucking Leo.

As the new moon descends, the sky caught in that dance

between day and night, the first streaks of burnished sunrise touch the horizon to cast shadows across the shore.

It should've shocked me more when Collins produced the scan. But I'd always known Leo was selfish enough to manipulate me for his own greedy gain. But damn—that was diabolical.

I'd like to believe he brought Collins here hoping to help me. That even if his guilt finally got to him, in the end, it wasn't purely to alleviate his conscience. Perhaps he didn't fully grasp the severity of the condition, or perhaps I really was becoming too great of a liability. A loose, unpredictable thread he was forced to sever.

Six years, and all the while the floodwaters were creeping in, a building tide of pressure eroding neurons, dissolving memories. I didn't need any results to validate what I'd always known after the wreck. That I was damaged; a glitch in my gray matter.

Even as the unbearable surge rises in my skull this very instant, I feel her there, carving a new channel—a passage for the dark tide to flow.

I adjust my watch, situating it until it feels right. I was able to recalibrate the astronomical clock while I searched for Leo's body along the shore. Clearly, Collins really hasn't spent time around the ocean, knowing little about tides. At least on that, she wasn't lying.

Dropping a body into a rip current during a perigean spring tide under the force of an eclipse is a terrible method of body disposal. The powerful tidal surge washed it right back ashore, pushed by the incoming swells.

"Night—?"

I turn toward the irritated sound of my name, watching as Prescott stalks my way. His dirty-blond hair is unkempt, his clothes disheveled, looking as though he spent the evening out after yesterday's festivities.

Perfect.

"I haven't even had coffee yet," he complains with an exasperated breath as he reaches me. "What are you doing out here? Did Banner message you, too—"

Without a word, I grab hold of his shirt collar and yank him forward. Stunned, he barely puts up a fight as I drop him over the side of the cliff.

His scream fades out, cut short as his body slams into a rocky outcropping, landing not far from Leo's bloated corpse.

Flexing my gloved fingers, I calmly straighten my tie, smoothing it along my shirt placket as I peer over the edge. "How's that for resolution, Dr. Holbrook."

I called myself a hunter.

Yet the terror in my victim's eyes just now makes me realize I am the thing she branded me, a sinister shadow of myth and nightmare.

Reaper.

I cast one last glance at the basin, ensuring the staged scene looks convincing. Along with the trail of evidence I've strategically left in place, the scene has to tell a specific narrative. Seems this was always Eugene's academic doom, such an insignificant death, barely an afterthought. Fitting, really. Just like his uninspired research.

Which is why he lashed out at Leo during the symposium, then attacked him in a resentful rage. Furious over being dismissed, easily replaced. His hack research stripped of funding.

I mean, someone has to serve as the scapegoat. Take the fall for the murder—quite literally, in Prescott's case. Might as well be my research-stealing rival. Besides, I'm fairly certain he was the one feeding information to the Feds. He always did show a bit too much interest in my work, hovering too close, a little too skittish around me. But I'll get confirmation on that soon enough.

I pick up my discarded astrolabe from the gritty earth, brushing away the sand. Lifting it to the clear sky, I align the sighting vane to that veiled pattern of stars—the hidden thirteenth constellation.

An ache burrows deep, and I instinctively touch my chest in mimicry of my little Serpent Bearer. Carrying her scar stitched of pain, just as the mythic healer bears the weight of a starry serpent, holding poison and remedy in eternal balance.

It's an intriguing story, one I'm looking forward to sharing with her. Intimately.

I warned her one taste would never enough.

Now there's something hungrier stirring with me, something darker that's emerged.

And it's insatiable.

Out of habit, my thumb sweeps the rule, its presence resonating like a familiar tune. Maybe Collins was right about how I made such a careless mistake, leaving the rule at a scene. Maybe it was cognitive decline, or maybe—

Sometimes, you have to lose something important to find it again.

And you have to be willing to risk losing it forever.

Ninety-nine percent science, one percent magical thinking. Like wishing on a star—or an entire fucking ocean of them, all scattered like grains of sand across the cosmos. An infinite sea of possibilities, each collapsing until only one inevitable outcome remains.

I slip the astrolabe into my pocket next to the queen, a smile pulling at the corner of my mouth. It's the knight that takes the leap, the mate inevitable, to deliver the final blow.

My firefly called checkmate too soon. This is far from over.

With my course set, I start back toward the university.

A heavy silence infuses the facility as I ascend the spiral staircase. Before I reach the observatory dome, the distinct trace of Collins's scent tightens my chest. A current of futile hope sparks, extinguished the moment I enter to see everything the same.

If she'd just stumbled in here before she left me bound to my bed with my own damn belt, things might've ended differently.

I look down, halting a few feet away from the gagged FBI agent shackled to my telescope pier. After a dismissive shrug, I sink my hand into my pocket and retrieve the capsule of smelling salts. Cracking it open, I wave it beneath his nose.

"But probably not," I say, speaking my thoughts aloud as I toss the empty capsule aside. I rip the tape away from his mouth, then smack his cheek to further rouse him. "She seemed highly determined."

He blinks a few times, his gaze slowly focusing on my face. "Where is she?" he demands, jerking weakly against the cuffs. "If you've hurt her—"

"So you did come here for her." I tilt my head, studying his dark eyes as I assess the truth there.

When I returned to the dark-sky preserve the next day to find the bodies removed, the entire site cleared of any trace of evidence, I questioned my goddamn sanity. It's possible I cleaned up afterward in my spiraled state out of compulsive habit. Or even more alarming—that I'd never been there at all.

"How did you recognize me?" the agent asks, interrupting my thoughts.

"Cops are pretty obvious to spot," I say, resting my forearm over my knee.

During my speech at the symposium—the one I was giving in order to keep away from the woman bound in my observatory—I noticed this guy skulking through the crowd.

I left mid-speech, shadowing him to the observatory, my thoughts turning violent the closer he got to Collins. And when I found her missing…that violence erupted. After I slammed his head against the window, I dragged him to the pier. Making sure to check him—thoroughly this time—for anything capable of picking a lock before I gagged him, then sedated him heavily for good measure.

And then, when I retrieved his phone near the window, that's where I watched it all play out between Collins and Leo. A perfect symmetry of violence and inevitability, her light dimming out.

There are still some gaps I need filled. Like who took care of the evidence at the dark-sky preserve, though I can now make a pretty good assumption on that. And while I'd like to believe she did it to protect me, that's likely just my poor, love-sick heart. No, Collins was willing to risk everything to keep not only me hidden at Stonehurst, but herself.

And whether it was my chaotic kill site that ultimately led this agent here, or if it was Prescott's doing, once the FBI appeared, I knew my time with Collins was limited. But I'd take every stolen second with her I could get.

Now, this agent and I are about to become very close friends.

"Since you apparently know who I am…" I say, cocking an eyebrow.

He hesitates before giving me his name. "Special Agent Zeke Darby." He jerks against the cuffs, frustration mounting. "Just tell me where she is," he demands once more, a resigned breath escaping. "I just need to know she's okay."

After studying him a beat longer, I grunt as I stand, striding toward the main console. "She's gone," I say bluntly.

"What the fuck did you do to her—"

"She left," I cut him off. "Got what she needed from me, then took off."

He releases a harsh curse beneath his breath. "Fucking hell, Hol."

A fierce knot of resentment tightens in my chest at the familiarity in his voice. I brace my hands against the desk, gloved fingers moving across the keys. Collins is good—impressively good—doing a hell of a job erasing her digital trace from my system. Almost perfect.

But echoes linger.

And those residual patterns are enough for me to follow.

My science once felt heartless—but it's never been without heart.

A purpose.

I didn't so much as code an algorithm as score one. Ada Lovelace referred to it as poetical science; the concept that an engine could weave algebra into music, that machines could create composition.

I'd like to think mine achieves something similar, only cast in a far darker register. Written in a minor key.

As I lock onto the pattern, I drum my fingers and tap a final key, the signal resonating deep within this dark, haunted part of me. The piece of my soul waiting, listening, suspended in breath-bated anticipation for the next notes of her melody.

Her whole song.

Our composition.

Once the system is closed out, I crouch down in front of the agent, producing the key. As I unlock one of the cuffs, his eyes narrow on me, expression wary.

"You're letting me go," he questions, suspicion threading his voice as I move to the second handcuff.

I halt for a brief moment, my gaze lowering to the worn, braided band circling his wrist. Clicking open the cuff, I meet his eyes. "Yes."

"Why?"

"Because I know what it's like to suffer for loving the stars too much."

The words scrape raw at the confession, knowing too intimately the wrenching agony when their light fades, their celestial bodies extinguished long before that light ever reaches us.

A conflicted look crosses his face. He rubs his freed wrist, watching me closely as his confusion morphs into contempt. "You think you're in love with Hollyn," he says slowly, the derision in his tone striking an exposed nerve.

My jaw hardens, a furious fire igniting my bloodstream. In an instant, I have his throat clutched. "Collins," I correct him through gritted teeth. "That's her name. The one she chose."

He holds my menacing gaze, defiant even under my ruthless grip, before finally conceding with a strained nod.

I release him abruptly and stand. "Let's go."

He remains rooted, unmoving. "Where?"

"You're coming with me."

Dragging himself upright, he scowls. "And why the fuck would I do that?"

I pause, casting him a cutting glare over my shoulder. "First, because you have information I need. Second, because I require your vehicle." I head toward the landing. "My girlfriend stole mine."

I'm not sure which part gives him more pause, but after a tense beat, his steps trail behind mine. "Tell me where the hell we're going first."

My gaze lifts toward the observatory windows, finding the shadowed horizon. I map her trajectory as instinctively as I sight the hunter in the sky, eternally stalking his prey across the celestial heavens.

There's nowhere she can run far enough to escape me.

I will hunt her.

I will find her.

A visceral, unrelenting ache pulses behind my ribs as my fingertips tap rhythmically against my thigh, matching the haunting staccato of her cadence, her melody scored deep.

Since the moment her name lit my screen, I've been consumed by one singular obsession—the one intrusive thought impossible to silence.

I can save her.

For all the luminous, light-giving bodies scattered across the known universe, there exists infinitely more darkness. The whispering void calling us to answer.

And with no fear to hold me back, I answer it. "To get her a heart."

AUTHOR'S NOTE

Lovely reader, where do we begin…

Honestly, I don't quite know, other than to say that, at some point, I literally had to pry this manuscript from my hands, or else I'd never stop layering and editing and iterating.

As Orion has said: obsession is like a fever.

You can go mad from it.

Thankfully, I have the most amazing, supportive readers who help pull me out of the writing abyss when it's time, so I can reemerge with a story that I hope will offer, at the very least, an escape. And maybe a little something more.

So let's dive into it (I couldn't help myself with one last ocean reference…)

Where *Lovesick* originated from —

After pouring my heart into the Hollow's Row series (the books of my heart), I admit, I was love sick. By the end of that series, I was so physically drained and just…*love sick* over Halen and Kallum that I needed somewhere to pour all those leftover emotions.

And there was one paragraph, one line in particular, from *Lovely Wicked Things* that I loved so much yet didn't make the cut, that I had tried desperately to make fit, but ultimately didn't feel right for the scene. So I held onto those words. I pasted them into a document. And when the dust settled, I pulled them out and started writing my love-sick heart out.

That one particular line was about "dark adaptation". Hence why, initially, this duet was titled the Dark Adaptation Duet.

This was the core of Collins and Orion's story. The gradual descent into darkness. How not only our eyes adapt to the dark, but our minds, our souls. How we can become desensitized to it. But it was more than about being submerged in the darkness, eclipsed by it—it was also about being able to find the light that is still always present there in that dark, if only we allow ourselves to adapt.

Over the course of many months, and many rewrites, this is where Collins and Orion's true story started to develop, like a negative in a darkroom under a safelight, bathed and washed until the image materialized.

And that first startling picture of them shook me.

While I gave Halen and Kallum so much of myself, in a lot of ways, I played it safe. I thought I had given them everything, all of me, every little broken piece—but I had held some painful breaks back. And, oh, I didn't want to go there... I actually walked away from *Lovesick* three times (Yes, Kallum, I know it's the magic number, thanks), before I accepted there was no other way through to the end without tearing some scars open and resetting the bones.

I guess we'll segue right to Orion from that comparison, and talk about how, at first, I thought Orion got the scraps. We know I gave Kallum Locke all my favorites—I built the MMC of my dreams—and I feared I had nothing left to give Orion but the leftovers. He got my OCD, of course (and when you and your character share a very similar obsessive-compulsive disorder, *oof*, the number of times we had to "start from the top!"; God, I'm amazed this book ever got done honestly, with how often we triggered each other ha)—but, he also got some hidden pieces of me, helping me realize those neurotic compulsions can also become strengths, if we just give them a little light and like, don't fear the pain of change.

cracks knuckles painfully

Which brings us to Collins.

I knew with her that we were going to explore some difficult topics together, and I thought I had braced myself. The years can give a false sense of closure, like assuming the distance of time heals all wounds. Yet, as Orion would clarify, time is an illusion. Trauma doesn't understand time, past, distance.

And I knew that her character would likely be, at least right at first, difficult to connect with. To understand and sympathize with and even to root for. Especially since much of her story isn't revealed throughout the book.

This was a facet of the story that I wrestled with—just how much of Collins's past to reveal up front, and even possibly in the end. Because, why wouldn't she tell her story? Why not give the reader all the details to her past trauma, to let them know about how the officials handling her case had "misplaced the SAECK kit", and also "lost the offender evidence" accidentally...of course. How, while being questioned inappropriately in the ER room by two male law officials, even the female conducting the mortifying evidence collection held a touch of their mirrored judgment in her eyes.

The answer was, quite frankly...

That she was done telling her story.

She was *tired* of telling it.

She was taking action.

But it is my hope that, even if you're unable to fully connect with Collins, that you at least give her grace. Give her time to tell her story in her own way, and to hear her.

Now, a short note on the science —

As always, I could ramble on about the research (and trust, the universe is vast; I barely scraped the cosmos in this book, making it difficult to be selective, to choose the motifs and elements that best connected to Collins and Orion…with a tic in my eye when I wanted to expound and get wordy lol), and I know, if an astrophysicist picks up this book, there will be much head-shaking at my attempt—but the truth is, I'm not a scientist. I had a story brewing inside me to tell, and I did so to the best of my ability. So thank you for having grace with me, and allowing me some hand-waving at the science. (Although, if you dive into it some, you'll start to see where it's terrifyingly plausible, even if only theoretical…for now.)

When Orion states early on that his previous focus was on dark matter, that wasn't a story device. It was the truth. This book was written near to its completion around dark matter…before I realized, very fucking painfully (and it still makes me cry) that it just didn't work. Both the science in general and as a backdrop for their story.

So, I fell into a black hole for about a week (ha—I'm so sorry, I just can't help it), and then set to work researching again all over. As the universe would have it, I was revising *Born, Darkly* at the time for audio, and I came across a passage that stopped me in my tracks. It was about gravity, which led into a metaphor of a black hole. And something just…connected.

I then went back through most of my books and searched for "black hole". Huh. There was a pattern—my very own. As it turns out, we were always heading here, drifting toward this dark, cosmic oblivion, a sort of writer's inevitability. Collins and Orion had always been there with me, just waiting for their moment— for the right time to tell their story.

The rewrite wasn't easy. That's an understatement. It's to-date the hardest writing project I've ever undertaken (sorry, Kallum, but you can't take the crown for *everything*), but again, I have the best readers, and I'm so grateful for your patience with me, and giving me your trust.

So, lovely reader, if you've made it this far with me—down the rabbit hole, into the farthest reaches—I hope you'll keep going with me on this journey. And as always, thank you so much for reading my words, especially the ones here in this note.

…from the bottom of my dark, dark heart.

Read madly,
Trish

Where do we go from here?

If you want to keep up with projects, characters, art piece reveals, and my daily madness, I'd love for you to follow me on Instagram @Trisha_Wolfe

If you want to dive down the rabbit hole of my backlist with more intense plots, characters, and thrilling twists, keep flipping the pages to see my preferred reading order.

If you want more Collins and Orion right now, here is a special gift to readers:

Get a copy of the **Deleted Tidal Lock Scene** between Collins and Orion from the Waning chapter. Also included, three printable character art pieces within. This deleted scene may contain spoilers for those who have yet to read *Lovesick*.

Find the Hollow's Row Series, and many other Trisha Wolfe titles, in duet style audiobook narration. Here's a tease from *Lovely Bad Things*.

KALLUM

Most obsessions start small, harmless. A tiny niggle in the back of your mind, an innocent fixation. The obsessive thought crawls under our skin and we begin to pick and pick until the desire overwhelms and we have no choice but to tear into it, claws raking and drawing blood.

The wound is a form of relief.

All great minds suffer this affliction. A torment that damns us to a monotonous existence.

But what is art and beauty if not pain? Anything which comes too easily is an insult to both the creator and the consumer.

With pain, we feel, we tear ourselves wide, and we allow the wound to heal over. We accept the scar. With obsession, we mutilate the skin until it's destroyed, never allowing the damage to repair.

Blood never clots. We want it to flow, to keep feeding the passion, the desire.

Little Halen St. James didn't start as a tiny niggle. From day one, she flayed my skin wide and buried herself deep.

And I can't stop scratching.

"Locke, you're up."

My name is called over the line of patients in the waiting room seated on a bench. It's dank and crowded in the small eight-by-ten holding area of Briar Correctional Institute for the Criminally Insane. The plain-white walls are dingy with age and neglect. There's a constant reek of bleach with a faint undercurrent of mildew, a stench that can never quite be masked.

The psychotic inmates smell worse.

Donning my neutral patient scrubs, I rise from the plastic chair and drag a hand through my slicked hair. A few loose strands creep over my eye, but the errant stragglers are forgotten when I'm ensnared by the sight at the visitation table.

I allow all five senses to absorb her fully before I step into the room.

Basic heather-gray thermal with three buttons undone at her collar. A simple, delicate white-gold chain drops a one-carat, teardrop diamond in the hollow of her throat. Her dark-brown hair is pulled back in a low ponytail, out of the way. A defiant streak of white frames the side of her unpolished face.

The only makeup she wears is a swipe of mascara to darken her lashes, and a hint of gloss on her plump lips. But why cover up her natural beauty with layers of toxic chemicals? I appreciate the simplicity, even if those dramatic hazel eyes make me want to draw blood.

As I move into the room, I watch as she observes me just as closely. I like the way she purposely tries not to blink, the way her cheeks tinge the slightest shade of pale-pink. It's deceiving on her part; she's not shy or meek or enraptured by me.

Oh, I know I'm a specimen to behold. There's no modesty in these bones. It would be pretentious of me to fake humbleness.

Since I was five, my mother's friends cooed and marveled over my eyes. My high-school girlfriends soaked their panties over my floppy black hair and crooked smile. Come to think of it, so did my mother's friends.

At six-one, my body is leanly cut and toned, honed to wreak havoc on the female mind and body.

Which is one of the many annoyances when it comes to the petite criminologist seated across from me; she never fell into my web. She escaped unscathed, unaffected. More so, she slammed a glass over me and trapped me like a common house spider.

A miscalculation I'm determined to rectify.

My bite has venom.

"Hello, Halen." The gravelly rasp of my voice curls around the syllables of her name. The first tremor of excitement rolls under my skin.

"Professor Locke," she replies formally. "I'd prefer if you addressed me in kind as Dr. St. James."

"This is the first time I've lain eyes on you in months, and here you sit, making demands. Impressive. Once you stepped out of those shadows, it seems you never returned." My gaze skims her composed features, probing for the crack in her armor. I thought I found it once, but I was *un*pleasantly surprised to stand corrected. Amid twelve jurors, no less.

"Am I being recorded?" I ask, not curbing the hard edge in my tone of voice.

"No. This conversation if strictly between us—"

"I thought the last one was."

She tips her chin higher and presents her phone, proving there are no recording apps, before she slips the device back into her bag. "But I'd like it if our conversation remains formal."

"Oh, come now," I say, "we can toss out nominal letters and propriety bullshit. We're both on equal ground."

She arches a fine eyebrow. "Does it rub you raw I won't refer to you as Dr. Locke? Because, given the doctorate in philosophy is the most common in academia, I only presumed you'd find it insulting. Although, I could always tack on the post-nominal lettering if it helps your ego, Professor Locke, *PhD*."

She's been a busy little bee investigating me to learn how I tick.

Ryder—who I suppose one may consider my closest friend—relayed how she'd been interrogating professional associates and what few friends I have left after this debacle. I may have used him to feed her some interesting morsels.

What tangled webs…

I lick my lips slowly, savoring the burn of her arousing scent as it stokes my senses. A mouthwatering combination of lily of the valley and ylang-ylang, a unique scent well-suited for her.

Poisonous. Toxic, but only if ingested. With a hint of aphrodisiac.

She could market the scent with her own brand: *Lure and kill*.

"Rubbing me raw, little Halen, has all the promise with no follow through." I spin the silver ring around my thumb.

She visibly shifts in her seat, refusing to be baited.

Scratch, scratch, scratch.

"What a waste of your doctorate," I press on, expelling a lengthy breath. "You should be working in academia yourself, fielding your own research. Instead, you're still traipsing around crime scenes, playing chase."

"Keeping tabs on me?"

I smile. "I have loads of time to kill."

Her mouth parts, as if I've said something to confirm a suspicion.

Daringly, I let my hand settle past the midway point on the table. There are no plastic dividers. No metal grates. I could reach out and touch her if I wanted—but I'm not yet ready to tear in and claw that itch.

Her gaze drops to my hand, to the faded inked celestial rose on the back of my hand and sigils that mark my fingers below my knuckles.

"I'm surprised you didn't request I be shackled." I drum my fingers on the surface of the hard plastic tabletop.

When she raises her gaze to meet mine, her resolve is firmly in place. "Should I have? Do you plan to hurt me?"

The vision attacks so suddenly and with startling fierceness—my hands collared around her slender neck; her breathy gasps for oxygen—I have to blink hard and push farther away from the table to escape her scent.

"Anger is an acid that can do more harm to the vessel," I say.

"That didn't answer my question."

"Mark Twain answered it, if you can surmise his meaning. Brilliant writer, horrible businessman."

With a clipped, sardonic laugh, she stands. "I don't know why I'm here. This was a bad idea. Apparently, you really are insane."

On impulse, I reach out and grab her wrist.

A charged pulse ignites a fire beneath my palm. The air, volatile and tense, suspends time for a mere blink, allowing my body to ravenously absorb the feel of her where I've only permitted my eyes to touch.

Our gazes collide on impact of that touch, and I see the conflict in her fearful eyes. I'm not the only one affected.

Her chest rises with uneven breaths as she twists her arm to break my hold, and despite the intense desire to keep her in my grasp, I let her.

My fingertips memorize the erratic beat of her pulse as she slips away. *Bah-dah-bump. Bah-dah-bah-dah-bump.* I want to carve it in my skin.

She crosses her arms, anxiously waiting for my rebound. I flex my hand as my gaze lingers on the visible imprint I left on her wrist. "It must have been difficult for you to come here," I say, sifting her from my thoughts to collect myself. "You should at least tell me why you came before you run away."

"I'm not running." Her strained swallow drags enticingly along the column of her throat to challenge her assertion. Then: "I need a philosophy expert."

"And how convenient you know right where to find one."

Meet Grayson Sullivan, AKA The Angel of Maine serial killer, and Dr. London Noble, the psychologist who falls for her patient, as they're drawn into a dark and twisted web in the Darkly, Madly Duet, the ultimate cat and mouse game for dark romance lovers.

TRISHA WOLFE READING ORDER

All Trisha's series are written to read on their own and pull you in, but here is her preferred reading order to introduce worlds and characters that cross over in each series.

Broken Bonds Series

With Visions of Red

With Ties that Bind

Derision

Darkly, Madly Duet

Born, Darkly

Born, Madly

A Necrosis of the Mind Duet

Cruel

Malady

Hollow's Row Series

Lovely Bad Things

Lovely Violent Things

Lovely Wicked Things

Dark Mafia Romance

Marriage & Malice

Devil in Ruin

Standalones

Marrow

About Trisha Wolfe

From an early age, Trisha Wolfe dreamed up fictional worlds and characters and was accused of talking to herself. Today, she writes full time, using her fictional worlds as an excuse to continue talking to herself.

Get updates on future releases at TrishaWolfe.com

Connect with Trisha Wolfe on social media on these platforms: Instagram | TikTok

Want to be the first to hear about new book releases, special promotions, and events for all Trisha Wolfe books? Sign up for Trisha Wolfe's VIP list at TrishaWolfe.com

Find audiobooks, character art, and merchandise on the storefront at TrishaWolfe.com